NO MATTER WHAT

JENNIFER CARR

Edited by
JENNIFER CROSSWHITE

JCARR WRITES

© 2022 by Jennifer Carr

All rights reserved. No part of this publication may be reproduced, stored, or transmitted in any form or by any means, electronic, mechanical, photocopying, recording, scanning, or otherwise without written permission from the publisher. It is illegal to copy this book, post it to a website, or distribute it by any other means without permission.

This novel is entirely a work of fiction. The names, characters, and incidents portrayed in it are the work of the author's imagination. Any resemblance to actual persons, living or dead, events, or localities is entirely coincidental.

Some Scripture quotations are used by permission from The Holy Bible, English Standard Version® (ESV®). Copyright © 2001 by Crossway, a publishing ministry of Good News Publishers. All rights reserved. ESV Text Edition: 2016

Some Scripture quotations are used by permission from the HCSB ©1999, 2000, 2002, 2003, 2009 Holman Bible Publishers.

First edition

ISBN: 979-8355976620

PART I

1

JESS

The knock at the door pulled my focus from the pages I was reading. A check of my watch told me it was almost 6:00. My stomach had been rumbling for almost an hour, but in my tunnel vision, I'd ignored it. I had planned on going to the store after work yesterday but had a stroke of inspiration in the car and headed straight home in hopes of squeezing out a few more hours of prepping for the defense of my dissertation.

Finals were also coming up for the undergraduate psychology class I teach on Mondays, and it had required far more of my attention than I had planned for at this point. That probably had a lot to do with the detailed final exam I was creating in addition to the research papers I was now grading. The lack of care with which the students approached the first half of the semester led me to apply more pressure toward the end of the year. This was a mistake simply because it felt more as though I was punishing myself than my students. It didn't matter; I was already in this deep. There was no turning back.

With my roommate, Stacy, at work and few options in the refrigerator for dinner, I'd decided to use a delivery app to order sushi from my favorite place not far from the house. When I opened the door,

Alicia, the girl who typically delivered in the neighborhood, was standing on the front porch. She was typically a bubbly coed, but today the girl had a fake smile plastered on her face.

Most customers might not notice, but I did. I notice everything.

Sadness. Fear. Anxiety.

It was clearly written on her face for me to read. "Hey, Alicia. Is everything okay?"

Blinking in surprise, Alicia attempted to fix her smile and said in a forced perky tone, "Sure. Here ya go!"

Taking the bag of food slowly from her hand, I gave her a sympathetic look and asked, "Are you sure?"

Alicia's mask fell away, and tears formed in her eyes as she shook her head. "My dad was in a car accident this morning, and I can't get home for several days. They say he's going to be fine, but it's making me crazy being so far away."

My heart was sad for her, knowing the struggles of being far away from family in these kinds of situations. "I'm sorry. Is there anything I can do?"

A sad but genuine smile crossed Alicia's face. "No, but thank you. It's nice to just be able to say it aloud and know someone cares."

I gave her a warm smile in return and raised the bag I was holding. "I know this is pretty much the extent of our relationship, but if you need anything, you know where I live."

Relief. Calm. Gratitude.

Alicia stepped forward and hugged me, causing me to hope she didn't take my stiff posture as a slight. Thankfully, the contact was brief, and she let go as soon as I gently patted her back and pulled away.

Alicia stepped back quickly and wiped at her eyes. "I'm sorry. That was completely inappropriate."

I tried to clear my expression and give her a reassuring smile. "No worries."

Clearing her throat, Alicia stepped back. "Thank you. You're really sweet. Have a good evening." She gave a small wave as she headed back to her car.

"You, too." I gave a small wave.

Finally situated on the couch with sushi and chopsticks in hand, I turned on the television and settled in to watch the news. I never watched the news to stay abreast of current events since it was a great way to find yourself either too scared or too depressed to leave the house. Instead, I watched for the people. People were my business, my passion, and sometimes my weakness. Technically, reading people and their emotions, intentions, and even their desires are all those things.

On the screen, the anchorman was reporting on an ongoing murder investigation while an over-the-shoulder graphic showed an outline of a body in shadows. His face wasn't familiar. He must be new, which always added a layer of challenge since there wasn't a baseline in my recollection.

As he spoke, my eyes automatically darted from his mouth to his eyes to his nose and back to his eyes.

Intrigue. Eagerness. Satisfaction. Confidence.

His voice was energetic and held just a hint of arrogance. My first thought was, *Interesting.*

The camera switched to a seasoned female anchor who introduced a story about a new panda cub born at the zoo that morning. Her pleasant expression was forced. The underlying truth was

Boredom. Disgust. Jealousy. Indifference.

My guess was she wanted the murder investigation story, but the new guy got it instead. It wasn't a great form of practice since my theories couldn't be tested, but it put faces in front of me, which helped me zero in on what I needed to see.

For as long as I could remember, I read faces like words on a page —not the obvious expressions everyone could pick up on, but micro-expressions, even micro-behaviors, involuntary leaks of emotion. Sometimes body language or involuntary gestures lasted only a fraction of a second but spoke volumes.

Over the years, I became increasingly aware I could also perceive a person's nature through physical contact. I was not the most affectionate kid, and I rarely sought physical affection, even from my mother. Handshakes were awkward, hugs made me feel trapped, and kisses made me extremely uncomfortable. As a child, if I found myself injured with a scraped knee or a twisted ankle, my mother would try to comfort me with an embrace or gentle hands on my back. I typically endured it because it made my mother feel better, not because it brought relief.

To the contrary, physical touch had always overwhelmed my senses with what felt like electrical currents pulsing through my body. Depending on the person, it could be a pleasant feeling or a painful one. The anticipation was usually worse than the experience since they were rarely painful. However, even the painless sensations could overwhelm me. Combined with my ability to transduce a person's facial expressions, I knew I was different. My mother called it a gift and said I was a true empath. I have simply considered it a tool that required use and practice.

It was this gift that put me on the path on which I currently found myself. After breezing through an undergraduate degree in psychological brain sciences and a Master's in applied psychology, some of my work caught the eye of a professor at American University, Dr. Derick Thorne. He was the one who convinced me to pursue a PhD in behavior, cognition, and neuroscience and work with him as a research assistant, which was where I found myself now.

The last two years had been spent focusing on determining how common or uncommon my abilities really were with the help of Dr. Thorne. Of course, the end of the school year also meant that in a matter of weeks, I'd be wrapping my research with him. Not only was I his research assistant, but he was also one of only a handful of people who truly understood the breadth of my abilities. Our research would hopefully allow us to expand the possibilities of utilizing my abilities and potentially seek out future students with similar skills or the potential to learn them. Just the thought threatened to send my heart into a rapid rhythm.

2

JESS

It was Friday night, and I found myself trying not to groan audibly as my roommate, Stacy, begged me to go out with her for the night.

"Please?! You have to come with me. I really want you to meet this guy. He's the hottest guy I have ever met." Stacy made a pouty face and batted her false eyelashes. "And he is so charming. Please, Jess! You just have to come."

She'd been dating the same guy for a few months, and honestly, she seemed happy. Which was the only reason I was even considering it as I sat on the corner of my bed and averted my eyes to stare at the floor. I tried hard to come up with any excuse not to go with Stacy. It would not have been the first time I gave in to end up being the third wheel. I also knew if I didn't go, there'd be a good chance Stacy would call in the middle of the night asking for a ride home. I stared at her and considered her words before answering.

"Okay, I will go, but under two conditions."

"Anything," agreed Stacy.

"We leave when I'm ready to leave, and you take it easy on the appletinis."

Stacy beamed and stuck out her hand. "Deal!"

Unconvinced, I shook on the deal and mustered a smile. Immediately, I found myself being pulled from the bed and dragged to my closet where Stacy proceeded to rummage through my clothes.

"You have zero clothes that even look ready for a club."

"We're going to a club?" I couldn't even hide the disdain from my voice.

Stacy whipped around and wagged a finger in my face. "We shook on it. You can't back out now."

Trying to keep my cool, I rolled my eyes and stared into my closet. "Fine. But remember, I decide when we leave."

Stacy smiled. "Yes, ma'am."

She walked toward the door before turning. "At least try not to dress like my mother, okay?" With a wink, Stacy left the room.

With a deep breath, I had to remind myself that Stacy and I were two very different people, but she was my best friend. I didn't have a lot of friends because being able to read people before they speak sometimes makes it hard for people to be themselves around me. Even when I didn't tell them what I could do, my reactions were sometimes misconstrued as either presumptuous or untrusting, and that had made it hard in the past to connect with people. I had spent years trying to hide my own feelings and reactions when I wanted to, and I had gotten quite good at it. I knew people, but people didn't really know me.

The longer I stared into my closet, the more frustrated I got with myself for agreeing to go to a club. The club scene had never been one I enjoyed. Clubs, bars, frat parties—none of these ever appealed to me. And being friends with Stacy had garnered many invitations to all these places. Sometimes as a guest and sometimes as a rideshare.

Aside from the noise and sea of faces that overwhelmed my senses, I despised the effect alcohol had on people. And where else were the effects of alcohol on people more obvious than a club? My dad had been an alcoholic. He rarely had a job as far as I can remember, but he always had a beer in his hand. He was a lazy drunk, and he was mean when he was sober.

Turning my focus back to my closet, I realized Stacy was right and it was a fairly boring place, full of knee-length, A-line skirts and coordinating blazers. If I wasn't dressed for work, I was in joggers, leggings, or yoga pants and T-shirts. I dug out a pair of black skinny jeans from behind my favorite gray ensemble that would have to do. Doing the skinny-jean shimmy, I had to wonder why women decided that this fashion was worthwhile. Even small legs were not made to squeeze into restrictive denim casings like sausages.

After a few minutes of picking through tops, I landed on a simple relaxed V-neck tee, added a short silver necklace and earrings, and slid my feet into my favorite black strappy heels. Hopefully, Stacy would think I was actually trying. I tousled my dark pixie cut before sighing at the reflection in the mirror. It was these moments that made me grateful to my mother's genetics that provided me with an almost unnaturally clear olive skin tone and dark lashes that framed mahogany eyes. I'd never felt the need to incorporate an abundance of cosmetics into my routine and I wasn't about to start tonight.

"That's as good as it's going to get, I'm afraid," I said to the empty room.

At the bottom of the stairs, Stacy was using the mirror by the front door to darken her already red lipstick. She took one look at me and rolled her eyes before looking back at her reflection in the mirror. "That's what you're wearing?" She wrinkled her nose.

Controlling my breathing, I made my way downstairs without answering.

Stacy stopped staring at herself and stared back at me. "It's just, you aren't going to get anyone's attention looking like that." Stacy gestured up and down my form.

"Why would I want anyone's attention? There is never anyone at a club whose attention I could possibly want."

Stacy put a hand on her hip. "What does that mean?"

I knew not to engage. I also knew that it wasn't anything I hadn't said before to Stacy. As calmly as I could, I replied, "I'm just not interested in guys who go to clubs. That's all."

Hoping Stacy would let it go, I grabbed my clutch, checked it for my ID, credit card, and keys, then glanced at Stacy. "Well, are we going?"

Stacy put her purse strap over her head and opened the door.

The twenty-minute drive was quiet. I tried asking Stacy about this guy she was meeting and how they met. The answers were short and not specific.

With a small huff, Stacy pouted. "Look, I know you are going to read Pete the minute you see him. Maybe take more than ten seconds to make your final judgments, okay?"

This behavior wasn't new. Stacy had a proclivity to cling to her youth. Not that she was old, by any means. We're both only twenty-seven. But Stacy lived in a very small bubble at whose center was Stacy.

When I moved to DC for college, I found myself a little outside my comfort zone. I grew up in Sunrise, California, just outside of Long Beach. The ethnic diversity of DC was a nice reminder of home. However, there was a different pace of life in Washington, DC than there was in California. Everything moved faster in the nation's capital. People were easily inconvenienced if they had to wait an extra minute for their venti nonfat mochaccino latte and made little effort to make eye contact. If I had experienced culture shock, Stacy had her world rocked to the core.

Stacy grew up in Blue Springs, Mississippi, population 400. She spent much of her childhood and teenage years competing in pageants and had been a lot of places. To Stacy's disappointment, she always went home to Blue Springs where life was less than exciting. Having spent so much time on a stage, Stacy knew when she graduated high school she was destined to live in New York. Broadway was her siren, her call to escape small town life. And while she had talent, she lacked experience. The closest school that would accept her—and Daddy's money—was the Corcoran School at GWU.

I met Stacy in a campus book and supplies store where she was working part time. Stacy was visibly upset as she was walking out of a door marked Employees Only. I didn't really have time to dive deeply into someone else's issues, considering my encroaching deadlines.

I've also never been one to intentionally ignore someone who appeared distressed.

Stacy had walked to the back of the store to some tables set up for people to work or just sit and read. *Sadness. Disappointment. Humiliation.* The emotions rolled off her in waves. Stacy pulled out her phone, stared at it, and began to cry. She put her phone down on the table then lowered her head down on her arms.

I walked over to her and gently put a hand on Stacy's back, causing her to jump. Her energy was light and airy with an undertone of malaise.

Moving my hand, I apologized. "Sorry. Are you okay?"

Stacy cried harder.

My planned purchases rested on the table as I took the seat across from Stacy. Two hours later, Stacy's condition suddenly made sense. She had been on academic probation and was now being dismissed from her program due to failing grades and too many missed classes.

"I just wanted to be an actress. I wanted to get out of Podunk, Mississippi, star in a few Broadway plays, and thank my mama in my awards acceptance speeches. Was that really too much to ask?"

I had to bite my lip to keep from laughing. This girl probably could have gone straight to Broadway and skipped college with her natural flair for drama. Stacy was a small—albeit dramatic—fish in a huge sea, but it didn't seem to faze her.

With a promise to return the kindness, we exchanged numbers and went our separate ways. A few days later, a text message from Stacy appeared on my phone asking if I wanted to meet up for lunch or coffee one day that week. We decided to meet at one of the small coffee shops in the area one evening after my classes were done. Our friendship solidified quickly, and it wasn't too long before we started making plans to find a place and room together.

As we pulled up to the club, Stacy's demeanor changed immediately as though a hidden reset button had been hit. She was beaming. "You are going to love Pete," was all she said.

The valet opened her door, and Stacy stepped out of the car. When he opened my door, he helped me out of the car before accepting the keys and handing me a ticket. He proceeded to move the car into the parking deck as we walked straight to the entrance rather than to the back of the line. Stacy handed the bouncer at the door what appeared to be a business card, and he unhooked the scarlet cord, motioning us inside.

The music was loud, and people were shoulder to shoulder, laughing, dancing, drinking, and trying to hear one another over the chaos. Stacy danced her way through the crowd, smiling and looking backward to make sure I was still close enough to follow her.

Trying to make myself as small as I could, I followed uncomfortably as people constantly bumped into me. Once on the other side of the crowd, Stacy showed another bouncer the same card she'd shown at the front door. He pointed upstairs and gave directions to what turned out to be a private room.

The room was spacious and dimly lit. There was a fully stocked bar to one side and a single round table in the center. There were several sleek leather couches on the walls flanked by modern angular armchairs. The room was insulated from the noise and only allowed in the occasional thumps of a beat. My ears were ringing, so, I appreciated the reprieve.

Stacy pulled out her phone and sent a quick text and received an instant reply. She grabbed my arm, and sounding almost panicked said, "He's coming. Do I look okay? How's my breath? Oh, Jess! You're just going to love him. I really think you will!"

I stifled a laugh and put a hand on Stacy's. She was humming with nervous energy. "Stacy, you have to calm down. You look amazing, your breath is fine, and—"

At that moment, the door opened and in walked a man who appeared to be in his early thirties. He had dark hair, hazel eyes, and a tanned olive complexion.

Stacy let go of me and moved quickly to the man, kissing him on the mouth then pulling him by the hand toward me. She introduced us. "Pete, this is Jess. Jess, Pete."

Pete reached out his hand, and immediately, as his hand embraced mine, I felt it. The painful current that warned of danger. I tried hard not to, but I tensed. All my senses were on high alert. The ringing in my ears grew louder, and my heart rate increased. The scent of his aftershave mingled with a hint of alcohol and mint turned my stomach.

Before I could retract my hand and end the handshake, Pete had both of his hands around mine and was smiling at me. "It is my pleasure to finally put a face with the name. Stacy has told me so much about you that I feel like I already know you."

Struggling to keep my reaction neutral, I attempted what I thought was a smile but my eyes attentive, never left this man's face.

Danger. Deception. Determination. Arrogance. Compulsiveness. Greed.

So many red flags, combined with the strong pulses of energy hitting my nerves, threatened to send my entire body from fight to flight mode. With a squeeze of my fingers on his, I attempted to signal that I'd like my hand free and was finally able to pull it out of his grasp. The warnings inside of my mind were blaring. This man should not be trusted.

"I wish I could say the same, but Stacy was determined to make the first impression a surprise," I said with a nervous laugh.

Pete smirked. "That sounds about right. She was telling me all about your ability to read people. I guess she wanted to find out what you really thought about me. Learn anything?"

My body went rigid at the idea of Stacy telling anyone, especially this man, about my abilities.

With a forced a smile, I said, "I always learn something, but I don't like to give my first impressions in case they are wrong. Know what I mean?"

When I glanced at Stacy, my face fell. I tried to communicate my concerns silently, but Stacy glared at me, giving a small quick shake of her head.

Pete beckoned Stacy, who immediately snapped back to the

moment and moved to take Pete's arm. "Pete, you have to tell Jess some of those stories you were telling me about the Army and some of the places you've been. Like the one about Mozambique. That one is hilarious."

Pete was checking his watch and not really listening. If he had picked up on anything I tried to convey to Stacy, it did not show.

The door to the private room opened, and all eyes moved to see who was joining our party.

"There he is!" Pete exclaimed.

Pulling free of Stacy, Pete walked toward the man who entered the room. There was a swagger in Pete's steps that emanated confidence and control. Pete extended his arms, and the men embraced, slapping each other on the back.

"Bryan, I would like to introduce you to Stacy."

Bryan dipped his head and shook her hand politely, causing Stacy to giggle.

She was interrupted when Pete forced Bryan's attention away from her to me. "And Jess."

I extended my hand and braced myself for another jolt, but when Bryan took my hand and squeezed gently, everything around us seemed to stop moving.

"Hi," he said, with the most beautiful smile I had ever seen. He was tall, broad shouldered, and clean shaven. There was a dimple in each cheek that immediately caught my attention, increasing the squeeze that had started at my hand but had quickly wrapped itself around my heart.

To say my senses went into overdrive would be an understatement. These sensations, however, were different from anything I had ever felt. Instead of the electrical impulses in my spine that warned of danger, I was engulfed in a wave of warmth that seemed to radiate through and around me. This was new.

"Hi," was all I could manage.

Though I let go of his hand, our eyes stayed locked for another beat.

Confidence. Self-Disciplined. Thoughtful. Warm.

Pete broke the silence. "Now that we are all here, let's sit. Everything is on the house, so make yourself at home."

"On the house? Is this your club?" I forced my gaze from Bryan to stare at Pete.

"It is." And with that, he directed the four of us to a table across the room and motioned to a bartender, who seemed to have appeared from nowhere.

Stacy reattached herself to Pete's arm as he led the way.

At the table, Bryan pulled a chair out next to the one he stood behind, and I stood there awkwardly unsure until he smiled and indicated with a slight head tilt it was intended for me.

Pete had already slunk into his chair leaving Stacy standing, watching the interaction.

As I took the seat, Bryan also pulled Stacy's chair from under the table and waited until she was seated to take his own seat. All I could do was watch with rapt attention as this stranger, who felt more familiar by the minute, behaved genuinely as though he was the least important person in the room. Which was the exact opposite of the image Pete seemed to portray.

Once we were all settled, the bartender joined us at the table to take drink orders. As he walked away and toward the bar, Pete assessed Bryan. "It is so good to see you, man. How long has it been? Three or four years?" There was a brashness to his voice.

My eyes focused on Pete's face when he spoke, watching as his outward shell attempted to cover the smugness in his eyes. A slight twitch in his lips alluded to some hint of amusement. What was the deal here? Clearly, there was a history, but what was going on right now? They hadn't seen each other for years, yet Pete was attempting to portray the two of them as good friends who had merely missed opportunities to see each other.

Bryan met his gaze. "Six, actually." *Detached. Guarded.*

Pete slapped a hand to the table causing me to jump. His voice was obnoxiously loud. "Six years? Are you kidding me? How did that happen? This guy, let me tell you." Pete turned to me and said with a sardonic tone, "He is the most dedicated soldier you will ever meet.

He pours himself into everything he does one thousand percent, and he doesn't care if he doesn't talk to a soul for six years as long as the mission gets accomplished." *Jealousy. Resentment. Bitterness.*

Bryan's ears turned pink. *Disappointment.*

He reached to straighten his already straight fork on the table. "Come on, Pete. You know that's not what happened. Besides, it's kind of hard to talk to someone who doesn't leave a forwarding number or address." His tone was calm but sharp. *Frustration.*

I turned my attention on Stacy, who looked as confused and uncomfortable as I was. There were a lot of emotions flying between Pete and Bryan, and I couldn't keep up. That was one of the disadvantages to being able to read people. I can read people of all kinds in all kinds of scenarios, but I work best one-on-one or in neutral territory. This was anywhere but neutral territory; this was Pete's territory, and he was acting like a man who had something he was trying to prove. I didn't like it, but I was simply a guest and outside observer.

The bartender came back with drinks on a tray, and Pete's face immediately morphed from a scowl to casual indifference and mumbled something to the server I couldn't hear. With a nod, the man walked out of the room again.

Pete stood and picked up his drink and reached for Stacy, whose demeanor bounced from uncertain to giddy in a single beat. She shimmied her short dress back into place before taking his hand and giving a shrug.

"We're going to go make the rounds. If the food gets here before we get back, help yourselves." Pete pulled his glare from Bryan and turned to me. *Calculating. Smug.*

Stacy grabbed her purse and her drink, and with a girly wave, she left with Pete. When he opened the door, the room grew louder with the sounds from downstairs, but it quickly returned to its state of quiet when it closed again.

Watching them leave left me feeling stunned. Several seconds that felt much longer went by, neither Bryan nor I acknowledging the events that had transpired. I continued staring at the door.

Then Bryan made a sound that could have been a laugh or a huff, maybe both.

Eventually I glanced over at Bryan, and I couldn't decide if he was angry or amused.

"You'll have to forgive Pete. He has never been one for great manners, or really manners at all. But he's usually good for a laugh." He paused. "Well, most of the time. He seems to be having an off night." Bryan studied the door as though he expected the two to return.

The beads of condensation rolling down my water glass made for a temporary distraction as I evaluated my feelings and next steps. This was just like Stacy. She rarely took anyone or anything else into account when she was getting attention. She behaved as though she was on stage, unable to be deterred from her spotlight role.

There was nothing about Pete that made me feel good about leaving her at his mercy based on our first encounter, but I also had no concrete reason to distrust him. Sure, I've got a track record that says there is a smaller than miniscule chance that my reading on him was wrong. However, I'm not arrogant enough to believe there is not a first time for everything.

Looking up from my water glass, I stared at Bryan who had turned his focus to an invisible point on the wall across from us.

Frustrated. Uncertain. Concerned. Uncomfortable.

It was at this point I decided that staying wouldn't be the worst decision I could make.

"So." I broke the silence while fidgeting with the edge of a napkin on the table. "A soldier?"

Bryan cleared his throat and moved his eyes to mine.

His bright-green eyes were stunning and threatened to derail any train of thought I may have been about to board. Had he not responded, I may have been relegated to making a list of everything less spectacular than his eyes. It would have been an extremely long list.

His face and shoulders both seemed to relax as his attention returned to the two of us at the table. "Yeah, a soldier. Well, these days, I'm what they call a 'digital soldier.' I mostly sit and stare at computer screens all day when I'm not in meetings with people more important than I am."

Examining his face for any and all markers, I found nothing indicating anything but openness and honesty.

"Do you enjoy your job?"

"I do, actually." He nodded as he answered.

He was not making this easy with his short answers, but I was unable to tear myself away from staring at him, so I asked another question. "Did you always want to be a soldier?"

Bryan thought for a moment but without much hesitation he said, "I always wanted to be in the Army. But I also wanted to work with computers. Being a soldier came with the Army."

"Why the Army?" At least he made it easy to ask the next question.

Bryan's answer was immediate. "My dad."

Maybe he was just being polite and didn't actually want to have conversation and I had misinterpreted his relaxing as willingness. This time, I just stared at him as though waiting for more. If he didn't want to talk, I'd take my cue.

Thankfully, he complied with my silent request. "My dad was in the Army, and the Army was always a part of my life. It felt natural to stay the path."

Not wanting to miss a beat, my next question popped out. "Would you choose differently if you had to make the choice today?"

Bryan took a minute to answer, which made me nervous at first. This was approaching deep-end territory, and I took us there much more quickly than I had intended.

Before I could suggest he didn't have to answer, Bryan said, "I might make different choices along the way."

Letting his answer sink in for several seconds, I drummed the table with my fingers. Voluntarily, I answered my own question. "I don't think I would."

Bryan interrupted before I could ask another question. "You'd live your exact life to this point again without changing anything?" He sounded surprised.

"I don't think I would change any of the major events of my life, no. Food choices, outfit choices, hairstyles, sure. But everything I've ever done has brought me to exactly where I am, and I'm happy with where I am."

"And where is that?" Bryan leaned forward, genuinely interested in my answer.

I looked around and motioned at the room and joked, "Well, maybe I'm not happy exactly where I am right this second."

Lifting a hand to his chest and dropping his jaw, Bryan feigned indignation. This first sign of banter gave me hope.

"Apologies. Present company excluded, this is not really my scene." I gestured at the room.

Bryan smiled. "How about when you aren't abandoned at a nightclub with a stranger? What makes you happy to be exactly where you are?"

Taking a long drink of water, I thought about the question. "Happiness is relative, is it not? If I'm doing what I love, then even when things are going differently from what I had planned, I'm happy. Honestly, I believe that everything I've ever done has led me to where I'm supposed to be. I feel like I have followed the path that I planned, and even when things haven't been what most would consider happy, it was all part of my journey. All the results of my choices? I've learned from them, good and bad. Decisions had to be made that I didn't want to make, but making those decisions was like adding another steppingstone on my path. I've taken what the universe has given me and made it my own. What good would it do to be anything less than happy with where I am? Life is far too short to live with regrets."

Bryan stared at me with a look of disbelief. "I have never met someone who was so sure of themselves with so little pretense."

Staring back, I was a little stunned by his sudden candor. "Really? You aren't sure of yourself? You seem so confident and self-assured. What would you change?"

"What would I change?"

"Yeah. What choices would you make differently?"

Bryan focused on the table as though the answer was hiding somewhere in the woodgrain. This conversation had moved further and faster than any I could remember having with someone I'd only known for an hour.

"That's a loaded question. Are you sure you have time for those answers?"

"I guess I have as much time as you," I said with a quick look at my watch and glance around the room.

It was at this moment the bartender-turned-server returned with a tray of plates filled with food that he set in front of us. He left once again, leaving us looking at each other and the food.

"And it would be a shame to leave and let all of this go to waste," I added with an amused grin and a flourish of hands as though I was making a presentation.

We sat and talked nonstop for hours before being snapped back to reality with a text message from Stacy that said, *Going home with Pete. Hope you're having fun. He's cute ;-)*

After reading her message, I looked at the time. It was 1:00 a.m. How was that even possible? Hadn't we just sat down? My eyes went wide before I spied Bryan checking his watch. He also appeared surprised.

"Yikes," he said with a chuckle.

"Yeah, I guess time kind of got away from us. Stacy said she's going home with Pete. I guess I should probably head out too." I reluctantly picked up my purse, feeling like I could sit at this table for several hours more.

"There's a good chance I'm going to be worthless tomorrow. Or today, I guess." The research proposal sitting on my desk flashed into my mind, causing me to inwardly groan knowing how much brainpower it would require and how little time I had to complete it.

Bryan picked up his phone. "I guess I'll see about getting an Uber. Want to share one?"

"I drove here. I could give you a ride. Do you live far?"

"Not at all. I just don't like walking through downtown this late. I don't mind getting an Uber. They are always in this area at this time."

"You frequent this area at this time?" I raised my eyebrows in mock suspicion.

I knew there was little chance that this strait-laced guy had questionable business in downtown DC during the early morning hours.

He laughed. "No, but I'm downtown more frequently than I'd like at this time for work. So, I'm familiar with the Uber availability."

Still smiling I said, "I see. Well, let me give you a ride this time, since I no longer have a passenger and I'm already here."

Bryan yielded and motioned for me to lead the way and followed until we were outside where he moved so we were standing next to one another while waiting for the valet. Watching the number of cars and people out and about after midnight made me grateful that I wasn't having to wait alone.

After the valet parked my car and exited the driver's seat, Bryan walked with me around the car and intercepted the valet with a smoothly exchanged handshake.

I turned to Bryan and asked, "Did you just tip him?"

The valet made no attempt to hang around as Bryan held out his arm directing me to the driver's seat. I moved in the direction but waited for an answer before getting in the car.

With one hand on the door, Bryan was now standing in very close proximity to me which made my insides tense before turning into Jell-O. He simply grinned and shrugged, once again motioning for me to get in the car.

I buckled my seatbelt and held the steering wheel as I watched him make his way back around the car, and I continued to stare at him until he was buckled. His only response was to raise his eyebrows and stare back at me. With a bemused shake of my head, I put the car into gear and began to drive away from the club.

"Where to?" I asked.

After several minutes of successful navigation, we pulled up to a set of townhomes. Bryan turned. "What do I owe you?"

"On the house," I said with my best imitation of Pete from earlier in the evening.

"That seems to be a popular phrase this evening. How about lunch Saturday?" he paused before quickly adding, "Wait, today is Saturday. How about lunch today? Would that cover my fare?"

My face grew warm, and I was glad it was dark inside the car. Before I could think about what I was saying I answered, "I think it would."

"Great." His smile was visible in the dark. "Want to give me your number and I'll call you later?"

Within seconds my phone buzzed with the sound of a new message.

"There. And now you have my number." He opened the door but turned to me before getting out of the car. "Thank you for this evening." He hesitated. "It was nice to meet you, Jess. I was expecting something very different. I'll call you later to plan lunch?"

Trying to hide my excitement, I bit my lip and nodded. "I look forward to it."

As soon as I pulled into the driveway at home, I texted Stacy.

Just got home. Please let me know you are safe. Lots to tell you.

I clicked the new message from a new number and smiled.

Thanks for a great evening. – Bryan Carsen.

Adding the number to my contacts, I went inside, took my shoes off inside the door, and carried them upstairs to my bedroom. The house was quiet, but my mind was racing. The entire night replayed in my mind. I hadn't even wanted to go and now I was feeling... what? Euphoria? Exhaustion? I was definitely feeling something.

My thoughts turned over on a loop, and then I remembered another feeling. The warnings emanating from Pete came rushing back. Thinking about them made the hairs on my arms stand and my breath catch. I had been blindsided by Pete and Stacy's exit and then had gotten caught up in conversation with Bryan and never revisited the uncertainty Pete's presence had given me. Should I be worried about Stacy? Yes, Stacy was a grown woman. But she was an immature grown woman who trusted attentive men far too easily.

I was definitely worried about Stacy.

3

JESS

The glow from the clock on the nightstand illuminated the room. I only knew this because my eyes were open, and I was staring at the ceiling. It was almost 2:30 a.m. the last time I looked, and I had a feeling if I looked again, nothing would have changed. The same would be true if I picked up my phone and checked it for any new messages. It didn't matter how many more times I texted Stacy, there was little chance she would respond. I had to try anyway. Maybe the next message would get a response.

Instead, when I picked up my phone, I hesitated. My thumb clicked the message under the one labeled Stacy. This time, I texted the only other person I knew who had a connection to Pete.

> Me: Hi. This is Jess. I'm sorry for texting at this hour and understand if you don't reply, but I am worried about Stacy. I know it's probably nothing, but I just have this feeling I can't shake. Is she safe with Pete?

Two minutes later an answer arrived.

> Bryan: I wish I could answer that for you to settle your mind. I would like to think she is safe with him. But I haven't been in touch with Pete in years. He doesn't have any kind of record of physical violence, but he has a temper when he drinks too much. It usually only makes him loud.

This was not the definitive answer I had hoped for, but he'd answered. Something warm inside me began to blossom, starting in my gut. The phone buzzed again a few moments later.

> Bryan: I just sent Pete a message. He said they were just getting back to his place, and he would call me tomorrow. I don't know what tomorrow means in this case, but if you want, I can call him.

A smile automatically spread across my face, and my nerves calmed as I stared at the screen and typed.

> Me: Thank you. I'm sure she's fine. Stacy thinks I worry about her too much and I'm sure you would much rather get some sleep than hear about my worrying so I will say thank you, again, as well as good night.

> Bryan: If it would help you sleep better, I will gladly listen to your worrying. But if you think you can handle a few hours before hearing from me, I will also say good night and we'll talk again, soon.

The warmth inside me grew into what felt like a cocoon surrounding me. Had I only met Bryan a few hours ago? Our conversations replayed for what seemed like the hundredth time in my mind. We'd naturally moved from one topic into another once Bryan started opening up and I wasn't rapid firing questions. On the one hand, it had felt like having dinner with an old friend. On the other hand, he was still a stranger—a handsome stranger, but a stranger, nonetheless. With those thoughts playing in my head, I drifted off to sleep.

A loud, vibrating sound coming from the nightstand sent my arm flailing to locate it. Startled awake, I reached the phone as the incoming call ended. Five missed calls. All from Stacy. What time was it? Looking at the digital clock, it read 9:14 a.m. The most recent message from Stacy sent a chill through me.

"Hey, Jess." Was Stacy crying? "I hope you're okay. Call me when you get this. I think I need a ride."

What time had she left the message? The call log listed the message as having been left at 8:49 a.m. Not even listening to her other messages, I jumped out of bed, grabbed the jeans I'd worn the night before, and called Stacy back.

Stacy answered, sounding like she was upset or drunk or maybe both and trying to hide it. "Hey, took you long enough to call me back," her words slurring together.

"Stacy, where are you? I'm getting dressed right now and will walk out the door while you tell me what's going on."

Slowly, with clipped words and a strained voice Stacy said, "Stop worrying, Mom. I'm fine. I must have had a little too much to drink, and it made me a little emotional. I'm fine, really. I think Pete went out for a run or something, and I'm just ready to get home and change clothes." It sounded like Stacy was having a hard time putting words together.

Grabbing a shirt from the drawer, I tried to temper my words while making it clear how serious I was being. "Stacy, do not lie to me. We don't have to talk about it now. Just tell me where you are, and I will be there as quickly as I can be."

"I'm sending you my location. I'm not really sure what the address is here."

Was she having trouble staying awake? This was not the first time Stacy had called from a new location needing a ride. It was, however, the first time I could remember her being this out of it this late into the morning.

With Stacy on speakerphone, I stared at the message with the pinned location and stared at the map in disbelief. "Stacy, you're in Southampton, New York."

Silence.

After a long pause Stacy sniffed.

When she didn't say anything else, I tried to assure her. "I'll get there as quickly as I can."

Stacy managed to say, "Thank you," but it sounded like it had taken a lot of effort.

Before letting her hang up I asked, "Are you hurt?"

Stacy took a deep breath and through tears said, "Please, Jess." It was pleading and almost a question.

Taking a deep breath, I tried to sound calm. "I'll see you, soon."

The room felt too quiet once I ended the call. Maybe I should have kept her on the line. I thought about calling her back, but the urgency building in my chest had me moving quickly in the direction of the door. On my way down the stairs, I called Bryan to let him know that I was not going to be available for lunch and caught him up on the situation.

"Stop by and get me on your way," he immediately responded, causing me to pause on the next-to-last step.

"I'm just going straight there and then bringing Stacy home. I think I'll be fine."

"It's what you might find between going and coming that concerns me."

I hadn't even considered what I might walk in on when I arrived. In all honesty, the thought of Bryan being there was a comforting thought.

"Okay. I'll be there soon." I grabbed my purse from the entryway table, walked out, and locked the door, and drove the short distance between our houses.

"Long time, no see," said Bryan warmly as he situated himself in the passenger seat.

I stared at him trying to read him before saying anything.

Warmth. Concern. Calm. Assurance.

"And good morning, to you. Did you get some rest?"

He screwed up his face as though he was thinking. "Let's say, yes," he said repositioning to lean against the door. "Have you had breakfast?" he asked.

I shook my head. "No. More importantly, I rushed out so quickly, I didn't have time to make coffee."

A look of shock crossed his face. "That's probably a criminal offense. We should address it immediately."

"I agree," I said, trying not to laugh. I held eye contact for several seconds as I considered him. Was he always this lively and charming? I let this line of thinking roll around in my mind while I drove us to one of the twenty-three Dunkin Donuts in a ten-mile radius from his home.

We made a quick stop for breakfast and coffee before heading for the highway. We rode in silence for several minutes before I finally said, "Thank you for coming with me. You really didn't have to."

He turned his stare on me for a moment causing the hairs on my arms to stand up and the familiar warm sensation flooded my entire body.

Bryan said quietly, "I'm sorry you're even having to make this trip, but I am not sorry to be going with you."

After taking a sip of my coffee, I took a deep breath and slowly released it as I tried to decide what to say next. Then I started talking and possibly ended up saying more than I should. I couldn't help it. This man seemed to weaken my typically fortified barriers.

"Stacy has a pretty terrible track record with guys. She had a boyfriend last year who couldn't keep his hands to himself, and I don't mean he was frisky. His hands landed Stacy in the emergency room with a fractured cheek bone after one of their arguments. I still don't know exactly what they argued about that night, but knowing Dale, it was probably about whatever Stacy was wearing. He was a controller. Stacy is a pleaser, but she has a stubborn streak. They didn't jive frequently. I suspected he was at least hurting her by grabbing her, because she would have small bruises on her arms. I asked her multiple times if he was hitting her, and she would tell me she could handle herself and Dale was just handsy. The night she went to the hospital she told me it wasn't the first time he had hit her, but it was the last. Unfortunately, he was not the only guy she let hurt her. He was just the worst."

I paused, knowing I'd said more than I should. He was going to think badly about Stacy if I kept on. "I'm not trying to sound critical. She's my best friend. I'm just really worried about her, Bryan. Pete is a different kind of guy from any of her past boyfriends. Physically, socially, financially, he is all around different. Do you think he would hurt her?"

Bryan adjusted the lid on his cup while he thought about his answer. "Like I said, Pete has always had a temper and a drinking problem. He wouldn't call his drinking a problem, but it definitely caused a number of problems when we were younger."

"Yeah?" I wasn't sure I really wanted to know the kind of problems Pete had caused, but it sounded like I probably needed to prepare myself for what we might be driving toward.

Bryan stared out the window and spoke to the cars passing us. "We were deployed together on a mission in Mozambique not long after we both enlisted. We were delivering humanitarian aid and helping the people bolster their intelligence abilities against ISIS. We had makeshift quarters on the embassy compound. The situation in the country was a lot worse than we had originally thought, but Pete can find a good time anywhere. He was not going to let the uncertain conditions hinder him in any way.

"There was one abnormally quiet evening. We were sitting in the rec, and Pete pulled out a flask and waggled his eyebrows at me as though he had a secret to share. I rolled my eyes at him because he knows I don't drink. He smiled his famous mischievous smile, took a swig, and leaned back in his chair. He sat there for ten seconds, maybe, before he took another drink. He closed his eyes, and I sat there and watched as he seemed to drift off to sleep. It was creepy. I knew something wasn't right."

Bryan closed his eyes and pinched the bridge of his nose. This was clearly not a memory he enjoyed reliving. "Had it just been the usual whiskey that he had somehow smuggled in from elsewhere, he would not have just fallen asleep like a narcoleptic. I called his name a few times, and he didn't answer so I walked over and patted his face and tried to wake him. He jerked awake, jumped up and grabbed his sidearm and grabbed me. He tried to pull me down to hide behind his chair with him, like we were taking cover. He was pointing his pistol and yelling something about needing back up, and the whole time his eyes were just glazed over.

"I finally realized he wasn't fully awake, but he wasn't asleep, kind of like a sleepwalk or hallucination. I got free of him and got him in a bear hug, and he lost the grip on his gun. He started flailing and was still yelling. Another one of the guys took Pete's legs, and we practically dragged him to the infirmary while I yelled for one of the others to pick up the dropped gun and flask and follow us. We had to help the doc get him restrained, and after five minutes of struggling, Pete stopped moving, closed his eyes and slept for three days."

When Bryan stopped talking, I took what felt like the only breath I had been able to take for the duration of his story. "What was in that flask?" I wondered aloud.

I felt him looking at me when he huffed. "Apparently, he had made a trade with one of the African soldiers -- vape pens for the flask. It took the doctor a while to break it all down, but it was apparently laced with LSD. Pete told our CO that he had no idea what was in the flask and assumed it had been whiskey. He just liked the flask. It was on that mission I learned that Pete was a better liar than I thought."

The thoughts in my head about who Pete really might be began to create a sense of panic inside me. Bryan was not painting his friend in a positive light, and he was not making me feel better about what could be awaiting us on the other end of this road trip. He must have realized what I was thinking.

"I know, that was probably not the best 'Pete story' to share in this exact moment. But I've known him a long time. He's done some pretty dumb things, but he never intentionally hurt anyone but himself with his antics."

Looking at the phone's GPS, we still had three hours to go before we found the location of Stacy's dropped location pin. I thought about the feeling I had when Pete shook my hand when we met at the club. Images came flooding back into my mind of the first time I'd felt the physical warning signs of danger from another person.

One morning in a middle school physical education class, we were learning how to play softball. The male teacher, Coach Drysden, was teaching us how to hold the bat and take practice swings. I noticed that it was only the female students who got hands-on help. The boys were shown from a distance how to hold the bat if they didn't already know. I had assumed it was because most of the male students played city league baseball.

When it came to the girls, however, the coach would hold out the bat until the female student would reach for it. When she did, he would pull the bat and the girl toward him and begin to wrap himself around her. As the girl placed her other hand on the bat, Coach Drysden closed his free hand around hers and began to move her arms and body through the motions of swinging the bat.

When it was my turn to hold the bat, Coach Drysden held the bat out, and when I put my hand out to take it from him, my hand inadvertently touched his. What felt like an electrical current shot through my arm, down my spine, and back up to my brain. I flinched and immediately let go of the bat.

Drysden's eyes bored into me as he snarled, "What? You already knew how to swing a bat?"

Without hesitation, I nodded without speaking, even though I had no idea how to swing a bat. I did know that if I had to choose between figuring it out on my own and experiencing the painful feeling that came with the coach's touch, I was determined to figure it out on my own.

I felt the coach watching me as I hoped that I had paid close enough attention to the other students to at least not make a fool of myself. The ball came toward me from the pitcher's mound, I swung and tipped the ball. A few more tries, and I moved the ball forward and back to the pitcher.

Coach Drysden seemed to accept my success by putting his hand on my shoulder and taking the bat from me. The shock hit me again. It wasn't a static electricity pop. It was a strong, painful current that moved deep inside me, as though every nerve in my body was on fire. I turned to move out from under his hand and immediately let go of the bat.

From that day forward, I watched his every interaction with every student. I studied his face when he would talk to the boys and when he would help the girls. I noted the differences in his posture and the movements of his face as he moved through the line of students. By the end of the week, I knew that there was something "off" about Coach Drysden.

I remember telling my mom about the experience and asked if I had to take PE. Of course, she told me I had to take PE, but if the coach made me uncomfortable, I needed to follow my instincts. Three weeks later, murmurings were rampant of Coach Drysden's escort from campus by the police during sixth period. The next day, we had a new female PE teacher. The next week, the news was reporting the arrest of a local coach for possession of child pornography. It was then my mom made it a point to remind me frequently to always trust my gift.

Bryan's voice from the seat next to me snapped me back to reality. "Are you all right? You look a little shaken. Did I say something to upset you?"

I noticed my grip on the steering wheel had tightened and my shoulders were tense.

I tried to smile, even though I was a little embarrassed. "No, sorry. I got lost in my own mind for a minute." Trying to lighten the mood I said, "You know, I've never taken a road trip with someone I've known for less than a day. I'm sure my mother would not have approved. I mean, she would have been fine with it after I told her you were safe. But she would have given me grief about it first."

Bryan cocked his head and gave me a half smile. "Safe?"

"Yeah." I laughed nervously, drumming my fingers on the steering wheel. I should not tell him this. I didn't know him; he didn't know me. I needed to change the subject. Instead, once again, words spilled out before I could stop them.

"I have what my mom called a gift." I glanced at him quickly before returning my eyes to the road. "It's really more of a skill that I've practiced and learned how to use. I can read people easily, and sometimes I can physically feel whether or not they're safe or can at least be trusted. So, she always trusted my choices when it came to the people I allowed into my life because I could tell if a person was safe or not."

"So, this gift," Bryan hesitated. "Did it tell you something about Pete? You seemed really upset about him when you texted me after you got home."

I nodded. "When he shook my hand, there was a very strong feeling that went with it, and I couldn't let go fast enough. And it must have shown, because Stacy had this look on her face when it happened. I think that's why she deflected and left so willingly. She wanted to spite me or to prove she was right about him, and I was wrong. She always says I act too much like her mother. But she needs someone looking out for her. Her judgment is typically very clouded."

"Well, she's lucky to have you to watch her back. Even if she doesn't act like it, she clearly trusts you enough to ask you to drive three hundred miles to pick her up from a bad date."

This was not the reaction I was expecting. I was expecting questions or laughter. Instead, he listened, believed me, and affirmed me. My heart fluttered momentarily before I could respond.

"I'm just glad she called." I tried to keep my focus on the road ahead of us.

There was another bout of silence. This time I broke it. "So, I've told you something about me. Now you tell me something about you. Then I won't be road tripping with a total stranger." I gave him a quick smile.

Bryan stroked his chin and scrunched his face as though he was thinking hard. "Well, let's see. I grew up in Kentucky. I'm an only child. My dad was in the Army. I played football. I enlisted right out of high school. I went to AMU where I eventually got my doctorate in strategic intelligence, which I use to work with computers and people all day every day. Most of the time I prefer working with the computers. And the most interesting fact I can think of about myself is that I once took a road trip with a total stranger to another state to pick up her friend."

I snorted a laugh. "That was an excellent start. I was hoping we might kill more than twenty seconds though."

Bryan shrugged with a grin. "I'm afraid I am not the most interesting person you could take on a road trip."

Surely, he remembered my propensity for asking questions. He wasn't about to get off this easily. "Tell me about growing up in Kentucky."

Bryan's eyebrows went up as he seemed surprised by the choice of topic. He tapped his chin before answering. "I will tell you about Kentucky, but you also have to answer the same question. Deal?"

"Deal."

We took turns volleying stories from our pasts. Bryan talked about growing up in what was basically a single-parent home even before his father died.

I shared with Bryan the story of my dad leaving and of my mom's passing from a short battle with an aggressive cancer during my first year of college.

As we took turns sharing about ourselves, I kept thinking how glad I was Bryan had come with me and how I didn't want anyone else in my passenger seat. Every time I stole a glance or he simply talked, I felt grounded and peaceful. This stranger was becoming more familiar with every passing mile, and this thought brought on a new but familiar warmth.

THE NEXT SEVERAL hours flew by, and the conversation flowed as naturally and easily between us as it had the night before. By the time we found the address Stacy had sent, we were no longer complete strangers.

"I think this is it." I pulled into a driveway of a bayfront estate. It was a massive structure with large glass windows and doors on all sides. "It's a fishbowl," I said without much thought.

"Yeah." Bryan considered the house in front of us. "Seems like it would be awkward to be naked in your own home."

We exchanged amused, horrified looks before looking back toward the house. I unmounted my cell phone from its holder and dialed Stacy, but there was no answer. I texted and still no answer. There were no other houses nearby. No cars around. No passersby to ask. Feeling helpless, I looked at Bryan.

"I don't know what to do other than hope she answers the door when I ring the doorbell."

Bryan tried calling Pete and was sent straight to voicemail. An uncomfortable silence settled between us as we assessed the situation. There was little to work with, but we had to get to Stacy, and this was the only place we knew to look.

Bryan opened his door and quietly got out of the car. He gently closed the door, so I followed suit. The atmosphere surrounding us suddenly felt tense. Bryan waited for me to come to his side so we could walk to the front steps together. We stopped at the front door which was, like the rest of the house, made of glass, and tried to peer into the windows. Sheer curtains lightly obscured a full view into the house, but we both saw what appeared to be a leg on the floor behind a coffee table.

I gasped, covering my mouth with one hand and gripping Bryan's arm with the other. Bryan tried the knob, which turned out to be unlocked, then turned to me and with a quiet, serious voice said, "Jess, I don't know what is on the other side of this door, but something feels wrong. I want you to wait here until you hear from me. If you see anything that looks wrong or out of place, it's okay to call the police and wait in the car."

My heart was pounding in my chest, and everything felt muted. How had it gone from a simple trip to pick up a hungover friend to

Bryan telling me I might need to call the police? I nodded in understanding and watched Bryan pull a handgun from his -- a handgun I did not know he was carrying.

He glanced back at me and gave what I took as a reassuring nod, and I watched as he eased open the door and walked inside with his gun drawn. He took slow, intentional steps toward the coffee table, scanning the room, sweeping his pistol as he scanned the room from side to side. He made his way through the open living space, and as he approached the coffee table, he holstered his gun and knelt before calling out to me.

"Stacy is here. She's alive, but she needs an ambulance. I'm going to check the rest of the house. Call 9-1-1." He retrieved his weapon and proceeded to sweep the rest of the house.

Fifteen minutes later, sirens and flashing lights made their way up the street. My entire body was trembling as I told the female officer everything, including the events of the previous night. The male officer and the EMTs followed Bryan inside to where Stacy was still on the floor.

Bryan exited the house first, holding what looked like Stacy's handbag in one hand and making a phone call with the other. He stood against the door, holding it open for the EMTs who were wheeling Stacy out on a stretcher. One of the policemen also walked out and shook Bryan's hand and handed him a card. Bryan nodded and handed the officer Stacy's handbag.

The sight of Stacy being wheeled from the house left me gasping and crying.

Immediately, Bryan jogged over and put his arms around me. All I could do was hug him back and hold onto him as though he was the only thing keeping my feet anchored to the ground. I was sobbing as they lifted the stretcher into the ambulance.

"What happened? Where are they taking her?"

With one arm holding me to him and the other gently cradling the back of my head, he spoke in a quiet voice. "The officer said they would take her to Southampton Hospital. We can follow them there. Do you think you can drive?"

Too stunned to say anything, I simply shook my head against his hand.

"Okay. I'll drive," he said, his cheek pressed to the top of my head.

I pulled away from him and straightened my shirt before wiping both of my cheeks with my shaking fingers. Bryan walked me to the passenger side of the car and opened the door for me, waiting until I was fully inside before closing the door and walking back to the driver's side. When the ambulance and police car pulled away, Bryan followed as I sat quietly staring out the window.

"I need to call Stacy's parents," I said abruptly. I wriggled my phone from my back pocket, having to wipe tears from my eyes just to see the screen so I could scroll through my contacts. I took a deep breath, trying to steady my voice when the call connected.

"Hello?" answered a woman's voice with a thick southern accent on the other end.

"Mrs. Carlisle, this is Jess Hayley, Stacy's roommate. I'm not sure what's wrong. I had to call an ambulance for Stacy, and we are on our way to the hospital. It looks like maybe she passed out. The details aren't clear, but she wasn't responding. She is with the EMTs now."

"Oh, my Lord! Which hospital is she going to?" Mrs. Carlisle sounded flustered.

"Southampton Hospital."

"Where is that?"

"Mrs. Carlisle, Stacy was in Southampton, New York last night and called me this morning and asked if I could come pick her up. When we got here, she was alone and unconscious on the floor, so I called an ambulance. We just got to the hospital. I need to go inside and find out more. Okay?" I knew I had just dropped a bomb on the poor woman, but I couldn't think clearly enough to choose words that weren't simply the truth.

"Oh, my Lord," was all Mrs. Carlisle seemed to be able to say.

There was an awkward pause when I wasn't sure if our call was still connected. I checked the screen and when I saw she was still on the line, I returned the phone to my ear.

Before I could speak, Mrs. Carlisle said, "Okay, thank you, Jess.

Please let me know what you find out. I'm going to find a flight out right away."

With that, I agreed to keep her updated and then we said goodbye.

By the time the call ended, Bryan had parked the car in the small hospital parking lot outside of the emergency department. I stared wordlessly at him, not knowing exactly what I was supposed to do next.

He put his hand on mine and in a calming voice said, "Let's go inside and see if we can find someone that is doing intake and learn what we can. It looks like they are still in the bay, so there's a chance she hasn't even made it into the system."

It was this simple gesture that provided me with the fortitude to face whatever came next. With a glance down at our hands and then back to Bryan, I whispered, "Thank you." Tears were burning my eyes, again.

He squeezed my hand and gave an almost imperceptible nod before letting go of my hand and moving to turn off the car. He opened his door and quickly made his way to my door to open it before I had the chance. He offered his hand to help me from the car, which I accepted after grabbing my purse. With a hand on my back, Bryan led me into the hospital.

Walking through the doors brought memories from seven years ago as I walked with my mom through her battle with cancer. The harsh lighting, the smells, the eerie silence were a lot to process on top of my already emotional state. I took a deep breath and stared ahead as Bryan guided us toward the front desk. When we stopped walking, I blinked several times before looking around the room. It was a small hospital, and the emergency room seemed deserted.

A nurse standing at the administration desk looked up and smiled giving us a cheery, "Hello." Her voice was sweet and her eyes kind. *Compassion. Genuity.* "Can I help you with something?"

Bryan smiled back at the nurse and quickly glimpsed her ID badge. "Hi, Mandy. Our friend was being brought here by ambulance, and it appears we may have beaten them inside."

About that time the phone on the desk rang.

"Excuse me for a moment," she held up a finger and answered the phone. Mandy studied Bryan and me as she listened. She gave a quick, "Okay, got it," and hung up the phone. "Your friend is just coming in. If you want to take a seat in the waiting area, I'll update you when I can." She gave us a reassuring smile.

We walked to the waiting area where vinyl cushioned chairs and sofas were positioned with side tables in between. Sitting on a two-seat couch, I pulled out my phone and sent a quick text to Mrs. Carlisle, letting her know we were at the hospital and Stacy was being brought in but that I had no other news.

Once the message sent, I checked the time on the phone screen. It was after 5:00 p.m. This day had been one long roller coaster ride and not the exciting kind that makes you want to stand in line for an hour hoping to do it all over again. Instead, I was waiting at a hospital in the Hamptons, feeling completely lost, rather than hanging out with Stacy drinking coffee and talking about the new feelings I had been excited to explore.

I couldn't write off the entire day since I had genuinely enjoyed the trip itself. The conversations and the laughs had given me the energy and resolve I needed for what had turned out to be a taxing day. I also couldn't ignore the attraction I had to Bryan.

This thought alone threatened to send me over the edge of panic that I had held at bay since my call with Stacy. Nothing about the last eighteen hours felt natural or in the least familiar for me. I was not prone to emotional displays, desiring of physical contact, or feeling a lack of control over my circumstances. Yet, I found myself having experienced all three and all in the company of a man I barely knew. And now, what I had expected to be a simple day trip was turning into a possible overnight wait in a hospital waiting room with the same man.

Before I could spiral any deeper into a black hole of anxiety, I needed to regain traction in my head and not allow my emotions to get the best of me. I started making a list of the facts I knew to be concrete. My best friend had been found unconscious in an empty house that belonged to Pete, a man I didn't know. He was also a man I did not believe to be the nice guy Stacy had wanted him to be.

Before I could make much progress, my thoughts trailed off and my mind buzzed with static. It was suddenly very apparent that I was tired, and according to the sounds my stomach made, I was starving. It growled loudly enough for the nurse at the desk across the room to hear, causing Mandy to look up and give me an empathetic smile. The heat in my cheeks rose.

"There's a cafeteria down the hall or vending machines around this corner." Mandy gestured behind her. "Honestly, if you're staying, I recommend the vending machines. The selections aren't healthy, and you'll probably be hungry again in an hour, but it's probably safer than the night shift in the cafeteria."

Bryan stood and stretched. "What do you think? Vending machine or hospital food?" he asked, weighing the options on invisible scales.

"I think with the way today is going, we should play it safe with the vending machines," I said, hearing the fatigue in my own voice.

"Agreed." Bryan held out his hand to help me up, which I accepted.

It was warm and steady. Warmth spread from his hand throughout my entire body as we walked around the corner where the nurse had directed us. As expected, we found two vending machines.

"She wasn't kidding about the selection." Bryan studied the options. "What will you have?"

I stared at the machine where our options were a variety of generic potato chips, rice cereal treats, candy bars, and sugar-free chewing gum.

"Decisions, decisions," I muttered. I was not a huge fan of snack foods because I always ended up starving and eating more than I would have if I ate real food. I picked up my purse to dig out my wallet as I made my decision. "I guess I'll go for the rice cereal treat. It's like eating cereal for dinner, right?"

Before I could get my wallet unclasped, Bryan had swiped his card and entered multiple numbers and letters into the machine.

"You really don't have to," I said.

He smiled. "I owe you for the ride last night, remember? It's the least I could do."

In disbelief, I smiled back at him. "I think all the events of today more than repay me. They probably put me in your debt."

We stared at each other wordlessly, and I found myself losing all sense of reality. There was a strength and assurance in those green eyes. Our surroundings seemed to dissolve around us. Had I really just met him yesterday? As cliché as it might be, it was starting to feel like I had known him my entire life. A thought entranced me as I was caught in his gaze. I was greatly anticipating settling any and all of my debts to Bryan, no matter how long it took.

The sound of footsteps coming around the corner pulled us both to the present. Turning, we watched the reception nurse walk in our direction.

"Dr. Lawson would like to speak with you," the nurse told us.

Bryan reached down to grab our vending machine purchases, and we followed Mandy back to the waiting area. I opened my purse for Bryan to shove the snacks in for the time being, which garnered a laugh from both of us. The much-too-small bag was overflowing with junk food as though we were attempting to sneak them into a movie theater.

A doctor was waiting for us as we approached the front desk. He motioned for us to follow him to a small private room with three plastic chairs inside the door. I remembered sitting in a room very similar with my mother and her oncologist. This was where families received the bad news.

The difference between the past experience and this one was that I wasn't receiving the news alone. Yes, my mom had been in the room when the doctor told us nothing else could be done for her. However, I'd had to process my own feelings on top of helping Mom cope with her own, as well as take on the logistics that came with receiving the news.

This time, there was someone here with me who had not only insisted on coming with me, but he had been rock solid every step of the way. Maybe I was putting too much pressure on a one-sided connection. But for now, it was all I had to cling to, and that was enough for me in this moment.

The doctor gestured to the chairs for us to sit, and he followed us inside.

"I'm Dr. Lawson. I was told that you are here with Stacy Carlisle. Is this correct?"

Bryan nodded as I answered with a croak, "Yes. How is she?"

The doctor held up his hand to allow for a collective moment of silence before answering.

His voice was calm and reassuring when he said, "The EMTs filled me in on what they were told by the police. I really shouldn't be telling you anything because you aren't technically family, but..." Dr. Lawson considered me as he carefully thought about his next words. "She is your roommate, yes?"

I nodded quickly. "Yes. For the last four years."

Dr. Lawson considered this. "That's close enough to family for me, but let's keep that between us."

"Right. Thank you."

"Your friend is very lucky you got to her when you did," explained the doctor.

Tears burned my eyes, again, but I had no control over them as they made their way down my face. Bryan reached for a box of tissues as the doctor continued to talk.

"I need to ask if you are aware of whether she was with someone last night or this morning."

Taking a tissue, I answered with the only information I had, which seemed meager in the light of his tone. "She left with a man named Pete Stewart last night. Based on what she told me this morning, he had been with her until sometime before nine this morning when I talked to her."

Dr. Lawson's face cleared as though this information settled something in his mind. "There was evidence of sexual activity but not rape. Does your friend drink?"

I nodded as I replayed in my mind a number of episodes involving drunken phone calls or texts Stacy had made over the last few years. "Unfortunately, she does, and with regularity. She doesn't have a dependency, but she definitely makes drinking a priority."

The doctor listened and thought before speaking. "Your friend, Stacy, had a blood alcohol content of .08 which means she either drank very heavily last night or this morning or both. However, she doesn't show the normal signs of toxicity. And alcohol does not explain the biggest part of the puzzle. Currently, Stacy is in a coma."

This news turned my insides to ice. I gasped, trying to cover my shock with a hand. Bryan's hand squeezed my shoulder, a reminder he was still there.

"We are running a CT, and we'll do a full MRI in hopes of finding the cause. I know none of this is really an answer, but I thought you would want to know we are working hard to find out what is going on with Stacy."

Tears continued to fall, and all I could do was nod. Dr. Lawson stood; Bryan did the same and extended his hand, shaking the doctor's. Then we were left alone in the small room.

Bryan turned to me with the sweetest expression on his face, and it was at that moment I wished my brain hadn't felt as though it had been replaced with fluffy cotton balls and my eyes weren't fully blurred by tears. Instead, I was unable to read anything more than the same kindness I had been experiencing all day. He offered his hand, and I took it as we walked back in the direction of the waiting area.

BACK IN THE waiting room I realized I should call Stacy's mother to give her the update we had just received. My thoughts felt a lot like static on a dead radio station as I tried to separate out the white noise from the sounds breaking through from other stations. There were thoughts about Bryan, and those were complicated in and of themselves. Then I needed to try and reason out what had happened to Stacy so I could pass along the information to her parents. I felt frozen in place by the weight of so much happening so quickly. The ding of an overhead speaker alerting us to a building-wide page pulled me out of my head and back to the moment.

"I need to call Mrs. Carlisle and fill her in," I told Bryan.

"Okay. I'll try to call Pete, again. I've been sent straight to his voicemail all day. Then, if you would like, we could walk over to a real restaurant and hold on to this load of snacks for later."

With a nod of affirmation I said, "That sounds good," before I moved to sit on the couch we had vacated earlier.

Before pressing the call button, I debated if telling Mrs. Carlisle about the coma was something she needed to worry herself with until they arrived. I decided that if I were in her place, I would want to know exactly what I was walking into when I got to the hospital. Mrs. Carlisle didn't answer, so I left all the details in a voicemail for her to listen to when they landed. With that, I put my phone in my purse and walked toward the automatic doors.

Bryan was in the parking lot talking on the phone. His face showed frustration and anger as though the conversation he was having was intense.

A wave of exhaustion rolled over me, and I sunk into one of the chairs close to the door. My eyes caught sight of a wooden cross hanging behind the nurse's station before I leaned forward, resting my elbows on my knees. I closed my eyes and rested my head on my hands, trying to force my mind to clear and my shoulders to relax.

The lingering image of the cross behind closed eyelids caused my mind to drift to one quiet Sunday morning about a year ago. It was sunny but not yet warm. The coolness of winter had not fully dissolved into spring. It was a rare Sunday that I had not chosen to work, and I desperately needed a break from reading another research paper. A walk sounded like a good idea, but I had no real destination in mind. As I was wandering down the sidewalk, I came to a large, old brick building with a steeple. The sign read Grace Presbyterian Church. From inside I could hear voices singing along with a piano.

Without thinking, I walked toward the front steps of the church, and before I realized what I was doing, I had walked up the steps, opened one of the large wooden doors, and slipped into a seat on the back row. A song was coming to an end, and the singing was louder and even more mesmerizing inside than it had been from the outside. I took in the room full of people around me to discover it was as diverse as the neighborhood I had lived in back in Long Beach. The faces were all joyful and kind. A man I assumed to be the pastor, stepped to the lectern and began to speak.

He talked about God and how he was the supreme ruler and king of the entire universe. He said that God has a master plan for all of humanity and that this should be a comfort to those who were considered to be children of God.

The words were beautiful, and as the pastor spoke, my spirit felt peaceful, lighter. When he stepped down from speaking, the piano began to play, and the people began to sing again. The words were rich and soothing as was the melody. I had never heard the song before, but it settled into my soul and made me feel warm from the inside out as though it was an old familiar tune.

When the song was over, another man led the congregation in a group recitation he called a confession. The words sounded old, and the people's voices echoed with conviction. When the group was once again quiet, the man leading them asked everyone to bow their heads to pray.

It was at this moment I took advantage of the privacy and made my way back out the way I had come in without being noticed.

The walk home was reflective. Questions swirled in my head. Did I believe there was a God? If there is a God, is he really in charge of the entire universe down to every element of some grand plan for humanity? I rolled them over in my mind and decided I would take more time to ponder it again later. I had already made so many plans and worked tirelessly to see them become reality that I didn't have time to let the idea of a higher power derail me. Even when I hit roadblocks, I had always seen them as opportunities for redirection and growth. In my mind, they had always been coincidence or a chance to make a different choice. I never considered they could possibly be divine intervention.

The memory was interrupted when I heard the automatic doors of the hospital open. Looking up, I saw Bryan walking back inside after his phone call. He was wearing a forced smile but was clearly upset.

"Everything okay?" I asked him.

Hands on his hips and shaking his head, Bryan's head fell forward and he took a deep breath then sighed. "That was Pete."

My eyebrows raised as I waited for him to continue.

"He says he's headed out of the country for a business meeting. He swears he told Stacy about it last night and left her a note this morning. I filled him in on everything I could, and all he could say was, 'well that sucks.'"

My eyebrows rose even higher, and I felt my eyes go wide.

With an unamused chuckle, Bryan ran a hand down his face. "There is no reason his attitude should surprise me. He's always been the kind of guy who looks out for number one. It's just really hard to imagine anyone being so callous."

I crossed my arms and struggled to make sense of it. "I can't imagine either. And I can't imagine why a girl like Stacy is drawn to guys like Pete. I've tried to reason it out, and the only conclusion I can ever reach is that she doesn't think she's worthy of better. And nothing I have ever said to her could convince her otherwise."

We stood in silence for a moment before Bryan abruptly changed course. He cleared his throat and attempted to sound upbeat, as though he could push past his feelings about Pete. "While I was outside on the phone, I noticed several restaurants right in this area. Are you up for a walk and some real food?"

Tired and hungry, I smiled. "I think that is just what the doctor ordered."

Bryan went to the desk and told Mandy we would be back shortly, but if she didn't mind, to call one of us if anything changed or there was news of any kind concerning Stacy. He left both our cell numbers, thanked her, and walked toward the doors where I was waiting.

Two blocks from the hospital was a bar and grill that didn't look too crowded. We got a table and settled into the booth facing one another and ordered drinks. After the waitress walked off, we sat in a comfortable silence until the server came back to the table with our drinks.

"Have you decided what you're going to have, sweetie?" The young waitress, whose nametag read Millie, flashed Bryan a flirty grin. She had positioned herself so that most of her profile faced me, and she leaned on the table, blocking from my view the side where Bryan was sitting. She kept her eyes trained on him. He was oblivious to the waitress's attempt at flirting with him as he glanced at her, handed her his menu, ordered a bacon cheeseburger and fries, and immediately peered around Millie to me.

Millie tried to convince Bryan she was more interesting than anything else currently at the table by leaning a little farther back still trying to block his view. She was practically sitting on our table.

"Are you sure that's all you want? Surely a guy with those muscles needs more than just a burger and fries."

Bryan shook his head and leaned sideways to see around her. "That's all. Jess? Do you know what you want?"

I had to bite my lip to keep from laughing. Millie slowly turned to acknowledge me but kept her eyes on Bryan as long as she possibly could. When she finally faced me, the look on her face threatened to make me laugh in spite of the vice my lips were clenched in between my teeth.

Exasperation. Disinterest. Frustration.

It was obvious that Millie had little interest in refocusing her attention, so I cleared my throat. "I'll have the same."

With that, she snatched my menu and walked off without another word.

When Millie was out of earshot, I laughed and said, "I think she likes you."

This brought a rosy blush to Bryan's cheeks which made the grin on my face grow even wider.

I couldn't stop myself from saying, "Like that doesn't happen all the time."

Bryan's sheepish expression warmed my heart. "I don't go out much."

I laughed. "I don't go out much either. But I know a flirty waitress when I see one." I studied his face. His green eyes were clear, though obviously tired. I found myself struggling to look away.

Calm. Honest.

His once clean-shaven face was showing signs of stubble. I'd be crazy to reach out and touch it, wouldn't I? My eyes wandered to his lips. They looked soft. I bet they were as warm and firm as I was imagining.

Secure. Hopeful.

Apparently, I had lost all concept of time and had no idea how long we had been sitting silently, but I suddenly became acutely aware Bryan had been staring back at me when his voice interrupted my thoughts, yanking my line of sight back to his.

"Do you believe in God?"

I blinked like it was the first time I had blinked in a long time. Trying to refocus, I took a drink of my water, aligned my silverware on the table, and stammered the question back to Bryan. "Do I believe in God?"

His face was hopeful.

"I don't really know. Do you believe in God?"

Bryan's eyes lit up. "I do believe in God."

Where was this coming from? And on the heels of the random memory about the church and a sermon that had clearly stuck with me, even if it was in the recesses of my subconscious.

"What made you ask me if I believed in God?"

Bryan's gaze was more serious and intense than it had been. "I'm sitting here with this beautiful woman I just met. And as I'm watching her, all I can think is that there has to be a God for this to be real. Twenty-four hours ago, I had no idea that my life was anything but complete. Now, I'm convinced that something has been missing."

My face grew hot. The silence lingered again, but the air between us felt charged. This was new and different. I'd think it was merely an extension of what I'd been feeling since he shook my hand when we met, but his face told me differently.

Hopeful. Interest. Vulnerable.

When Millie came to the table carrying two plates of food, she set them down in front of us, placing her hand on Bryan's shoulder. "Need anything, sweetie?"

Without taking his eyes from mine, he lifted his chin as though to indicate he was speaking to her. "No, thank you."

"You?" She turned her attention to me briefly.

I shook my head.

With a roll of her eyes, Millie left us and walked back to the kitchen.

My phone buzzed with a message. I dug it from my bag and read the screen. The message was from Mrs. Carlisle. I read it to Bryan.

We found a private pilot who is willing to fly us tonight. He says it's about an eight-hour flight.

The events of the day once again rolled over me, reminding me that I wasn't simply out to dinner with a cute guy. I held the phone to my chest as my heart felt the ache knowing the Carlisle family was about to face an incredibly challenging time.

"I'm sure she's relieved to be moving in this direction, but that is going to make for a long day for them tomorrow." I put the phone back into my purse.

"I'm afraid they may be in for a number of long days at this rate," Bryan said with a heavy sigh.

After several beats of silence, I decided to return us to our previous conversation. "So, what's another reason you believe in God?" I tried to keep my tone light, but I was genuinely curious.

Bryan swallowed and thought before answering. "Sometimes it feels like I've just always known God was real. My mom took me to church every Sunday my entire childhood. I watched her pray for my dad and for me and for everyone she met. She read her Bible and talked about God being in the mundane things like laundry. It wasn't until I was in high school that it clicked. I was sitting at the kitchen table doing homework one evening, and Mom was listening to some preacher on the radio talking about God. He said something like, 'You can't see the wind, but you know it's there because you can feel it and you can see what it does, and sometimes you can even hear it. The same is true for God.' And somehow at that moment, I just knew that God was real."

All I could do was stare at him, my eyes burning with tears. With a shaky inhale, I attempted to get my already volatile emotions in check. I wiped my eyes with a napkin as I asked, "Just like that, huh?"

Bryan smiled gently, "Just like that."

We ate and talked briefly about different things, not staying on any one topic for very long but moved away from talking about God.

Millie brought two separate tickets to the table, and Bryan reached for them, but I grabbed them before he could, which surprised our server.

Giving me a quick sideways glance, she turned to Bryan. "I hope I see you in here, again, sweetie," and she gave him a wink. "If you ever find yourself lonely, you know where to find me."

Bryan stared at her as though she had materialized from thin air and he struggled to compose a sentence. The best he could manage through his embarrassment was, "Uh, thanks."

Millie sauntered away looking back at Bryan and giving him what was probably supposed to be a seductive grin.

A laugh tried to escape, forcing me to bite my knuckle until the server was out of earshot. "Wow. I have to hand it to Millie. She's confident."

Bryan rolled his eyes and then reached out his hands with an unspoken request for the tickets.

"You bought breakfast and the snacks at the hospital. I'm buying dinner."

Bryan turned his face upwards and sighed in exasperation. "Fine. But the next one is mine."

"I don't think so." I shook my head. "I believe that today alone has put me in your debt for a very long time."

Bryan considered me for a moment before responding. "While I don't agree that you owe me anything, I do think that I am open to exploring some repayment options."

Acting as though Bryan had made some wild innuendo, I splayed a hand over my chest and dropped my jaw. This reaction caused Bryan's cheeks to turn red, which made me laugh. He was too easy to fluster, and it was really cute when he blushed.

He stammered, "That's not... I mean... I was thinking more like you would pay for dinner again." He dragged a hand over his face.

"I know." I gave him an exaggerated wink like Millie had. "I thought it might be fun to watch you squirm for a minute. It was, for the record."

After I paid our tickets, we made the journey back to the hospital mostly in silence. There was a new nurse at the desk when we walked back inside. Becky was not nearly as amiable as Mandy had been upon our meeting. She told us she would talk to the doctor and let us know if she could tell us anything, then gestured for us to have a seat as she picked up the phone.

Several minutes passed before she called out, "Miss Hayley, Dr. Lawson would like a word with you and Mr. Carsen."

We walked to the desk where Dr. Lawson met us. His face was hard to read, but his voice was kind when he spoke.

"I have good news and bad news, though I will tell you that the good news probably won't sound very good."

I held my breath as Bryan took up the space behind me, his hands on my shoulders.

"I've concluded that Stacy suffered from what appears to be a mild stroke."

It felt as though I had been punched in the stomach. All the air I had been holding in rushed from my lungs leaving me feeling dizzy. Bryan's hands tightened on my shoulders.

"Like I said, the good news doesn't sound very good, I know."

"If that's the good news, what's the bad news?" Bryan asked.

"Stacy is in a fairly deep coma."

I was speechless. Bryan spoke instead. "How long will she be in a coma?"

Dr. Lawson's eyes darted from me to Bryan. "There is no way to know. Chances are she was having a slow stroke where a blood clot was slowing the flow of blood down but had not completely cut it off. But it had been happening long enough to cause some damage to the brainstem. It's rare but it does explain what we are seeing in this situation."

Bryan nodded. "Can we see her?"

Dr. Lawson smiled and nodded. "Of course."

He led us to a room and opened the door. Once we were both inside, Dr. Lawson followed. "You can go to her. She won't respond, but I personally think coma patients are aware that there is still a world around them and that they can hear you." With that, the doctor left the room with a nod.

My steps felt wobbly as I walked to the bedside and gently took Stacy's hand. "Oh, Stacy. I am so sorry. I never should have let you leave last night." Sobs shook my body as I rested my head on her hand in mine.

After several minutes of my holding Stacy's hand and crying, Bryan gently rubbed my back and asked, "Do you need anything?"

I sat up and let go of Stacy's hand, sniffling and wiping my eyes. "I need to call Mrs. Carlisle."

"Okay," he whispered. Bryan led us back to the waiting room and grabbed a box of tissues from one of the end tables as we made our way to one of the couches in a dark corner of the room.

"Thank you," I said as I took the box of tissues from him. I tried to dry my face as best I could before I started rummaging through my bag for my phone. The phone battery was low, but I was sure it wouldn't matter. Chances were, Mrs. Carlisle wouldn't have her phone on while she and her husband were on the airplane. I left a message relaying the details from the doctor. The phone died as I was ending the call. I sat and stared at it blankly as though I could force it through sheer will to turn on again.

"What's wrong?" Bryan stood in front of me, his brow furrowed.

I sighed and tossed the phone onto the seat next to me. "My phone died. I don't even think I have a charger in the car."

"I have one. I'll be right back." Bryan walked out of the sliding doors, toward the parking lot.

Knees drawn up to my chin, I wrapped my arms around my legs and closed my eyes. I played the morning over in my mind, wondering if things would have been different if I had answered the phone sooner. A tear rolled down one cheek before I could stop it.

Back from the car and holding a white charging cable, Bryan located an outlet behind the table next to the couch. He took my phone, plugged it in, and set it on the table next to the couch before sitting down next to me.

"What is it?" he asked, his voice quiet.

I let my legs fall over the seat and leaned over on Bryan's shoulder. He raised his arm and put it behind me, so I curled up next to him, repositioning my head in front of his shoulder, my cheek resting on his chest.

"I should have tried harder to warn her last night. At the least I should have been able to answer my phone the first time she called this morning." The tears were falling hot and fast.

Bryan wrapped his arm around my shoulder, gently smoothing my hair down. He spoke quietly with his cheek pressed to the top of my head, "You could not have stopped Stacy from leaving with Pete. From what I understand of Stacy, she wasn't one to be told what to do. Even if you tried, I'd have expected Pete to put up a fight. You can't blame yourself, Jess. Stacy made her own choices and all we can do is be ready to support her as she deals with the consequences."

I nodded wordlessly. I could feel his heartbeat, constant and rhythmic. It occurred to me that I couldn't remember a single time I had sought comfort through physical contact with another person, and here I was seeking it out and accepting it with no hesitation from someone I barely knew.

But it felt like I did know Bryan, like I had always known him. I felt him move his arm to hold me more securely against himself. Within minutes, I was lulled to sleep by the steady beat next to my ear.

4

BRYAN

Resting my cheek on the top of her head, I held Jess against me, wanting her to feel safe and supported. With my face practically buried in her hair, I breathed in, her citrus-vanilla scent making me want to stay right here in this seat forever. How was it even possible I had only known this woman for a single day and felt the intense need to protect her from the world? From the moment we locked eyes, my heart was pulled toward her as though we were connected by a thread.

Leaning my head back on the wall, I breathed deeply. I rolled through our conversation from dinner. She was everything I didn't know I wanted, and yet she couldn't be mine. Not right now. But for this moment, I was going to take care of her and help her through this situation with her friend. And in the meantime, I would have to work hard to guard my heart.

Closing my eyes, I sent up a silent prayer.

God, I don't know what's at play here. I know you are at work in my life and Jess's. I pray that you will heal Stacy. And thank you for allowing me to meet Jess, if for no other reason than to realize you may have bigger plans for my life than I could have imagined. And if Jess could be a part of those plans, I would be grateful. But first, show her who you are and that you are real.

5

JESS

A buzzing sound came from the hard-top table next to us, and before I was fully able to open my eyes, Bryan reached for the phone. The screen read Linda Carlisle.

I felt my head lower and rest on a warm vinyl surface as he maneuvered himself to a standing position as he quietly said, "Hello?"

I tried to rouse myself enough to reach for the phone, but my eyes closed again, not yet wanting to fully function. The sound of a male voice speaking quietly was dim in the background of my foggy mind.

Bryan moved away from the couch and spoke a little louder, but his voice was still hushed. "Yes ma'am. This is Bryan Carsen. I came to New York with Jess yesterday when Stacy called."

There was a pause before Bryan said, "Yes, ma'am, she is. She is asleep on one of the couches here in the waiting area. Do I need to wake her?"

Another pause.

"Yes, ma'am. We will be here when you arrive."

Groggy and with a slight headache forming behind my eyes, I was fully awakened to my name being whispered close to my ear and a hand on my back. I sat up and rubbed my face. The room came into focus as did a piercing duo of green eyes. Immediately, I was completely aware that I had fallen asleep pressed against Bryan's chest. Discretely, I attempted to wipe my face to remove from view any signs of drool followed by a quick run of a hand through my hair. I probably looked about as good as I felt, and in that moment, nothing felt very promising.

It was still dark, but there was light starting to brighten the doorway causing Bryan to appear as more of a shadow than a person.

"Good morning," I managed to whisper.

He smiled and handed my phone to me.

"Good morning. Stacy's mother called. I hope you don't mind that I answered. She said they will be here within the hour."

I nodded and rubbed my face again trying to stand. With an uncomfortable stretch, I felt every bit as though I had slept on a far-too-small couch with little padding.

Trying not to wince, I asked, "Did you sleep?"

With a look that said, 'Not enough,' he replied, "Some."

Still feeling bleary-eyed, I said, "I'm going to go try to make sense of all of this before more people see me," gesturing to my face and hair. "Maybe we can find some coffee before they arrive?"

Bryan smiled and nodded.

I pulled myself together as much as a hospital bathroom would allow after only sleeping a few hours on a vinyl couch before walking out to find Bryan holding two foam coffee cups with steam rising out of them. A boyish grin on his face sent my heart into rapid flutters and put a smile on my face. It had been an emotional couple of days, but standing here with these feelings flooding over me had me questioning my mental and emotional fortitude.

My dating history may as well be considered nonexistent. I went on a few group dates in high school, but the emotional and mental tumult that came with it when paired with my ability to read people made dating a relatively tedious -- if not traumatic -- process. A lot of it came with the territory, seeing as how high school is naturally predisposed to drama, particularly when it comes to the mingling of the sexes. Having to constantly question and process emotions I didn't even fully understand myself was exhausting, which caused me to resign myself to put off dating. Which is what I did, indefinitely.

Even if my adolescent experiences had been favorable ones, I hit the ground running when I got to college, and I left little time for a social life. Academics had always been a platonic lover who never lied, cheated, or became overly attached and never required me to interpret its expressions. Those scholarly intellectual arms never failed to provide an easy, undemanding safe space when I needed one. The deeper I fell into those arms, the less room I had for other things—like people. Now, however, standing here I had a sudden urge to make time for a very specific person.

Bryan extended one of the coffees to me, which I happily accepted with a smile and a thank you as we made our way back to the waiting area.

"Have you seen the doctor at all this morning?" I scanned the surrounding area.

With his cup at his lips, Bryan shook his head and sipped his coffee. He swallowed before answering. "No, but I checked in with Becky." He indicated to the nurse at the admin desk with his head. "She said Dr. Curtis is on rotation and will meet with us when the Carlisles arrive."

Shortly after finishing our coffee, a woman in her mid-sixties who appeared to be an older version of Stacy came rushing through the doors to the waiting room. She immediately locked her eyes on mine and made a beeline for me with her arms outstretched. As her arms closed around me, she began to cry. When a gentleman of about the same age walked up behind Mrs. Carlisle, she let me go and stepped back to introduce her husband and herself to Bryan who shook Mr. Carlisle's hand.

Bryan and I led the Carlisles to the reception desk and introduced them to Nurse Becky, who gave them a polite smile. She stood and asked our group to follow her to a private meeting room.

Sadness. Sympathy.

My heart sped up as we followed. The room to which we were led to was larger than the one Dr. Lawson had taken Bryan and me to the night before.

"Dr. Curtis will be in very soon. Can I get anyone anything?" Becky asked the room. This was the most bedside manner she had shown since we had met her after shift change the previous night.

Something had changed. I could feel it and I knew Bryan felt it, too, because it was written on his face when we exchanged a look.

Concern.

He closed his eyes and gave a slight nod to acknowledge he felt the same thing.

Mr. Carlisle smiled at the nurse after he sat down and said in his thick southern accent, "You wouldn't happen to have any black coffee would ya, darlin'?"

She smiled at him. "I will see what I can do. Anyone else?"

Mrs. Carlisle nodded silently in agreement as she sat between her husband and me.

Reaching over to take Mrs. Carlisle's hand, I tried to fill the silence. "How was your flight? It was lucky that you found a private pilot on such quick notice."

Mrs. Carlisle squeezed my hand and turned to face me. "It wasn't luck; it was God. We tried to use that blasted Google to find a flight, and neither of us is very good with computers. After several minutes of getting frustrated, I stopped what I was doing, put my hands in my lap, and prayed, asking God to provide us with a flight as soon as possible. Ten minutes later, Marvin came in and told me he had gotten ahold of one of his buddies who is a pilot. He said he could have his plane fueled up and ready in the thirty minutes it would take us to get to him."

Tears came to her eyes as she continued. "All I could do was say 'thank you, Jesus' over and over while I threw my clothes and toothbrush into my bag."

Tears began to fill my eyes, but I was given a chance to gain my composure when Nurse Becky came to the door with two foam cups filled with steaming black coffee. She handed the cups to the Carlisles. Mr. Carlisle thanked her quietly.

She smiled, but it never reached her eyes. "Dr. Curtis is right behind me. Please let me know if I can do anything else for you."

As she walked out, an older doctor with salt-and-pepper hair and serious dark eyes walked in. Mr. Carlisle moved to stand, but Dr. Curtis motioned for him to stay seated as he extended his hand. "Mr. Carlisle." He gave a nod.

Dr. Curtis took Mrs. Carlisle's hand and covered it with his other hand. "Mrs. Carlisle, I am sorry you have had to come so far. I know the two of you must be tired. But I am glad you are here." He released her hand. "As I'm sure you know by now, Stacy has had a stroke that has resulted in her falling into a coma."

At this, Mrs. Carlisle began to weep silently. I placed a hand on her back and rubbed with small circles to offer whatever comfort I could.

Dr. Curtis continued. "There is no way to know how long a coma will last. It could be hours or days, and in the worst cases, years. What is important is to make the patient as comfortable as possible. In the meantime, we monitor them for other signs or symptoms of any other condition. We don't know exactly how long Stacy was suffering from a partial clot that prevented substantial blood flow to the brain. We do know that had her friends here not found her when they did, Stacy may not be here with us at all."

Mrs. Carlisle reached for me and patted my leg in gratitude. I continued rubbing her back as she asked the doctor, "Can we see Stacy?"

"Of course," replied Dr. Curtis. "We will need to talk again because at some point you will need to make some hard decisions. But right now, let me take you to your daughter's room."

As we all exited the private room, I held Mrs. Carlisle's hand. "Mrs. Carlisle, now that you two are here, we need to get back home. And you both need this time with Stacy. If it's okay with you, we're going to excuse ourselves."

Mrs. Carlisle pulled me in for another tight hug. "Oh, Jess, thank you so much for being the wonderful friend you are to Stacy. She always talks about how you look out for her and how much she adores you."

When Mrs. Carlisle let me go, she hugged Bryan who gently hugged her back.

Mr. Carlisle placed one of his large hands on my shoulder as he shook Bryan's hand. "Thank you, both," he said.

Wanting to be supportive I said, "If there's anything we can do for you, please don't hesitate to ask. We're just a phone call away. And please keep me updated when you know more."

Mr. Carlisle squeezed my shoulder. "We will, darlin'. Y'all be careful heading home, won't you?"

I nodded, trying to keep the threatening tears at bay and hugged Mrs. Carlisle one more time. The Carlisles followed Dr. Curtis down the hall toward Stacy's room, leaving us in the hallway as we watched them turn a corner.

We returned to the waiting room in silence until Bryan stopped at the reception desk and thanked Becky for her help.

She smiled warmly this time. "You're welcome. Their whole world is about to change. They are lucky to have friends like you two."

Bryan returned her smile then turned to me. "Are you ready?"

The heavy sigh that escaped betrayed my nod. Bryan wrapped his arms around me, and I let the tears I'd been holding in release themselves. So much had changed in so little time, and there was nothing I could do about any of it. My heart hurt for Stacy, my best friend, young and beautiful, battling uphill in uncharted territory. I hurt for her parents and all the unknowns they were now facing as they watched their only child fight for her life in a strange place.

I was overwhelmed by the graciousness of the nurses and doctors who made Stacy a priority and allowed us to be there for her. I ached with gratitude for the arms holding me and that he had made this experience part of his own journey even though we were perfect strangers.

When the tears subsided and with the reality that I had left a large wet spot on the front of Bryan's shirt, I sniffled and laughed before fruitlessly dabbing at his shirt with a tissue I pulled from my purse.

"Don't worry about it," he said with humor in his voice.

We walked through the sliding doors one last time, my heart in my throat. In the parking lot, Bryan guided me to the car with his hand hovering at my back. He didn't have to touch me for me to feel the energy that had become a constant hum between us.

An involuntary shiver ran over my spine as a warmth slowly pulsated over every nerve in my body starting in my chest and spreading outward.

At the car, Bryan opened the driver's side door for me. I stood in front of him before taking my seat and asked, "Breakfast and a gallon of coffee then home?"

Bryan nodded. "I'm in. Do you want to trade places halfway?"

I shook my head. "I think I'll be okay to drive. I have plenty of thoughts to keep me company."

After a quick stop at a diner called The Bay-gull that served a wide selection of bagels and mediocre coffee, I drove us southward down I-95.

6

JESS

As I merged onto the interstate, my thoughts zipped around in my mind as though a pinball machine was engaged. Instead of a single pinball at play, however, there were multiple balls bouncing and pinging around simultaneously, making it impossible to focus on any single thought. The guilt of leaving the hospital loomed over me. It had been the right choice, but it had also felt like abandoning my best friend. Additionally, we wouldn't have even been at the hospital in the first place had I stopped Stacy from leaving the club with Pete.

And then there was the fact that a man I had known for fewer than forty-eight hours was sitting in the car next to me. A man who gave up sleep and rescheduled his entire day to ensure my safety in a situation for which he held zero responsibility. A man who had put his own safety at risk, not knowing what he might encounter when he stepped foot into Pete's house. A man who, despite my typical aversion to physical touch, provided the very comfort and security I needed through contact, and for the first time I could remember I had not only tolerated it, but I also welcomed it.

Initially, I had been interested in Bryan enough to agree to have lunch with him after what I couldn't even definitively call a first date.

Now, I was kicking myself for wondering if there was a way to prolong this road trip because our time together had been far too short, albeit intense.

This thought alone was reason enough to make absolutely certain I drove him straight home, thanked him, and headed straight for my house where I could process and clear my mind. Shared trauma and stress were not grounds for attachment, and this entire experience would be considered textbook trauma bonding. But, and maybe I was reaching, but I was certain the moment I saw him in the dimly lit room of the club, something happened inside me. And when his hand touched mine, there was a connection made that I had never experienced with another person. Just thinking about it sent my heart into overdrive.

"Jess?"

I jumped slightly and blinked hard at the sound. The silent chaos swirling around inside my head was interrupted.

His voice was quiet, as though he had been debating whether or not speaking would scare me.

His answer came when I realized I had been gripping the steering wheel much harder than necessary and had to slowly lessen my grasp to prevent the painful sensation running through my fingers. I turned my head and tried to give him a casual look that wouldn't betray my current thoughts that had been focused on him.

"Hm?" I asked.

"Sorry," he said with a soft smile. "I didn't mean to pull you away from your thoughts. I was just going to ask if you were okay to drive or if you wanted to trade at some point."

Focusing on the road ahead of us, I said, "I'm good. Why don't you lean back and maybe get some sleep? I'm kind of wired right now and could use the quiet to clear my mind. If I need to switch, I'll let you know."

I felt Bryan watching me for several seconds before I glanced back over at him. It was probably a dangerous thing to do, but I lingered on his green eyes, taking in the sensation that buzzed around me. Forcing my eyes back to the road, I felt my face heat slightly.

Before I could start tumbling down another vast canyon of thoughts, Bryan cleared his throat and shifted in his seat. "Okay. But promise you'll let me know if you change your mind."

I bit my bottom lip so as not to show the goofy smile trying to plaster itself on my face. "I promise." I raised my hand as though to make an oath.

As he leaned his seat back a few inches, I watched Bryan from my periphery drop his head back. Within minutes his breathing was slower, and with a quick glance, I saw his features relax.

With a heavy sigh, I let my head hit the headrest for a few seconds. It was times like this I wished I could call my mom. I imagined her disbelief melting into laughter before implying that somehow fate had brought the two of us together. Was this fate? Or was this the God thing I had been reminded of at the hospital? I spent the next several hours fighting a losing battle with the cacophony of thoughts and words swirling around my mind.

We were about an hour from home when the sound of a person shifting and a groan from the passenger's seat grabbed my attention. When I stole a look and caught a glimpse of a waking Bryan, I had to stop myself from reaching over and smoothing down the back of his hair. The ruffled hair and sleepy eyes gave him a boyish appearance that threatened to distract me from my current task at hand—driving. He was running both hands up and down his face when he realized I was watching him.

To hide the effect his attention had on me, I quickly returned my eyes to the road before saying, "There you are, sleepyhead."

"Hey." His voice still hoarse with sleep.

"Feel better?" I asked.

"Yeah, thanks. Looks like we're almost home. Did I miss anything?"

"It's been a quiet drive. I'm definitely ready to be home. There's a nap and a shower – each with my name on them."

A comfortable silence hung in the air until Bryan asked, his voice clearer than before, "Have you heard from Stacy's parents?"

With a shake of my head in disappointment I answered, "No. And I guess I really didn't expect to hear anything so soon. I'm sure they are still reeling and are exhausted from their traveling. I can't imagine seeing your only child in that condition and especially with such little information. Knowing all the questions I have, I imagine they have more."

Bryan nodded as he listened.

"They have quite a journey ahead of them. Nothing could have prepared them for this, but I know they are grateful you were there when Stacy needed you."

"I still can't get over everything that has happened in such a short amount of time. I have played it on repeat in my mind almost the entire drive and it seems surreal. How can any of this have really happened? Stacy is twenty-seven years old, and as far as I could tell she was in great health. Sure, she made terrible choices when it came to men, but that shouldn't have landed her in the hospital with a stroke."

It was as though I couldn't stop myself from verbalizing everything I had been processing for the last few hours.

"I should have told her right away how many red flags I picked up on when I met Pete. Or maybe if I had tried to stop her from leaving or been more insistent that she stay when I got her message—"

"Jess," he interrupted my downward spiral. "What happened to Stacy was not your fault. It just as easily could have happened while she was in her own bedroom as it did at Pete's home. You aren't allowed to blame yourself, okay?"

My eyes burned with tears that I forced back as I nodded. I knew it wasn't my fault and that Stacy's choices were her own. But the helplessness I felt made it hard to accept that.

The rest of the drive was uneventful and silent until we pulled into the driveway of Bryan's townhouse. After putting the car in park, I turned to Bryan to find him staring at me.

Nervous. Curious.

Shifting in my seat to face him, I reached across and placed my hand on his. He quickly turned his hand over, enveloping mine. My pulse quickened and warmth seeped into my skin.

"Bryan, I cannot say thank you enough for going with me. I could not have done it by myself knowing now what I didn't know when Stacy called me yesterday. I really am in your debt." It was getting hard to think clearly with those green eyes on me.

Those same eyes seemed to be searching for something.

Uncertainty.

After several quiet moments passed, he swallowed. "Can I call you later?"

Trying to hide the eagerness I was feeling, I tried to sound casual. "I might be offended if you didn't."

The smile that spread across his face sent a strong, soft current through my hand, up my arm, and into my chest.

He squeezed my hand before letting go. "Then I will definitely call you later."

"Good," I replied. Not smiling was not an option.

He hesitated before opening his door and exiting the car. I watched him walk to the door where he turned and gave a small wave before he went inside. When he was gone from view, I pulled out of his driveway and headed for my own.

It was almost 10:00 a.m. when I arrived home. When I got out of the car and began to walk toward the front steps, my entire body felt as though I was wading against a strong current. I dragged myself up and into the house, each step more exhausting than the last. Without much thought, I opened the door, dropped my bag just inside, lumbered up each step until I made it to my bedroom. Without hesitation, I crawled into my bed fully dressed and closed my eyes.

I had no idea what time it was when I sat up. The room was full of light pouring in from behind the sheer curtains that covered the blinds, but it was the yellowing light of late afternoon. When my eyes finally focused on the clock next to my bed, it read 4:00.

After several minutes of staring blankly and orienting myself, I slowly made my way from the bed to the shower. Between the car rides and spending the night in a hospital, not only was my entire body stiff, but I felt the need to wash every part of me at least twice. I stood under the hot water until I had used every ounce of it, replaying the last two days in my mind.

When I finally turned off the water, I was feeling much more like myself. I threw on my favorite joggers and an oversized T-shirt and picked up one of the journal articles I had been meaning to read and notate before going downstairs where I thought I might curl up in my reading chair and get to work.

As I turned to sit, my eyes happened to land on the bookshelf across the room where light was reflecting off metallic letters on the spine of a book. Not able to remember having a book with such lettering, I walked to the shelf where I found a black leather-bound book with gold letters that read, *Holy Bible*. My surprise escaped me in the form of "Ha."

Book in tow, I returned to the chair where I had initially planned to sit while I ran my thumb along the outside of the pages. I remembered buying it on a whim at one of the campus bookstores soon after my experience of wandering into the church, thinking I might take a look at some of the things I'd heard that Sunday. Instead, I put the book on the shelf and, until this moment, hadn't touched it.

The front cover was inflexible, which made it difficult to navigate the first few pages, so with slight trepidation, I attempted to crack the spine enough to keep it open. Once it stopped flopping itself closed, I swished through the first few pages until I came across a Table of Contents. Skimming over the list, I recognized Romans as the reference point the pastor had used that particular Sunday. It seemed like the most familiar place to start, even if familiar was the last thing I felt toward the book as a whole.

The words on the page almost seemed like a different language as I read. Yet, the foreignness gave way to familiarity as something inside me stirred. My heart was beating hard in my chest as though it was trying to communicate and make contact with something outside of my body.

The more I read, the stronger the impulse I had to continue reading until I was struck by a single paragraph.

They know the truth about God because he has made it obvious to them. For ever since the world was created, people have seen the earth and sky. Through everything God made, they can clearly see his invisible qualities—his eternal power and divine nature. So they have no excuse for not knowing God.

My eyes kept reading the same set of sentences until I finally processed the words. If I was reading it correctly, and I try not to be prideful, but I do think I can credit myself for being relatively skilled in reading comprehension, the author of these words was saying that it's obvious that God exists because God himself makes it obvious through nature.

In that moment it made complete sense. I've never been one to ponder the why and how of nature. I can say that I have always appreciated a cerulean sky full of puffy clouds and the sounds of the ocean's waves. I would even agree that rainy days have their place.

But I can't say that I really ever wondered where it all began because it was never relevant to the here and now. Since the world has always existed, I have merely accepted that it was put in place as some sort of universal playground for humans. Now, however, it occurred to me that my thinking was extremely limiting.

Allowing my mind to wander away from the words on the page, I felt a sudden pang of futility as I considered the insolence of all the times I'd chalked life events up to happenstance, luck, human nature, or some other unknown impersonal metaphysical force. The probability and statistics required to reject the idea that there was actually a higher power in control of the universe were far too improbable. The more I sat there and attempted to process the idea that there was a God and that he wanted people to know he was real, the faster my heart began racing with the thrill of discovering something new.

There were so many things I had attributed to fate or luck, good and bad. I thought about everything I had ever learned about the complexity of the human mind and the brain itself. And now, I knew I could no longer attribute those things to the universe doing its thing. I fast-forwarded through all the memories and snapshots to just one day ago. Had there not been a higher power at play, would I have gotten to Stacy in time? Would Stacy's parents have gotten a flight to New York when they did? Would I have met Bryan? A shiver ran through me. How could my entire life have been mere coincidence? It wasn't possible. And the comfort that idea alone brought me was almost overwhelming.

I was pulled from my thoughts when my phone chimed with a text message. My smile was automatic when I opened it.

> Bryan: How do you feel about Chinese food?

> Me: I'm a big fan, actually.

Five seconds later, my doorbell rang. I laid the Bible on the table before moving to answer the door. From the window I passed, I noticed a black Jeep in the driveway that I didn't recognize. At the door, I peered out the small window next to the door and saw a very familiar face. My pulse quickened as I tried to compose myself with several deep breaths before opening the door. Unable to contain the smile on my face, I opened the door to find a handsome, smiling man holding a large, brown paper bag.

"I was wondering if you were free for dinner." Bryan held up the bag.

Caution. Hopefulness.

The grin on my face had to be ridiculous, but I could no longer control it. "Lucky for you, I seem to be completely free this evening." I pulled the door open and motioned for him to enter.

Once inside, I led Bryan to the kitchen where we sorted the takeout containers and laid out our plates before returning to the living room. As I shimmied back into the armchair and crossed my legs in the seat, I closed my eyes and inhaled the aroma of the steaming dumplings on my plate. In addition to making my mouth water, I was transported back to my childhood.

When I opened my eyes, I found Bryan smiling at me with raised eyebrows.

"So, you like dumplings?" he mused.

"Like is not a strong enough word for how I feel about dumplings. And it's not so much about the dumplings themselves as it is the nostalgia that goes with them."

"Sounds like a story I'd like to hear." Bryan skillfully lifted one of the soft, doughy pouches with chopsticks and bit it in half.

I really wish I was as graceful when it came to chopsticks, but instead, I'm forced to either use a fork or shove the entire dumpling in my mouth in one bite. I opted for the fork. The problem with using a fork over chopsticks was that I didn't have the benefit of ineptitude making sure I didn't inhale my food.

Tonight, however, I found myself wanting to take all the time in the world, if it meant spending time with Bryan. And if he wanted to take a walk down memory lane with me in the process, who was I to deprive him of the experience?

"I was eleven when my mom was promoted to the manager of her department at the hotel where she was working. When her first manager's paycheck hit the bank account, she raced home as soon as her shift was over and told me to put my shoes on because we were going out to dinner. There was a Chinese restaurant around the corner we had never been to, and I insisted I had heard it was the best one in town. I was only repeating what I'd overheard a couple of the neighbors saying because I had no idea what I was talking about, but my mom didn't care. She was always game for anything.

"Money was a foreign concept to me, and I never knew how little of it we really had, so it wasn't until years later that I understood what happened when we arrived at the restaurant. The day it happened, I had assumed everything was exactly as it was supposed to be. As Mom eventually told me, when we walked in, she took one look around and knew that even her new paycheck would not go far. But

Mom did what any good parent would do in the situation and played along.

"Mom told me that she had heard that the dumplings, which were coincidentally the most affordable item on the menu, were what made them so famous. She ordered waters for each of us and the dumplings to share. The server was a pushy college-age kid, and he scoffed and rolled his eyes when we didn't order anything else. Again, I was clueless. I was just ecstatic that we were at a restaurant that didn't involve paper wrappers or cardboard boxes.

"When the dumplings arrived at the table, they were steaming hot and served in a beautiful bamboo steamer. The server set down two pairs of chopsticks, two plates, and the check and told us to enjoy. I spent several minutes breathing in the steam, not allowing Mom to remove the lid until she convinced me we should eat them before they got cold."

"We sat in that dining room and talked about Chinese food, school, work, and Mr. Hernandez's cat from down the street. I couldn't remember a time before that day seeing my mom's shoulders so relaxed. I begged Mom to make eating at that restaurant a payday thing. When she agreed, that's when I fell in love with dumplings and looked forward to every payday after that one."

When I finished talking, I took another bite and savored it.

Bryan was quietly watching me from his seat on the couch, his plate resting on the coffee table in front of him. "You and your mom were close?"

"The closest. It was just the two of us from the time I was six until seven years ago."

His eyes were soft and his smile thoughtful. "Moms are pretty incredible," he said in a voice so gentle it was almost a whisper.

"I remember you saying your dad was gone a lot. Were you and your mom close?"

Bryan nodded. "We were. And she was the strongest person I knew until the day she died."

At a loss for words of my own, I repeated his back to him, "Moms are pretty incredible."

We sat there for a while in silence, each of us lost in our own thoughts until Bryan cleared his throat, getting my attention.

"Doing some light reading?" He indicated the Bible I'd left open on the coffee table.

I stared at the open book, almost thankful for the change of subject. While thinking about my mom came with a bittersweetness, it was a topic I was well acquainted with, unlike the one Bryan just raised. I traded my empty plate for the book and smoothed out its pristine pages just to have something to do with my hands. The feel of the cool onion skin page under my fingers gave me a sense of comfort I didn't know I was seeking.

With a slow nod I said, "Yeah. I had actually forgotten it was on my shelf until this afternoon."

"Did you read anything interesting?"

My voice was weak when I tried to speak so I swallowed and tried again. "I want to believe that there is a God. Honestly, I'm almost convinced there is a God. I just don't know what to do with that information."

"Would you be willing to talk more about it with me? I'd also love to share with you some of my favorite verses." He sounded almost cautious, but it was clear he genuinely wanted to share this with me.

"I think I would like that very much." I tried not to sound as overwhelmed as I felt.

Bryan held out a hand, and I handed him the Bible, which he transferred to his other hand and held out his hand once again, this time it was for me. I accepted the offer and let him pull me to the seat next to him on the couch. He stared at me with a look that I struggled to read.

The bloom of warmth that washed over me combined with the hum of the current that passed through me where our shoulders touched had the potential to unnerve me. I was pulled out of my thoughts and back to the moment when Bryan looked away and down toward the book in his hands.

The next two hours disappeared as Bryan turned pages and spoke more animatedly than I had seen since meeting him. He would read and sometimes ask questions while other times I would ask questions.

It wasn't until I stifled a yawn in the middle of one of his explanations that he paused and checked his watch. It wasn't late, but after the two days we'd both had and knowing the next day was Monday, it may as well have been midnight.

His smile was warm and sent a flurry of sensation through my core. "Maybe we should pick this up later." He closed the Bible and set it on the table.

"Do you always get this excited when you talk about God?" I asked.

"Trust me, when you become aware of everything he has ever brought you through without you even realizing it, you'll get excited talking about him too."

"Hm," was all I could think to say as I regarded him and his sparkling green eyes that seemed to be holding on to a secret.

Reaching for the two empty plates on the table, Bryan stood and took them to the kitchen.

I followed and started repackaging the leftovers on the counter. Since he had brought the food, I intended for him to take the rest with him.

"You should keep those. I won't be home to eat them, and I would hate for them to go to waste," he said before I could put the containers back in their bag.

My eyebrows raised in question. "Too much excitement for one weekend, so you're skipping town?" I smirked.

He attempted to hold back a grin and remain serious as he placed the dishes in the sink. "That's definitely it."

I leaned my hip against the counter and crossed my arms. "That's too bad. I had just decided that I might look for something else less dramatic and maybe even more exciting to do since I'd found a decent road trip partner."

The words were out of my mouth before I had time to think about what I was actually saying. These kinds of things never left my brain much less my mouth, and here I was implying that I wanted to take an actual road trip with a man I barely knew. Realizing how it might have sounded, I felt the heat creep up my neck and into my face.

Bryan's lips twitched in amusement. "A decent road trip partner?" He mirrored my posture against the counter. "Just decent? I thought, all things considered, maybe I'd rank a little higher than decent."

The flicker of amusement that crossed his face made me think he was enjoying the banter as much as I was. At least, I hoped I was reading it correctly. I was moving into unfamiliar territory, and it was both exciting and terrifying.

"Fine. You were an excellent road trip partner. I just didn't want the compliment to go to your head."

With a pleased expression on his face, he turned to the sink and began to wash our dishes. "Thank you. I'll try not to let the flattery get to me."

"So, if you won't be home to enjoy these leftovers, where will you be?"

"Atlanta."

"Business or pleasure?"

"Business. I'm speaking at a symposium on cyber intelligence and leading breakout sessions this week and next. I don't love public speaking, but sometimes it beats sitting at a desk behind a wall of computer screens or sitting through meetings all day."

He was going to be gone for two weeks. A pulse of something akin to sadness flickered through my chest. It was not a sensation I immediately recognized in this context. Disappointment, maybe? Why would I be disappointed that he was going out of town? I told myself this feeling was not an appropriate response to the situation and that I needed to regroup my thoughts.

Clearly, the process was easier said than done as I realized Bryan was looking at me and saying my name. How long had I been standing here arguing silently with myself as he watched? My cheeks felt warm.

"Huh?" was the best I could do.

Concern. Hesitation.

"Where'd you go?" He hung the towel he had been using on the drying hook next to the sink.

That was a loaded question. "I was just thinking that two weeks of public speaking sounded like a lot," I lied, hoping my words didn't completely betray my feelings.

"It's definitely longer than I care to be away from home. Especially now."

His gaze was fixed on me, and I was letting myself get lost in it. Then my mind kicked into overdrive. What did he mean by *especially now*? What was holding him back from wanting to go? Maybe he had a new puppy at home. Who'd want to leave a new puppy? I mean, he hadn't mentioned a puppy, but what did I really know about this guy? That had to be it.

My heart was racing, and I was spiraling and needed to get a grip. This was not how I responded to extraneous variables.

With a slow inhale I forced my heartrate back to normal, before attempting to speak. Trying to sound nonchalant, I asked, "Why especially now?" My nerves were buzzing with an anxiety different from anything I had ever experienced.

His eyes never left mine. Instead, they seemed to intensify their watch momentarily before they softened. He took a step toward me causing me to drop my arms to my side and stand straighter.

Vulnerability. Apprehension. Hope.

"I mean, I've spent more time with you since we met than I have away from you. And now I'll have to wait two weeks to see you again. That just seems way longer than I care to be away from home. Especially now."

The idea of swooning had been a ridiculous concept until right in this instance. All the blood in my body seemed to have rushed to my feet, leaving me slightly dizzy and making the room appear to shift slightly. Before I could make my silent apologies to all those who'd ever swooned and I'd had the audacity to roll my eyes at, a hand wrapped around my own, sending a stream of subtle vibrations through me. The room straightened and my vision fixated solidly on a pair of jade green eyes, and in that instance, I could not stop the words that poured from my lips.

"When we met the other night, I had no idea who you were. And if I'm being completely honest, I still don't really know who you are. Your face was foreign to me, but something inside me was drawn to you as though you were familiar. And it was as though I did know you or at least I was supposed to know you. I watched you walk toward me, and I searched your face and your eyes in hopes of finding some recognition that maybe I had just forgotten. And then you shook my hand and there was a feeling I had never had. It was like a strong current was rushing from your hand to mine. Not the kind of harsh shock that makes you want to let go and scream. It was the kind that was so strong, but also low and painless, that made letting go feel impossible."

I took in our hands and intertwined our fingers. "Then we spent those hours talking and laughing; it was comfortable. I didn't want to go home because I felt like if we went separate ways, I would never see you again. I was afraid that would feel like I might never breathe again. And then you were there, again. And the longer I was with you, the pull got stronger. I let my guard down. I never let my guard down. But somehow with you, I feel vulnerable, but I also feel safe. And now here I am, not only unguarded but empty of coherent thoughts and wondering if I've made a huge mistake because I realize everything I've said probably sounds crazy."

Bryan raised my hand to his lips and gently kissed the back of it. "When you dropped me off the other night, I sat on my couch for an hour and prayed, 'God, just let me see her one more time.' I couldn't clear my mind or think about anything else. And after the worst night of sleep I've had in a long time, you called. There was no way I was going to pass up the opportunity to see you again. That sounds really selfish now that I think about it, but it's true. The longer we were together, even in the circumstances we were in, I prayed in the back of my mind, 'When this is over, please let me see her again.' I can stand here and tell you I honestly believe God put you in my life for a reason, and I am going to pray every day he will let me see you, again and again."

Tears blurred my vision as I freed my hand from his and placed it on his cheek before pulling his lips to mine. My arms reached around his neck as his hands wrapped around my waist and pulled me closer. His lips were warm and soft, carrying a sense of urgency behind them.

A shot of adrenaline rushed through my veins, causing me to feel like I was floating. The current running up and down my spine moved outward down my arms and legs leaving me weak in the knees. I could feel my pulse in my head and the blood rushing behind my ears. Breathing almost seemed optional until I thought my heart might explode from the lack of oxygen I was allowing into my lungs.

When it was clear that oxygen was no longer a mere choice, I slowly pulled away and opened my eyes. His were already looking back at me.

Bryan rested his forehead on mine as he tried to control his breathing. My eyes fluttered closed, and my arms slid around his waist as the heat between us simmered to a comfortable warmth. I could feel his heartbeat attempting to return to a normal pace alongside my own.

We stood there for what seemed like hours, though it had clearly only been minutes. I would have stayed in that moment had one of us not come to our senses.

"I really should get going. 4:30 comes early in the morning," Bryan whispered.

With a sigh of resignation that was much louder than I had intended, I lamented, "These will be the longest two weeks of my life."

Bryan let out a chuckle, and I raised my eyes to his.

"Does that mean I get to see you again in two weeks?"

I felt myself blush. That had been a huge assumption on my part, which was out of character for me. Due to the nature of my work and research, I was usually very careful not to make assumptions without sufficient evidence toward a point. However, I was apparently not holding my personal life to those same standards and just assumed Bryan would want to see me again. He must have sensed my unease when I tried to take a step backward, but Bryan's arms held me in place.

"Jess, I'm glad you want to see me when I get back. I don't make it a habit of kissing women in their kitchens so soon after meeting them. You seem to bring out something in me that makes me feel impulsive, which is probably a good reason for us to call it a night."

With a huff of relief, I rested my forehead on his chest and squeezed a little tighter for one last hug before releasing Bryan and putting space between us. We stared at each other, both of us grinning like complete goofballs until I let out a latent sigh that sounded like something a swooning person would make.

Before I could silently berate myself, Bryan also breathed a heavy sigh before rapping his knuckles on the countertop. "Okay, I'm really going, now." He reached for my hand.

Accepting it I said, "I'll walk you to the door."

On the front porch, Bryan fidgeted with his keys and struggled to focus on any one thing for a moment before deciding it was safe to look me in the eyes.

"Thank you for dinner and for the company. It was a really nice way to end an eventful weekend," I said.

"You're welcome," he said before turning to go. He immediately turned back to face me and asked nervously, "Would it be okay if I called you later? Not tonight, but maybe tomorrow if our schedules line up?"

Attempting to appear completely unvexed while feeling quite enamored, I gave him a wink. "I'd be offended if you didn't."

With a one-sided grin that threatened to buckle my knees, Bryan stepped forward and placed a gentle kiss to my lips. "Goodnight, Jess," he said in a low, almost whisper.

"Goodnight, Bryan."

I watched him leave before closing the door and locking it. It took a minute to begin processing the evening and when I did, all I could think was how much my face hurt from smiling and how still the space was around me.

7

JESS

Sleep had never been an issue – until it was an issue. Whether it was that I was too tired to sleep, had slept too late in the day, or could not stop thinking about a certain pair of green eyes and a soft set of lips, sleep was now an elusive creature. If I was completely honest with myself, I would say it had everything to do with the fear of waking up to realize it was all a dream. After turning over and adjusting my pillow for what seemed like the tenth time in two minutes, I sat up and picked up the journal article I had attempted to start earlier in the day. I didn't even make it to the fourth sentence before my eyes drifted closed with the thought flickering behind my eyelids of two very strong arms holding me.

When the alarm on my bedside table sounded, I struggled to open my eyes. My head was heavy and my mind hazy. As the room came into focus, I reached to shut off the alarm, knocking my phone off the table in the process. The commotion sent enough of a jolt through my system that I immediately recalled the events from the previous night, allowing them to fill my thoughts. The memories sent a flood of warmth through me that made me want to curl back up under my blanket and relive them over and over for the next two weeks. Before my dream could become a reality, my backup alarm went off, reminding me it was Monday.

There had always been a love/hate relationship between Mondays and me, and truthfully, it was a very one-sided relationship, in which I had been a victim for two years. Most days, I would pride myself in my ability to rise and shine at any hour. Mondays, however, were not usually those days. Technically, it was the 8:00 a.m., two-and-a-half-hour freshman psychology class I taught on Mondays that created the feelings of angst deep within me. I never understood why classes would be offered at 8:00 a.m. for any underclassmen. Yes, some students needed the early class hour to make the rest of their day schedule work accordingly but offering a one-day-a-week class at such an hour to freshmen was and always would be absurd. Sure, they might show up the first two weeks of class if I was lucky, but once the syllabus had been read, all bets were off when it came to attendance.

As a student, I rarely opted for early morning classes and would instead choose to work mornings and take classes in the evenings. Whether accurate or not, I always felt like evening classes were both more laid back and attracted more mature students, both in age and personality.

As an instructor, I appreciated the faithful early morning class attendees and sympathized with other early morning instructors. My philosophy from behind the lectern was that if you could do good work without attending class, then kudos to you. There were no attendance policies for my class, but even for freshmen, the work was rigorous. I found it to be a fair trade-off.

One might think such standards would encourage class attendance. One would be wrong. However, there were only two Mondays left in the semester, and after the last final was graded, my penance would have been served and I would have my choice of classes to teach and time slots in which to teach them.

I rolled out of bed, put on my running clothes, grabbed my gym bag and my backpack, and headed for my favorite running path. I had tried to find a new one once I graduated from undergrad, but none of the alternatives could live up to the familiar trail even after having to make accommodations for the extra twenty minutes required to relocate from George Washington to American University. I stretched and loosened up then checked my laces one last time before heading out on my daily run.

This route took me eight miles, adjacent to the Lincoln Memorial, alongside the Potomac River, around the entirety of East Potomac Park, and past the Jefferson Memorial. I always tried to time my runs in accordance with the sunrise as it came up behind the Jefferson, and this morning did not disappoint. My favorite runs were at the peak of the cherry blossom season when the pink fluffy flowers were in full display under the golden light. A late freeze had been unkind to the fragile blossoms this year, but the trees were still just as green and beautiful, and this morning the pinks and purples of the sky were a pleasant complement in place of the flowers.

After a shower at the campus fitness center, I walked across the street to the small café where Talia began working on my usual order as soon as she saw me walk into the building. Talia was one of my faithful early class attenders last year and had remained on my radar in hopes of getting her on Dr. Thorne's in the next couple of years. Her work was always above average in most cases, and she took advantage of office hours to discuss her future on a regular basis. She once told me she considered me her mentor, which is why I think every Monday morning since her semester in my class, she had tried to ensure quick and efficient service. It was selfish of me, but I couldn't bring myself to tell her I'd be happy to mentor her even if I had to wait a normal amount of time for my coffee and bagel.

We chatted briefly as I paid my tab, and I suggested she stop by one day this week to catch up if she had time. Then I made my way to my classroom in the building one block away. My phone buzzed in my backpack as I walked through the door, so, as soon as I could set my coffee on the rolling cart next to the podium, I swung my backpack around to the side and dug out my phone before attempting to situate the bag elsewhere. I rarely received messages this early on any day, which is why I was intent on retrieving it in such a hasty manner.

I found my efforts rewarded and my cheeks flushed when I saw it was a message from Bryan.

> Bryan: Good morning. I hope your night was more restful than mine. I kept dreaming I was kissing a beautiful woman and had to leave her for two weeks. Then I woke up to find it was true. It made it hard to leave this morning.

My heartrate picked up and I felt the dopey smile take over my face as I held the phone to my chest. I quickly typed out a reply.

> Me: Sounds familiar. Is it possible we were sharing a dream?

I set down my phone as the first two students walked in and took their seats. My mind was racing and distracted with the hope of another message. A glance at the clock said there were ten minutes before class officially started. Never had I ever been glad that today's class was a review for the upcoming final and wouldn't require my strongest focus, because now I wasn't sure I'd be able to give that.

Another buzz had me grabbing my phone.

> Bryan: I would share a dream with you anytime. Call you later?

Biting my lower lip and trying not to let my smitten expression show, I responded.

> Me: I look forward to it. I'll be free after 1:00.

On the way to my car after my class and a lunch meeting with Dr. Thorne, my phone buzzed with an incoming call. At the thought it might be Bryan, my heart skittered slightly. It plummeted when the screen read Linda Carlisle. A knot formed in my stomach as I answered.

The call hadn't lasted long, but it packed a punch. Mrs. Carlisle recounted their plan for transporting Stacy to a hospital close to their home in Mississippi. The kicker had been that Pete Stewart, Stacy's boyfriend, had offered to pay for it and they had accepted his offer. I kept my opinions about Pete to myself since it was probably a lessened burden on the Carlisles, but I still didn't like it.

I was glad to know Stacy's doctors felt confident she was stable enough to make such a transition so soon. Unfortunately, nothing had really changed, and Stacy was still in a coma. With that news, Mrs. Carlisle also informed me they would like to relocate Stacy's belongings and were willing to pay a moving company to handle it. Rather than deal with the hassle of scheduling and monitoring packers, I agreed they could send a transport service, but I would take care of the actual packing.

When we hung up, I sat in my car for a long time processing the conversation. A wave of sadness washed over me. So much had happened in such a short amount of time. Beginnings and endings were butting up against one another, and it was a lot to take in. Hot tears began to fall, and I let them. When the tears finally subsided, I took a deep breath and decided if I was going to have Stacy's room packed up in such a short time, I should get started on it. The search for good quality boxes began, creating an excellent distraction from the ache in my heart.

8

BRYAN

I was restless. After packing the suitcase that now rested next to my bedroom door, I sat on the edge of my bed with my elbows on my knees that refused to stop bouncing. I stared at the floor as though it knew a solution to the restive feeling that had a hold of me. The events of the weekend replayed themselves in my mind, and I was left reeling. How had I gone from reluctantly visiting an old friend to meeting the woman of my dreams in the same night?

As these thoughts bombarded me, my phone buzzed loudly on my nightstand with a text message shocking me back to reality. I hoped it was from Jess. My blood pressure seemed to spike when I discovered it was from Pete.

> Pete: Hey, man! Sorry about this weekend.
> Let's get drinks this week.

I groaned not only because of who the message had come from but also that he wanted to meet up again. Why? The first meeting had been completely pointless. Maybe not completely pointless since it was how I'd met Jess. But Pete had not stuck around long enough to carry on a full conversation aside from his snarky jibes before taking off with that poor woman, Stacy. Thankfully, my schedule was booked solid for the next two weeks. Maybe that would be enough time for Pete to move on to his next target.

> Me: In ATL for 2 weeks.

I had hoped this would deter additional attempts at unsolicited invitations. I was wrong.

> Pete: Dude, send me your schedule. I'll be in ATL this week.

Great. What were the chances? Why was Pete trying to reconnect after all this time? Surely it was just a coincidence. I sent one last message before setting the phone to Do Not Disturb.

> Me: I'll let you know.

Pete had been my best friend from the moment we met in basic training. I was pretty sure that if not for the Army, Pete would have been on a path of destruction as parties and alcohol were nearly his downfall in high school. As he tells it, Pete walked into his local Army recruiter office on a whim after a night of heavy drinking and enlisted before he had fully sobered. Within two weeks, he was standing in line behind me waiting his turn for a haircut and uniform. We served alongside each other through good times and bad until Pete decided he'd had enough. I remained enlisted, though I eventually transferred from an active soldier to a cyber warrior.

They say basic training is where you make lifelong friendships, and you learn whom not to trust. Pete had never given me reason not to trust him, even though he had a long list of poor choices under his belt. I could only hope that his newfound desire to reconnect was not one of them.

Checking the time on the phone screen, I resigned to forcing myself to fall asleep even with the nervous energy coursing through me. I walked the phone to my dresser where I left it before switching off the lamp and sinking into the bed. As soon as I closed my eyes, I knew that falling into a sound sleep was going to be a challenge.

In that in-between state, right after closing my eyes and drifting to sleep, all I could see was Jess in my arms. Her body was strong but gentle. I felt her hands soft against my face, her breath warm next to my lips. It was everything I had ever imagined and more. As real as this felt, maybe it had all been dream.

My eyes popped open as heat enveloped me under the blanket. I threw off the covers and swung my legs over the side of the bed, holding my head in my hands. My thoughts were taking control of my senses. As much as I desired to give in to these thoughts, it wasn't what I wanted. I took several deep breaths and prayed silently.

God, I can't go down this path for too long before my heart and mind cause my body to betray us all. Give me self-control and wisdom.

Sleep eventually came as did my alarm. It was not the best sleep I'd ever gotten, but it was by far not the worst. I had spent enough time sleeping in hot, cramped spaces in full gear that it took a lot for me to consider several hours of sleep in a comfortable place to be poor. Even the vinyl couch I'd fallen asleep on at the hospital two days ago was an upgrade from some of the abandoned buildings I holed up in with ten other men in active war zones.

The thought of that vinyl couch had my head clearing quickly, and it wasn't because it had been a comfortable option for sleep. Instead, I was thinking about with whom I had shared the space. It had been an extremely long day, and as tired as I had been, Jess had been emotionally and mentally taxed, leaving her physically drained. I was not surprised she practically passed out the moment her eyes closed. I was, however, surprised when she made herself comfortable curling up next to me. And it had felt completely natural.

As tempting as it was to dwell on those memories that threatened to revive the emotional tidal wave of last night, I knew if I did not get myself in gear, I risked throwing my entire day's schedule off track. I got dressed and headed for the gym at my office. There was more than enough time to get through my usual workout and shower before heading to the airport. It was at the airport where things began to unravel the day's schedule.

What should have been a comfortable built-in buffer became a sweaty, frustrating wait on a packed aircraft. The only saving grace had been my ability to snag emergency row seating. I always aimed for the highly coveted row, but not for the reason most people did. Sure, extra leg room was a bonus. I, however, took the emergency row responsibilities very seriously. It sounds a little dramatic, and I have never experienced an emergency requiring the exits on a commercial flight, but I have little desire to leave such responsibilities to chance. If it couldn't be me ready to pull that red emergency handle, I would accept fellow military, law enforcement, or a Kindergarten teacher. Because let's face it, any man or woman who could herd a room full of five-year-olds outside for a fire drill in under sixty seconds was fully competent and capable in a full-blown emergency on an airplane. This time, I had scored the coveted seat. Thankfully, my services were not needed.

The flight was full, but it was also early enough that everyone was still quiet, so as we sat on the tarmac waiting for the pilot to show up —because it's almost never an actual mechanical issue that keeps you on the plane during a delay—I pulled out my phone and replied to a few emails. Before I shoved it back in my pocket, my thumb kept hovering over the Messages app wanting to send Jess a quick text since I wasn't sure when I'd actually get to call her. We hadn't talked about her weekday schedule. Giving in, I pressed the icon and opened our text thread.

After several attempts at trying not to come across as creepy, desperate, or dramatic, I went with sincere. I held my breath, felt my pulse quicken, and hit send. The flood of relief I felt when I got an almost immediate response was welcome. I knew the smile on my face had me looking like a dope, but I did not care. Had she really dreamed about me too? I might be a grown man, but I felt like a kid at Christmas. At this moment, I was dumbstruck to the point I didn't care if we had to sit on the plane another ninety minutes.

Thankfully, that didn't happen. Before I could put too much

thought into my next message, an announcement gave a heads-up that we would finally be on our way shortly thereafter. I sent a quick reply asking if I could call her later and powered down my phone, tucking it back into my pocket.

By the time we landed, I had an hour to get an Uber, grab lunch, and check in at the convention center. Normally, this would have me coming unhinged. I appreciate schedules and routines more than most people, and when the schedule I am following is knocked off course, I tend to get easily frustrated. Today was different, and I was crediting the new message I had awaiting me when I turned my phone back on upon landing. She was looking forward to my call, and I was more than anxious to be able to make said call. Unfortunately, it was going to have to wait until after the afternoon rush of the conference.

THE FIRST DAY'S agenda was not as full of speaking engagements as the remainder of the week and instead boasted a welcome presentation from the conference host, a security briefing from the head of the FBI, and a panel presentation on ransomware. I was grateful the conference eased us into the event because it took everything I had to keep my mind from wandering to a certain woman I was dying to talk to again.

According to the schedule, there was a break for dinner between the panel presentation and a networking event for all the leaders in the cybersecurity community. A check of my watch told me all I had to do was force myself to focus for another two hours. I let out an internal groan of frustration before catching myself.

It was almost comical how a woman I had known for three days had already gotten under my skin, in a good way. All I wanted to do was relive last night, and if I couldn't do it in person, my imagination was more than happy to repeat it on loop. Granted, just thinking about Jess made it difficult to engage in anything the presenter on stage was saying. I needed to compartmentalize and engage my mind, especially if I had any hope of surviving this week mentally. Trying to shut out those beautiful invasive memories, I forced myself to remain present and aware of the speaker's words.

The two hours passed as expected—slowly. Before leaving the table where I had been sitting, I powered on my phone and was greeted by a text from Pete.

> Pete: Dinner/Drinks Wednesday?

I had to take a deep breath before sending my reply. My gut reaction was to deny him the request. There was no good reason coming to mind to agree to meet him. I was still a little put out by the flippant attitude he'd had about Jess's friend, Stacy. Maybe I could use the opportunity to talk sense into him or at least understand him better. Though, I had enough experience with Pete to know I could do all the talking and chances were good he would still leave thinking he had been wronged in some way. With reluctance, I made a suggestion in response to his message.

> Me: Sure. Blue's, 8 PM?

Blue's was my favorite hole-in-the-wall diner close to where I was staying. I wouldn't have to try hard to get there or back from the hotel.

> Pete: Great.

There were several hands I had to shake and conversations that held me up before I could make the trek to my hotel room where I planned to hang out for a couple of hours before the networking cocktail hour. I grabbed one of the prepackaged box meals provided for the attendees and headed upstairs.

The room was basic but comfortable with a view of downtown Atlanta from my window. I had left my luggage with the front desk for them to deliver it to my room, and I was glad to see it had indeed made it to my room. I tossed the leather satchel that held my laptop and other important materials onto the bed before allowing myself to collapse next to it. I released a breath that seemed to take all the tension from within me along with it. My body relaxed, and a sense of quiet calm washed over me. The day had not been a bad one, but it had been draining.

I laid there with my eyes closed for several minutes before an image of Jess appeared behind them. I was immediately energized and reached for my phone.

> Me: How do you feel about video calls?

The reply was immediate.

> Jess: I hate them.

Within seconds my phone buzzed with an incoming video call. My heartrate spiked, and I had to take a moment before answering to allow it to regulate.

"Do you always do things you hate?" I asked once the call connected.

She joked back, "I was forgetting what you looked like."

It felt as though we had known each other a lot longer than we had when I considered the level of comfort and familiarity between us. The next hour went by quickly after we took turns filling each other in on the events of the day.

She told me about Mrs. Carlisle's phone call, which had seemed to take its toll on her emotionally. Her tears threatened to undo me and made me wish I was there to hold her hand and help her pack.

I told her about Pete's text, which caused her to respond pretty much how I had. It was actually really cute to watch her speak her mind about Pete. She was too nice to be mean, but she was spunky, I'd give her that.

When my phone alarm alerted me I had thirty minutes to get ready and head downstairs, I hung my head in displeasure.

"Looks like it's time to get back to it. Can I call you when I get back to my room if it's not too late?"

"Definitely," she answered with the hottest smirk I've ever seen, as though she was daring me not to call her again.

"Then I will talk to you later." I winked.

When the call disconnected, I spun around in the desk chair and ran my hands through my hair. Seeing her face again had ignited the feelings I had tamped down the night before.

"Get it together, Carsen," I told myself, once again pushing my feelings back down.

I took a quick shower before getting dressed and heading for the evening's event. Networking was probably one of the worst parts of my job since it was technically glorified brown-nosing. My position was secure, and I was happy to stay in it exactly as I was, and the expectations for the evening were clear. All I had to do was touch base with my higher-ups, make vendors feel important, and highlight the US Cyber Force as the eminent defense of cyberspace. Every event I'd ever attended where these were the expectations, I could have been the poster child for the organization. Tonight, it was a slightly different story.

My mind kept wandering to Jess and the next time I was going to get to talk to her. The number of times I either pretended to hear what someone had said or asked them to repeat themselves should have been embarrassing. And I did not care. I should have cared, but I was so wrapped up in my own thoughts that I practically muddled through the hours of speaking and listening with very little recall of most of my interactions with people. Tomorrow would have to be different, and I would have to be at my best and brightest. Tonight, I practically ran back to my room when I had made the rounds and shaken the most important hands.

From the elevator, I sent Jess a message hoping she was still awake.

> Me: Any chance you're still up?

I could barely maintain my composure when she replied. Within minutes of being back in my room, I was answering a video call from the only person in the world who had ever made it this hard to remain in control of my emotions. Every time I thought of her or talked to her or even read a text from her, I was flooded with what felt like hope mingled with excitement. My heart, pounding with anticipation, made it a point to ensure I had to make a real effort to steady my breathing. This was a feeling I could get used to.

As soon as I saw her face on my phone screen, I could tell something was wrong. The amount of time Jess and I had spent together would not even rank me as a novice in regard to reading her mood, especially through a screen. Her eyes, however, told me a lot. The same big brown eyes that seemed to pick up on everything in detail seemed unfocused. When I asked her about her evening, she gave a noncommittal answer about packing boxes and writing test questions. It was clear something had changed since our earlier conversation.

"Is something wrong?" I asked when her answer seemed vague.

Jess took a deep breath and sighed before answering. "No, not really. Maybe everything." She paused and pressed a thumb hard against one of her eyebrows before continuing.

"It's quiet and I realized earlier today that it's always going to be quiet because Stacy isn't coming home tonight or this week. She'll probably never call this home again. And I don't know how to feel about that." Tears rolled down each cheek. She stared at the wall beyond her phone.

Not sure what to say, I let the quiet linger. If only I could reach through the phone and wrap Jess in my arms. "I wish I was there with you."

She stared back at me through the phone and smiled, but it did not reach her eyes. "That would be nice. Then maybe I wouldn't feel so alone." Her gaze turned to me and grew intense.

I felt as though she was studying me for a final exam.

Jess sniffled before letting out a breath. Wiping the tears from her face she smiled and apologized. "I'm sorry. You did not call to hear me lament about my emotional state. Tell me about the rest of your day."

She was hurting, and I felt helpless.

"Hey, if something is bothering you or upsetting you, I want to hear about it. I want to listen."

There was a hesitation in her next words but also relief. "Thank you. That's really nice of you."

This reminded me how little we knew each other. She thought I was just being nice when the truth was, I wanted to take on this pain for her and make it go away. That probably made me sound pathetic, but there was something about this girl, this woman, that made me feel things I don't remember ever feeling. It was as though she'd worked her way under my skin and into my heart after such a short amount of time, and I was trying not to come across as creepy or clingy.

"I'm not just saying that, Jess. I genuinely care about your feelings. If you want to talk about anything, I'm here."

Her face seemed to relax at this. "Thanks. I'm still just processing everything that happened with Stacy over the weekend. When her mom called this afternoon to let me know they wanted to move Stacy's stuff home with them, it was like a sucker punch after the initial blow. I'm fine, really. It's just a lot. And I have even more coming up at work and school for the next two weeks, so it's all hitting hard and fast at the same time."

That she opened up to me gave me a sense she believed what I had said. She trusted me, and I knew from some of our conversation at the club, it didn't seem that was something she gave easily. I asked her to tell me more about the things causing her stress and I listened.

I knew Jess was special. She told me about her gift on our way to New York. I had no idea, however, how incredible she was. When she described the thesis she was gearing up to defend, I got a taste of what it must feel like when I talk about technology with some people. I wanted desperately to understand, but all I could do was nod along, ask questions, and attempt to grasp at least part of what she explained. Jess had a better grasp on people than I had on computers, which was saying something.

"Jess." I hoped I sounded awed and not overwhelmed or lovestruck. "You are unlike anyone I have ever met."

Her cheeks pinked as she scrunched her nose. "Is that a good thing?"

"It's amazing. You are amazing. I won't pretend to understand everything you just said, but I believe most words would be insufficient to describe you."

She gave me an exaggerated eyeroll even though the smile on her face was big. "Let's talk about something else. You choose." Her mood was lighter.

I tapped the desk I was sitting at as I searched for a topic. "Okay, yeah. I wanted to ask you sooner if you would go to church with me when I'm back in town."

"Oh." Her face brightened at this. "Yeah, I would love to go with you.

"Good. One more thing to look forward to when I get back." I waggled my eyebrows.

We spent the next hour talking about God, the Bible, and church. Neither of us realized how late it was until Jess covered her mouth and tried to stifle a yawn. A quick look at my watch made me chuckle.

"It is definitely past my bedtime." She repressed a yawn.

"Good night, Jess." I desperately wished I could tell her in person.

"Good night, Bryan."

After ending the call, I sat at the desk and stared at the black screen in front of me. So many thoughts and desires whirred to life inside me. I needed to pray.

God, I want your will to be done in my life more than anything. Let the desires of my heart be from you. Give me wisdom and strength to pursue you alone. I know you are working in Jess. Thank you for giving me front row seats. Continue to reveal yourself to her and keep me from being a stumbling block. My heart longs for her more deeply than it ever has for another person. Please don't let me put that ahead of your will for either of us.

With a heavy sigh, I left the chair, readied myself for bed, and fell into a dreamless sleep.

9

BRYAN

Pete was already seated at a table when I walked into the diner, standing as I approached. After a one-armed back-slap-handshake combo, we each sat.

"It's so good to see you, again, man!" Pete oozed charisma and charm. None of it felt genuine.

Trying to mirror his energy, I said, "Yeah, hate that we didn't get to hang out longer last weekend."

I watched him, wondering what was going on inside his mind. Immediately, my thoughts went to Jess. The fact that she'd had Pete profiled from a single look boggled my mind. I couldn't help but wonder how it felt to be able to know a person so intimately without the person even knowing what you knew about them.

Now I was thinking about what she saw when we met. Clearly, I didn't scare her off or give off the wrong signals. Had she seen the instant attraction I'd had to her?

Before I could let myself get derailed on this train of thought, Pete threw himself back in his chair as though he had been punched.

"Dude, what happened to Stacy was brutal. I mean, don't get me wrong; we had a great time. But, geez, she was fine when I left the house. When I got your call, that tore me up. I liked her."

Pushing thoughts of Jess from my mind, I eyed Pete. "Have you heard how she's doing?"

Leaning forward and putting his elbows on the table Pete shook his head. "Nah, I talked to her mom for a couple minutes and got her to let me pay for the medical transport. It felt like the least I could do after everything that happened. But I don't think I'll be getting regular updates."

Trying to keep a neutral look on my face, I nodded. "Yeah. Well, definitely a sad situation."

The server approached the table and we ordered. As soon as she turned to walk away, Pete stretched back in his chair. "So, what's going on with you? Still soldiering along at a desk, working for Uncle Sam?"

There was a tingle of hope in the back of my mind that if I kept my answers short and simple, Pete would get bored, and we'd say goodnight and go our separate ways. However, as he was never one to be lacking in words, Pete carried the conversation most of the night. That of course meant the topic of conversation was mostly Pete and his business venture.

He was starting his own technology investment and development firm with a plan to find companies or even individuals wanting to push the envelope when it came to technology and to provide capital if necessary to help develop their ideas. The more Pete talked about his company the more aware I became of Pete's real motives for wanting to meet, though he had yet to come right out and say it.

After almost two hours of practically nonstop listening, I checked my watch and unintentionally let out an audible sigh.

Pete looked at his watch too. He seemed to have as much energy as when the evening started with while I was mentally drained. "Man, look at me, just talking your ear off. I'm sure you've had enough talking for today. I'm really glad you had time to hang out. I've missed you."

My smile was forced but I tried to sound genuine. "Yeah, man, it's been a long day, but I'm glad we could catch up."

Thinking I might have been wrong about Pete having ulterior

motives for meeting, I moved to stand, but Pete caught me one last time.

"Hey, before you head out, can I ask you something?"

Positive I knew what was coming, I hesitated before sitting back down. "Sure, Pete, what's up?"

"Think you'll be wrapping up your time with the Army any time soon? I could definitely use a guy like you to head up the tech side of my company. I know there are plenty of other guys out there, but I want the best. And I know you are the best. And not that this is a good reason, but I can definitely pay better."

There it was. I stared at my hands, folded on the table. "Thanks for that, Pete. But I love my job, and I like doing my job as a service to my country."

Returning my focus to Pete, I saw the displeasure on his face. He'd taken it as an insult. Scoffing, Pete leaned back in his chair, his face morphing between disdain and apprehension. "Yeah, always the perfect soldier."

That was my cue to excuse myself. I stood and offered my hand, but Pete did not return the gesture.

"It was good to see you, Pete. Good luck with your venture. I hope you find what you're looking for." I tapped my knuckles on the table.

Pete huffed and scanned the diner trying to get the server's attention without another glance in my direction. I paid the check at the counter before looking over my shoulder to see Pete sulking at the table with a beer in hand.

Back in my hotel room, I got ready for bed. The mental fatigue was heavy, but the rest of me was on edge. Fidgeting with my phone, I wondered if it was too late to send a message to Jess. I missed her. How could I feel so strongly about someone I had known less than a week?

Before I could think too hard about it, my phone buzzed first.

> Jess: I hope it's not too late or that you're sleeping soundly enough to not be disturbed. Missed talking to you this evening. Maybe we can talk tomorrow.

My chest grew warm inside and out. I quickly replied.

> Me: I was just wondering if it was too late to message you a good night. I missed talking to you too. Let's talk tomorrow. Have a good night.

I could only smile when I was thinking about Jess. Knowing she was thinking about me sent my heart soaring.

10

JESS

It was finally Saturday. The week had crept by so slowly that I wondered if it had only been one week. The sun was peeking through my bedroom curtains as I debated how much longer to stay in my bed. The only thing on my to-do list for the day was to finish packing Stacy's room. I had tried to make progress on it in the evenings after work, but my heart had not been in it. It was too close to the equivalent of saying a final goodbye, and I just didn't have that in me right now. I knew it needed to be done because a moving van would arrive sometime next week for the boxes. If I didn't finish today, I wouldn't have anything for the movers to take with them.

With a groan, I heaved myself out of bed. Before heading to the bathroom, I checked my phone, hoping I might have a message from Bryan, but there was nothing. It had been a long week for both of us. Maybe he was sleeping late. He deserved a break. If the weather in Atlanta was as beautiful as it was in DC, the day held a lot of potential.

As I brushed my teeth, I thought about how he might be spending his day. I'd never been to Atlanta before, but it was a fairly large city so there had to be plenty of options. I wondered if we could both go to a park and take a walk together while we were on the phone.

Wiping my mouth with a towel, I stiffened when there was a knock on my front door. A slight wave of panic rushed over me as I wondered if I had gotten the date wrong for the movers to come. Grabbing a hoodie to throw over my slept-in T-shirt, I scrolled through my calendar and verified that nothing was scheduled for Saturday.

Jogging down the stairs, I ran a hand through my hair, hoping it came across as intentional bedhead and less like actual bedhead. Without thinking to check, I opened the door and froze. It took me a moment to process the fact that Bryan was standing in front of me.

"Hi." His voice was warm with a hint of tired.

My face immediately broke into a smile. I had to stop myself from leaping toward him. "Hi."

My heart had apparently stopped at his appearance but decided to finally beat again causing me to feel a little lightheaded. A familiar warmth spread through me as I reached out to hug my early morning visitor.

Bryan hugged me back, lifting my feet off the ground as he walked inside.

Needing to see his face, I let go, and he set my feet back onto the ground. When he did, I took a small step backward without letting go of his arms.

"What on earth are you doing here? I thought you were still another week away."

He reached to shut the door with his foot. "I decided since I don't have to be there until Monday and you could use less time alone, maybe I'd make a quick trip back. I hoped you wouldn't mind the company."

Still processing his presence, I hugged him again, this time tighter than the last. When I finally pulled away, I tried to use my sleeves to dry my face before looking back at him.

"I had finally pulled myself together before you showed up and surprised me. Hadn't cried in days." I laughed through my tears.

He took my hand in his. "If I had known that my appearance would drive you to tears, I would have stayed put." He kissed my hand, gently, squeezed it and let it go. "Would it be better if I went home?" He playfully reached for the door.

Stopping his hand, I laced my fingers with his, and stared into his eyes. "That would quite possibly make it worse."

Returning my stare, he squeezed my hand. "I wouldn't want that." He leaned down and kissed me.

My entire body hummed at the contact. This man kicked all my senses into overdrive, and while I didn't think it was possible, the feelings were more intense today than they had been a week ago. And he was here. He was here because he didn't want me to be alone. This was completely new territory for me, and I scrambled to make sense of it all. I was getting lost in him, in his kiss, and in his hands.

As though he was reading my thoughts, Bryan pulled back and rested his forehead on mine. We stood together in silence for several moments before he took a step backward, holding onto my hand to maintain contact.

He smiled and I became acutely aware that I probably looked like I just rolled out of bed. And it was most likely true since that's exactly what had just happened.

"So, did my arrival wake you?" He eyed my attire.

"No, but I definitely hadn't planned to have company so soon after getting out of bed." I laughed.

Running a hand through my hair, I hoped I was helping and not making it worse. I had taken a quick glance in the mirror before running to open the door and couldn't remember what I had seen. How could I not remember the state of my hair or even my face at the time? I felt my cheeks turning pink.

"Got any big plans today?" Bryan still held my hand and rubbed his thumb over my knuckles.

"I was planning to finish packing up Stacy's room. So, I wouldn't say I have big plans."

"Would you like help?"

"I wouldn't say no if you are offering. But I would hate for you to have flown all the way back here just to end up packing boxes. And by the way, what kind of flight got you here this early?"

Bryan's eyes smiled back at me. "One that I would take again in a heartbeat, but only for you."

I was warm all over and had a hard time looking at him for a moment. Emotions were running through me like a smoldering fire. In this moment, I was positive it would take very little to fan the flames growing inside of me. For a moment, I was certain we had been on the verge of creating an inferno between us. And then he pulled back. While deep down I knew it had been for the best, it didn't fully stamp out the sparks within me. I suddenly felt too warm in my hoodie.

I snapped myself back to the moment. "I'm going to go upstairs and change. There should be coffee ready in the kitchen. Make yourself at home," I said before running upstairs.

Home. I had not felt close to home since I left California. My mom's house, the house I grew up in, the house where we made countless memories, just Mom and me for so long, that was home. When I first got to DC, I lived in the dorms on campus and was always surrounded by hundreds of other students. It had its moments of comfort and familiarity, but it had never been home.

I bought this house after Mom died because I needed to be out of the dorms, and I had met Stacy who wanted to be my roommate. As close as we were and as nice as my simple house was, it had never felt exactly like home. Until. When I thought about Bryan spending the evening here, on my couch, sharing a meal, talking, even when he kissed me, it had made me feel like he belonged here. Once again, that's exactly how it felt now that I had said the word *home* to him.

When he was with me, I felt at home. He made me feel safe, grounded, and sure of everything. This was crazy, wasn't it? It had been 180 hours, give or take an hour, since I laid eyes on Bryan. Seven and a half days of conversations, car rides, text messages, and phone calls, and I was in a place I had never been emotionally. There had never been a time, past or present, that I remember thinking I felt at home with someone aside from my mom. The longer I thought about it, the more I wondered if he felt the same way or if my heart and mind were running away from me.

WE WORKED all morning and into the afternoon packing up Stacy's room. We had surprisingly managed to empty the room of everything that needed to go, and I had even made a trip into every room in the house to make sure nothing had been left out. As I finished taping the last of the boxes closed, Bryan picked it up to carry it downstairs.

"I guess that's it." My words came out shakier than I had meant for them to.

Bryan's face was etched with concern. "Are you okay?"

I was suddenly exhausted and wanted to fall over on the empty bed next to me, curl up, and go to sleep.

"I will be, thanks to you. I don't know how many more times I could say thank you to you before I feel like I have thanked you enough. And not just for today. Though today requires just as many thanks as the entire last week. I feel like facing this empty room alone would have been impossible. And you have done more for me than you could know, just by being willing to listen. It was like God knew I was going to need someone. That I was going to need you, this very week." My thoughts and words trailed off.

Bryan swallowed hard. His hold on the box in his arms tightened. He opened his mouth to say something but instead of speaking, he set the box down on the bed and reached for my hands.

Taking a deep breath he said, "Jess, I know that we have only known each other for a week... a single week out of our entire lives. And this is probably going to sound corny and cheesy."

He paused. I held my breath.

"From the minute I walked into that room and met you, I have felt differently than I ever have about another person. My heart is set on you, and I'm afraid that if I don't tell you this right now, I don't know what will happen. And if you don't feel the same way or have not even thought about me in that way, I will understand. But until you tell me otherwise, I am going to pursue your heart in hopes of making it mine forever."

Heart pounding and breaths shallow, I realized I had a death grip on his hands. I slowly released his fingers and moved my hands to his face. Words didn't come. Instead, I pulled his face towards mine, tiptoed, and kissed him. In that moment, I felt more than warmth. Moving my arms around his neck to hold onto him, what I felt was heat, it was fire, it was everything I didn't know I wanted but knew I could never live without from that moment forward.

Bryan wrapped his arms around me and kissed me back. It was slow and deep and meaningful. Every emotion, every word, every thought wrapped up in this one moment being spoken silently from one soul to another.

When all that needed to be said had been said, our lips slowly broke apart. Breathing felt like a foreign concept for a moment as we both struggled to compose ourselves.

I spoke first. "It's yours. My heart. It's yours. I had almost convinced myself that I was crazy for feeling anything, much less something so strong in such a short period of time. But it was like I just knew you were supposed to be here." I put my hand on my heart.

He pulled me into a firm warm hug, and we stood there for what seemed like years, as our hearts found the rhythm of one another and began beating in unison. And then, as though it should not be outdone, my stomach growled loudly.

We both laughed, breaking the precious silence but the sound was just as sweet.

Trying not to laugh again, Bryan said, "I think that sounds like something we should address sooner than later."

"Agreed."

My face was beginning to hurt from smiling.

SETTLING into a booth at the sushi place not far from the house, I finally felt as though my feet were back on solid ground once again.

There were feelings and emotions I have never felt before coursing through me, and it felt like it might take a small eternity to process all of them. Until a week ago, I had never had a boyfriend. Today, not only had a man I met eight days ago confessed his love for me, but I had returned the sentiment. And meant it. It should have terrified me or in the very least convinced me I was losing my mind. Instead, with every passing minute, I was without a doubt falling in love with Bryan Carsen.

After we ordered, Bryan watched me intently, neither of us speaking for quite a while. The silence was not heavy, but it was full. It was full of questions, and I really hoped they were questions that could easily be answered. I felt completely out of my element at this point.

"What happens next?" I asked.

His eyes, never leaving mine, seemed to sparkle brighter than before. "Well, I'm not sure there's an instruction manual or a field guide available. So, I guess what happens next is up to us to decide."

"Hm." I nodded slowly.

We sat quietly for a while longer until the food arrived. After our plates were set in front of us and the server had gone, Bryan reached out his hand, and I placed mine in it.

"This doesn't feel real." I hadn't meant to say the words aloud.

I felt the need to continue when Bryan's lips twitched to conceal a smile.

"Seriously, if you had asked me nine days ago what this week would look like, I would have told you it would look like every week before. Work, write, research, work, and write. Today, it's like I put everything I've ever thought about my future in a snow globe and shook it really hard, and now I'm watching the little pieces of fake snow settle back down."

Bryan listened and nodded and stared at our hands. "Is that good or bad?"

"Good, I think? This part is definitely good. I have never not known what I was going to do next. Everything I've ever done has been a clear plan with clear steps. I've never had to take into consideration anyone else's plans. And now all I can think about is doing whatever keeps this like this." My hand gripped his tighter.

His gaze moved to mine. "I get that. Schedules, regimens, plans, tactics, procedures, everything always in place for me. The Army spoiled me. The unexpected always hits differently. When my dad died, it was unexpected. I struggled with that for years. He had been my hero, even though he was MIA for a lot of things. I always imagined him off saving the world when he was deployed or at work. His heart attack seemed to come out of nowhere. Looking back, I know he was not in great health. But as a kid, he was just there one day and gone the next.

"When my mom died, it was expected. She'd been diagnosed with ALS, and it was aggressive. She was gone sixteen months from her diagnosis. I watched her decline, but I was deployed so I wasn't even really there. But it was a combination of shock, sadness, and relief. I knew it would come eventually, and when it happened, I knew she wasn't suffering anymore."

His voice trailed off; his gaze unfocused.

I watched him for a while until his eyes found me again.

"I'm sorry, I got carried away in my thoughts. I was just trying to say that I understand the dichotomy of expected versus unexpected life changes. And we can take as much time as we both need to make any decision about us, because I plan to be right here no matter what."

I smiled and squeezed his hand one more time. "Me too."

Taking a deep breath and letting it out slowly, I looked at our full plates in front of us then back at Bryan. "So, tell me about yourself." I smiled as I let go of Bryan's hand and picked up my chopsticks.

We made our way through our plates of sushi, taking turns talking about our families and our hometowns, finding we had even more in common than we had initially known. We both loved running, being outdoors, and learning, for starters.

Three hours later, we decided it was time to give up our table. On our drive back to my house, he asked if I would go to church with him the next day. I'd agreed immediately.

We sat in his Jeep in my driveway for an hour, holding hands and still talking about anything that popped into our minds just to stay close to one another.

Bryan yawned mid-sentence, making me laugh.

"You are probably exhausted after today. I should let you get home and rest."

He smiled sheepishly before getting out of the Jeep and hurrying around to open my door. After another half hour standing on the front porch together trying to find any reason not to part ways, I asked if he wanted to come in.

Bryan began to pull himself away. "Yeah, I do. But I won't. What I'm feeling and what I know is right are battling it out right now, and before my willpower crumbles, I should go."

I nodded but before I could open the door, he put his hands on my hips and pulled me to himself. He slid his hands up to my waist, never taking his eyes from mine. My hands landed on his chest, and as we stared at each other, time seemed to warp and slow. Sounds around us silenced.

He leaned down and brushed his lips softly against mine. It was warm, sweet, and gentle. I wanted to hold onto him more tightly, reach for more, but I understood the unspoken request when he pulled away. The longing was intense and desperately wanted to become more. Instead, I ran my hands down his arms until my hands were in his.

He rested his forehead on mine.

"Goodbye, Bryan."

"Goodbye, Jess."

11

JESS

The music was just as peace-inducing as I had remembered it being the last time I was in this very church. My soul was practically trembling as the choir sang. The sermon was evocative and deep. The pastor had started a series called "The Will of God" in which, he related in his introduction, God has a plan for every life he created, and it's a good and perfect plan. That sounded too good to be true. This entire week had been a massive reminder that I thought I had a perfect plan for my life, and now I was hearing that God actually had a better plan than the one I'd concocted.

"This is good, and it is pleasing in the sight of God our Savior, who desires all people to be saved and to come to the knowledge of the truth," he read from a book called First Timothy.

He explained that any person who did not know God personally, who had not made Christ the Lord of their life, could ever know the will of God for their life. The message was abundantly clear. Before I could ask God for anything else, I needed to know him.

Through the entirety of the service, I felt like I was going to squirm right out of my seat. If Bryan noticed my restlessness, I didn't know. As we were standing for the final prayer, my mind wandered, and I had apparently taken a firm grasp of the seat in front of me.

After the pastor gave the benediction, Bryan turned to gather his Bible and I just barely registered him watching me. He put his hand on my back, the sensation slowly dragging me back to where I was.

With a shaky voice, I said, "I think I need to know God personally."

When I turned to look at Bryan, his eyes had gone watery. He pulled me into a hug and all I could do was hug him back, tears pouring down my face.

A woman with beautiful tan skin, dark hair, and dark eyes placed a hand on each of our backs.

Bryan and I released our hug, but he held onto my hand as the woman put her hand on my arm. In a thick Spanish accent, she said, "I heard you tell your young man here that you need to be saved. Do not wait another minute if you have not already asked Jesus to be your Savior. Time can get away from you and life will pass you by before you know it." Her eyes sparkled with tears and the truth. She patted my arm and walked away from us without another word. Where her hand had been was warm.

I cut my eyes to Bryan. "Do you know her?"

With a confused smile on his face, he shook his head. "No, but she seems like a wise woman. Want to talk about it over lunch before I head to the airport?"

"Sure." I smiled at him.

HAVING a serious conversation over lunch is a good idea. Having a serious conversation over lunch in a restaurant when every church in the DC metro area lets out at the same time is not a good idea. Everything was rushed and noisy, and by the time we got our food and eaten, we had to hustle to get me home before Bryan had to be at the airport. I was disappointed to say the least when we pulled into my driveway, not having had enough time.

The time to say goodbye came too quickly. Holding hands, we

walked up the steps to my front door. I think we were both feeling the weight of having to say goodbye for another week.

"Hey." He lifted my chin so he could see my eyes. "It's just a week, right? And we'll talk every day, and then I'll be back Saturday. And you know what we should do?"

I smiled up at him, trying to memorize every line of his face. "What?"

"Go on a real date. One that we planned. And it should be somewhere nice."

My smile widened. "I think that is a very good idea."

He leaned down and kissed me before wrapping his arms around me. He held on as if letting go would take his last breath from him.

I whispered, "I don't like letting you go."

He kissed the top of my head. "I don't like it, either."

We held each other in silence for several minutes before he loosened his hold.

Leaning back so I could see his face, I felt my heart skitter slightly. "I don't know how it's even possible, but I love you, Bryan Carsen. And I need you to come back home as soon as possible."

The smile on his face sent a jolt of warmth completely through me. "I promise, no matter what, I will be back here as quickly as humanly possible. And I love you, Jess Hayley."

We kissed one last time before he walked to his Jeep and headed back to the airport.

Without opening the door, I stood in the doorway and leaned against the frame watching long after Bryan's Jeep was out of sight. The afternoon was warm and sunny. Honestly, I was glad it hadn't been a gloomy day, as it would have made this part of the day that much harder.

When my thoughts turned to the upcoming week, I decided it would be best to go inside and review the final exam that would be issued tomorrow. I reached into my bag to find my keys and discovered an envelope that had not been there earlier. I pulled it out and saw JESS printed in blocky capital letters on the front. Unlocking the door and moving inside, I set my bag on the table in the entryway and walked to the couch, opening the envelope as I sat.

Jess,

I can't remember the last time I sat down and actually wrote a letter. It's late and I have many things I want to say to you but calling or even texting at this hour would be rude of me. A letter it is, then.

I'll start with what may sound unoriginal, but I mean every word of it. From the instant we met, I felt connected to you like I have never felt to another soul on earth. If you had asked me prior to that night if I believed in "love at first sight" I would have immediately said no. That's not true anymore. I fell in love with you the moment our eyes found each other and have continued to spiral into a depth of feeling that is new and overwhelming every minute of every day. To say I hope you feel the same is an understatement, but I won't pretend to know your heart, and I would never attempt to force your heart to feel anything other than what is real. I will, however, work hard every day to make sure you know mine.

You told me hours ago that your heart was mine. I hope you meant it, as nothing would bring me more joy. More importantly, I want you to know that as I strive to honor you and protect your heart, I will first and foremost trust God to lead me in those actions. I have committed my body, heart, and mind to be saved for my wife. I plan to fulfill that commitment and won't allow the passions I find creeping up inside of me when we are together to change that commitment. I care for you too much to let my desire to be close to you dictate my faithfulness to God and to you.

At the word *wife*, I dropped the letter in my lap and my breath caught in my throat. *Wife.* That was a loaded word; a word I had never given much thought to in reference to myself. Was he using it in reference to me? My face was warm, and my heart pounded in my ears. I picked up the letter, hand shaking, and finished reading it.

God has and always will be my first love. It's only by his grace that I found you. I don't know what the future holds for us. I know that it will be full of love, joy, and hope if we are allowed to grow closer to one another with God at the center.

I can't wait to see you again. I love you.

Bryan

I read the letter several times before tucking it back into the envelope. Curling up in my seat, I gripped the envelope, letting my eyes close and my breathing slow. Having always been a planner and an organizer, I rarely allowed my thoughts to flood my mind all at once. It was even less common an occasion when I would find myself overwhelmed with feelings and plans that seemed to contradict one another, but now I can't fight the urge to let it all rush through me, letting my mind wage the battle because it was imperative I make sense of the perplexity.

How could I have let myself become distracted by another person? How could these feelings possibly be real? They had manifested themselves instantaneously and such a short time ago. There was no way they were genuine. It had to be infatuation or lust. Questions and doubts rose to the surface, and my logical mind began to emerge. The tendency to overthink began to pull me downward as tears trailed down my face. Every tear was the result of a feeling that threatened to overtake me being released for processing.

Slowly I began to direct my thoughts into a meaningful picture. Creating a big picture inside of my mind allowed me to work through the complicated roadmap that initially felt full of roadblocks and detours. The hard part was allowing all the hidden and forgotten things to come to light. The things I compartmentalized neatly into the *I'll deal with you eventually* category needed to make an appearance. My priorities had been school, work, and research for so long that personal relationships, the future, and any divergence from the path I was on had been put into that category.

Amid the swirling thoughts, words came into my mind from earlier in the day. *This is good, and it is pleasing in the sight of God our Savior, who desires all people to be saved and to come to the knowledge of the truth.* At these words, my mind went blank. The commotion and chaos that had been battling for attention faded away, replaced by the sound of my heart beating in silence followed by the words of the last song I had heard in church. *Child of weakness, watch and pray, Find in Me thine all in all. Jesus paid it all, All to Him I owe; Sin had left a crimson stain, He washed it white as snow.*

Everything inside of me began to hum with what felt like electricity. I had no idea if I spoke the words aloud or if my mind was so clear it just felt like my thoughts were audible.

"God, I need you. I believe in you. Forgive me for my sins. Be in control of my life."

My entire body felt warm from the inside out, and the tears came more freely, but these tears felt different. These were tears of freedom and hope. My breaths were deep and full. It felt like the weight of a thousand worlds had been lifted from my chest. It had been a weight I didn't even know I was carrying.

I opened my eyes and peered down at the envelope still sitting on my leg. Gently picking it up, I held it to my chest and whispered another prayer.

"Your will be done."

Feeling completely drained of everything, but too restless to sit still, I picked up my phone and sent a message to the only person I wanted to talk to.

> Me: Bryan, thank you for the letter you managed to put in my purse without me knowing. After you left, I asked God to save me and to show me his will for my life. I'm still not sure what that means or what that looks like, but I know it happened and it was real. I miss you, already.

I knew he wouldn't get the message until he was off the airplane, but it was nice to have been able to share it. One more week. I just had to wait one more week.

12

JESS

After spending two days in a cramped conference room with multiple PhDs and professors answering multitudes of questions about the research I had completed and published over the last several years, I was mentally exhausted. Even though I had known it was coming and was as prepared as I could have been, I still felt a hint of trepidation knowing I had shared a lot of information that skirted around the very edges of a topic that I was not ready to share with the world.

While I very capably explained information that sounded peripheral, the truth was all my work and research had revolved around my ability to read people, and I'd had to defend all of it without ever having disclosed said fact. I'd had to dodge questions that probed the degree of my familiarity with the topic. Though it never felt like an outright lie, it took a lot of energy to externalize the information without letting any part of myself appear in the equation.

There had originally only been two people in the world to know the truth, and when my mother had passed away, Dr. Thorne had become the sole holder outside of myself to know about my "gift". That was the case until I'd shared it with Stacy who had apparently shared it with Pete though I highly doubted he believed her. Now that Bryan knew, there were once again only a small number of people who held my closest secret to themselves, and I was certain I could trust them to keep it that way.

After the second day of presentation, Dr. Thorne, who had been my advisor, was a former professor of mine, and was now a partner in my research, asked if I had some extra time to discuss some things privately. In all my years of school, Dr. Thorne was my absolute favorite professor. Not only was he interesting as a teacher, but he himself was an intuitive person who had his own ability to communicate with people. He was a body language expert as well as a self-proclaimed empath, and I never questioned it as it was clearly true. Dr. Thorne not only interpreted body language, but he could also feel and interpret other people's emotions when they were engaging him.

The first time I introduced myself to him during an advisory meeting, Dr. Thorne called me out for being hesitant and hiding something from him. I was completely taken aback, as I had become quite adept at masking the tells that suggested I could read others. When I asked him how he could tell, he explained he had a certain set of skills that allowed him to read people. This of course got my attention and encouraged me to suggest I may have my own set of skills.

That initial advisory meeting ended up lasting three hours, and we both laughed when he realized he'd failed to show up to teach one of his classes. Before leaving his office, he offered me a job as a research assistant, and I was doubly shocked when he also offered me the leeway to head up my own projects.

We had wrapped up our most recent project and submitted it for publication a few weeks ago and had not agreed on our next steps, so it was possible he had a lead on a new one. I let this be the primary assumption as we walked into his office.

"Jess, you did a fantastic job on your presentation. You always do great work. Congratulations. I don't think there is anyone who would question that you deserve the committee's seal of approval," he said as I walked by him into the office.

The office was a small room with walls of books and a large window overlooking a small concrete courtyard. There were two old leather wingback chairs that faced a large wooden desk positioned in front of the window. Dr. Thorne directed me to take a seat in one of the old chairs.

"Thank you. That means a lot coming from you," I said proudly as I took my seat.

Dr. Thorne returned the smile and sat down in his desk chair. He clasped his hands and leaned forward on his elbows. "Jess, I want to tell you first, I have enjoyed working with you these last few years. I have learned much from you and still don't feel like I know everything there is to know about what you can do and how it works."

This sounded more like the beginning of an exit interview than a project discussion. My palms began to feel clammy. Was I being let go? I searched his face for any sign of what was coming.

Calm. Sincere. Confident.

"Thank you," I said less confidently.

"As much as I would like to keep you here and continue working and learning with you, I wanted to ask if you had considered that there are other places, people, and organizations that could benefit from your skills and knowledge?"

My heart skidded to a halt, and I felt my face turn red. "Dr. Thorne, are you trying to tell me that I can no longer work here?" This was starting to feel more and more like a "We're sorry, it's just not working out" speech than anything else.

Dr. Thorne shook his head with certainty. "Not at all. I'm sorry if it sounded that way. I have a friend who works for a certain three-lettered government agency that I talk to regularly. Your name and abilities may have come up in conversation once or twice over the years, and last week I may have mentioned that you were in the home stretch of your education. He has said on more than one occasion he was very interested in learning more about how your skills could benefit his agency."

I sat in stunned silence. The idea that anyone outside of my very small circle, which was really more of a triangle, knew anything about my gift felt strange. I wasn't sure if I should feel flattered or angry. Maybe I was feeling a little of both in this moment.

I knew it was a unique skill and knowing how to use it efficiently and effectively made it even more valuable. However, I always assumed I would be "patient zero" and others would learn from my research, not directly from wielding my abilities actively and certainly not publicly. I never considered I'd be asked to use my gift independently outside of a lab or a classroom. It was what had always felt like the safest plan.

"Jess, I would hate to lose you. The university would hate to lose you. But I truly believe that you could do so much more just by being you elsewhere."

There was a slight burn behind my eyes as I scrambled to consider his words without taking it personally. "I've never considered anything beyond teaching and research. I like learning and understanding how things work, how I work, so other people can utilize the information. I wouldn't even know how to use my abilities practically outside of normal life."

Dr. Thorne leaned back in his chair and with his hands still clasped he rested them on his abdomen. "Jess, you are special and gifted, you know this. You are also brilliant and so full of potential that I'm afraid that you will one day find yourself bored here. I also believe that what you are capable of is something that could help a lot of people. And not that there is anything wrong with who you are, but because you are who you are, you refuse to take a single step from the path you created, the path you think you are meant to be on forever. This may be exactly where you want to be, but how will you know if you don't take into account the possibilities of something different? I know you won't leave the path without a reason. I want to offer you a reason."

It became apparent I had been holding my breath when air rushed from my lungs. I slowly nodded in acknowledgement, yet I was feeling a little affronted by the truth in his words.

I stared down at my hands resting on my legs for a long beat before looking back at my teacher, coworker, and mentor. "What is it your friend is wanting to offer and what does he expect in return?"

His eyes were hopeful though his face passive. "We only ever spoke in generalities. I'll send him an email this afternoon and let you know what he says about your possible entertainment of his offer and let you know something soon if that works for you."

I gave a single nod as I stood and exited the office, unsure to what I had agreed.

I was sitting in my car, my head resting on the steering wheel, when my phone buzzed with a message.

> Bryan: I've been praying for you today. I can't wait to hear how it went. I'll be free the rest of the afternoon.

My heart fluttered. I really wanted to call him, but I needed to work through the conversation I'd just had with Dr. Thorne. On the drive home I let my mind wander to possibilities that could take me from the road I had been on for so long. Thinking of the journey, did I even have a destination planned, or was Dr. Thorne right? Had I been meandering aimlessly because I was comfortable on my chosen way? Would I miss out on better things by following the thoroughly planned route? What better things were there?

Bryan had not been on my chosen path, yet I was not disappointed in the least by his appearance. But was his appearance part of a new path or an extension of my current one? And what were the expectations? We both had very strong feelings, and we were both adults who were secure in their ability to make good decisions.

Were we on the same page, however? His letter said he was committed to his future wife. Was that a general statement, or did he intend it for me? Love? Wife? Commitment? None of these things had been part of my plan, and the thought of them excited me and simultaneously scared me.

What if Dr. Thorne's contact had an offer that required me to diverge from my current path? And what if that path required me to choose between the one that included Bryan and one that didn't? What if the path that didn't include Bryan allowed me to use my gift to help more people than I could help by staying in a research lab? Did I even want to consider making my abilities common knowledge? There would definitely be consequences for letting that happen, and many of them I would not be able to control.

I gripped the steering wheel tighter.

I was wrapping up a fairly logical argument with myself as I pulled into my driveway and stopped when I noticed a long square box was propped against my door. I retrieved my bags from the backseat and made my way to inspect the box. Not recognizing the return address, I went into the house on a hunt for a pair of scissors. Upon opening the box, I was greeted by the most beautiful arrangement of peonies, roses, and hydrangeas ranging from blush pink to mauve and from white to ivory. There were sprigs of eucalyptus and fern throughout.

I rifled through the box to find the card. It read *I have found the one whom my soul loves. Song of Solomon 3:4 – Bryan.* My heart melted. Saturday suddenly felt light-years away.

I found a vase in the back of one of the kitchen cabinets and situated the flowers in it. After adding water, I positioned the vase in the center of the dining table and sat in one of the spindly chairs admiring it. I had never been sent flowers before, and honestly, the butterflies in my chest told me I wouldn't mind it happening again.

After staring at the soft petals and inhaling the scents of flowers and eucalyptus for several minutes, I dug my phone out of my bag and texted Bryan.

> Me: You said you'd be free the rest of the afternoon. Still true?

He responded almost immediately.

> Bryan: 100% true

Seconds later we were on a video call. I showed off the arrangement and gushed over it, thanking him no fewer than three times.

He seemed pleased with how happy I was to have received them.

When I asked Bryan to tell me about his day, he explained the conference had been cut short due to a presenter needing to leave early, but he had been brought onto a new project at work that was going to start when he returned from Atlanta. He seemed excited but didn't say much else as it had been labeled classified.

Then it was my turn. Not sure I wanted to start with Dr. Thorne's conversation, I gave him the short version of the committee's thorough grilling of my thesis.

"Jess, that's great! It sounds like you really impressed them."

When I didn't return the enthusiasm, Bryan asked, "Everything alright over there?"

My words were tangled thoughts in my mind contending for first to be spoken. "Yeah, yeah. I just had an interesting conversation with one of my mentors today, and before I tell you about it, I wanted to talk about something else first."

My words did not land right, which was very clearly written on Bryan's face.

Concern. Surprise. Seriousness.

"Oh, no! It's— it's not bad. It's just that I would rather talk about it with you here in front of me. But I also want to talk about it now," I said, hoping to reassure him.

Relief. Concern.

Tracing the designs in the wood of the table, I drew in a deep breath before saying anything else. "In the letter you left me you told me that you were saving yourself for your wife." My cheeks burned. This was not a conversation I felt prepared for, but it felt necessary before I could make a solid decision about my future.

Bryan's face turned pink, as well.

"Is that commitment meant for someone else or...." I trailed off and looked back at my phone screen to see Bryan swallow hard.

Excitement. Nervous. Hesitant.

Clearing his throat after a long minute he asked quietly, "Do you want it to mean you?" His face had gone white.

Nervous. Anxious. Hopeful.

My heart threatened to leave my body, it was pounding so hard.

We sat and stared at each other on our screens. Did I want it to mean me? If I said yes, was I going to look too eager? Because my instincts were saying, *Yes, I absolutely want it to mean me*, but the more reserved logical part of my brain was laughing at me uncontrollably. Which was ironic because my logical side was usually very serious. I should have waited until he got back to have this conversation. It was too late, now. I had started it.

How much time had passed? I had no idea.

Rather than answering him directly, I told him about the conversation I'd had with Dr. Thorne. I told him the details weren't many, but it had me thinking about now and the future. I wanted to know if it would change things if at some point in the near future I ended up being offered a job and wanting to accept it.

Bryan was smiling a smile that told me he was relieved. He also had a look of pride on his face. "Jess, that sounds fantastic! And it changes nothing for me. I love you regardless of the job you choose or don't choose. If you take a job that requires you to travel across the country every other day, I'd find a way to be with you, no matter what." He paused before asking, "Does it change anything for you?"

Tearing up I shook my head slowly. "I love you, and I would probably marry you tomorrow if you asked."

"Good to know," he said with a small laugh.

With the heaviness of the conversation behind us, we talked about the upcoming week for each of us. I had the moving van coming for Stacy's things on Wednesday and final exams had to be graded and submitted by Friday afternoon.

Bryan's last big presentation for the week was Friday with several smaller group sessions before then.

I didn't mean to let the yawn escape, but it had already felt like an entire week had gone by since Sunday and it had only been two days.

As we were saying our goodbyes Bryan asked, "Jess, did you mean what you said? About marrying me?"

Giving him my coolest shoulder shrug with a wink I teasingly said, "You should ask and find out."

"Okay." He paused and stared intently into the camera. "Jess?"

My heart was in my throat within milliseconds.

"Goodnight," he said with his sweet silly grin.

Giving him a smirk and a side eye, I replied, "Goodnight, Bryan."

13

JESS

The movers took the last of the boxes to the van and the driver handed me a receipt noting what and when they had loaded and left with the boxes. I missed Stacy. The last update I had gotten was that Stacy had made it back to Mississippi but was still in a coma. It hurt being so far away from the girl who had been like a sister to me for so many years. As I thought about the events that landed me here watching a moving van drive away with the material possessions of my best friend, I remembered the doctor saying that he thought patients in comas could hear the world around them. It was then I decided I would write an email to Mrs. Carlisle and ask her to read it to Stacy.

It took me over an hour to type out all the details I could remember about the last two weeks. I wrote about the trip to New York, including the details that involved taking a road trip with and telling a man I hadn't known for very long that I wanted to marry him. Stacy would have laughed for hours over that one. The self-controlled, motherly, boring Jess was in love with a guy she just met? I could hear Stacy now in her loud southern drawl saying, "Girl, hell must be freezin' over!"

I wrote about going to church and told her how I had become a

Christian, and then I wondered if Stacy was a Christian. It was all so new to me I didn't know how to tell if someone was or wasn't one, so I asked in my email.

Staring at the computer screen, I hovered over the Send button. It felt strange sending an email to someone in a coma. It was a one-sided conversation with someone I'd had countless conversations with every day for so many years. Several emotions crashed over me in that moment, but before I could process any of them, my phone buzzed with an incoming call.

Clicking send on my email, I changed my focus from my laptop to my phone.

It was Dr. Thorne. After initial pleasantries, he got to the point. "I spoke with my friend this afternoon, and he wanted to know if you were free to meet tomorrow evening after work. I told him you had office and lab hours until 4:00 p.m. I hope you don't mind. He said he would gladly meet you in your office at five if that worked for you."

The certitude of his words left me a little taken aback, but I found my voice. "Oh, yes, five is good. Do I need to do anything or bring anything with me? I don't have a résumé or anything like that, but I can create one if I need to." I fidgeted with the cord of the computer charger, unsure of what I was really agreeing to in this moment.

"I think he just wants to meet you and maybe learn more about what you can do and how it works."

Relieved that my part seemed easy enough I said, "Sounds great. If you will, pass along my confirmation, I will plan to meet him tomorrow."

With that, we said our goodbyes. I rested my head on the table and sent up a desperate prayer.

God, make your will abundantly clear tomorrow. Sooner would be good too. But I want to do what you want me to do. I don't know exactly what I want to do beyond what I'm already doing. If you want me doing something else, I will.

I was sitting at the desk in the office I typically only used on Friday afternoons to grade papers and occasionally meet with students who came in to beg for extra credit work when they found their grades were bad at the end of semesters. With little success, I was attempting to read a research paper about interpersonal neurobiology and adolescent brains, hoping to calm my nerves about the meeting I had agreed to with a man who works for a government agency and knows about my abilities.

The knock on the open door at 5:00 p.m. on the dot stopped me from reading the same sentence I had been reading for the last ten minutes. Standing there was Dr. Thorne and a man who appeared to be in his mid-thirties. He was wearing a light-gray, long-sleeve dress shirt unbuttoned at the collar with the sleeves rolled to the elbow, and jet-black dress slacks. His skin was fair, and his cropped hair sandy blonde. His eyes were a piercing blue that rivaled the sky outside. His face was serious.

Arrogant. Confident. Skeptical.

Before the men stepped a single foot through the door, I'd read him and made an initial assessment. I moved to stand in front of the desk and smiled what I hoped was a professional-but-charming smile. This man might be a skeptic, but he didn't have to remain one.

"Dr. Thorne, good to see you," I said with a nod.

"Jess, this is Special Agent Mark Collins of the FBI."

I turned to shake his hand. "Agent Collins."

"Mark, please," he replied with a surprisingly friendly tone.

"Okay, Mark. Please come in and have a seat." I gestured to the chairs I had arranged into a sitting area.

We all observed one another for a few seconds before Dr. Thorne motioned for the agent to speak first.

"Miss Hayley," the agent started, leaning forward, putting his elbows on his thighs and clasping his hands together.

"Call me Jess, please."

With a stiff nod, he cleared his throat. "Jess."

Anxious. Arrogant.

"Dr. Thorne has told me a lot about you and what you call your gift. Can you tell me about it? I'd like to hear your explanation."

"Sure, I can do that. I'm not sure what there is to tell more than what Dr. Thorne has shared with you. If there is something specific you would like to know, feel free to ask."

"Tell me how you decided you had a gift."

The word *decided* irked me, but his tone was tentative, which is why I watched him intently for several silent seconds while he made his own unspoken observations. When I did speak, I tried to temper my words with tolerance.

"I realize anything Dr. Thorne has told you must sound highly improbable, especially out of its full context unattached to an actual person. What I am able to do may seem unheard of, but I can assure you, not only are my abilities real, but I also believe they can be taught, learned, and reinforced through the proper training. The research Dr. Thorne and I have completed in the short time we have worked together is groundbreaking and has potential to provide service and assistance to a number of groups and organizations if utilized correctly."

The next several minutes were spent with me giving a brief autobiography and a basic summary of the research and possibilities that stemmed from said research while Agent Collins stared blankly without making any indication in his features or gestures that he was or was not listening.

When I finished speaking, he leaned back in his chair and crossed his arms over his chest using one hand to massage his face. A five o'clock shadow had started forming on his otherwise flawless face. His rough hands rubbed across the prickly hair.

"So, you either think what I can do is not real, or you just think it's a party trick." It was a statement rather than a question. "Regardless of which is true, you have come in here a blazing skeptic. You have attempted to conceal your skepticism by projecting a harsher image, which in turn looks like arrogance and boredom. You want to believe what I can do is real, but you are afraid your colleagues would think poorly of you for seeking alternative methods to investigations and closing cases. There is something that requires answers, and you are reluctant to ask for assistance, especially from someone with unconventional capabilities."

He recognized his defensive posture and returned to his original more casual position and gave an amused smirk.

Dr. Thorne held back a smile, but his eyes told me I had called it correctly.

"Miss Hayley, uh, Jess, have you heard of Enrique Rodriguez?"

Running the name through a catalog in my mind, I shook my head. "No, that name doesn't sound familiar."

"Enrique Rodriguez is an NFL player accused of murdering his girlfriend's ex. The motive, the evidence, even his faulty alibi all line up to say he is not guilty. None of it makes sense."

"Not guilty? But he's been accused of murder?"

"Correct. He claims he killed the man, but his stories contradict themselves. And while it would be very easy to simply take his word for it and call it a closed case, if he didn't actually kill the guy, then there's still a killer out there."

There was very little I knew about law enforcement outside of television shows. What I did know was the need to find the truth. However, he had yet to ask for my help, and even if he did, his skepticism made it hard to want to help.

Wading through skeptics and critics on the academic level had been hard enough. The countless hours and effort it had taken to make the first breakthrough and get the first grant had been grueling. It took fortitude I didn't know I had to prevent taking the numerous rejections personally, because that's what every ounce of energy I poured into my work was—personal.

Trying not to sound flippant but not knowing what Agent Collins was angling for I said, "Sounds like you have an interesting time ahead of you."

Annoyed. Frustrated. Desperate.

I'd unintentionally struck a nerve.

"Don't get me wrong, interesting is good. It beats monotony any day. But cut and dried is also good."

My curiosity was growing. "Why are you telling me this?"

Yielding. Self-Doubt.

Agent Collins shifted forward in his seat. "Three reasons, really. First, I wanted to see if what Dr. Thorne has told me on multiple occasions was as phenomenal as he made it out to be. Secondly, I wanted to see if you could get a read on Mr. Rodriguez based on his interviews."

The look on my face must have given away my confusion.

"Third, if your gift, as you call it, is as amazing as Dr. Thorne thinks it is, and if it looks like it could be utilized in similar ways in the future, it might be worth having you consult for the FBI on a regular basis."

As I maintained eye contact with Agent Collins, the room was silent as we studied one another.

Expectant. Eager. Guarded.

It was clear that he wanted me to accept his request. It was also clear that he was not convinced I would be able to help. The fact of the matter was his ask was nothing like anything I had done before, and I couldn't guarantee that the answers he was looking for were something I could provide.

That being said, I was intrigued by the prospect of a practical application of the years of work that led to this moment. There was also a twinge of doubt in the back of my mind telling me this was bigger than what I was capable of.

Before I could think myself out of it, I took a deep breath. "I will watch his interviews and give you my feedback. Keep in mind, I've never worked in these circumstances before, so obviously, I appreciate any grace that may be necessary in the end."

For the first time since meeting him, Agent Collins cracked a small smile.

Satisfaction. Arrogance. Restraint. Relief.

He stood. Dr. Thorne and I followed suit.

"Good. I will be in touch soon. Do you have a card?"

"I don't. But I can write down my contact information, and I will look forward to hearing from you."

We exchanged information and shook hands before Agent Collins and Dr. Thorne exited the office. I stood in the doorway momentarily after they left, rubbing my forehead, trying to make sense of what I had just agreed to. My phone buzzing on the desk caught my attention.

> Bryan: Some of the higher ups want to have dinner and talk business. Not sure what business they are referring to, but I've been told that my attendance is mandatory. I probably won't be in contact again tonight, so I wanted to tell you I love you and goodnight.

With a slight pang of disappointment, I decided it was probably for the better. I could use the evening to think through some things.

> Me: Just finished the most bizarre meeting. Looking forward to telling you about it. I'll miss talking to you. Sounds like an exciting evening ahead. I love you.

Packing up books, papers, and my laptop, I made sure that Agent Collins's card didn't get lost in the shuffle and put it in my wallet. The drive home was thankfully uneventful. I used the time to think and pray over the day.

God, I don't know what I had been expecting, but I left that meeting with mixed feelings. Give me clarity and peace as I make the next decision. I need you to guide me so I don't fall off a cliff or hit a speedbump I can't recover from. I believe that you know everything before it happens. I believe that you can make good from bad. I also know that I am just as likely to make the wrong choice as I am the right one. Help me make the right choice.

14

JESS

Rather than trying to catch the evening news as I settled in for the evening, I decided that if I had found peace in reading and remembering the Bible before, it was worth diving into it again, just in case. Just like one of my old textbooks, there was a topical index in the back of the Bible, so I skimmed it until a word jumped out at me. It was not the most academically proven method of research, but I frequently worked on information and intuition, and it seemed like a good method for a newbie.

The list was alphabetical and much more extensive than I thought it would be. Until I reached the D's, I wasn't convinced this tactic was going to prove to be very effective. Then as though it had been bolded and highlighted for my eyes only, a single word stood out—*desire*. Below the word was listed several verses with small snippets of the reference containing the word *desire*. The first one in the list was Genesis 3:16. *Your desire will be for your husband.* A bark of laughter escaped. Not there, yet. The next verse listed was Psalm 37:4 *Will give you your heart's desires.*

"Huh."

There were several others that I wanted to go back to, but the verse in Psalms pulled at me. It conjured up the most basic question that could very well be the most important one. What were my heart's desires? Did I even know? I considered it as I navigated back to the Table of Contents and located Psalms. Flipping through to page 789, I scanned for the large print 37 and started reading.

Fret not yourself because of evildoers; be not envious of wrongdoers! For they will soon fade like the grass and wither like the green herb. Trust in the LORD, and do good; dwell in the land and befriend faithfulness. Delight yourself in the LORD, and he will give you the desires of your heart. Commit your way to the LORD; trust in him, and he will act. He will bring forth your righteousness as the light, and your justice as the noonday. Be still before the LORD and wait patiently for him; fret not yourself over the one who prospers in his way, over the man who carries out evil devices!

The language was beautiful and heartfelt. It felt like poetry and a promise, whose sole purpose was to produce courage. And to think, these words were written to people thousands of years before I ever existed who were clearly asking the same questions I was asking. Until now, asking myself what I wanted seemed selfish and shallow. Clearly, it was not an original question. My heart reached out in desperate need for answers.

God, what does my heart desire? I think my heart tells me that I want Bryan, and if I'm being honest, my body tells me the same thing in a different way. My mind gets in the way, and I fear taking the wrong path. I do believe he loves me, and I am certain that I love him too. I've never been in love, nor have I been loved by someone who wasn't my mother or my grandparents. I can only assume you brought us together and put what I feel for him in me. Because I don't know if I could feel this way on my own.

What about my job? Do I stay at the university, or do I work somewhere else? The more I learn about you, the more I understand you gave me the gift I have. It's confusing and overwhelming sometimes, and the thought of using it outside of a controlled situation like a lab scares me. But if you have a different plan, a better plan, I know I should want that for me. Help me make the right choices.

I sat on the couch with the Bible in my lap and flipped through, skimming different chapters and verses in Psalms. So many of them sounded like a cry from the heart of someone who was lost on a journey and confused just like I was, maybe even more desperate than I. Some of them felt like forlorn pleas, while others felt like joyful and happy songs. All of them, however, filled me with a sense of tranquility and peace.

With my mind and spirit at peace, I realized I had forgone lunch and it was well after dinnertime. The weight of the afternoon had drained me of any motivation to cook and it was far too late to have something delivered. Since I wasn't expecting a call from Bryan that evening, I grabbed a pack of peanut butter crackers from the cabinet in the kitchen, a glass of water, and sat down at the dining table with my laptop to get some work done.

When I opened my email, there were two that caught my attention. One was from Linda Carlisle, Stacy's mother. The other was from Mark Collins. I started with Mrs. Carlisle's.

Dear Jess,

Thank you for your letter to Stacy. I agree with the doctor that she can hear everything we say to and around her. We are very careful to stay positive and upbeat when we talk in her room. The moving van arrived with all of Stacy's belongings. Thank you for taking care of that for us. It was a huge relief to have one less thing to worry about, though being honest, it was a tough wave of heartache to see the boxes full of her stuff at first.

I know you wrote your letter to Stacy, but as I am the one to read to her every day, I was made privy to your life's current events. I know I am just an old woman you don't really know, but I wanted to tell you I am very proud of you for making the choice to follow Jesus. He will change your life for the better if you let him, even in the hard times.

One last thing. I don't want to pry or stick my nose into business it has no place being, but I think your young man is a marvelous catch. I only met him briefly, but I would have sworn he had loved you much longer than a few hours after watching him with you. A week may not sound like a long time, but in the grand scheme of things, a week can be an eternity since we aren't promised tomorrow.

Take care, sweetie. I look forward to reading your next email to Stacy.
Sincerely,
Linda Carlisle

P.S. I only knew Mr. Carlisle for three days before we eloped, and I was only seventeen. So, I like to think that when you know, you know.

Mrs. Carlisle's email sent a jolt of both happiness and sadness through my heart. It was another reminder that my best friend was farther away than she ever had been since we had met. It was also a surge of comfort and encouragement reading the older woman's words. I made a mental note to reply sooner than later, but right now I was more than a little interested in the other email awaiting me.

Miss Hayley (Jess?),

It was a pleasure to meet you this afternoon. I know you are aware that when I met you, I was a skeptic. Though I did not leave fully convinced of your abilities, I am open to learning more about you and what you could offer. I have attached three video files of the interviews I mentioned in our meeting. When you have time, please review them and send any notes you think would be of relevance to the case as soon as it is convenient for you. Feel free to reach out if you have questions.

Mark Collins, Special Agent, FBI

Double clicking the first video file, I watched the ten-minute clip of what appeared to be Enrique Rodriguez's first interview. The camera had been set up directly in front of the man so there was a clear view of his face, and when he put his hands on the table in front of him, they were also fully visible. It was a good vantage point to get a strong read of the interviewee.

The officer questioning Enrique started with the basic questions, his name, birthdate, why he had been brought in to be questioned.

The officer's reaction deemed the basic information accurate, so that was what I used to get what would be considered a baseline. It was the last question the officer asked that led to what I considered potentially interesting feedback. He asked why Enrique thought he had been brought in for questioning. It was a simple question that elicited a simple straightforward answer.

It wasn't Enrique, however, who caught my attention. It was the reflection behind him. The officer had stood behind and to the side of the camera, and all I could see of him had been a reflection in the glass behind Enrique. Initially, it was a reflection of the officer's torso with his arms crossed over his chest. When the officer asked Enrique why he thought he had been brought in for questioning, the reflection moved with him. The officer leaned down and put his palms on the table, which brought his face clearly in view in the reflection.

Enrique showed recognition, fear, confusion, and exhaustion. When the officer leaned in more closely, Enrique's eyes flashed almost imperceptibly and grew subtly larger. His lip gave an involuntary quiver. He was terrified of the man questioning him. When Enrique answered, "I'm not sure," it was more of a question than a statement.

There was a flash of something that crossed the officer's face. It was hard to read from the reflection that distorted with his movement. Between his body language and the anger in his eyes, I decided it was worth coming back to when I finished watching the entire video. Grabbing a notebook from my laptop bag next to me, I made a note of the video and timestamp.

The interview continued with the officer asking Enrique about his known list of associates, his recent jobs, if he had committed crimes in the past. For almost ten minutes I watched a scared and confused man answer questions. There was nothing about the man being interviewed that indicated he was being deceptive. What's more, there was nothing that indicated he knew why he was being interviewed in the first place.

Moving on, I clicked open the next video in the email. This time, a different officer was interviewing Enrique Rodriguez. Enrique's demeanor was drastically different. He was calmer, appeared better rested, and had clearer answers to the questions he was asked. Again, nothing indicated that he was lying or hiding anything. He seemed better informed of the circumstances surrounding his questioning. His reactions, expressions, and body language all conveyed confidence with only the slightest hint of natural defensiveness.

The third video was another interview between the officer from the initial questioning. Enrique showed signs of being worn and dejected. There was a resignation about him. The officer was on the same side of the table as the suspect and had placed a yellow legal pad in front of him. He bent down and spoke to the side of Enrique's face with a spitting tone.

"You thought you would get away with it, but I got you. And you're going to write down every word you just confessed."

He threw a pen on top of the notepad.

I paused the video, and though I could only see part of the officer's face, it was clearly marked with satisfaction and smugness. It did not sit right with me, and something stirred in the pit of my stomach.

Going back to the original video, I scrolled through to the timestamp I had written down then backed it up four seconds and clicked play. I watched it multiple times focusing on Enrique and the officer separately each time. The process was repeated with the other two videos. Click, watch. Click, pause. Rewind. Click, watch. Click, pause.

I wasn't sure what exactly I was supposed to say in my report, if it could be called a report. Without solid guidelines, I wrote what I had seen and left it at that.

Special Agent Collins (Mark?),

After having watched all three videos multiple times and looking carefully for any signs of deception or indicators of suspicion, several items jumped out at me. In the first video, I made a note of the facial expressions of both the questioning officer and Mr. Rodriguez.

Mr. Rodriguez seems to be unaware of why he is being interviewed, but his behavior and appearance demonstrate he is familiar with and possibly scared of the officer interviewing him. This is especially evident when the officer is in close proximity to him (videos one and three).

If you observe the officer's reflection in the glass behind Mr. Rodriguez, he makes a brief expression of what appears to be anger, possibly rage. It seems out of place in the context of an initial interview. It appears personal. In video one, the body language of his hands on the table and putting his face closer to Mr. Rodriguez would reinforce this supposition.

In video three, similar expressions and behaviors occur. However, when a different officer is questioning him, Mr. Rodriguez's demeanor is very different. He's more confident and defends himself, producing no signs of deception. I don't know if this is at all helpful. It's all based on observations I made in a short amount of time with limited resources. If I can be of additional assistance, please do not hesitate to reach out to me.

-- Jess Hayley

With a click and a *whoosh,* my email was on its way to its recipient. I closed the laptop and looked at the clock on the wall. How was it already 11 p.m.? My brain was wide awake, though the rest of me felt tired and stiff from having sat in one position for so long. After spending hours staring at a computer screen watching the same three videos over and over, I was convinced that's all I would ever be able to think about again.

Pushing away from the table, I took my plastic wrapper from the crackers and the water glass to the kitchen. Walking back through the dining area, I picked up my phone, turned off the downstairs lights, and headed upstairs to get ready for bed. I desperately wanted to message Bryan, but I wasn't sure my brain and fingers would coordinate with one another to type out a coherent message. Instead, I put my phone on its charger and called it a day.

That night I dreamed I was being questioned in a sterile room by a faceless voice. He kept asking me what I desired deep down in my heart, and when I answered, "I'm not sure," the voice would answer, "Yes you are." This seemed to be a continuous cycle until I woke groggily to my alarm going off the next morning.

I think my deepest desire is to stay in bed the rest of the day, I thought before slowly tossing the covers back and making myself sit up. If I couldn't have that, then extra coffee would have to do.

15

JESS

Since it was the last day to submit final exam grades for the semester, I was grateful Fridays were typically quiet in the lab. My calendar reminded me I had a meeting with Dr. Thorne to talk through some ideas for the next year's lab studies. I let out a huge sigh as I lugged my backpack and what would be my third cup of coffee into the office. That third cup of coffee almost left my hand as I walked in to find Agent Collins waiting for me in a chair in front of the desk.

He stood when I entered, and when I was closer, he extended his hand in greeting. I had to move my phone to the same hand as my coffee to shake his hand.

"Good morning, Agent." I corrected myself. "Mark. I wasn't expecting company this morning."

Situating my coffee, phone, and backpack on the desk, I took a seat in the chair behind the desk.

Mark smiled briefly and with a nod took his seat across from me. "I got your email last night. You were working late?"

"I didn't actually mean to work so late. I just started watching the videos and time got away from me."

He nodded in understanding. "That happens. I read your report on the videos several times and decided that it would be easier if I spoke with you in person. I noted your posted office hours yesterday and thought if you had a few minutes this morning, I would stop by on my way to the office. I'm sorry if I should have called first."

Apprehensive.

His visit hadn't been part of my plan for the morning, but I was more interested in his feedback than I was annoyed by his presence. "No problem. What can I do for you?"

Nervous. Uncertain. Self-conscious.

This was a much less confident man than the one I had spoken to just the day before. "I don't like being wrong, Miss Hayley," he finally said, looking me in the eyes. "I don't like when someone could be better at my job than I am. Especially when I have been doing the job a lot longer."

I wasn't sure if I was being scolded or if he was reprimanding himself.

"After I read your notes and went back to watch the videos, I still had to watch it three times just to catch the reflection. And even then, his face did nothing for me." He took a deep breath and let it out through his nose slowly. "I had not caught the reflection or Mr. Rodriguez's reaction to the questioner. Because you brought it to my attention, I decided I would follow the crumbs you dropped and do some digging on the officer. Do you know what I found, Miss Hayley?"

With raised eyebrows and a slow shake of my head, I waited for his answer.

"That officer had personal connections to the murder victim. Now, I don't know what will come of this information, and technically, I probably shouldn't even be telling you this much. But I thought you would like to know I am much less of a skeptic than I was before. And your help has given me some new leads, so hopefully, I can find some traction on this case again."

Because of the admission of his waning skepticism as well as the idea I could be assisting in getting a bad guy and dirty cop off the streets, I sat in stunned silence. Even if that wasn't the outcome, I had helped give hope where it was needed. It took several seconds for me to respond, and when I did, all I could hope was that I didn't sound like a complete idiot.

"Well, I'm glad to know that one way or another, I could be helpful."

It was hard to say for sure what he was thinking as reluctance and nervous tension defined his face. He reset his features before replying. "Yes, I plan to dive in as soon as I get to the office." He adjusted his tie. "Jess." There was an awkward stop at the end of his sentence, as though he had planned to say more.

"Yes?"

"If I have additional questions or interviews that could use your input, would you be open to that?"

"I guess it depends on the context. Are we talking as a personal favor to you or in an official capacity for the FBI?"

His ears went pink. "I can't officially give you any kind of compensation, so technically, I guess, it would be a personal favor." He stopped talking abruptly and his gaze dropped to his shoes.

Trying to ease the tension that seemed to be building around him, I attempted to make my next comment lighthearted. "I've never been owed a favor by the FBI. That sounds like it could be useful someday."

He breathed a laugh still studying the floor. He took a deep breath, raised his eyes to mine, and with hesitancy asked, "You wouldn't happen to accept payment in the form of drinks after work, would you?"

It was my turn to blush. I regained my composure quickly and gave him a sympathetic smile.

His face showed that he knew what was coming.

"Agent Collins, I am flattered, really. But, I'm not single. And I don't drink."

He sighed heavily, then stood. I followed suit.

He smiled and reached out to shake hands. "That is the story of my life," he muttered with a disappointed smile.

I moved from behind the desk to walk him to the door where he stopped in the doorway.

"Would you really be interested and willing to help in the future if I need it?"

Narrowing my eyes at him, I said, "You must be a more reformed skeptic than you claim to be. If you'll really owe me a favor one day, I'll see what I can do if you find yourself needing a fresh set of eyes, again."

"Deal." With a smile and a nod, Mark headed for the exit.

I walked back to the desk, picking up my coffee with one hand and my phone with the other. I had missed a call and two texts from Bryan.

> Bryan: How do you feel about having dinner with me tonight?

My heart jumped. Tonight? Wasn't he slated to come home tomorrow? Excitement pulsed through me.

> Bryan: I'll pick you up at 5. Wear something nice.

I quickly typed out a reply.

> Me: I'll see you at 5.

Giddiness threatened to overtake me. The clock on my phone said it was almost 10:30. If I focused, I could wrap up in the office early, and maybe if Dr. Thorne was flexible, we could meet early and knock out plans for next semester. I called Dr. Thorne's office and left a message asking him to call me back then set out to grade the remainder of the exams. I may have kicked myself more than once for being so thorough when it came to creating exams that weren't simply multiple choice.

Dr. Thorne called me back after lunchtime and said he needed to reschedule our planned meeting anyway, so we agreed to work together the following week. It was just as well, as it took until after three to finish grading and posting my students' final test scores. As soon as I verified the last posting, I slammed my laptop closed harder than I meant to, packed up, and set a direct course for home.

I TOOK my time getting ready. Dates were not something I was accustomed to, but thanks to Stacy, I did know how to get dressed up. After showering, I scoured my closet trying to find a balance between uptight nerd and lazy college student. I settled on a black pencil skirt that came below my knees and a short-sleeve white blouse with black buttons. Shiny black stilettos, pearl stud earrings, and a simple pearl necklace that hung right below my collar bone rounded out the look. The shoes not only accentuated my calves, but they made me taller. And being taller would put me closer to Bryan's lips. Butterflies fluttered awake inside, making me feel lighter.

While completely impractical, dressing this way never failed to make me feel confident and maybe a little sexy, if I was being honest. And since this was technically our first real date, I wanted to make a memorable impression. After styling my hair, I did my makeup, adding just a little eyeliner to my eyelids and mascara on my lashes for a more dramatic effect.

I stared at myself in the full-length mirror on the bathroom door. It had been a long time since I had spent this much time getting ready for anything. Stacy had always hassled me about at least wearing mascara every day because she thought it made it look like I at least tried to put some effort into my appearance. That habit lasted about a week before I gave up on it. Stacy had rolled her eyes and taken it upon herself to make sure the makeup did not go to waste by adding it to her personal collection.

When one of my colleagues invited me to his wedding, I made the mistake of asking Stacy for makeup advice. We spent two hours and far too much money at a boutique cosmetic store one afternoon. When we got home, Stacy forced me to sit still while she applied layers of makeup in a wide variety of colors and textures. The person

I saw in the mirror had not been recognizable, though Stacy said it had been her best work ever.

The day of the wedding, Stacy convinced me to let her do my makeup but had promised to keep it more natural. I had been pleasantly surprised when Stacy handed me the mirror and the reflection was a face I did recognize. My heart ached at the thought of Stacy, and I desperately wished she was there with me.

My memories were interrupted by a knock at the door. It felt like all the blood in my body was rushing to my head and my heart was pounding against my ribs. After several deep breaths to calm myself, I grabbed my black-satin clutch from the bed and tucked it under my arm and headed for the door. I hadn't stopped smiling since hearing the knock, but my smile soon turned to what had to be a look of shock and confusion when I opened the door.

There on my front porch was Bryan, wearing a dark suit with a bright-white button-down shirt and a silver tie. But he wasn't standing. He was kneeling on one knee, holding up a black velvet box.

As reality started to sink in as to what was happening, I felt my eyes grow at least two sizes, and one of my hands landed over my heart. All the calm I had managed to produce upstairs flooded back in exhilaration as my entire body began to tremble, and my breaths turned shallow and quick. This was a joke, it had to be. But I didn't think Bryan was the type to joke about something so serious.

Before I could say anything, Bryan spoke. "Jess," his voice wavered with emotion at first. He cleared his throat and started again. "Jess, I know that we have only known each other for a very short time. I have prayed and wrestled with this idea since it came to me just a few days ago. To some, it might look insane, but to me, it feels like the most natural thing in the world, next to breathing. So, if you feel the same and if you would do me the greatest honor, will you marry me?"

He opened the box, and inside was the most beautiful ring I had ever seen. It was a vintage platinum ring with a large emerald cut diamond in the center surrounded by six single cut accent diamonds and four rectangle cut sapphires.

The only thing I was able to do in that moment was stand there looking back and forth between the ring and Bryan. I must have remained silent long enough to cause concern because Bryan tilted his head, raised his eyebrows, and leaned forward slightly causing me to realize I hadn't made a sound since opening the door.

Slowly, I nodded my head, then more quickly until I finally managed to whisper, "Yes."

Bryan smiled and rose to stand. My eyes followed his as he reached for my hand. He took the ring from the velvet box, and after putting the box in his pocket, he slid the ring onto my finger.

Immediately I threw both arms around Bryan's neck and held on to him like letting go could mean death. We were both laughing and sniffling through tears. He picked me up and walked inside before setting me down. As soon as my feet were on the ground, I grabbed his face and kissed him hard, giving no thought to the tears or the snot. It was then I knew I had found exactly what my heart desired.

Bryan was my heart's desire.

When I was able to pull myself away from his lips, I found myself getting lost in his gorgeous green eyes. I wanted to say a million things, but nothing seemed sufficient.

When I did manage to speak, all I could manage was, "How? What? You're not even supposed to be back until tomorrow."

Bryan laughed. "Yeah, it was a weird week. Suffice it to say, I convinced the men I went to dinner with last night that it wasn't important for me to stick around after my presentation. When I mentioned there was someone I needed to get back to ASAP, they all slapped me on the back and told me to get out as soon as I was done. And here we are."

I stared at him incredulously and mystified and then looked down at the ring on my hand and back up at him. "And this? It is the most beautiful ring I have ever seen."

His eyes sparkled almost as much as the diamonds in the ring. "I was hoping you would like it. It was my grandmother's."

I held up my hand to watch the stones glitter in the light. "Like it? I love it almost as much as I love you. And that's saying something."

Bryan placed both hands on my face and found my lips with his, leaving me breathless.

Once I regained my ability to breathe, I said the only thing that came to mind. "So, now that I've been completely blindsided, is there any chance you have plans to feed me?"

With his heart melting smile, Bryan replied, "As a matter of fact, yes. I've made us some pretty spectacular reservations."

"You're a good man." I winked. "Let me go upstairs and hit reset on all of this." I motioned to my face. "Then, I'll be ready to go."

Bryan drove us to a charming two-story brick building at the District Wharf perched right next to the Potomac. He parked at the valet station and handed the keys to a young man waiting for him before hurrying to the other side to escort me inside. Bryan spoke in almost a whisper to the maître d', who quickly escorted us to a room on the second floor.

The room's walls were a dark teal and light cream-colored Spanish ceramic tiles adorned the floor. Combined with the sparse, heavy mahogany furniture, the room had an old-world feel. Much of the light came from the wall of windows that overlooked the river while the rest came from lanterns placed around the room.

Our escort led us to a single table with two chairs that sat at the end of the room. Bryan spoke to the man in fluent Spanish, which left me both shocked and mesmerized as I listened and watched. The man simply nodded his head and turned to leave the room.

"You, sir, are full of surprises." I marveled at him.

Bryan sheepishly ducked his head and asked, "Did I not mention that I speak several languages? I could have sworn that had come up in the last two weeks."

I stared at him at a loss for words. There were so many things I did not know about this man. Yet, I was ready to spend every day learning something new about him.

He stood and offered me his hand, which I gladly accepted, and guided me to the window where we watched the boats on the river and people milling about the Wharf. Standing beside me, Bryan wrapped one arm around my waist pulling me into him.

I slid an arm under his and around his waist. The air around us was warm and comfortable.

After several minutes of watching in silence and simply enjoying the presence of one another, Bryan said, "I have another question for you."

Turning toward him, I wrapped both arms around his waist and waited for his question. His gaze, his warmth, the hum of energy pulsing between us threatened to unravel every thread of my being.

"Will you marry me?" There was a sparkle in his eyes that sent chills over me.

"You've already asked me that. Did you forget? I said, yes." I waggled the ring in front of him.

"Tomorrow. Will you marry me tomorrow?"

Without letting go, I leaned back so I could see Bryan's entire face. Had I heard him correctly? "Tomorrow? As in tomorrow, Saturday?"

Bryan put his hands on my shoulders and slid them down my arms to my hands, which he held gently in his own, running his thumbs back and forth over my knuckles. "You don't have to say yes. But I wanted you to know that it was an option and that I was open to it."

Staring down at our hands looking for an answer. The hands that held mine were warm, strong, and steady. They made me feel like his strength became mine when they held me.

Shifting my gaze to meet his, I immediately knew the answer. "I think tomorrow would be a good day to get married."

His eyes lit up as he wrapped his arms around me. Resting my head against his chest, we stood there until the door opened and a server with a large tray loaded with food and drinks entered.

For the next several hours we sat eating, drinking, and talking excitedly. Bryan explained how he had called Pastor John the week before, explaining his desires. He had even gone so far as to ask, if somehow, I said yes to both questions, if the pastor would be willing to marry us on short notice.

Pastor John had agreed with one condition. He normally required couples to go through premarital counseling, but because he trusted

Bryan's judgment, he would perform the ceremony if we agreed to post-wedding counseling. It was a foreign concept to me, but it sounded like a good idea. From there, our conversations became more of a speed dating event with each of us tossing out questions.

Your house or mine? Joint accounts or separate? Future career plans? Kids or no kids?

As I got into bed that night, I replayed everything leading up to today in my mind as I stared at the ring on my hand and traced the stones with my fingers. Nothing about the last two weeks made sense on paper. Honestly, it made little sense to the logical left hemisphere of my brain, which was trying very hard to grant my newly awakened amygdala some leniency.

My phone buzzed on the nightstand next to me.

> Bryan: Tomorrow at 4 at the church? I'll be the guy trying to hold it together.

I laughed as I wrote back.

> Me: This has to be the easiest wedding to plan in the history of planned weddings. I'll be the girl in the dress trying to refrain from running toward the guy trying to hold it together.

My heart was happy as warmth enveloped me as I fell asleep.

16

JESS

This was it. Today was the day. I had one mission and that was to find a dress. If there was time after, I'd shoot for a mani-pedi. Throwing on a pair of leggings and an oversized plain T-shirt, I headed for Leslie's Bridal Boutique. It was the one bridal boutique whose website said they were open this early on Saturdays. The store was a sweet one-story, white-painted brick building. It had a pink awning and two large windows on either side of the entrance. One of the windows had Leslie's Bridal etched into the glass. A bell jingled as I walked inside.

"Welcome to Leslie's!" a sweet voice echoed from behind a rack of dresses of different shades of white.

"Thank you," I called out, looking around for the voice.

A petite woman with bright blue doe eyes and long blonde hair pulled into a sleek straight ponytail appeared from behind the rack.

With a genuinely bubbly smile, the woman asked, "What brings you in today?"

Most little girls tend to have their weddings planned by the time they're twelve. I was not most little girls. Most modern women my age have a Pinterest board packed full of ideas for the perfect wedding. I was also not most modern women. With nothing to go on, I decided to give Leslie a short version of my story, to which the woman's jaw dropped and slowly curved into a smile so big, it almost showed every tooth in her mouth.

"Oh, my word! That has to be the best story I have heard in forever," she gushed. "I'm Leslie, by the way. And this," she motioned to the storefront, "is my baby. And if you give me thirty minutes, I'll have you squared away and ready to marry the man of your dreams."

Options were limited, as was time, so I decided to give in to Leslie's whims. The next thirty minutes involved being peppered with questions about myself and my sense of style. She asked about the venue, Bryan's style, my favorite flowers, my decorating style, my ideal date night, my favorite memory, and other seemingly meaningless things. Before all was said and done, I felt like I should be leaving with a date, not a dress. Throughout the process Leslie had only brushed by with a flash of white chiffon here and satin there as I followed her around the store.

Finally, after several instances of pulling and replacing dresses on and off racks, Leslie turned to me empty-handed and instructed me to wait for her in a dressing room. Two minutes later, Leslie handed me a dress through the curtain.

"This is the one. Put it on and step out here on the pedestal, and I'll zip you up," Leslie said through the curtain.

Running my hands over the thin white satin, a cool breeze swept over my skin, a gentle refreshing breath. I undressed, folded my clothes, and placed them on the shelf in the dressing area. As soon as I pulled the dress on over my head, chills rushed over my skin. It was flowy, like water moving over my body. The flutter sleeves and ruffle hem that created a faux wrap to the knees in the front fit my casual style perfectly, while the deep V-neck gave the appearance of having some semblance of cleavage making it appropriately sexy. It fit like a glove without clinging. It was perfect.

When I stepped out of the dressing room, Leslie helped me onto the pedestal and zipped the dress up the back. Stepping back, she eyed me up and down before sighing dreamily. The pedestal on which I stood was in the center of the room surrounded by floor to ceiling mirrors, and my attention had been solely on Leslie until I realized she was motioning for me to turn and look at myself in the mirror.

The woman staring back at me was almost unrecognizable. The dress was perfect. The size, the fit, the style, all of it. But more than that, she looked relaxed and happy. The best part was that I actually felt relaxed and happy. Before I could stop them, tears pooled in my eyes with one escaping down my cheek.

"It's perfect," I whispered.

Fighting tears of her own, Leslie said, "It absolutely is."

Within an hour of arriving, I had purchased a dress and shoes and thanked Leslie for a wonderful experience. I left feeling as though I could have made a friend had there been more time.

At this thought, I was reminded of the most important people I wouldn't have with me on the biggest day of my life. My mom would be beside herself making a fuss, and Stacy would be pushing for everything to be more over-the-top, bigger, and brighter. I smiled at what could have been, allowing this to be my motivation to enjoy every moment I'm given with the people I love. Today, I will enjoy marrying Bryan, the man that I love.

17

BRYAN

If someone had asked me three weeks ago if I believed in love at first sight, I would have laughed and said, "Only in the movies." In my mind, love has always been a goal to work toward or a strategic match that requires planning and systems that work together over time to develop into something.

Love at first sight was never on my radar because I only thought it to be the result of a lack of impulse control. I have never made an impulsive decision in my life. My mother had instilled in me the importance of thinking through every action because actions, as she always said, came with consequences, and I had to be ready to own whatever consequences I invited by my actions. I learned this early enough in life that it stuck with me.

Since I grew up in a small town in Kentucky, there were very few options for entertainment without driving thirty minutes out of town in any direction. Even then, you had to be a lot older than fourteen to make it into most of those places. Though most of the kids I grew up with were decent kids, every town has its troublemaker. Ours had two—Jimmy and Dayton Brewer. They were a couple of brothers from the rougher side of town and had reputations for picking fights and leaving a wake of destruction in their paths when they were angry.

One Friday after a high school football game, I was hanging out with some of my friends in Mr. Barnett's field where we'd have a bonfire after every home game. The Brewer brothers had shown up with some extra attitude and steam, which was never a good combination. Each had swaggered toward the group as though they were guests of honor while everyone present knew they had not invited them.

After several instances of the brothers physically and verbally harassing most of us, Dalton, the younger brother, picked up the can of gasoline we had used to soak the newspapers at the bottom of the bonfire. Much to the amusement of his older brother, Dalton made several swings of his arm, allowing the gasoline to spurt from the old metal can toward the already high rising fire, causing the flames to flare even larger in his direction.

Everyone's reaction of gasps and hurried movement away from the fire caused both brothers to laugh and taunt anyone who reacted. After one excessive swing of his arm and an attempt to empty the can, a lick of flame shot out and latched on to Dayton's skin, lightly coated with the gasoline he had been distributing.

It happened so quickly that none of us knew exactly how to react until the screaming and yelling attracted the attention of Mr. Barnett's old hound inside his house. Jimmy was trying to help his brother strip off his clothes while forcing him onto the ground without catching himself on fire. Minutes that felt like hours went by before Mr. Barnett had been able to put out the last of the fire with a large saddle blanket he had dragged from his porch swing when he'd realized what was happening.

The immediate results were just as devastating as the long-term impact. Dayton Brewer spent several weeks in the burn unit at the Cincinnati Children's Hospital before he developed and succumbed to an infection that cut short his already too-short life. Jimmy Brewer was never the same either, exchanging his brazen aggressive demeanor for a more dangerous quiet and simmering presence that led him to several arrests and a stint in juvie before he dropped out of high school.

It was that night I truly understood and embraced my mother's warnings about making hasty decisions, especially regarding anything that might affect someone else. Those warnings and memories of the accident also worked as helpful reminders on numerous occasions both when I was home and when I was deployed. Every choice I made was eventually filtered through weeks of deliberation and prayer.

My choice to ask Jess to marry me was no exception. From the moment we met, I had prayed constantly for two weeks that God would allow me to make Jess mine forever. I had just never considered that forever would start so soon after the first time I asked for it. It was this that drove my heart to pray once again.

God, thank you. Thank you for hearing my prayers and answering them with the deepest longings of my heart. Thank you for Jess's salvation and the love you have for us both. Thank you.

With that I made my way to the closet and retrieved my dress blues. Today, I was marrying the woman of my dreams.

18

JESS

Finding a nail salon that didn't look too busy for a walk-in had been easier than I expected. Within minutes of entering, I was greeted and in a chair with my feet soaking in warm water. A woman immediately started working on my fingernails with speed and efficiency as she carried on a conversation with one of her colleagues on the stool next to her.

Sitting still and letting my entire body sink into the soft leather massage chair reminded me I had skipped breakfast in my rush to get to the boutique. There was no way I could skip lunch, too, so I would have to make a plan to grab something on my way back to the house. As the massage chair vibrated behind me and adept hands worked on my hands and feet, I was lulled into a repose. Leaning my head back, closing my eyes, I let my mind wander.

As my thoughts drifted to the significance of what was planned for the day, I couldn't help but think once again about my mom. I was transported to the side of Mom's hospital bed that a hospice team had brought in a few weeks before I was scheduled to be home for Christmas break. I had known that Mom's time was not long for the world. The cancer had taken hold aggressively, and by the time the doctors had caught it, it was terminal.

They had tried a few rounds of chemo, but all it did was wreak havoc on her already declining body and caused a mental fog that made her incoherent for days at a time. When given the choice, Mom had decided that if she could choose, she wanted to have her mind about her so she could be present for as long as possible.

We talked on the phone every afternoon before I was free to fly home for a few weeks. It had taken every ounce of willpower every single day not to fly home and disregard my finals. Our daily calls were my only source of motivation to stay and push through the massive distance and heartache that had threatened to hollow me.

When I was finally home, our afternoon talks continued with me lying next to her, holding her hand though the conversations that were rarely long, as Mom would become rundown quickly with the effort. But they were some of the deepest, most meaningful ones I had ever had with her. Any time I thought over those talks, I recognized Mom was trying to pass on her lifetime of wisdom and experience in the short time we had left together. How I'd wish I had taken notes or recorded the calls.

The sounds of the nail salon faded away as the memory of one particular conversation trickled into my awareness. It was a rare occasion that either of us ever spoke of my father after he left us, but there was one dreary afternoon as I was sitting on the bed, holding Mom's hand that she said to me in her quiet, dry-throated voice, "Jess, never let your memories of your father distort your view of other people like I did."

This single statement hit me in the chest like a ton of bricks. Turning to look at her, I saw her eyes fill with tears that threatened to fall at any moment. To that day I could count on one hand the number of times I had ever seen my mother cry.

I held her feeble cold hand more tightly and stroked the top of it with my other hand, unsure of how to respond to the situation. My hands were hot compared to hers, making me very aware of the contrast in the moment.

"All of these years I think I let my anger and my fear of getting hurt again hold me back from opening my heart to anyone else. I didn't trust people and ended up isolating us. I thought I was protecting you. I wouldn't trade all the time and attention and love that you and I have been able to share, just the two of us, for anything in this world. But I look around and know that when I'm gone, I will have left you alone." It was then tears escaped her eyes.

My tears followed shortly after as I tried to assure her I would be fine no matter the circumstances. "Oh, Mom, no. Don't say that. I won't be alone. I have Stacy, I have my study groups, and who knows, maybe one day I'll have time for a boyfriend. But don't for one minute think that you are leaving me alone." Unsure if she had even heard me, I squeezed her hand.

When Mom began to stare into the distance, that was the end of the conversation.

When I opened my eyes, I found myself back in the nail salon. My face felt hot, and my eyes stung as though I was on the verge of crying. It was then I realized I had done the same thing Mom had carried guilt over for so long. I had isolated myself. Sure, I'd had Stacy, but we always lived two very different lives. My social life was nonexistent, and I justified it by pouring every extra minute I had into my education and work.

Being able to read people before ever getting to know them had been a major issue when I was younger. Rather than allowing anyone a chance to prove me right or wrong, I always assumed I was right, and people were exactly who I deemed them to be. Over time, I did learn to make multiple assessments of others before making final judgments, but I also allowed myself to become skeptical and closed off after being proven correct more often than not.

This led to a creeping void inside of me I continually filled with temporal activity and people I knew I would never have to open up to personally. If I was distracted with academics and teaching and research, I was convinced that I was content with the life in which I had chosen to exist.

It wasn't until I met Bryan and had spent time with him that I had felt what it was to genuinely connect with another person. The unnamed void I had been filling with superficial acquaintances and academia had been loneliness. And now I was getting ready to commit to opening my heart more deeply to a single person than I had to a multitude of people in my entire life. The thought overwhelmed, excited, and thrilled me.

A year ago, even a month ago, I would have balked at the idea of marriage. Not because I didn't think it was a good thing. It just wasn't something I had seen in my future. Marriage sounded like a good way to get distracted from my goals.

But what were my goals? Had I really planned to teach unexcited, uninspired college kids forever while spending hours on end reading and writing scientific papers? Would I count myself successful if I had to cycle through the same schedule alone everyday inching toward having my name added to one more study just to start over the next day?

The last two weeks had made me very aware of the banal existence I had been living. Sharing about my days, my thoughts, my ideas with someone else who actually listened and reacted with sincere interest had melted away the idea I had solidified in my mind that making any journey alone was right for me. I could not imagine having orchestrated this beautiful detour on my own.

And what a detour it was! Because not only was I seeing the landscape around me differently, but I was picking up a traveling companion who had already proved his love for and dedication to me numerous times. It was humbling and electrifying simultaneously.

Before I got swept up in my thoughts again, the woman who had been adding the last touches to my freshly polished nails was ready to help me to the nail drying station. I shuffled over to the chair the woman pulled out for me and sat. My phone started buzzing in my bag but not wanting to risk smudging my nails, I let it go to voicemail. After waiting half an hour with my hands and feet under fans and lights, I decided I desperately needed to eat, even at the risk of my nails.

In the car I checked my phone before leaving the parking area. I had missed numerous messages and calls. Bryan had messaged to check in and share his excitement for the day. That made me smile, and a blanket of warmth enveloped me at the thought of seeing him. I typed out a quick response.

> Me: Been a busy bee trying to make myself presentable. 4 can't get here fast enough.

Checking my voicemail, I had one from an unrecognized number.

"Jess, this is Deborah Parker, Pastor John's wife. I was hoping to get together with you before this evening just to get to know you a little. If you could, give me a call back..." and she left her number.

An uneasiness replaced my previous calm as I debated returning the call. I had only been to church with Bryan one time, and we'd been in such a hurry to get him to the airport on time, we hadn't had the chance for him to introduce me to the pastor or his wife. Not wanting to risk something being wrong or overlooking anything before getting to the church, I decided to return the call.

A female voice answered halfway through the first ring. I greeted the woman and introduced myself.

The voice on the other end was syrupy sweet. "Jess! Yes, this is Deborah. How are you? Getting ready for your big day?"

It felt friendly but forced.

"I am. I was at the nail salon when you called so I couldn't answer. But I wanted to call you back."

"Thank you for calling back. I feel like I already know you as much as Bryan has talked about you to John and me. But I wanted to ask if you were going to have any free time before you went to the church. I would love to meet you and just talk."

The impression that Deborah had something she wanted to talk about specifically but didn't want to do it over the phone was strong. I hesitated before making my invitation.

"Well, I was actually about to go on the hunt for lunch. Would you like to join me?"

"What did you have in mind?" asked Deborah.

We arranged to meet at a café not far from the salon before disconnecting the call. My nerves were on full alert as I sent Bryan another message before heading to the restaurant.

> Me: Is there anything I should know about Pastor John's wife, Deborah? We're meeting for lunch, and I feel like I might be headed to the firing squad.

His response was waiting for me when I arrived at the café.

> Bryan: I think she just wants to make sure you aren't feeling pressured into anything. Pastor J didn't seem concerned at all. Deborah is very traditional, so I think she was just surprised by the timing.

A second message followed almost immediately. It felt panicked.

> Bryan: DO you feel pressured?

The timing of his concern made me laugh.

> Me: Trust me, zero pressure. I tried to tell you a week ago. you could have asked sooner... T-4 hours...

There was a woman in her early fifties standing at the hostess stand when I walked in, and she must have recognized me as quickly as I recognized on her face everything she was thinking.

Distrust. Distant. Suspicion.

However, even with her less-than-genuine smile, the woman held her hands out and said with earnest, "Jess?!"

Trying to match her enthusiasm, I closed the embrace. "You must be Deborah."

The hostess led us to a small table where we ordered lunch. As soon as our menus had been taken away, Deborah commenced with her actual motives for wanting to meet. She was clearly nervous but pressed on in a rapid cadence.

"I know this must feel strange. You don't know me, but like I said on the phone, I feel like I know you a little. Bryan has called John several times in the last couple of weeks. They do a sort of discipleship mentor thing regularly. John doesn't tell me everything they talk about, but Bryan said it was okay for him to tell me about you. And I just thought I needed to meet this girl that came in and swept our Bryan off his feet."

My face grew warm, and I took a long drink of my water. Trying to sound gracious and not defensive I said, "Well, I don't know if I did all the sweeping. I'd say we're both on the same page."

The silence we sat in was awkward as Deborah took a long survey of my face. I interrupted her nonverbal interrogation.

"Mrs. Parker, I love Bryan. He is clearly special to you and Pastor John. I never expected to meet him when I did, much less find myself in this whirlwind with him. But we have both prayed about this, and I know he feels the same way. I have never felt more certain about anything in my entire life."

Deborah listened and watched me with intensity until I stopped speaking. After a few quiet beats, Deborah's demeanor changed, and a darkness lifted from her face.

Relief. Warmth.

She must have heard what she had come to hear because for the next hour, Deborah told me about their relationship with Bryan and asked questions about my family. By the time we had come to a natural ending to the meal and our conversation, we had both relaxed immensely. With one last hug, Deborah ensured me she would see me again at the church and that I could call her if I needed anything at all. We weren't parting as friends, but it was nice to know someone cared enough to be present and available if I needed her.

Looking at my watch, I decided I had plenty of time to run one more errand before going home to shower and get dressed.

∼

IN THE PARKING lot of a small jewelry store, I stared at the front door, unable to still my nerves but strongly compelled to take this step.

When I walked in, an older gentleman with silver hair stood from his stool and greeted me with a warm smile. "Hello, young lady. What can I do for you, today?"

For whatever reason, I felt an affinity for the man as though we had known each other for a long time, which brought an immediate smile to my face. "Well, I'm getting married in a few hours, and while nothing has been traditional about the entire situation, I think I would like to find a ring for the groom in keeping with some tradition."

"Ah." His gray eyes sparkled. "Well, tell me about this lucky gentleman."

I rattled off facts like, he's in the Army. He works with computers. He likes things to be simple and streamlined.

The older man nodded as he listened then said with a knowing grin, "Now tell me how you feel about him."

A slight blush covered my cheeks as I thought for a minute. "I knew from the moment we met that we had a connection. And when he shook my hand the first time, electricity moved between us. When he's with me, I feel complete and whole and safe. When he went out of town for work, I couldn't wait to talk to him, and I counted down the hours until I would see him again. I didn't believe in love at first sight until I met him. Now, I don't want to imagine my life without him."

The older gentleman's eyes had rimmed red and were glassy with tears. He pulled out a handkerchief and wiped his eyes and then tucked it back into his pocket. He cleared his throat.

When I noticed his tears, I began to apologize. "I'm so sorry. I—"

He interrupted with a sad smile that crinkled his old eyes. "Never apologize for being in love, my dear. I had a love like that once. My Ethel was my everything. We met in first grade, and we grew up together. When I lost her, my world fell apart. Stories like yours remind me of her and the way things used to be."

He gazed into the distance as though he was lost in thought, probably a lifetime of memories, if I had to guess. And as much as I didn't want to intrude, I was on a schedule. After a few quiet moments I interrupted his thoughts. "I hope one day I have those kinds of memories that bring me joy when I need them."

He nodded slowly and blinked as though waking from a dream. "Yes. But for the present, cherish every single moment. Now, you are here for a ring, correct?"

I nodded.

"I see your ring is platinum. I presume your band will be platinum as well?"

I glanced at the ring on my hand and then back at the man with a shrug. "I honestly don't know."

He nodded, again as he thought for a moment. "Do you want his ring to match yours or are you open to a style more tailored to him?"

"Let's find something more his style."

After about twenty minutes of staring at shiny silver and gold rings, I was drawn to a black band that had smooth, rounded edges. It was simple, classy, but unique.

The jeweler noticed where my attention had landed. "Interesting choice. This is one of the newer bands on the market. It's made with a technology that uses one million pounds of pressure and high heat to fuse millions of black diamond particles into a solid band. It makes it more durable than titanium, harder than tungsten, and it will outlast silver, gold, or even platinum. It's guaranteed to last forever, looking just like it does today every day."

I didn't need to hear anything else. "This is the one I want."

It felt right. Nothing about my relationship with Bryan had been anything resembling traditional, yet it was special and unique. This ring was the perfect representation of us. I paid and thanked the man for his assistance and left holding tightly to the small bag that held the precious band.

It felt like I had been moving through the day in a daze, and by the time I was home again, I only had about two hours to rest, shower, and do my hair and makeup. As I put the car in park, it occurred to me that I had spent all day getting ready for a wedding ceremony but had not considered what I needed to plan for the wedding night. My stomach tied itself into about fifty different knots, and I wasn't sure I was capable of taking a full breath.

In the car, I sat gripping the steering wheel for ten minutes until the pressure of the situation threatened to cause me to pass out. I swallowed hard and forced myself to let go of the steering wheel, taking a deep breath before picking up the garment bag sitting next to me. Finally able to open the door and step out, I carried the dress inside, laid it across the back of the couch, and stood in the living room massaging my temples as I surveyed the room for an answer.

My phone buzzed, pulling me from my panic.

> Bryan: I'm sending a car to pick you up. Is 3:30 OK?

It was already two. I needed to make a plan and fast.

> Me: Sure.

Loneliness crept up around me. Should I message Bryan and ask him? That would be beyond awkward. I can just imagine trying not to sound eager but also not wanting to sound disinterested.

Hey, what's the plan for tonight? Pizza and movies or....?

Yeah, I wasn't about to ask him. Forget that idea.

Was there anyone I could ask for advice? My heart began to ache. Once again, I was reminded how badly I wish Mom was still with me. Then a thought came to me. It wasn't ideal, but I was out of options. Scrolling through my call history list, I touched the most recent missed call and texted the number.

> Me: Deborah, this is so awkward, but I have spent so much time thinking about getting ready for the ceremony, I have no idea how to plan for AFTER. Help???

Several minutes later I had a new message.

> Deborah: John talked to Bryan (discreetly, of course). Pack an overnight bag. I don't have details, but I do know that much. Do you need to talk about anything specific?

My heart raced and I felt lightheaded. Yeah, I probably did need to talk about a lot of things, but I couldn't bring myself to say that.

> Me: That's what I needed. Thank you.

The hand on my forehead felt as though it was the only thing keeping me upright in the moment. I had to pull myself together because this was it. This was crunch time. Taking a deep breath, I picked up the bag with the dress inside and went upstairs.

After taking a shower and shaving my legs three times, I put on my bathrobe and started digging through my dresser drawers trying to find the expensive matching white lacy bra and panties set that Stacy had given me for Christmas two years prior. Stacy was always telling me that I needed to be ready for anything at all times. When I asked her how fancy underwear was going to make me ready for anything, Stacy had just rolled her eyes and called me a prude. I found the set, still with the tags attached, in the back of the drawer.

"Thank you, Stacy!" I said victoriously.

Trying to steady my trembling hands as I worked, I threw all the necessities I could think I might need in a small weekender bag. By the time I was done packing, I had thirty minutes to get ready. Sweat threatened to bloom on my forehead and under my arms with a new rush of adrenaline. The first half of the day had been so leisurely and relaxing. Now, my nerves were starting to set in. I sat on my bed, took a deep breath, and prayed.

God, I am scared to death. All the anticipation is starting to overwhelm me. The unexpected is creeping up on me, and I don't know what to do. Calm my nerves and give me strength. You have brought me to this point. Please don't let go of me now.

At 3:27, a horn honked outside. With one last look in the mirror, I ran my fingers over the pearls around my neck before turning to pick up my suitcase and making my way downstairs. Purse in hand, I locked the front door, and headed for the black town car waiting in the driveway.

19

BRYAN

It was creeping up on four as Pastor John and I sat on the front pew of the church. After Jess messaged me about meeting with Deborah, I asked John if he could meet me a little early for us to talk. Not only did I want to talk through the nerves that had been building in my gut all day, but it was important that I had the chance to assuage any doubt John or Deborah had about the choice I had made to marry a woman I had known for such a short time.

When I first moved to DC, I knew I wanted to find a church where I could lay down roots. Church had always been a large part of my life when I was growing up. Mom and I were there every Sunday and Wednesday, for every revival and potluck in between until I turned eighteen and joined the Army. Even then, I made it a point to attend the weekly worship services on base.

My first Sunday in town, I visited Grace Presbyterian, and it was that Sunday Pastor John and his wife Deborah invited me to join them for lunch after the service. That day was the beginning of one of the most meaningful relationships I'd had in my life. They became surrogate parents in the absence of my own, with John acting as a mix of father/brother/friend. He would call every week to just check in, and some days I would stop by the church, and we would talk about a variety of things like current affairs, theology, and when she came into the picture, we talked a lot about Jess.

Deborah had not been thrilled when I shared with them my desire to marry Jess, especially after such a short time. She thought it was a rash decision and made her point very well known to both John and me. Her initial reaction had hurt at first until John explained that it was out of the need to protect rather than doubting my ability to make good choices. He assured me he trusted my judgment and promised to talk to Deborah and calm her fears. In the meantime, John had been the one to pull together everything I couldn't while I was out of town. Deborah had not been thrilled but had eventually agreed to be supportive.

John and Deborah were not my parents, and I was an adult. These were simply the facts. However, because of how deep my love and respect ran for them, it mattered to me that they trusted my judgment. I knew once they got to know Jess, they would understand what I already did. She was the one for me.

The connection I felt to Jess was one I could only describe as a tethering of souls. There was an immediate bond connecting us to one another the moment our eyes locked across a dimly lit room, and every conversation, stare, kiss, and quiet moment had strengthened that connection. There was a force that pulled us toward one another and continued to pull us together. It was that force that made me certain beyond a shadow of a doubt, Jess was my forever, no matter what.

20

JESS

Deborah was waiting for me on the front steps of the church when I arrived. This time, when her arms wrapped around me, it felt like the embrace of a mother. When she let go, I was left dabbing my eyes, hoping I wasn't ruining my makeup. I followed Deborah into the church where she led me to a small hidden room that had a sign on it that read Bridal Suite. The thought that I was walking into a room meant for a bride stole the air from my lungs. I was the bride. I was getting married.

When Bryan had walked into the private room of his friend's nightclub, I was convinced of three things. Time had stopped, the world around me had ceased to exist—with the exception of a perfect set of green eyes—and my heart was going to detonate inside my chest. The feelings I had immediately experienced in that moment were unlike any I had ever known. The idea of falling in love had always been one of a slow process that involved an extended period of time and effort. Now I knew that love could happen in an instant.

By all measures of reason and logic, I should not be getting married to a man I met in a nightclub two weeks prior to today. Nonetheless, I knew in the deepest recesses of my heart, mind, and soul that Bryan Carsen was the one I had always wanted and never known

I needed. From the moment we met, I knew my life would never be the same.

Once inside the small room, Deborah closed the door behind us. She took both my hands in hers and squeezed them. With a teary smile, Deborah said, "I'm going to pray for you, and then you're going to go marry one of the most wonderful young men God ever created."

All I could do was nod as I bit my lip, begging my tears to stay inside. As her words wrapped around me, I tried to level out my breathing and send up my own silent words of thanks. When she ended her prayer, Deborah handed me a small bouquet of peonies, hydrangeas, and roses almost identical to the one I had on my table at home. I had to stop myself from hugging them to my chest so as not to damage the delicate flowers.

"Thank you," I said quietly.

"Are you ready?"

"One minute." I turned to dig through my purse, where I found the small velvet pouch. After wrapping it around the stems of the bouquet, I took a deep breath, and walked arm in arm to the door of the sanctuary with Deborah at my side.

21

BRYAN

At the sound of a throat being cleared, John and I turned to see the source and immediately stood to our feet and faced the back of the church. There she was surrounded by the remnants of the soft light trailing in through the doors behind her. Our eyes locked, and I was afraid to even blink for fear of missing a single step she took.

I'd been through basic training, deployed to war zones, and worked for the US government, and not a single one of those ever sent my heart into the rapid speed it was in as I watched the most beautiful woman in the world walk toward me. My breathing turned shallow, and if I'd locked my knees, I would have plummeted to the floor. My hands stayed crossed tightly in front of me to keep them from visibly trembling.

I hoped the smile on her face was indicative of the one on mine. It felt as though my face might crack. When my vision began to blur, I was forced to use one of my traitorous shaking hands to wipe the building moisture from my eyes.

When she was finally standing in front of me, still not having taken her eyes from mine, she whispered, "Hi."

A full breath left my lungs before I could inhale and whispered back, "Hi."

This was now my only reality—Jess standing in front of me, perfect in every way, smiling, letting me know we were the only thing that mattered here in this moment. The thread between us pulled tighter and reinforced in the beats of time passing by us. We stayed in our own bubble communicating wordlessly until we were snapped back into reality by John clearing his throat, causing all four of us to chuckle.

The next fifteen minutes passed in a blur. I vaguely remember repeating our vows and saying, "I do." As we proceeded to exchange rings, there was a gaff with juggling the flowers and watching Jess attempt to pull my ring out of a small pouch attached to her bouquet. Every time she would reach into the bag, the drawstring would go taut and pull the bag closed.

Once Jess had freed the ring, Deborah stepped up to take the flowers, and Jess had to bite her bottom lip to keep from laughing which threatened to send us all into a fit of laughter. After she repeated the words given to her by Pastor John, I watched her hand slide the black band on my finger. It fit as though it had been made for my hand, a reminder that everything about this day and everything leading up to it had been orchestrated perfectly.

And now, after making vows, promising to love, cherish, and protect one another until we were parted by death, after exchanging rings and more promises to honor and respect one another through our faithfulness, we waited together in the heavy silence of the sanctuary.

As we waited, I took in the sight before me. Standing there was a woman I didn't know, yet I knew everything I needed to know. She was the one—the one who invaded my thoughts first thing every morning and the one who walked with me into sleep and through my dreams. She was the one I craved to talk to, to share my days with and my nights. She was the one to whom my soul had attached itself as an anchor, securing it in a safe harbor. She was the one I swore to love for the rest of my life. My wife.

Lost in my thoughts, I almost missed John's directive and was only pulled from them when I heard, "Bryan, you may kiss your bride."

A wave of relief, excitement, promise, and every emotion in between crashed over me and through me. Releasing her hands, I wrapped one of my arms immediately around her waist to pull her to me as I took her face in my other hand. Before we sealed our promises, I made one final declaration against her lips as I waded deeper into the depths of her dark eyes.

"I love you."

Before she could respond, I claimed her smile with my lips, allowing the sacredness of the moment to captivate us, my heart in full surrender to hers. The moment imprinted itself on my mind and heart, and I knew we were at the beginning of something beautiful and eternal. Though the experience had been ephemeral, it had been searing and full of more promises to come.

As our lips drew apart, our eyes immediately connected. Watching one another in awed silence for several breaths, we both broke into wide grins before turning to face John. With an arm still around Jess, I put my hand out for a handshake. He pulled me into a hug which I returned happily. Deborah, who had been standing behind us, moved forward and the four of us formed a circle of warmth and trust and family.

When we had all righted ourselves and dried our tears John said, "Before you two disappear, I need you to sign the marriage license." Pulling a piece of folded paper from the pocket inside his suit coat, he retrieved a pen from his shirt pocket.

And just like that, I was married to the woman who stole my heart the moment I met her.

22

JESS

Papers signed, huge smiles plastered to faces, Bryan asked John and Deborah if they would join us for a celebratory dinner before they called it a night. At first, they declined, but Bryan told them he had already booked the private dining room at The Lafayette. It was not a hard battle to win. They agreed to meet at six, which gave us an opportunity to decompress and see each other, which we had not done since the day before.

We walked hand in hand to the town car waiting in front of the church to take us to the restaurant, my heart crashing inside of me like powerful waves on a bright and windy summer day. My thoughts and emotions were running rampant, leaving me breathless and dizzy with joy. When we were both settled inside the quiet car, we each expelled a rush of air, causing us to turn to look at each other.

Then we laughed, and I was blanketed in familiar warmth even with half a seat between us. It was the first time I had ever heard Bryan's real laugh, and it was glorious. His eyes always held a gleam behind them, and when he smiled, there were small creases at his eyes. But in this, his laugh, all of it compounded into a single effect that threatened to launch my heart into the stratosphere. It was a culmination of every question, every experience, every anxiety, and every emotion. The release was pure magic.

The quiet fell around us, and the energy shifted from sheer adrenaline to something deeper. I felt it in his gaze and his voice. He lifted my hand to his lips and kissed it for a long moment before locking out fingers together. "You look..." He trailed off, running his eyes from my head to my toes I had slipped out of my shoes.

His eyes drank me in as though he was just seeing me for the first time. His words stuck in his throat before he finally whispered, "You are exquisite."

The heat crept from behind my knees to my cheeks. "And you..." I traced the badges on his uniformed chest with my free hand. "I like this look. It's true what they say. There really is something about a man in uniform."

He winked and kissed my hand again. "Why do you think I joined the Army?"

This made me laugh, causing me to realize that I was seeing a completely different side of Bryan. From the moment we met, our interactions had been relatively serious, though sweet, and pleasantly amiable. His easy-going nature was attractive from our first conversation, and his ability to fluidly alternate from depth to surface had been refreshing from the get-go.

The flirty, teasing side of Bryan was captivating. It turned something inside of me over, making me want more of everything he had to offer, and I was eager to uncover all of it. And now he was mine to unearth.

Unable to keep my hands to myself, I ran my hand over his chest and up his neck where my hand rested, locking my eyes on Bryan's, fighting to keep my breathing steady. Slowly, he bent to meet my lips with his, and the embers that had sparked from the beginning were being fanned back to life. Our hands pulled at one another and moved in desperation trying to fill the longing between us, only intensifying the need with every passing second.

Bryan's lips left mine and traveled as far down my neck as our limited space would allow before returning to my lips. I was exerting almost as much will power to stay in my seat as I was trying to paw my husband.

The immensity of that thought, the idea that I was making out in the backseat of a car with my husband, packed a punch so strong it caused me to freeze on the spot. We were both panting when I slowly leaned back to survey the man in front of me. The backseat had grown warm with the heat we generated, leaving me with a light sheen of sweat that immediately cooled in the breeze of the air conditioner. Before we once again settled into our own seats, Bryan rested his lips on my forehead, his hand gripping the back of my neck, holding me to him.

Several moments of silence passed between us, and I struggled to read Bryan through the mist of my own clouded mind. All I could really hear was the sound of my own breathing as the blood rushed back to my head leaving me dazed.

"Those uniforms might look good, but they are not conducive to making out in the backseat of a car," I joked, breaking the silence.

Bryan laughed, and I tucked the sound away in my heart.

"You're telling me." He reached up to brush my hair back in place.

"I can only imagine what I look like. I might need to grab my makeup bag before we get to the restaurant and freshen up. I would hate to show up and let Pastor John and Deborah see me looking like this."

"You're breathtaking. And I like this look."

"This look? What would you call it? Mauled?" I teased as I attempted to smooth out my dress.

"I'd call it a lovesick newlywed who couldn't keep her hands off her husband," he teased back, running a finger down the side of my neck before he leaned over and kissed my shoulder.

An involuntary shiver ran down my spine as my hands brushed down my dress. The shiny metal band on my finger caught my eye. "Was this your grandmother's too?" I held out my hand.

Bryan kissed it and rubbed his thumb across the ring. "It was. She died before I was born, so I never knew her. Mom always told me stories about Gran and how she and my grandfather had made it through the Great Depression. They had sold practically everything, including my grandmother's original engagement ring and wedding ring to survive. He always promised to replace it. And he did."

A sucker for a good story, I raised my eyebrows waiting for him to share. Still holding my hand in his, I scooted to the middle of the bench seat and listened.

"After the Ford plant closed, my grandfather went on the hunt for work. He found and made a deal with a local man who owned hundreds of acres, which was more land than he could work by himself. The man had originally been growing cotton, but with demand shrinking so drastically and being unable to afford workers, he was on his own. So, my grandfather bartered services. He agreed to work the cotton field if the owner would let him plant tobacco to sell and live on the property. The owner agreed but only if Granddad paid him a percentage of the tobacco profits.

"Before long, the owner had given up on cotton completely, and he and my grandfather became partners of a huge tobacco farm. His partner died a few years into the venture and left his share to my grandfather. By the time most people were just getting back on their feet, Granddad was one of the wealthiest men in Kentucky. He made sure my grandmother was swimming in jewels and fur coats. But she didn't care about any of that. The only jewelry she ever wore were these two rings. Mom said it was Gran's reminder that no matter how hard life got, there would always be something beautiful on the other side."

Something fluttered inside my chest and my throat tightened. "That's beautiful. Your grandmother sounds like she was a smart lady."

Bryan fidgeted with the ring on my hand. "I would have liked to have known her more than just the stories I heard growing up. Both she and Granddad were strong people, good people." Bryan's gaze moved to his own hand. "Speaking of rings, this one is great."

"Do you like it? I know it's kind of different, but once the man told me how it was made, I knew it was the right one."

I told him about my experience at the jewelry store that afternoon and about how the ring was made. "I thought it sounded a lot like us and what I hope our marriage is like fifty or a hundred years from now—indestructible and just as solid as today."

He leaned in and kissed me slowly. There was a crush of disappointment when the car came to a stop signaling the end of the kiss. We put ourselves back together and walked inside where we met John and Deborah in a private alcove in the corner of a hotel restaurant.

For the next couple of hours, I got to know the people Bryan had been taken in by as one of their own. I was beginning to understand Bryan's fondness of them both. They were kind and encouraging, and Pastor John was surprisingly funny. Spending time with them felt like inhaling a breath of the freshest beach air, and as I sat and listened and watched, I knew I had been sitting with family the entire time.

After dinner, John and Deborah said their goodbyes and made their way to the valet. Holding on to Bryan's arm, I peered up at him and couldn't help but smile. "I like them."

Returning my smile Bryan said, "Good. Shall we?" He gently tugged my arm linked with his, escorting me toward an elevator.

My nerves were smoldering under my skin, and my entire body tensed.

Bryan must have felt it, as he covered my hand on his arm with his hand. "Hey," he whispered against my temple. "No pressure, no expectations. I just want to be with you, okay?"

My eyes burned as I leaned into him.

He moved his arm to wrap it around me, and when the elevator doors opened, his hand rested on the small of my back and guided me inside. We rode up in silence, Bryan's arm around me, and my thoughts whirring inside me at breakneck speed.

I had zero reference points for anything beyond this point, and for me, that felt a lot like bungee jumping without a cord. My entire world had revolved around reference points and baselines for so long, and now I was back to relying on intuition and instincts, and it was unnerving. My insides felt as though they were winding themselves into a coil, leaving me with a feeling of anxiety.

When we exited the elevator, we walked to the end of the hallway where Bryan pulled a room key out of a pocket. He flipped it over in his fingers several times before inserting it into the lock. Opening the door, he stood to the side allowing me to enter first. I felt my eyes go wide as I took in the large, plush room. I walked through the room, unsure of what else to do, running my fingers over the soft furnishings. Staring out the window, not really taking in the view, I gathered my thoughts, my insides trembling.

I turned and let my focus stay on Bryan, who had shaken his heavy uniform jacket from his shoulders and was draping it on the back of a chair. He put his hands in his pockets and watched me with a look of contentment on his face.

Unable to stop myself, my eyes slowly swept over him, over every muscle defined under his close-fitting undershirt, before locking onto his gaze.

"How did you do all of this?" I motioned without removing my gaze from his and taking a step toward him.

"Do you like it?" he asked hopefully as he took a step toward me.

"The room? It's beautiful. But I mean all of this. Everything in less than a day?" I took another step.

His lips quirked up on one side and he took another step. "I took a chance," he said softly. "I knew when I got on the airplane last week, I was going to do everything in my power to spend forever with you, starting sooner rather than later. I prayed God would give me this one thing. I made calls all week between meetings, and the only thing I couldn't guarantee was whether you would say yes. I hoped you would, and deep down I thought you would. But there was always a chance I had misread things and had gotten caught up in my own feelings."

He stepped forward again, putting us close enough I could feel his breath on my cheeks. My breathing had slowed, and I could no longer differentiate between his breath and mine. Bryan's hand cupped my face, and he brushed his thumb gently across my cheek.

His eyes were steadfast on mine as he leaned down and kissed me. It was deep and full of heat and longing and in that instance, I kissed him back.

The tug on my heart told me I would never be able to be close enough to him, even when there was no space between us to be had. We clung to each other as though the dream might end at any moment, and I knew I would love Bryan Carsen for the rest of my life.

PART II

PART II

23

JESS

My phone rang as I clicked Send on an email. Even after two years, my heart fluttered when his name showed on the screen.

"Jess Carsen," I answered in a playful but formal tone.

"Mrs. Carsen, this is Bryan Carsen. I was hoping I'd catch you. Is now a good time?"

"You caught me just in time. What can I do for you today?"

"It has come to my attention that you and I are long overdue for a date, and I was hoping to rectify the situation by offering you a romantic dinner, and if I'm lucky, a romantic rendezvous after."

Pretending to check my calendar, I paused before answering. "Hmm, I think that can be arranged. How does seven o'clock work for you?"

"I'll see you then." Then he added, "I love you, Mrs. Carsen."

"And I love you, Mr. Carsen. See you tonight."

The warm tingles I always felt when it came to Bryan ran through me. It had been a few weeks since our schedules had lined up to allow us a chance to spend more than an hour together before going to bed. And it was a constant battle between wanting to catch up on one another's day and being unable to keep our hands off one another. A date night sounded like the best of both worlds.

Weeks after the wedding, I sat down with Dr. Thorne, and we talked through some of the questions and concerns I had about the future of my work at the university and my career. I really liked the security and consistency of the university and the research lab, and I enjoyed teaching, but the more I thought about it, the more I wondered if I was being selfish keeping my ability insulated after I became aware I could use it for so much more.

What had started as a test of my abilities when I demonstrated my people-reading skills for a case as requested by Special Agent Mark Collins of the FBI, evolved into repeat consultations then broadened into consulting with the FBI, DHS, ICE, and several other acronymic government agencies as well as several local police departments.

Within six months, I had convinced my mentor and colleague Dr. Derick Thorne to branch out and partner up to do part-time consulting. A year later, Carsen-Thorne Consulting was born. In eighteen months, we had helped close twelve cold cases and forty-three open cases.

The work was exhausting. The mental and emotional strain took its toll. Some days were harder than others, and some cases were more devastating than others. Being able to see the difference we were making in families and society, however, provided the motivation to keep pressing on along this new path.

Bryan had driven to work that morning, so it was easier for me to take an Uber downtown. I shut down my laptop and went upstairs where I took my time getting ready.

When the Uber pulled up to our favorite restaurant, The Wharf, Bryan met me outside. After a long kiss hello, I thought about suggesting we skip dinner and head home but thought better of it when I spotted the lightness of his presence. Instead, I let him lead me to a table on the outdoor patio that overlooked the marina. It took the entire walk to the table to settle the butterflies that formed in my chest when he kissed me.

"You look amazing, as always," he said in a low almost growl in my ear as he pulled the chair out for me.

And he could still make me blush. "It's all for you," I whispered before sitting.

He shook his head slowly as he took his seat, his eyes, full of pleasure, wandering over me. "How did I get so lucky?"

Running a foot up his leg under the table, I smirked and gave him a seductive wink. "You haven't gotten lucky, yet."

He closed his eyes as they rolled into his head. "You are killing me."

After we ordered, Bryan watched me, a conspiratorial look on his face. I knew him well enough I didn't need to read him, but this time it was written very clearly on his face.

"So, what is it you are dying to tell me?" I asked.

He laughed. "You know I've been working on this project for the last two years, and we finally wrapped stage one today." He was trying to keep the excitement out of his voice.

"Yeah?"

"Yeah. I didn't think it would ever get here. Now that there's a definite break between stage one and stage two, I've been cleared to take PTO."

Hope flared inside of me.

"So, I submitted my leave request and got approved for two weeks. If your schedule will allow it, I think two weeks would be a good start on the honeymoon we've yet to take."

It took everything in me not to jump out of my seat and tackle him right there on the patio. "Yes. Absolutely. I will burn my calendar and plead the fifth."

Bryan was trying to suppress his smile. Something else was happening under the surface, and I couldn't pinpoint it. "The approval came in maybe an hour after I had submitted it. Which is highly unusual. Leave never gets approved that quickly if it isn't for an emergency. But I took it as one of those God moments where he had unexpected mercy on me. Then about five minutes after I read the email, I got called in to see the General."

The hope inside of me threatened to wane.

Bryan continued, "I immediately made my way to his office. After he invited me in to have a seat, my mind started racing. There were so many things I thought he was going to say, that I almost missed what he actually said."

He stopped talking as our server arrived and set our food in front of us.

Trying to be patient, I focused on the plate being set in front of me, but as soon as the server stepped away, I prodded him to continue. "And?"

"Jess, I'm being promoted. Lieutenant Colonel."

My hands flew over my mouth as I gasped with excitement before reaching for his hand. "Bryan! That is fantastic! I am so proud of you."

By the time we had finished dinner, we had a tentative plan in place for how to spend our two weeks together. When I initially asked Bryan how he wanted to spend our time, his first response was, "Naked with you."

I'd rolled my eyes and laughed then promised to make plenty of time for that. When he made his second suggestion, my heart warmed, and I knew it was exactly what I wanted to do.

"I'd like to show you where I grew up."

Two days later, we were boarding a plane. After we landed, we drove for an hour and a half after leaving the Louisville International Airport. The farther away we drove from the city, the more beautiful the scenery became. After driving through a quaint old downtown, we left all signs of civilization. There were hills and pastures that stretched for miles. Houses were few and far between. I saw more cows in a single hour than I had in my entire life. It was peaceful.

After we turned off the main road and onto a long, packed-gravel drive, it took almost three minutes to arrive at a huge farmhouse at the end of the lane. My jaw dropped as I stared at the large house.

Bryan opened my door with a sweep of his hand and a smile on his face. "Welcome to Owenston, Kentucky."

It felt like I had stepped into a different time as I surveyed the endless pastures. "This is beautiful."

He held out a hand to help me from the car. "I had a feeling you might like it. Come on, let's go inside. I want to introduce you to Cal."

My hand in his, we walked up the wide front steps onto a huge wrap around porch.

"Cal?" Bryan called out into the house through a screened door.

There was movement from inside before a man who appeared to be in his early sixties came to the door, smiling.

"Bryan Carsen? Is that you?" He came out onto the porch and the two men embraced one another like old friends.

"Cal, it's so good to see you."

"You, too, son," said the older man in his thick southern drawl. "And who is this here pretty lady?"

"Cal, this is my wife, Jess."

"Well, I'll be. That's wonderful. I am pleased to make your acquaintance, ma'am." Cal bowed his head, took off his cowboy hat, and held it to his chest.

"It's nice to meet you." I felt an immediate surge of familial connection to Cal as I watched him and Bryan interact.

Cal turned to Bryan. "I'm headin' off here in just a minute. I wanted to let you know that my right hand, Carlos, will be here and there every day, takin' care of all the things. If you need anything, you can flag him down or I left his number on the fridge. You can give him a call anytime. He's a nice fella. Gotta passel of youngins so you might see one here or there helpin' him out. But they shouldn't bother y'all. I want y'all to make yourselves at home, seein' as how it's still your home, son. And I'll be back in about a week. I'm headin' up to an auction north of here, then out to see my sister. If I don't get back before y'all are gone, it was right nice to see you, again, son. It's been too long."

He gave Bryan a long look before he turned and tipped his hat to me. "And it was nice to meet you, Mrs. Jess."

Bryan hugged Cal, again. "It's good to see you too, Cal. Thanks for letting us have the house."

"The timing works out for me to be able to make this trip, and y'all can have your private time without feelin' like you have to tip toe and sneak around." He winked.

I felt the blush in my cheeks.

"Alright, now, the keys are on the table, there are cookies on the counter – I promise I didn't make 'em."

"Thank you, Cal." I extended a hand to shake his.

He accepted and gave me a conspiratorial wink. He turned to Bryan. "Keeper."

Bryan smiled as his eyes locked with mine. "I plan to, as long as she'll have me."

He took me on a tour of the house after we had stowed our luggage in the guest room. The house had obviously been updated with modern fixtures in the last decade. But the old charm from the original hardwood floors and walls was undeniable.

We made our way back to the front porch looking over a large yard enclosed by a wooden rail fence.

"Bryan, this is amazing. It's so beautiful and peaceful. How could you ever want to leave?"

His smile was one of contentment and satisfaction as he wrapped his arms around me and kissed the top of my head. His warmth radiated through me. "If I had never left, I would never have met you."

I made a quiet hum and leaned my head back on him.

"But honestly, leaving was hard. I felt like I was choosing between my mom and my future. If Cal hadn't been around, I probably wouldn't have left."

We watched the leaves falling from the trees.

"Now that you're here, is it completely different or does it feel like coming home?"

Bryan took a deep breath of the cool air. "It's familiar, but it's not home."

We stood there in silence just staring out over the landscape. The sun was getting lower in the sky, and the air was getting cooler. A shiver ran over me as I tried to hold in a yawn.

Bryan squeezed me. "It's been a long day. How about you go take a bath, and I'll figure out dinner and get a fire going in the fireplace?"

I turned to face him and moved my hands slowly from his chest up to his shoulders then around his neck pressing myself against him. Placing a short kiss to his lips, I smiled. "You always have the best ideas."

With a roguish grin and a growly voice he said, "You haven't heard half of them."

I soaked in the tub for almost an hour before convincing myself it was time to get out. The idea of curling up next to Bryan in front of a fire was finally enough motivation for me to pull the plug. I'd been battling a headache for a few hours, blaming travel fatigue and cool weather. The warm bath helped relieve the tension that had been building in my back a little, but my head still felt achy. After I got dressed, I rummaged through my toiletries case and found the medicine kit, taking a couple of pain relievers with water from the bathroom sink.

Bryan was in the kitchen taking plates from the cabinet and setting them on the table when he spotted me coming down the stairs. "Better?" he asked.

I sighed as I rolled my neck and shoulders. "It was heavenly. I could have stayed another hour, but the water got cold. And that made me think of how warm you always are, so I hurried out and got dressed so I could do this..." I put my cold hands under his shirt, causing him to jump and let out a loud grunt. I laughed as I dug my fingertips into his sides trying to make his escape harder.

"Oh, that's dirty," he said in disbelief. He turned around quickly, wrapping me in a bear hug that resulted in a squeal. He laughed as he found my lips with his. Everything slowed as the warmth he always provided spilled over me.

My hands roamed farther up his back, this time to pull him closer trying to eliminate all space between us. Bryan's hands, hot against my skin, threatened to melt me with his touch.

A couple of hours later we found ourselves starving and deliriously happy on the couch in front of a crackling fire. When my stomach growled loud enough for us to both hear it and laugh, I located Bryan's discarded hoodie and went back to the kitchen to reheat the dinner we had abandoned.

A week went by quickly, though the days were languorous as we roamed the property. One morning Bryan took me fishing, which I decided was not going to become a new hobby any time soon. He showed me how to use some of the different firearms Cal had in the safe. Apparently, I had a penchant for them, which impressed Bryan immensely.

One afternoon Carlos took us to the barn where baby goats were bouncing around and running to us in search of treats. My smile felt permanently etched on my face. We found no reason to leave the property the entire week. Falling asleep together in front of the large brick fireplace became a nightly ritual.

"Promise we'll come back here often," I pleaded with Bryan.

"I promise we'll come back here often." He crossed his heart and kissed my forehead before putting our suitcases in the trunk.

Bryan asked several times on the flight home if I was feeling okay as I had been quiet.

I finally explained I'd had a headache on and off all week, but I was sure it was the change of routine and fresh air that had put my system on alert. When we got home, he insisted I shower and head straight to bed, and I was not too proud to argue. So that's what I did.

24

JESS

When I woke up with a worsening headache, Bryan insisted I call the doctor in case I had a sinus infection or something that could get worse. He still had a few days off, so when I got an appointment for that afternoon, he offered to go with me. We arrived at the doctor's office a few minutes before the appointment time and settled into a couple of the chairs in the waiting room.

"Remember the last time we sat in a waiting room together?" Bryan put his arm around my shoulders.

"A lot has happened since then, huh?"

"It really has."

My mind drifted to the day we spent in a hospital waiting room in New York where we waited after I had gotten the call from my best friend Stacy that she was in trouble and needed help. It was in that waiting room I fell in love with the man sitting next to me. He had been the epitome of strength and dedication. He supported me, held me, and walked with me through one of the darkest days I'd experienced.

I was then reminded of the day I got the call from Stacy's mother telling me that Stacy had another stroke that had been fatal. Bryan had been there, his arms around me, shielding me, loving me through it. He went with me to the funeral and held my hand as I said goodbye to the woman I'd loved as a sister. His constant support and care even now overwhelmed me. And I loved him for it more and more each passing day.

I was about to tell him this when a voice from across the room called my name.

I squeezed the hand I'd been holding in silence and whispered, "I'll be back," before

following a nurse to a triage room.

After verifying all my basic information, the nurse took a medical history. "We need a urine sample, and we'll draw some blood when you come back out here. Then we'll get you situated in an exam room."

It had been a long time since I had been in a doctor's examination room as the patient. I didn't feel comfortable sitting on the exam table since my only symptom was a headache, so I sat in the extra chair in the exam room to wait for the doctor.

When she came in, the doctor's warm smile made me feel instantly better. "Mrs. Carsen?"

"Yes, that's me."

Warmth. Sincerity. Reservation.

The doctor studied the chart in her hand and then at me. "I see here that you've had a persistent headache for several days. Have you had any other symptoms that concern you?"

I shook my head. "No, just the headache. My husband thought it would be a good idea to see you to rule out anything or maybe get something stronger than Tylenol for it."

The look on the doctor's face told Jess she wanted to say something but was struggling to come up with words. Her expression gave me pause.

"Is something wrong?"

The doctor smiled. "Mrs. Carsen, you're pregnant."

25

JESS

Bryan had always been thoughtful and doting. He would leave notes on the mirror for me to find some mornings if he was going to be gone when I got out of bed. He sent flowers on a weekly basis because he enjoyed seeing how happy they made me, even though I called them frivolous. When we found out I was pregnant, his doting went into overdrive.

We had talked about having children one day, and he was always excited at the idea. I had no concept of how much more excited he would be when the idea became a reality. If there was a book he thought we should read, he would read it to me as we sat on the couch with my feet propped in his lap. He had a morning sickness survival kit readily available in the bathroom with crackers, bottled water, ginger candies, and peppermints neatly arranged in a basket. Dinner for the next day was always planned and prepped before we went to bed.

There were days when I had to stop him from hovering, and he would simply wrap me in his arms, kiss me, and tell how excited he was to experience this with me. Of course, I would swoon, and he would smile and continue to smother me with love.

Seven months after hearing those words in the doctor's office, I gave birth to a precious baby girl we named Hayley Grace. She had Bryan's green eyes and my nose. She was perfect.

I planned for and took several weeks of maternity leave, though most of those days I found myself spending the early morning hours reading through Dr. Thorne's notes on cases and making some of my own as I nursed and rocked Hayley. I was thankful for the flexibility of my job and for Dr. Thorne's willingness to pick up the slack when necessary.

Bryan had taken our first week home off from work, but even as he was home, he worked more than he didn't. I knew the timing had been stressful, and as sympathetic as I tried to be, it was hard because I had no way of predicting his increased workload would have coincided with the birth of our child.

For several weeks I really tried to be understanding because I knew his job was very stressful, and he was in the middle of major development of a project. But I was exhausted and needed him to realize I more than wanted his help. I needed it. There were days when I would have to make demands of his time just so I could get a shower, and when I'd come downstairs, I'd find him trying to unsuccessfully multitask with Hayley and his computer, leaving me frustrated.

Over the next six months, Bryan slowly transformed from the strong, confident man I knew him to be into a persistently tired and frazzled stranger. He spent his days at work and then came home and sat at his computer in our shared office for hours.

Initially, when he would wave off my suggestions to come to bed, I would gently try to persuade him, and sometimes it worked. Most of the time, it didn't. I tried seducing him, I tried making demands. Eventually, when he stopped responding, I stopped trying. And he didn't seem to notice.

THE MORNING I walked downstairs and found him sleeping with his forehead resting on the desk and had to forcefully shake him awake, I

was done. Not because he had fallen asleep at his desk but because the look on his face scared me.
Paranoid. Fear. Exhaustion.

26

BRYAN

I heard her voice, but it sounded far away. My head felt as though it weighed at least a ton, and my eyes struggled to blink anything around me into focus.

"Bryan, you are going to call in sick today. Right now. Then you are going to go upstairs and get a shower. I'm going to call Deborah and ask if she can watch Hayley while you and I go out."

It took several seconds for her words to register. Slowly and wordlessly, I nodded and stood. Another beat passed before I took a step and then another before I finally left the room.

When I had finished tying my shoes, I sat on the edge of our bed, uncertain of how I had gotten there. Running both hands over my face, I caught my reflection in the mirror over the large dresser against the wall. A stranger stared back at me. I had lost weight. My skin was sickly pale. There were large, dark circles under my eyes. I hadn't slept more than three hours on any given night in the last several months. I didn't remember the last time I ate more than two bites of anything Jess had put in front of me.

Jess. I couldn't remember the last time I said her name aloud. Jess. Hayley. My heart ricocheted inside my chest. My face felt hot. How could I have let things get this far out of my control? I let my elbows fall to my knees and buried my head in my hands.

An hour later, we were in the car. After a silent drive, Jess found a park that was mostly empty and swung into a parking spot in the shade of a small oak tree. She sat and stared at me as though she was trying to read a stranger.

A pain pulsed behind my ribs making it hard to breathe. I had become a stranger to my own wife, and it was my own fault. I tried but couldn't hold her gaze for more than a few seconds. The shame attempted to drag me under.

When my gaze fell from hers, she opened her car door and spoke softly, "Come on."

I opened my door and followed her to a small pond on the opposite side of the park. We stood silently staring out across the water for a long time. I was holding back a torrent of emotion that had been building inside of me for so long.

"Bryan."

When Jess said my name, the hurt, the longing, the desperation I heard in her voice pierced me at my core. I forced myself to look at her.

Tears were streaming down her face, and I was moving closer to the precipice.

"Bryan, I need you. I need you to talk to me, to trust me with whatever is going on with you. I see you every day, and I miss you more than if you were half a world away. Hayley needs you. She needs to know her daddy loves her and is there for her no matter what. At first, I thought it was the stress of a new baby, one that we hadn't planned. Then I thought it was me because we couldn't be intimate for so long and maybe you had found someone else."

A guttural sob erupted from deep within me, and her words broke off. I couldn't take a full breath, and my entire body was shaking. My arms immediately reached for Jess and held on to her as though she was the only link I had to this life. I buried my face in her hair as the words tumbled out.

"I'm so sorry. Jess, I'm sorry. I thought I had it under control. I thought I had it figured out. And then it got away from me, and I couldn't let that happen. It wasn't you. Oh, God, it wasn't you, and I am so sorry you ever felt that way."

I held her and allowed the warmth of her seep into me as she clung to me. When my breathing had leveled out, I slowly loosened my grip on Jess. I needed to see her and was terrified of what I might find when I did. I took a step backward, keeping our hands locked together.

She appeared guarded and afraid. Her mouth moved several times with nothing happening. "Bryan, what are you talking about?" Her voice was shaky.

My thoughts were racing, and I struggled to know what to tell her. I had to pull my gaze from hers in an effort to make sense of the words I needed to say. Staring out across the small body of water, I ran a hand through my hair and inhaled deeply before slowly letting out the breath. I took a minute to survey the park around us, trying to avoid anyone who could eavesdrop on our conversation then spoke in a hushed tone.

"Several months ago, right before Hayley was born, we hit a snag on the project at work. These things happen. One wrong keystroke and hundreds of lines of code are rendered useless. I sent the problem to one of the best guys in the group, and he came back a few days later and said that it wasn't anything that happened on our end. It had come from the outside."

My eyes darted around the park as I spoke. "That shouldn't have been possible, but the more I poked around, the more of a possibility I realized it was. So, I started watching and waiting. And like clockwork, things started happening that shouldn't happen. Little things at first. I made reports, and we upped our security, but the system stayed under constant attack. I have spent the last six months trying to find the perpetrator or some kind of trail that might at least point me in the right direction. And nothing."

Jess sucked in a deep breath as her eyes searched my face. She reached up and put her hand on my cheek, forcing me to look at her.

When I leaned into her touch, she pulled my lips roughly to hers. It felt forced at first, angry, frantic.

When I realized what was happening, my trembling hands moved to her waist. Her body slowly relaxed against me, and her warmth moved through me providing renewed life and energy. It had been so long, too long. She pulled me closer and deepened the kiss.

My hands moved and pressed into her back, holding on to her as though I could wake up from a fevered dream at any moment. I felt like I was in the middle of the ocean trying to hold on to a life preserver as waves crashed over and around me. In that moment, I knew Jess would do everything in her power to keep me afloat.

When she pulled away, I stood with my head bowed and eyes closed. I couldn't look at her, yet. Tears spilled from my eyes once more. "Jess." I could barely form a whisper. "I'm so sorry. I—"

Jess put a finger on my lips. "Don't. Just listen, okay?"

I nodded.

She put her hand over my heart. "I love you. I have always loved you. I will always love you. Neither of us can change what has happened in the last six months. But we can change what happens from this moment forward. I need you. I want you. Hayley needs you. Promise me that you'll come back to us. Today. Right now. Promise me you'll never leave me, again. I can't live like this. I won't. Until I felt your heart beating against mine just now, I didn't know how empty I had become. Don't take my heart away, again. Promise me."

Covering her hand with mine, I rested my forehead on hers. "I promise. No matter what."

She wrapped her arms around my waist, and we stood there, sharing heartbeats for a long time before driving home in silence.

27

JESS

"You go upstairs and try to get some rest. I'm going to talk to Deborah and check on Hayley," I said as we walked toward the front door.

Bryan obeyed silently.

Deborah, who had been sitting on the couch reading her Bible, put the book on the table and stood to face me. "How is he?" She rested her trembling hand on my arm.

I covered Deborah's hand with my own and stared into the face of the woman I had grown to love as I had my own mother. After Bryan and I married, Deborah discipled me and through the process had become more than just a friend.

"Honestly, Deborah, I don't know. I won't pretend to understand everything he said today. He's wrapped up in something at work that just took over and—I don't know. He's scared and paranoid. I'm worried about him, but I'm hopeful. He talked to me, and that's more than I can say for a long time. But I think we have a long way to go."

Though fewer than they had been, the tears were back.

"We haven't stopped praying and we won't. You have an army of prayer warriors behind you who are ready to go to battle for you."

"Thank you. You have no idea what that means to me. And I

know it means something to Bryan, whether he can see it right now or not. And thank you for being here today. I know it was last minute."

Deborah beamed through watery eyes and reached for me. "I would be here in a heartbeat to love on that sweet baby. You don't know how much she means to John and me. How much all three of you mean to us. God put all of you in our lives at different times for different reasons. I wouldn't want to miss a minute of it."

As our embrace ended, Deborah reached for a box of tissues and went into mothering mode. Though never having been a mother herself, Deborah was a natural.

"Now, I laid Hayley down about fifteen minutes ago. We played, she had a bottle, and I rocked her until her little heart was content. I found a frozen lasagna in your freezer, so I put it in the oven, and the timer is set. You need to go upstairs and be with your husband. Talk if you need to. Be silent if you need to. But what's important is that you are with him right now."

A breath left my body in a woosh. "Thank you." I hugged Deborah again.

After walking Deborah to the door, I turned and stared up the stairs toward our bedroom. With a few cleansing breaths, I slowly walked up the stairs.

Bryan was lying flat on his back on top of the covers fully dressed, his shoes on the floor next to the bed.

I walked to the other side of the bed, slid my shoes off, and crawled in next to my husband. Facing him, I slowly moved my trembling hand under his shirt and across his abdomen.

Bryan released a long breath and moved his arm to cover mine as he turned his head to face me. His face was red and swollen, streaked by tears. We laid there silently taking in each other for a long while. Wordlessly, his hand slowly moved up my arm and rested on my face, his thumb gently stroking my cheek.

I moved myself as close to Bryan as I could, wrapping my arm around him until I could tuck my head under his chin. Curled up in the space that held me perfectly and securely, we laid together and wept as we began to heal the sacred space that had grown between us.

THE NEXT SEVERAL months rekindled a hope in my heart that I hadn't felt in a long time. I watched as shadows of the man I had married emerged. He started going to church with us again. We read the Bible together and prayed together like we had before. Bryan embraced fatherhood with enthusiasm, and as I knew he would be, he was a natural.

My favorite time of day was watching him come home from work. He would find me first to kiss me, and then immediately he would swoop Hayley into the air and hug her while she giggled. This was the man I remembered. This was the man I had fallen in love with at first sight.

There were still days that Bryan would seem distant, almost an empty shell. Other days he would check the front door lock ten times before he went to bed, where he would toss and turn for hours before going back to the downstairs office.

I prayed for him every day; sometimes it was every hour.

Hayley turned one, and we invited John and Deborah over for dinner and cake. Even though it was only for a few hours Bryan had been every part his old self. My heart had overflowed with joy and confidence that the future was full of promise.

Bryan had started meeting with Pastor John every week for counseling, which helped immensely. But some days were just hard. Those were the days I prayed harder, cried harder, and loved my husband harder. I refused to let the hard days win. It was the hard days when I remembered our wedding day when Bryan shared his grandmother's wisdom.

No matter how hard life got, there would always be something beautiful on the other side.

28

JESS

I worked hard to balance work and home, but there were days I still felt like I was drained of every ounce of effort I had inside of me. There were days I functioned as a single parent in addition to struggling to find strength to encourage my husband. Working from home was hard too. When I thought about putting Hayley in daycare just to feel less guilty about dividing my time and attention, the guilt of sending her away would overwhelm me.

At one of our weekly Tuesday night ladies Bible studies, I wrestled with whether or not to mention the additional stress the decision about daycare was causing. Finally, before the prayer time began, I asked the group to pray I could find peace about making the decision concerning daycare.

Later, after the group had adjourned, one of the ladies in the group approached. Marí was a stout Dominican woman with a strong Spanish accent, even though she had lived in DC for thirty years. She liked to say, "You can take the girl out of the Dominican, but you'll never take the Dominican out of the girl!" She was right. Marí was a spitfire who loved Jesus and never held back when she had something to say. The thing with Marí, however, was that she would serve selflessly and give endlessly even if it left her destitute.

"Jess! I need to speak to you."

I turned to see Marí making a beeline for me with a look of determination on her face.

Smiling, I held out my arms to receive an embrace and a kiss on the cheek from my friend. "Marí, it's so good to see you. How are you? How's Sadie?"

Sadie was Marí's granddaughter whom she was raising after Marí's daughter had fallen victim to a drug overdose not long after Sadie was born.

"She is good. Growing like the weeds just like your little one seems to be. How is Bryan? I noticed you did not mention him tonight. I am still praying for him, every day, you know?"

Smiling was a natural response to this sweet soul. She exuded love and compassion. "He's doing better. Every day is a new day, you know?"

"Yes, it is. I do know, better than most. But that is for another time," she said with a wave of her hand. "I wanted to tell you that you do not have to worry about daycare. I will take care of it. What time do you work every day?"

My brows furrowed in confusion. "I start working at five-thirty before Hayley wakes up so I can take a break when she does get up. Why? What do you mean you'll take care of it?"

Marí held up a hand. "What time does your niña wake up?"

"Around seven. Marí, what is this all about?"

"You have enough to worry about right now, and I only have Sadie and I do not worry about her. She is seven and as happy as she can be. So tomorrow, Sadie and I will be at your house by six-thirty, and you will not have to think about daycare until you know it is what God wants for you to do."

My hand went to my heart and my chin trembled. "Marí, no. That is so generous of you, but I can't let you do that."

"You are not letting me do anything. It is already done. I will see you tomorrow morning." With that, Marí gave me a kiss on the cheek and walked off to speak to Deborah.

For Marí to make such a generous commitment was a true sacrifice of her time and energy. But after six months of our new routine, I felt like a new person. I had more energy for my family at the end of the day, which seemed to have a positive effect on Bryan too.

Though I hoped with all of my heart, I sometimes wondered if things would ever be as they were before between Bryan and me. Regardless of the future, I knew God was working our story out for our good and his glory. I was thankful God had given me friends who taught me what it meant to trust him to always be there, even in the dark times.

29

JESS

It had been a year of heartache and struggle intermingled with grace and hope. Bryan and I had made great strides in our marriage, with much of the credit going to the regular counseling sessions we began attending together. We still had not fully rekindled the spark that had existed in the beginning, but progress was progress.

Bryan had left for work before I was out of the shower and found that he had left a note on the counter in front of the coffee pot telling me to have a great day and that he had enjoyed our alone time the night before, ending with a winky face and a heart. The smile on my face that had been left over from said alone time doubled in size after reading his note. I stood there reading and rereading it until I heard the front door lock being turned.

Folding the note, I slid it into my pocket and poured my coffee before turning to find Marí and her granddaughter Sadie walking toward me from the living room.

Sadie skipped over and hugged me as she did every morning before I greeted Marí with a cheek-to-cheek air kiss.

"Good morning, ladies," I said in a sing-song voice.

"Oh, sounds like you are having yourself a good morning, mija." Marí gave me a knowing look.

I attempted to hide my face by taking a long drink of coffee, but it only added to the heat already in my cheeks.

Marí chuckled and patted my face. "Good, good. Now, I am thinking I will take the girls to the park this morning before it turns too hot, and then we will come home for lunch." Marí rattled off their plans for the day as I started putting bagels into the toaster for breakfast.

Once everyone had been fed and Hayley had been dressed, Marí set off with the girls and I settled in at my desk to begin my day working through some emails. When I stood to stretch after being seated for a couple of hours, I pulled Bryan's note from my pocket and smoothed it out on the desk next to my computer, reading it one more time, remembering the kiss we shared before we had fallen asleep wrapped up in each other's arms.

I was pulled from the memory by a knock on the front door. Marí had a key, and I wasn't expecting any deliveries, so I was almost immediately annoyed at the idea of a solicitor at the door. Upon opening it, I froze.

Instead of a salesman, there were two men in military uniform standing on my front porch. My heart lurched in my chest. The pit forming inside of my stomach threatened to take me to my knees. Gripping the doorknob tightly enough my knuckles turned white, I leaned on the door to steady myself.

"Mrs. Carsen?" one of the men asked.

"Yes." I nodded slowly.

"May we come in?"

At first, nobody moved. I couldn't remember how to breathe. My throat ached, and a sharp pain formed in my chest. "What's going on? What's happened? Where's Bryan?"

"Mrs. Carsen." The man lowered his voice and his gaze before looking back at me. "May we come in? I think it would be best if you were seated."

I didn't remember moving to let them in or even leading them into the living room. Their words sounded foreign, and I felt as though I was watching from outside of my own body as the uniformed men told me that Bryan's body had been found on a sidewalk earlier in the morning.

"It looks like a mugging gone wrong," the older of the two men said before asking if there was anyone they could call for me.

Shaking my head, I asked, "Where is he? Can I see him?"

The chaplain explained that he would make arrangements with the morgue, but they strongly encouraged me to call someone to go with me.

When the chaplain excused himself to call ahead to the morgue, I walked to the office on trembling legs to retrieve my phone. I stared at it as though I had never seen the device before and fumbled it several times before the younger officer who had accompanied the chaplain helped me unlock it. When I could finally still my hands long enough, I scrolled to Deborah's number and pressed Call.

The rest of that day became a shadow in my memory. In the coming weeks, I barely held myself together through the deluge of phone calls and messages from our friends at church. At the funeral, I put on as stoic a face as I could manage for no other reason than our beautiful two-year-old daughter. By the end of the first week, there was an obscene number of casseroles in my freezer. I didn't eat any of them. Instead, I sent one home with Marí almost every night.

My business partner, Dr. Thorne, generously suggested I take as much time as I needed away from work. It was work that brought me sanity most days, but on the bad days when I was unable to focus on work, the pain became almost unbearable. Breathing felt like a choice I was forced to make. The emptiness inside me was an endless cavern, dark and cold.

One night as I was rocking Hayley to sleep, my tears escaped without warning. Hayley's soft, warm hand reached up and rested on my cheek. Choking back a sob, I held the small hand in mine and kissed it through the tears. I had no idea how we were going to get through this when every day was a struggle to want to wake up in the morning to an empty bed and daily reminders of the life that would never be.

What I did know was that the sleeping beauty in my arms, the little girl with her daddy's green eyes, was all the motivation I needed to take the next step and walk through to the next day.

30

JESS

Exactly fourteen days after my world began to implode, I was awakened by a loud knock on the door. I had fallen asleep on the couch after Marí had taken Hayley and Sadie out for ice cream. The days felt longer and the nights shorter as I was constantly battling my mind for sleep. Wiping the drool from my face, I dragged myself from the couch as the knock on the door turned to pounding.

"I'm coming!" I growled.

Outside the door was a man dressed in a nondescript uniform holding a box wrapped in brown paper. "Jess Carsen?" The man seemed hurried.

"Yes."

He pushed a clipboard and pen toward me. "Sign this." His mannerisms were rigid, and his face gave away nothing.

I stared at the clipboard for several seconds as though it was a foreign object in my hand before scribbling my signature on the page.

"Here," he said quickly and shoved the box at me.

I had barely taken hold of it before he was back in his black, unmarked Mercedes Sprinter van and was pulling away before I had turned to walk inside.

As I stared at the box then at the van growing smaller in the distance, the shock eventually wore off, and I carried the package inside. There was no address on the box. Just a thick envelope taped to the top with my name written in a familiar block lettering. JESS.

My heart skipped several beats as I set the box on the couch and pulled the envelope from its tape. Holding the envelope in one hand, I traced the letters on its front with the other.

My hands shook as I gently unsealed the flap and removed its contents. The sight of the familiar handwriting left a tightness in my chest. The words were there, but I could only focus on the page itself. I knew once I read the content, I'd be driven to another level of grief I wasn't sure I was ready to face. The longer I lingered, the harder it was to ignore the words.

My dearest most precious Jess,

This is the hardest thing I have ever done in my entire life. The reasons I'm doing it will most likely make little sense to you as you read these words. My hope is that one day, you will find comfort and peace in knowing that my reasons were good.

If you are reading this, it means that something has happened to me. I hope that it was not overly traumatic. My heart aches at the thought of you suffering in any way. At the time of my writing this letter, you and I are working to rediscover the passion for one another that at one time consumed us.

I feel the need to once again tell you how deeply and truly sorry I am that I ever put us in the situation to need to do such a thing. I got caught up in what almost became an unsolvable puzzle. It drove me to the brink of losing everything. Even now as I think about what it almost cost me, and what it did cost me, I am overwhelmed to the point of being paralyzed by my emotions. You have been my everything since the night we met. I vowed to love and protect you and your heart forever. And knowing that at some point I failed to keep that promise threatens to end me right here and now.

But I can't let that happen because I am on a mission to set right the wrongs of some very bad people. And if I succeed, even in my death I will have protected so many more. I think you would agree it's a good cause.

The box that is now in your possession is very important. Its delivery was part of a strategy I had in place in case something happened to me and I could no longer pursue my mission. Inside, you will find mountains of evidence that should lead to the last pieces of the puzzle I have been working on. Chances are good that you might find answers to questions you didn't know you had until now. I pray that they bring healing and not more heartache.

Because of this box, my life was in jeopardy. If I thought you or Hayley would be in danger because of it, I never would have sent it to you. But I truly believe that the people I've been working to stop are convinced they have won. I know for a fact they have not.

There are only two people in my entire life I would trust with any of this. You and Cal. I know this is going to sound impractical and maybe a little crazy, but I need you to finish what I started. I wouldn't ask you to do this if I didn't think it was important. It could be a matter of saving the world.

Jess, if you can find the strength within you, I need you to trust me. What I am going to ask of you will be one of the hardest things you have ever done. I know this. For now, I want you to close your eyes and remember the trip we took together and the memories we made. Think about the joy and the peace we found with each other in front of that fireplace. I promised we would go back, and I now realize we will most likely never have that chance. I'm so sorry for breaking another promise to you. But I want you to go back and show Hayley. I think she would love it.

I know that apologizing again won't change anything, but I truly am sorry for the heartache I caused you and our family. I love you, Jess. I love you more than words would ever be able to convey. If I could go back and change anything aside from the obvious, it would be to love you better, hold you longer, kiss you more slowly, and savor every minute ever spent with you more deeply. The thought of you and protecting you keeps me moving forward every day. Please know that I will always love you, no matter what.

Yours Always,

Bryan

I read and reread the letter allowing the fresh waves of grief crash over me every time, each one bringing about more tears I didn't know I had. And I cried until there were no tears left. When the last tear had been dried, I slid the piece of paper back into its envelope and held it to my heart.

God, I'm not going to pretend with you because you already know. This hurts and I hate it. I feel like one minute I'm going to be okay and the next I'm struggling to breathe. I need you like I've never needed you before. Help me to make sense of everything because right now I feel lost. Give me wisdom. Thank you for the time I had with Bryan. I'm thankful that if I can't have him here with me that he is there with you. Part of me is jealous while the other part knows I need to be here for Hayley. Help me. I'm begging you.

The sound of a car door startled me to alertness. Marí was back with the girls. Grabbing the box, I ran upstairs and hid it in my closet behind a suitcase. I was back downstairs in time to see the door open and my precious girl chatting away with Sadie.

"Mama!" The sweet-faced toddler squealed as our eyes met.

"Hey, baby girl! Did you eat all the ice cream?"

Hayley giggled and kept chattering, insisting on getting down to go play.

"Did you get any rest? We stayed out as long as we could, but I think Little Bit there is going to crash soon from the sugar. I thought it might be a good time to come back home."

I wrapped Marí in a hug trying to communicate how grateful I was for her. "Yes, I did rest, thank you. Marí, I don't know what I would have done without you. Not just these last two weeks but for all these months. You are remarkable, and I owe you more than I could ever repay."

Marí waved her arm as though to brush me off. "Jess, when God tells you to do something, you do it without any expectation of thanks or payment. That you have provided payment at all is simply a blessing from God for my obedience."

I didn't know how to respond. I wanted that kind of faith. I wanted to be able to let go of whatever might be holding me back and grab ahold of anything God handed me, no questions asked.

"Marí, I don't know what the future holds for me. And I won't pretend to know God's will for you. I don't even know God's will for myself, right now. I do know that it would mean the world to me if you and Sadie would come live with us. That is, if you wanted to. I know that you call your neighborhood your mission field. But I can move my office to my bedroom upstairs and—"

Marí put her hand up, and I immediately stopped talking. The woman stood with her hand up and eyes closed for several minutes. I was left standing in place and staring around the room, unsure of what was happening. When I started to speak, Marí flicked her hand toward me, so I remained quiet. Finally, she opened her eyes and smiled broadly.

"I would be honored to make this my home. Though I need to tell you God has told me it will not be my home for long. I don't know what that means, but he will allow us more time together right now, and for that I am grateful."

A confused laugh tinged with tears of relief escaped me as I hugged my Dominican angel once again.

THAT NIGHT I sat on my bed with the brown-paper wrapped box in front of me. A feeling of dread mingled with anxiety began to fizz inside me as I slowly tore the paper away and tossed it to the other side of the bed. Pausing to consider the repercussions of my next action, I wondered if I was about to open Pandora's box. With a heavy sigh, I lifted the lid from the plain white banker's box. Inside was a stack of manila folders and envelopes with labels that meant nothing to me. It was no different from something that would be found in any office on any given day. My eyes landed on an envelope labeled Start Here.

Emptying the envelope's contents onto the bed, I discovered

another handwritten letter and a USB thumb drive. I immediately grabbed the letter in hopes of another message from Bryan.

Jess, I love you. I hope you have never questioned that.

Now, an explanation, sort of. This box is the culmination of over a year's worth of work. When I came home from those two weeks in Atlanta, and after marrying the most beautiful woman in the world, I was slated to start working on a project that remains classified. Suffice it to say, there is technology that has been created that could cause a lot of problems in a lot of places if the wrong people gained access to it.

About two years into the project, some global anomalies were brought to my attention that I attempted to address myself. I monitored as many applications as I could until I believed that these were not flukes of human error. The problem was that our NIDS wasn't sending out alerts to the operators. I know some of this jargon is foreign to you right now, but I'm hoping that you can make enough sense of it.

Long story short, someone has been making some very diligent efforts to access some very sensitive information. I am 99% sure I know who and I know how. Unfortunately, they know that I know. And now everything I know is in your hands. If you can think of a single person you can trust to help you work through this box and what I have told you, I want you to reach out to them as soon as you feel comfortable doing so. This really is a matter of national and maybe global security.

I also want you to consider selling the house and moving to Kentucky with Cal. I know this sounds extreme, and I don't believe you are in imminent danger. However, I know you would be safe with Cal. Pray about it, please. If you are to this point, then we both know that my opinion no longer matters in the grand scheme of things. I have sent Cal a letter just as this box arrived to you. He'll be expecting you if you decide to go.

Three final things. One, there is a phone and multiple prepaid cards in the box. Only use this phone to make any contact concerning the contents of this box. And when you use it, do so in a public place.

Two, only trust who you need to. Be sure they can be trusted with your life and Hayley's. I know this is not something you need to be reminded of considering the number of bad guys you've helped put away but be careful.

Three, destroy this letter after you have read it. There are names and information that no one else needs to know exist.

Jess, I said it before and I will say it, again—I love you. You are the most extraordinary human being on the planet. I hope you will one day forgive me for plunging your life into such uncertainty. It was never my intent. Stay safe. I love you, no matter what.

Bryan

He was joking. He had to be joking. Because what he was asking me to do sounded insane. I read it, again, trying to imagine how he might have felt as he wrote this letter. I closed my eyes, and his smiling face swam into view. *Warm. Kind. Confident.* A shaky breath left me as I opened my eyes and traced his name at the end of the letter.

I read it at least twenty times before going to the closet and finding a pair of scissors in a sewing kit. I cut out the first line of the letter and set it on my nightstand. *Jess, I love you.* Then I went to the bathroom, opened a drawer where I kept a lighter for candles, read the letter one more time, then lit the corner of the paper, set it in the sink, and watched the remaining words burn away.

As I watched the paper turn brown and break into smaller blackened pieces, I wondered if I really had to do this. I could burn everything in the box, and no one would know. There would be zero danger in that.

But Bryan had called it a matter of global security. What did I know about global security? My job was to analyze people based on their facial expressions and body language, not bring down an evil conglomerate. But if Bryan had died protecting the information in the box, it had to be important.

"No pressure, huh?" I thought out loud.

Sitting back down on the edge of the bed, I noticed the thumb drive. My laptop was downstairs. Marí, who had insisted on staying the night even though I hadn't finished moving my office upstairs, was asleep on the sofa in the living room. Creeping slowly and quietly, I painstakingly made my way to the office and grabbed the computer and its charger.

Back upstairs, I quickly plugged in the drive and a box opened that contained one video file. When I opened the file, I had to cover my mouth to stifle a scream. On the screen was Bryan's handsome face, and I was immediately entranced by two dark-green eyes.

After several moments I remembered it was a video and clicked Play. At the sound of his voice, I melted into a puddle of tears and snot. I hadn't ugly cried like this since the day of the funeral.

"I love you, Jess. I'm so sorry that I'm not there to tell you in person. My love for you has never wavered. I may not have always shown you or told you, but my love for you has burned inside of me since the instant our eyes met. I can't imagine what the coming days will look like for you and Hayley as you navigate the unthinkable. I want you to know that I have and will always trust your judgment. You are one of the wisest people I have ever met. I'm sorry that things have not gone the way we planned. We had so many plans. I hope you will continue to make plans and live out some of our dreams. Jess, I know it isn't much comfort right now, but no matter what happens, I have loved you and will love you until the day I die."

At his last few words, Bryan's voice cracked and then the video ended. I watched it on repeat for over an hour until I fell asleep to his voice next to me.

31

JESS

The next morning, I woke up feeling as though I had been run over by a steamroller and my head had been stuffed with cotton. It wasn't until I saw the computer with its black screen on the bed next to me that I remembered the video, the letters, and the box. I was instantly jolted awake, and a surge of adrenaline made quick work of the heaviness with which I had awakened.

After throwing on my running clothes and shoes, I rummaged through the box and found the disposable cell phone and a prepaid card and shoved them in my jacket pocket. Placing the box back in the closet in its hiding place, I quietly tiptoed downstairs in case Marí was not yet awake.

It was 5:30 a.m. And much to my surprise, Marí was already up and sitting at the dining table with her Bible open and her eyes closed. She must have heard me; her eyes popped open, and she smiled.

"I'm sorry if I interrupted you. I need to go for a run and clear my head. I should be back before Hayley wakes up."

Marí nodded without speaking and closed her eyes again.

I grabbed my keys and took my ID and a business card from the wallet in my purse and headed for the car. Sitting behind the wheel of the car, I mentally flipped through all the places Bryan and I would go running. Those mornings pre-Hayley, we would wake up and wordlessly dress and set out together early in the mornings before our hectic schedules would send us separate ways.

As I let my mind wander, I remembered the last half mile we would always spend holding hands and walking back to the car, the post-run showers together, the lingering kisses in the doorway before Bryan would leave for the office. My heart ached as I fought back the tears.

Unable to bring myself to run our favorite trail, I headed for my old familiar trail at George Washington. Before getting out of the car, I loaded the phone with the card and zipped it into one of the jacket pockets then tucked my ID, the business card, and car key in the other pocket. After a few minutes of stretching, I headed for the trail.

It had been a year since I had run any distance. There had been little energy or time in excess lately. Thankfully, my feet found their rhythm, and while it was slower than my usual pace, I felt my mind begin to clear.

Four miles later, I was back at the car. Grabbing my bottle of water, I took a slow cool down walk toward one of the large cherry blossom trees along the path. It was still early so there were few people milling about but I inventoried the area anyway to make sure I was alone. I pulled out the card and made a phone call.

"Collins," the sleepy voice answered.

"Mark? Oh no, did I wake you? I'm so—"

He cut me off. "Jess?" The tired gravelly sound left his voice.

"Yeah, hey, sorry, I did not mean to wake you."

"No, don't worry about it. It was a late night and…" There was a pause. "Listen, Jess, I was really sorry to hear about Bryan. I wanted to be there at the funeral but, uh, I was in LA for a case."

I hated this part of every conversation. "Thank you," was all I could come up with as a reply.

There was a long silence.

"If you're making calls this early, something must be up."

I should have made a better plan other than *grab the card, go for a run, call Mark*. In hindsight, it seemed lacking.

"So, do you remember that favor you said you'd owe me a couple of years ago?"

"Sure."

"I need to call it in. And it might be a big one. But I can't talk about it here. Can I come by your office later?"

"How early can you be there?"

Hayley woke up crying. I heard her as I was walking by her room to mine once I had gotten back from my run. Tiptoeing around Sadie who was on a pallet on the floor, I scooped Hayley up and took her with me to my room.

Even though I was still damp with sweat, Hayley nestled down on my chest.

"Mommy, where's Daddy?" Her voice was sad and sleepy.

I had to take several deep breaths before I could answer.

"Sweet baby, Daddy isn't here, remember? He's in heaven with Jesus."

At two years old, I knew she didn't comprehend the concept of death and its permanency. I did not, however, doubt her sadness over Bryan's absence. They'd had routines and activities they had claimed for their own. Saturday mornings they would spend on the couch watching television and singing along with the brightly colored characters on the screen. Sunday afternoons were for playing in our tiny backyard, which involved many piggyback rides and squeals. While Hayley was too young to put words to her feelings, she was fully feeling all of them.

Hayley sniffled against my neck and sobbed. This was my undoing. We sat on the floor next to the bed where I rocked and cried with my little girl. We were both desperately missing the same man whom we both loved dearly.

Hayley stilled, her breathing deepening. She had fallen back asleep. I enjoyed the moment a little longer before I attempted to stand back up to take Hayley to her bed. After a few awkward shimmies and stretches, I was successful.

Once Hayley was tucked back in, I went downstairs to give Marí an update on my day's schedule.

"I should be back by noon, and then I have a meeting every hour until four-thirty. If you'd like, I can take care of dinner when I'm done with my last call."

Marí waved her hand. "I will take care of it."

With the plans for the day in place, I gave Marí a tight squeeze before she pushed me away making a face at me. "Go shower. You smell like a sweaty monkey."

This made me laugh, which sounded foreign to my own ears. I thought I saw tears in Marí's eyes before I jogged upstairs to get a shower.

IN THE PARKING lot of the J. Edgar Hoover Building, I wrapped up a call with Dr. Thorne and made a mental note to stop by the university to meet him and a few of the new interns after I left Mark's office. I grabbed the box from the backseat and carried it inside.

Mark shot up out of his seat in the lobby atrium and intercepted me as I scanned my consultant ID badge.

"Jess!" His hand raised in a wave. "Can I take that for you?" He gestured toward the box.

I hesitated before catching a glimpse of Mark's face.

Nervous. Curiosity. Eagerness. Reserved.

Handing him the box, I repositioned my bag on my shoulder. "Sure, thanks. And thank you for meeting with me this morning. I know you're busy."

He gave a polite smile. "I was glad you called."

We rode the elevator in silence before I followed him through a glass-laden hallway of offices. Some were occupied with people already busy working while others were like glass cases of solitude with little to no movement inside.

I was pulled from my observations when Mark stopped in front of me and opened a glass door he held open so I could enter the room. Once I was in front of a chair across from the pristinely organized desk, Mark closed the door and set the white box in the chair next to me.

He pulled the blinds on all the windows and door for privacy, stopping abruptly and looking in my direction. "I assumed since you didn't want to talk about anything over the phone and it sounded urgent, I thought maybe—" He gestured to the blinds.

I nodded. "I think privacy is good. Thanks."

He finished and sat at his desk, looking flustered. His hands fidgeted with the edge, his eyes flitting back and forth between me and the box.

I mostly stared at the box.

"Want to tell me about this favor I owe you?" Mark's words brought my attention to him.

I took a deep breath before delving into it. For the next twenty minutes, I talked and Mark listened. He tried to keep his face as neutral as he could, but there were moments where his mask slipped.

Shock. Alarm. Apprehension.

"Bryan was very specific that whatever was in this box needed to be known by as few people as possible. I don't understand half of what's in it. I need help, but I also only trust very few people. And you are one of them. And you are the only one who would most likely have the resources needed to make sense of all of this."

Mark tried to keep his face unreadable, but a blush crept up his neck. "I'm glad you feel you can trust me. You can trust me, and I will help any way I can."

There was a momentary silence as we studied one another.

Mark cleared his throat then motioned to the box. "Where do we start?"

Standing, I moved the box to Mark's desk. "I don't even know. I'm sure there is a rhyme or reason to how the box is arranged but to be honest, I didn't make it very far into it." My voice cracked, and tears welled in my eyes as I thought about the video I had fallen asleep listening to the night before and again when I woke up this morning.

Mark stood and grabbed a box of tissues from the filing cabinet behind him and handed them to me.

With a slight shake of my head, I sniffed away the tears and gathered myself. "I'm fine. Sorry. Thank you."

"Okay. Well, do you want to start on it now or...?" He trailed off looking to me for answers.

I checked my watch before answering. "My schedule is clear for about another half hour. That probably isn't enough time to dive too deeply into anything, is it?"

He tapped the small calendar on his desk with the day's schedule scribbled on it. "Geez. Today is slammed," Mark seemed to be talking to himself. "Any chance you're free after work? I can be wrapped up and free by seven. I'd hate for you to have to drive back down here, but it's probably the most secure place to talk about things of this nature," Mark suggested.

"Okay, sure. I'll be back at seven. And if you find time before that to get started, feel free to do so without me. Who knows? Maybe you'll have it figured out before I get back." I tried to sound positive.

With another glance at my watch, I ran my fingers through my hair. "I need to head to the university and meet with Dr. Thorne. I know you two talk, but I'm not ready to loop him in on any of this, so, if you do talk to him, maybe don't mention this?" I gestured at the box.

"You got it."

Sincerity. Warmth.

Back in the atrium, Mark stood with his hands in his pockets as we parted ways. "I'll see you tonight, then."

"I'll be here."

32

MARK

The white box stared back at me as I stood behind my desk. It was a stark contrast in the space typically void of any personal effects. This box, while insignificant in appearance, was highly personal. Though I had yet to open it and determine the significance of its content, I was not oblivious to the magnitude of its presence. Jess had come to me for help. She trusted me.

I reached toward the box and slid it to the edge of the desk, my hands resting on its top. My thoughts kept jumping from the box to Jess. Her brown eyes were still just as sure of themselves as they were when she was staring a person down to pull the truth from them. I knew she didn't mean to let her mask slip, but I saw the vulnerability in them when she was in my office. To anyone else she would have seemed serious and focused during our meeting. But I saw through it. I knew her. The sadness seemed to cloud her naturally sunny personality.

The first time I met her, I was a raging skeptic. Her long-time mentor turned business partner, Dr. Thorne, had relentlessly talked up a potential asset for the FBI in the form of a young woman who was capable of "cutting through the crap" as he put it. When he finally convinced me that I should at least meet the woman he had come to hold in such high regard, I walked into the office expecting some kind of circus performer.

Instead, I came face to face with a set of piercing dark-brown eyes I would have sworn saw directly into my soul. I was shaken, and it had taken every ounce of fortitude I could muster to steady myself, locking into place what I thought had been an impassive front. I had been wrong, of course, and she had seen right through it.

I left her office that day conflicted professionally and personally. Personally, I didn't care if she sat behind a crystal ball and wore a turban on her head. Jess had gotten my attention before I made it across the office in which I met her. She was confident and beautiful, and her smile sent a jolt of something hot through my core. When I'd agreed with Dr. Thorne to meet with Jess, it was more out of courtesy than expectation. Once I met her, I knew I couldn't leave that office without another reason to see her again.

Professionally, however, how was I supposed to admit that there was someone naturally capable of doing the things I'd spent years learning to do? What would my colleagues think if I even suggested considering the possibilities?

That's when the idea of a test case hit me. I'd been struggling with a case for several weeks that hadn't set right with me from the beginning. It was a high-profile case, and I hated those because the expectations were compounded by public opinion, which always complicated things. An extra set of eyes was never a bad thing, so I suggested Jess take a look, and if she could offer insight, then I would be grateful. If she couldn't, I wasn't out anything and I still had an inroad with her, which meant maybe I had a chance.

What I had not expected was the speed and accuracy with which Jess performed. Overnight, my weeks of investigations and analysis had been condensed into a single short email. I also had not expected the next day's revelation that she was not single, as I had hoped. My ego took an even bigger hit a few weeks later when Dr. Thorne inadvertently disclosed Jess was married. I'd asked her out and taken the rejection, but at his revelation, I found myself regretting my choice.

All I could do was hope I hadn't hindered the chance Jess would agree to work with the FBI in the future.

Fortunately, my pursuit and her rebuff were never mentioned and had no impact on her decision to accept the offer to become one of the FBI's most sought-after consultants. Her abilities were quickly recognized and widely coveted, which required new channels of operation to be opened. Jess and Dr. Thorne established their own consulting firm, and I gladly volunteered to be the liaison between their enterprise and the FBI.

Over the next year and a half, my admiration and respect for Jess grew as we worked together. She was always warm and friendly to everyone, regardless of their position at the agency. The days she came into the office, people were naturally drawn to her, and she was always welcoming. Sometimes I wondered if it was because she could truly see them, and she still received them as equals. I know that's one of the many reasons I found myself wanting to be around her.

Jess and I never associated with one another outside of work. Through our work, however, we became acquainted with one another's personal lives as is the natural progression of working closely together. Though I never met them, I knew her husband, Bryan, was a cybersecurity specialist for the Army and their daughter, Hayley, was two. I also knew that after Hayley had been born, there were some struggles in their family that had required Jess to pull back from work for a while. She was always careful to keep the details private, but it was regularly obvious she was stressed more often than she was not.

My life was far less notable than hers, but she was repeatedly offering up encouragement and asking about my personal life. She made it a point to ask every Friday about my weekend plans and making alternative suggestions after I had casually mentioned on a random Friday that I'd be spending the weekend barhopping. She lived by different rules than I did, which was not a bad thing. In fact, her drawing attention to my lack of intentional connections with people made me reconsider parts of my existence. Unfortunately, old habits died hard, and I regularly found myself in a revolving door of extremely short-term connections.

Even with our differences, I considered us more than just close acquaintances, though I was not the kind of guy to make friends with married women. I had principles. Some lines just didn't get crossed. When I learned Bryan had been killed, I'd been across the country working through some leads on a case. I'd called Jess and she hadn't answered, which had not surprised me.

According to Dr. Thorne, she was back at work almost immediately after the funeral, though she was not making plans to be in the office any time soon. Even as I considered Jess to be a friend, I was in unfamiliar territory. Part of me had wanted to push for her to answer my call, while the other part of me said I needed to let her move at her own pace. I was thankful for the distraction of work that forced the latter. When she called with the sound of desperation in her voice, I was more than ready and willing to be available.

Still staring at the box, I took in a deep breath and lifted its lid, setting it to the side. Inside, it was stacked with manila files and envelopes neatly organized. Removing the folder from the top of the stack, I flipped it open and scanned the page. The first page read like a table of contents. Flipping to the next one, it was a glossary of terms that went on for several pages. An investigation summary report followed the index. I didn't know Bryan, but I liked his style. It was organized and thorough.

My desk phone rang before I could make it through the report. After hanging up, I closed the folder and put it back into the box and placed the lid back on top. Not wanting to leave the box out in the open, I scrambled for a place to store the box. I settled on putting it inside an empty cabinet that locked. If a man had been killed over what was in this box, it seemed like it might be worth protecting. I dislodged the keys from the cabinet and wound them onto my keyring before heading to my first meeting of the day.

My mind was full, preoccupied with thoughts of Jess and the box for most of the day. I was sitting in an office almost identical to my own not hearing the man's voice directly in front of me.

"Collins, hey! Where'd you go?" My partner, Washburn, was snapping in my face.

I was jerked back to the present. "Sorry. Say that again."

"You alright? Something bothering you?" Washburn was sixty-three and counting down his days to retirement. But he hadn't lost his drive and ability to focus when there was a job to do.

"No, sorry. I was at the office until one this morning working through the Brink's file, and then I was here again, early. Probably should have just slept here. Anyway, I think we've got him. Just need to check on a few loose ends. What were you asking?"

Washburn shook his head. "You young guys think you don't need sleep. But you gotta take care of yourself. That's how you stay sharp. I was asking you about the Brink's case. But if you're onto something, run with it. I'm going to make a few phone calls, and then I'm out the rest of the day."

With a nod, I picked up the folder on the desk in front of me and walked out of the office.

33

JESS

Marí was folding towels and singing passionately in Spanish when I walked in the door. She didn't stop singing and just waved and winked. The scene made me smile. I didn't speak Spanish, but Bryan had. I remembered being surprised the first time I'd heard him do it. It was the night he had proposed after we had only known each other for two weeks. I'd also been shocked to learn he spoke Russian, Mandarin, and some Arabic.

One of the things I loved about Bryan was he was an actual genius, but he never flaunted it. Had he wanted to master fourteen languages, he could have, and it would have taken no time at all. Instead, he only focused his energies where he thought they would be most useful. The smile faded to sadness the more I thought about it. Bryan's focused energy ended up physically costing him his life and emotionally costing me everything.

When I didn't move from the spot where I had stopped to place my bag on the table, Marí stopped singing and turned to see what was happening. She either sensed or saw something that caused her to leave her place on the couch. Walking me back to the place she had been sitting Marí asked, "What is it? What has taken you from smiling to this sad face?"

There was no point trying to restore the smile as it wouldn't come. "I was just thinking about Bryan. Your singing, which is beautiful, by the way, reminded me of Bryan speaking different languages, and it spiraled to much darker places. It happens a lot, actually. I will feel like I'm finally floating on calm waters into the sunshine, and then all of a sudden, I'm being sucked under by these dark rapids. And then I have to hang on for dear life, because I can't find my life jacket. It's mentally and emotionally exhausting, and I'm scared that I will never escape the rapids." My voice wavered as I spoke the last sentence.

Marí patted my leg. "You can and you will escape the rapids. And your life jacket is Jesus. He can never be taken off or lost." She gave a heavy sigh and stared out a window behind me. "When I moved here a long time ago, I had my husband and my infant daughter. That was all I had. We were offered a chance to make a new life, so we took it. At first, it felt like a fairytale. There was more money, and we made friends, and we were happy.

"When my daughter was fifteen, a group of local gang members attacked her when she was taking out the trash. They did terrible things to her." This time, Marí's voice wavered with emotions. Her gaze dropped to the floor as her haunted memories flickered across her face.

My breath caught as my hand gripped my chest.

"We had known there were gang members in the area, but they had left us alone until then. They began to harass my husband at his store, and they broke windows too many times to count. My husband tried to keep it under control himself. He thought he was protecting us.

"One night after he had locked up and was packing up the money for the deposit, these boys, they were children, broke the glass door and attacked Ernesto in his office. They beat him until he was unrecognizable and took all of the money for the deposit. My sweet Ernesto never regained consciousness."

My hand found Marí's. "I had no idea."

"I do not tell you this to make you feel sorry for me. I could tell you more that would break your heart into millions of pieces, but you already know what that is like. I tell you this, Jess, because I have been in those rapids myself. I have felt like I would never be able to come up for air. But I am here today to tell you that if you are wearing that life jacket, you will not drown. Do you hear me?

"The Lord tells you and he tells me in Isaiah chapter forty-three verse two, *When you pass through the waters, I will be with you; and through the rivers, they shall not overwhelm you; when you walk through fire you shall not be burned, and the flame shall not consume you.* He did not say there would be no water or fire. He said when there is, he is there, and you will live. I had to cling to this verse for many months when it felt like there was no way through. Now you must do the same. Because if he says that he will take you through, that means there is another side where there is no water. Do you see?"

Tears were pouring from my eyes. I could only nod my response as I reached across and hugged my friend tightly until Marí let go and moved me away.

"Now, that's enough of that. You need to eat. Go dry your face, I will go get the girls, and we will eat lunch together."

Later as we cleared the dishes, I told Marí about my meeting scheduled with Mark for that evening.

Marí raised an eyebrow. "After hours?"

"It's not an official case so we had to plan it around both of our schedules."

Marí pressed her lips together as though she was thinking. "Pastor John and Deborah are coming for dinner this evening," she said.

"Oh, I thought dinner tonight was just the four of us." I stopped drying the plate in my hand and looked at Marí.

"Don't worry about it. I have it covered. I thought it would be nice for them to see Hayley and you, of course."

I don't know why this irritated me, but it did. Being social had been so far down my list of things I wanted to do and now I had this pressing matter looming over me. It felt like another rug being pulled out from under my feet.

Trying not to sound upset, I forced my tone to sound calm. "I wouldn't have made plans to work late if I had known they were coming."

"They wanted to come by and check on you, and I offered to feed them. They will understand. Besides, you know they love to spoil Hayley like their own, and they are so good to Sadie too."

With a frustrated huff, I studied my watch. "Okay, what time will they be here?"

"Five-thirty. I promise to have everything taken care of. Now, get back to work. You have a busy schedule."

She was right. My afternoon was the fullest it had been in a while. When I ended my last call at five, my head was pounding, I massaged my temples before making my last notes and calling it a day.

At the top of the stairs, I could hear multiple voices coming from below including Hayley's giggle in the entryway. I really thought I would have to fake a smile, but the sight of these people in my home, loving on my daughter, brought a real smile to my face. As soon as I was down the last step, I was enveloped in a full group hug. I told myself I was not going to cry, but I didn't listen to myself.

Marí had made the right call, and I owed her an apology. The food was delicious, and the company was more than I could have hoped for after a long day.

Deborah noticed me checking my watch for the third time. "Marí told us you had a meeting this evening. Do you think John and I could steal a few minutes with you alone before you go?"

With a wave of her hand, Marí motioned us away. "I will take care of them. You go talk." She stood and shooed the little girls up the stairs for baths.

John and Deborah sat on the couch while I sat on the edge of the armchair. They silently communicated with each other for several moments before John spoke. "Jess," he paused, again.

My nerves tingled.

Sadness. Regret. Uncertainty.

"Jess, Bryan sent us a letter. It was a very nice letter, and one or both of us read it every day. You know he was as much as a son to us as one we might have raised, and we hope you know that we love you as we would love our own daughter had we had one."

Every eye in the room was welling with tears.

He swallowed hard and cleared his throat before continuing. "He left a lot of things without explanation, and that's okay. We don't need one. We have always trusted him and his judgments completely. He did make it very clear he thought it would be in your best interest for you and Hayley to make a move elsewhere. Bryan loved you more than his own life, and from what I read between several lines of his letter, his life was given to preserve yours and Hayley's and many more. We wanted to tell you face to face we will support you and help you do whatever you need to do, regardless of the decision you make to stay or go. We also wanted to encourage you to pray about it and trust Bryan had done the same. If he thought you going somewhere else was the best choice, it wasn't something he came up with impulsively."

My ragged breathing threatened to unsteady me. I stared at the floor and took several deep breaths slowly. When I raised my eyes to meet theirs, my tears were not the only ones to escape.

"I can't imagine leaving. This house, you two, our church family, any of it. It's home. The two of you, Marí and Sadie, and Hayley are the only family I have."

Deborah smiled through her tears. "Jess," she whispered, though her voice grew stronger as she spoke. "Distance won't change that. We will always be here for you and Hayley. Christmases, birthdays, graduation, all of it. We'll be there, or you can come here. And apparently, my phone will make calls with videos, which is almost as good as being together."

This made me laugh.

John said, "We want you and Hayley taken care of. Your safety and well-being were Bryan's priority, and now they're ours."

As I considered the wonderful people sitting across from me, I realized Deborah was right. A lot of families lived far apart but were still close. I had lived across the country from my own mother when I was in college. I released a breath I didn't realize I had been holding and glanced at my watch.

John stood first. "We know you have somewhere you need to be, so don't let us keep you. Pray about it, Jess. We're praying for you and for Hayley. Change is rarely easy, but sometimes it's necessary."

The three of us embraced for several minutes. The warmth felt like a soft cocoon where I wanted to stay indefinitely.

"Thank you, both. You mean the world to me, and I know Bryan loved you both so much. And you are the best grandparents to Hayley. I'll go tell Marí I'm leaving for the evening. You should stay for dessert. I don't know what it is, but you know if she made it, you definitely want to stay for it."

34

MARK

The building was empty, and the ticking of the large clock on the wall echoed off the walls. Jess scanned her ID and walked in my direction. Her smile was forced. Her eyes were empty and held dark circles under them. She looked tired and defeated. This was not the same woman I'd come to know over the years.

"You survived your full schedule, I see." Jess's voice sounded strained.

"Yeah, closed a case, even. I'd say it was a success."

"Nice."

The elevator door opened. Once inside, we rode upwards in silence.

Unsure of what to say, if anything, I let the silence settle between us as I watched her. Jess stared at the floor appearing lost in her own thoughts. The elevator's loud *ding,* indicating we had arrived at our floor, was the only sound to penetrate the quiet.

In my office, I unlocked the cabinet in which I had stored the box and walked it to the desk.

"Did you have a chance to look at any of it?" she asked.

Shaking my head, I set the box to one side of the desk and

removed its lid. "I pulled out the folder on top and flipped through it. If everything is as clear and thorough as the first ten pages, things might just fall into place that much easier."

"That sounds about right." Her tone was distant and her face somber. Her eyes roamed around the room seeming to take in the blank walls and empty surfaces as though she had never seen them before, when in reality she had been in this same office dozens of times.

When she noticed I was holding one of the folders in my hand, her eyes locked with mine. In that moment my lungs felt like they had permanently sealed off, and the heart in my chest was on the verge of leaving my body. This feeling was new, and I wasn't sure what it meant.

"Does it tell us where to start?" She didn't indicate whether she had read.

I cleared my throat, needing the moment to force myself to breathe. "Not sure. He wrote this like he knew someone who understood investigation reports would read it. That helps. The glossary of terms is nice. I can use a computer to send email, that really is the extent of my computer abilities. But if I'm reading this right, he stumbled onto some pretty big stuff way above my paygrade."

She reached across the desk for the folder, and I relinquished it. After several silent beats, she said, "Drones that can be controlled remotely to deliver EMPs? That sounds like something from a sci-fi novel."

Taking back the folder, I closed it and placed it face down on the desk. Pulling the next folder from the box I said, "I have a feeling that Bryan started risking a lot before recent events took place. He could have been imprisoned just for taking this information outside of his office." Realizing what I was saying, I stopped talking. My face heated at the unfiltered thoughts I said aloud. "I'm sorry. I should not... I... Sorry." My gut twisted with mortification.

Her smile, though sad, was reassuring. "Hey, it's okay. Really. I hadn't thought of that. Which makes this something even bigger than I thought before now."

Fully removing the stack of manila envelopes and folders revealed an ivory envelope taped to the bottom of the box. On the front in block letters was written SPECIAL AGENT MARK COLLINS. Trying not to draw attention to the inside of the box, I moved the box to the floor next to my chair and placed the lid on top.

"I think we should make sure nothing was shuffled about in transport or is missing by comparing the contents list with the actual contents before we dive in completely. What do you think?"

Jess shrugged. "I defer to you. I feel so lost in all of this. Lead the way."

We spent two hours comparing the list to the contents. When she had gone silent, I looked up to see Jess pressing her fingers into her eyes.

I checked my watch then rubbed a hand over the back of my neck. "It's been a long day. We can pick this up later if you want," I suggested.

Jess's expression was torn. "Are you sure? I feel like we barely accomplished anything."

I gave her a knowing smile. "These things take time. It's not like on TV where the case is solved, the bad guys are put away, and the day is saved by the roguish FBI agent in forty minutes."

This got a small laugh from Jess, which bolstered my spirit.

"Yeah, I know. It just feels like we're trudging through knee-deep mud heading for more mud." She tossed the list in her hands onto the desk.

"Sometimes it starts out that way. I think Bryan left us plenty to work with; we just need to figure out what it means. It's possible we're going to have to get some help from outside this room though."

Jess's eyes darted straight to mine. I knew what she was thinking without her saying anything. Bryan had made it clear she couldn't trust just anyone with this. He had been right. I, however, was not fully equipped to work through any of this on my own and neither was Jess.

I put both hands up. "Hey, it's okay. You said you trust me. Did you mean it?"

She watched me. I knew she was reading me, even though there was nothing that would ever indicate she couldn't trust me.

"Yes."

"Then you can trust who I trust. Okay?"

She gave a reluctant nod. "Okay."

I put down the folder I'd been holding and stepped around the desk. "I'll walk you to your car, and then I'll come back and clean this up." After we left the room, I locked the office door behind us.

As soon as I was back in my office, I pulled the attached envelope from inside the box. There was a lead weight in my gut as I opened it.

Mark,

This is hard for me to write for several reasons. For starters, I don't know you and you don't know me. Let's cut through all pretense and understand that everything I have done has had one goal and one single intention —to preserve and protect my family.

I am also writing under the assumption that you are the one Jess has chosen to trust with all of this. The list of people she trusts is shorter than my own. Deductive reasoning led me to you. She spoke highly of you many times and was impressed with your ability to sort through information quickly. As you can see, there is a lot to sort through. I tried to make it as simple as possible, but there are several holes that need to be filled.

Thirdly, thank you for helping Jess. If I hadn't needed to involve her, I wouldn't have. But I need her to understand the magnitude of my decisions. You have no obligation to get involved in any of this, and I understand if you choose to decline. However, I have a feeling that you and I are not different from one another in enough ways to make me believe you would do so. There's a reason Jess trusts you, therefore, I trust you.

Finally, and this is the hardest part for me to write. I am pleading with you as a man who realizes he is on borrowed time. If it is in your power, protect Jess and Hayley at all costs. I can offer no reward nor issue any threats. My appeal to you is as a man and a soldier who would die a thou-

sand deaths if it meant preserving my family. It will be a debt I will never be able to repay, but I would be eternally grateful.

Sincerely,

Bryan Carsen

I scrubbed both hands down my face as I tried to imagine the resolve Bryan had needed to write this letter. He had known what he was doing was dangerous, but he did it anyway. And it wasn't just to protect his family; they had simply been his driving force. I admired the bravery written in every word on the paper in front of me.

Even if Bryan had not appealed directly to me, if Jess had asked, I would have helped, no questions asked. This letter, however, solidified in my mind the urgency and significance of the situation. Lives were at stake. This was not a new concept to me, as protecting innocent lives was part of my job. But this was different. This was bigger than anyone could fathom. And now it was now up to me to see it through while keeping Jess and her daughter safe.

35

JESS

When I walked in the door I tried to move quietly, as it was far later than I had planned to get home and I didn't want to disturb Marí if she had already gone to bed. Marí, however, was on the couch reading her Bible.

As I set my purse on the entry table, I quietly said, "I'm sorry for getting back so late. I hope everything went smoothly for bedtime."

Marí nodded wordlessly, and she motioned for me to come join her in the living room.

After sliding my shoes off at the door, I headed for the armchair where I sat, pulling one leg under me, waiting for Marí to speak.

"I will go with you." She turned to look at me. "Sadie and I will both go with you. Wherever you need to go, we will go with you."

I felt my eyes widen.

Marí continued, "I am not a nosey person. This house is only so big. And remember when I said God told me this would not be my home for long? I believe he meant that I would be going with you wherever you need to go."

In dismay I blurted, "Marí, I can't ask you to do that. I wouldn't. To uproot Sadie, and what about church and the ladies group?"

The debate between staying and leaving had plagued me since

reading the suggestion in Bryan's letter. I told myself if Hayley and I left, we would be alone and giving up the people and places we had grown to love, therefore, staying was the right choice. Then I'd argue with myself that being alone but away from the threat of danger was what mattered most. I hadn't had this conversation with anyone else because I didn't know what I needed or wanted to hear.

When John and Deborah brought it up this evening and they encouraged me to consider leaving town, I was confused and a little hurt. After the conversation I had with Mark about the gravity of Bryan's discoveries, I was teetering closer to the edge of considering the option of leaving town. The number of reasons for leaving were starting to override the reasons to stay, but the weight of leaving my home, my friends, my church, my job kept the scales balanced.

Marí held up her hand to interrupt my protest. "I don't know everything that you know. I don't need to. What matters is that you and Hayley are my family too. The girls are like sisters. And family should be together whenever possible."

How was I supposed to respond to that? I agreed, of course. But Marí was connected to our city and our church and had been a lot longer than I had. The selfish part of me wanted to immediately tell her it was the best idea and load up a moving van first thing in the morning.

Instead, I hesitated because I knew that Marí was a giver, and in this moment, I was ready to be a taker. "Let me pray about it tonight. And if you will ask God to give me a clear answer by tomorrow, I would be grateful."

Marí gave a slow nod of her head and closed her eyes.

Slowly I walked toward the stairs, stopping behind the sofa to place a kiss on the top of Marí's head. "I don't know what I would do without you," I whispered.

In my room, after I readied for bed, I knelt beside my bed and prayed.

God this is the hardest thing I have ever walked through—harder than my dad leaving, my graduating then moving across the country to go to school, my mom dying. None of it was this hard. None of it scared me like this does. This feels so much bigger. And now I've lost the one person I could hold onto for strength. He would have made the right choice. He would have known whether leaving or not was the answer. And now I have to decide. If we move, I will leave behind so many people I care about. My job will be harder.

And Marí wants to go with us? I don't want to be responsible for ruining her life. What if we move and she's upset after we get there? What if Sadie struggles with it? It wouldn't be fair to either of them.

I know I'm rambling, but my heart and mind are jumbled with so many questions and it feels like answers are so far away. All I need is peace and wisdom. You have always been faithful when I have asked for it. I'm begging you to do the same tonight. Please.

When I opened my eyes, I noticed the thumb drive with Bryan's video on my nightstand. My laptop was on the desk I had moved upstairs from the home office where Marí now slept. I brought it to the bed and plugged in the thumb drive before curling up under the covers next to the computer. At the sound of Bryan's voice, hot tears swelled in my eyes.

Staring at the screen, I traced his face with my fingers, missing his warm skin against mine. It never failed that he always had warmth to give, and now all I had was a cold computer screen to connect us. There was a constricting squeeze around my heart. The rapids of emotion began swirling up around me, ready to pull me under. My breathing shallowed. I tried to swallow but it was hard. I squeezed my eyes closed tightly. I was so close to giving in to the darkness.

God, save me from this. Get me to the other side.

The squeeze on my heart loosened, my breathing slowed, my heart steadied its pace. There were still hot tears leaving trails on my face, but there was a calm to go along with it. Closing my eyes, I fell into a sound sleep.

36

JESS

The sky was clear and blue. The air was cool and crisp. There was a cold breeze rustling through the red and golden leaves still hanging onto the tree. There was a smell of a working fireplace somewhere in the distance. The handfuls of dried brown leaves being tossed into the air flew in every direction. Hayley's squeals and giggles rang out, carried on the wind so the neighbors could hear. I struggled to keep my hair out of my face but was fighting a losing battle to the wind, which only made me laugh more.

We chased one another through the leaves until we were both breathless. Dramatically, I collapsed to the ground and rolled to my back, flinging my arm over my head. Hayley did the same. The rosy cheeks and red nose in front of me warmed me through, settling a smile on my face. My beautiful green-eyed girl. She had her daddy's eyes. I saw the same sparkle, the same joy I had grown to love in his eyes.

Sadness tugged at my heart, threatening to steal the moment as thoughts seeped in about the man whose eyes I would never get lost in again.

Then a small, cold hand touched my cheek, pulling my face towards those shimmering eyes. "I love you, Mommy."

A wave of peace flooded through my soul. Breath filled my lungs more deeply than it had in so long. "I love you, my baby girl. Are you ready to go inside and warm up? I think there are cookies."

"Yessss!"

Smiling, I jumped up and pulled Hayley with me, lifting her over my head with a spin before lowering her to my chest. Wrapped in my arms, Hayley rested her head on my shoulder, and we turned to walk toward the large white farmhouse, together.

A buzzing sound from the nightstand pulled me from the dream. I reached for the phone trying to read the screen through sleep-weary eyes. There was a text lighting up the screen. Sitting up quickly, I scanned the room. Only one person had the number to this phone. Heart racing, I forced my eyes to focus.

> Mark: Call me when you can.

Why was he texting at this hour? Had he found something? I texted him back.

> Me: Is something wrong?

As I waited for a response, I thought about the dream I had awakened from. I recognized the yard and the farmhouse. In the dream, I had felt peace there with Hayley, who had never been to the farm. Wasn't peace what I had just been praying for? Was this my confirmation?

Mark responded almost instantly.

> Mark: I'm so sorry. I lost track of time. Nothing urgent. We'll talk later.

With the phone back on the table, I fell back to sleep and picked the dream right back up where I had left off. When my alarm rang, I felt better rested than I had in weeks.

THE TRAIL I decided to run was longer but not as steep as some of the others, which made it easier to focus on my thoughts and not my steps. I needed more confidence in the choice I was leaning toward making. There was a constant volley between the urge to stay and knowing we needed to leave, which was exhausting my heart and mind.

God, I feel like I know where you are leading me. I think I've known since reading Bryan's letter. And you have sent me nods through multiple people and now this dream. I am not testing you but begging you to please, give me one more confirmation.

At the end of the trail, I opted to take a cool down walk over a stone bridge that led to the other side of the park. It was still early but I was sure Mark would be up, so I pulled out the burner phone and pressed Call.

He answered on the second ring. "Collins."

"Mark, it's Jess."

"How are you?" he asked, his tone softer.

"Fine, thanks. Please tell me you were not still at the office at two a.m. when you sent me that text."

"Yeah, sorry about that. In my defense, I lost all track of time after you left and thought it couldn't be later than ten o'clock when I sent it."

This made me laugh. He was known for getting caught up in his work, and I had been the recipient of many emails sent at ridiculous early morning hours.

"I'll let it slide this time. Maybe check the clock before sending texts at night."

"Yes, ma'am. Got it. What's your schedule like today? Any chance you're free for lunch?" His tone was casual, which helped settle the anxiety that had been forming in my gut. Whatever he'd wanted to talk about must not have been urgent. That was good, right?

We made plans to meet at the coffee shop around the corner from his office after lunch, and I headed home.

∼

MARÍ WAS ONCE AGAIN on the couch reading her Bible when I walked in.

"Good morning," I said quietly, not wanting to interrupt but wanting her to know I was home.

As she had the day before, Marí motioned for me to join her, so I made my way to the living room where I leaned on the arm of the chair to keep my sweat off the furniture. "Did you have a good run?"

"I did. Running always helps me clear my mind."

"Did you find any specific clarity while you were out there?"

I paused and dropped my eyes to examine the same rug that had been in the living room for years before answering. There were so many reasons to stay; two of those reasons lived under the same roof I did. But every day there were no answers to the evidence in Bryan's box meant there could be more risk involved by staying. I couldn't and shouldn't put Hayley or myself at any unnecessary risk, which meant I knew leaving was wiser than staying. Still, my heart warred within me.

Looking up I watched Marí, whose eyes had remained fixed on her Bible. "I did find clarity. And before I tell you, I would like to know if God gave you any answers."

Marí turned her gaze to mine. "He did. And I have written it down so you can see I have not been persuaded by whatever you tell me. Because I know you and what you might think if our answers matched without this." She waved a small sheet of paper in the air.

I couldn't help but smile. "You know me so well, Marí."

"I do. I know you because you are a lot like me in some ways. Especially when I was a baby Christian. But that is not for us to discuss right now. For now, you tell me what clarity you were given and then you can read this." She flapped the paper toward me.

Forgetting about how sweaty I was, I moved to sit on the couch next to Marí, our knees touching. "I think Hayley and I need to go. I would never ask you and Sadie to make such a big move in such a short amount of time. But if you really wanted to go with us, nothing would make me happier."

Marí gave a sly smile and flapped the paper again.

Grabbing it from the air, I opened it and read it. Tears immediately flooded my vision.

Family should be together whenever possible.

"Thank you, Marí."

She gently patted me on the leg then shoved my shoulder gently. "Now go shower before I can't get your sweaty smell off the couch."

37

JESS

Coffees in hand, we found a table near the door of the coffee shop before Mark picked up our conversation from the walk over.

"I finished reading through the first folder and that led me into the second and so on."

I pulled the lid from my cup and watched the steam swirl upward. "What folder are you on?"

"I read all of them."

My jaw dropped as my eyes lifted to meet his. "All of them?" I asked, incredulously.

"You're not the only one with superpowers around here." He winked.

A small shiver ran over me followed by a warm pulsing at the base of my spine. My heart picked up its pace as I realized Mark was still speaking. He had lowered his voice to almost a whisper, and I had to lean in to hear him.

"Anyway, it looks like Bryan found evidence of foreign hackers going after the drone technology. He's connected a lot of dots that have created a nice road map pointing in a very specific direction. I'm going to talk to a buddy I have at the NSA later today. We may be looking at some bad actors on the inside. Jess, this is huge, and it's not good. This has some potential to go south very quickly on a lot of fronts.

"And according to his personal notes, it's no wonder Bryan was paranoid. Apparently, his office and Jeep were broken into and searched multiple times. Jess, I'm concerned that you and Hayley may not be safe here once the other guys realize that they didn't succeed. They may think you know something or have access to something just because you were married to Bryan. I have a friend in WITSEC, we can get that ball rolling…"

I held up a hand to stop him. My mind was struggling to keep up and process all the things he had just said. Bryan never mentioned the break-ins. Had they happened at the house? Had someone broken into the Jeep in our driveway? Then Mark's last sentence rang in my mind.

"WITSEC? Like witness protection?" I tried not to sound panicked.

His tone serious but sympathetic, Mark said, "Yes. It's not easy, but if it keeps you and your daughter out of harm's way, it would be worth it, right?"

This could not be real. I stared into the dark liquid inside my cup, watching the tiny bubbles floating around the edges. How could I possibly go into witness protection with my daughter and maintain my career? I'd have to give up even more of my life than if we headed for the farm in Kentucky. There was no way I could take such drastic actions when I had a perfectly sound solution. That was when I knew with complete certainty what the next step was going to be for Hayley and myself.

After several minutes of silence, I took a deep breath and tore my gaze from the cup to find Mark watching me as I fought my internal battles. "Hayley and I are leaving town. We have a place pretty far away from here."

Mark leaned back in his seat and studied me, drumming his thumbs on the table.

"I've been wrestling with it for days because at first, I didn't think it was necessary. Then I struggled with leaving behind my few connections. But I know, especially after hearing all of this, that this is the right choice. If it were just myself I had to worry about, I'd stay. But my daughter doesn't deserve to be raised in danger or in the lies that come with witness protection."

Mark nodded along slowly. His expression was neutral, making it hard for me to get a read on him.

We stared at each other in silence before he responded. "I think that's wise." He stretched his hands wide then clenched them shut a few times before sliding them into his pockets. "I'm not gonna lie, I will miss working with you directly. It's never boring."

His words affected me more than they probably should, and I scrunched my nose trying to stop the burn of tears. "I do a lot of consultation over video calls. That's kind of like working directly with someone, right?" I tried to sound assuring.

Mark snorted, and his gaze fell to the table. "Yeah."

Disappointment. Concern. Restraint.

His face betrayed him for a split second, and when I registered what it was I'd seen, I asked, "Everything okay? Did I say something?"

Once again, his expression went blank as he leaned forward, both hands in front of him. His index finger on his right hand twitched several times before he leaned back again. "This is a lot all at once for you. Is there anything I can do for you?" His voice was gentle.

"Aren't you already doing enough? I mean, I kind of dropped this on you like a giant bomb and now it looks like I'm running away from it."

Mark's face softened. "You are not running away from anything and I'm doing my job."

I considered his offer. What more could I possibly ask of him than asking him to step into a world of unknowns based on a mysterious box of information my murdered husband sent me? "Can I let you know?" I asked, unsure.

"Of course."

With a look at my watch, I started to gather our trash and stood. "I have to go. Thank you for this." I held up my empty coffee cup. "And for everything. I guess I'll be owing you a favor after all of this." We stepped out of the shop and onto the sidewalk.

Mark stopped and studied me. "Or we could just stop owing each other favors and be friends like normal people."

I laughed. "Like normal people? Huh. I guess we could try that. But there really is quite the power trip when the FBI owes you a favor."

Mark chuckled as we began walking again. "Technically, it was just a guy who happens to be in the FBI that owed you a favor."

"I guess that's true." I shrugged.

When we arrived at my car, I unlocked the door then turned to Mark with my hand outstretched. "Friends?"

His smile showed the lines next to his eyes. Taking my hand in his, he said, "Friends."

I froze as the warm pulse flowed through me. It was new yet familiar. Before I could dwell on the nerves in my body that had gone into action, I withdrew my hand and used it to push my hair behind my ear.

"I'll see you later," was all I could think to say before getting in my car and driving away.

38

MARK

She was leaving, and she wasn't just driving away; she was leaving DC, and I wasn't sure how I felt about it. Honestly, I wasn't sure how I was allowed to feel about it. I'd known Jess four years, and since the day I met her in that office at the university, she'd never ceased to hold my interest.

It was obvious how much she loved her husband by the way she spoke about him when he came up in conversation. When she got pregnant, she was radiant. Until then, I had never understood the idea of a woman glowing when she was pregnant, as I hadn't been around many pregnant women for an extended amount of time. Jess had glowed.

I felt like a moth flying aimlessly around a candle when she was in the office. Everyone did. Her excitement overflowed into her conversations, and even when she was in the midst of a tough case, there was an underlying contentment that quietly accompanied her satisfaction in her work. People were drawn to her, and she welcomed them into her sphere unconditionally.

After her baby was born, she changed. There was a shift in her attitude, her smiles became less frequent and forced, and her overall demeanor had faded from its natural enthusiasm to weariness. Not feeling close enough to ask her about it, I wrote it off as having a thriving career that brought its own special stress and having a newborn at home. Now, knowing what I know, I wish I had asked more questions sooner.

Until today, I made it a point to respect our professional boundaries, refusing to insert myself into her personal life. As attracted as I'd always been to her, I respected Jess far too much to consider crossing into anything more than work acquaintance territory. I never asked questions, I didn't pry, or even asked anyone else about her aside from casework.

Today, however, something was different. Something about her, or maybe something in me, had changed. As we sat at the table and talked, it felt less restricted and more casual. I wanted her to let me in, to let me help her. And maybe it was wishful thinking on my part, but when I shook her hand and accepted her offer of friendship, there was an intense feeling of affection that rooted itself in my gut.

There were many reasons I could think of to ignore these feelings. For starters, she was leaving. And I was going to help her get to wherever she was heading. If that wasn't enough of a reason, her husband was killed weeks ago, and there was no way I would ever take advantage of the vulnerability that came with a loss like that. I didn't care how attracted I was to her, even I had my limits. What I would do was anything that ensured Jess and her daughter were safe and out of harm's way and work as hard as I needed to in order to bring this case to a close.

39

JESS

I pulled out of the parking lot and turned in the direction of home, my entire body still humming after Mark shook my hand. I'd shaken hands with countless men and women in my life, and very few had had such an impact on me that I had to physically withdraw. Until now, all but one of the strong reactions I have experienced to physical contact have been painful jolts of electricity shooting through the points of contact, and they typically accompany an already heightened sense of danger or threat brought about by an assessment I'd made prior to contact. They act as warnings, confirmations of my initial judgments of a person.

The fact that I didn't have such strong reactions to every form of contact made me grateful. The strong negative reactions were always overwhelming when they happened and forced me to need time to recover. As I got older and was able to be more selective in the touches I received, I eventually became proficient at avoiding contact from strangers altogether.

Until the night I met Bryan, I hadn't known how positively impactful a single touch could be. The first time I locked eyes with Bryan, I'd had an unprecedented desire to know what his touch felt like. The moment our hands had touched, there was a flood of warmth, tranquility, and promise engulfing my entire being. From that night forward, his mere presence was palpable to the depths of my soul, until it wasn't.

The year before his death had led to a slow fade into numbness. The warmth became cold, the tranquility turned turbulent, and the promises felt hopeless. Even after we had set off toward reconciliation, there was a veil of uncertainty between us, a fear of relapsing and of Bryan caving back in on himself. My heart had broken every day for so long that I was having to learn to trust him again, and just as hope had taken root in my heart that we were finally being restored, he was taken from me. Once again, he was gone, and this time there would be no reconciling. And the worst part was the sense of relief, which carried with it a load of guilt.

No longer was I hanging in the balances each day, wondering if the man I married or the stranger who had taken his place for so long would be coming home from work. I wasn't exerting every ounce of strength within me to keep all of us afloat while still maintaining my job and my sanity.

The glue on my barely mended heart had not fully dried the day I learned Bryan had been killed, causing it to shatter into pieces once more. But for the last two weeks, I found myself mourning more for the *what had been* and the *what should have been* rather than what my reality had been when he died. This came with its own remorse and a completely separate grieving process.

I loved my husband with my everything until the day he died, even when I didn't know if he still loved me. I fought for us and for him to the end, and I would do it again if it meant I would have him back. But he was not coming back, and my life as I now knew it went on. And that scared me almost as much as living in the uncertainty of the last two years. It especially scared me now that I was having to question what happened in that parking lot when I shook hands with Mark.

For the last four years, Mark and I had been colleagues, a dynamic duo of case closers through our collaborations. When we met, I had almost convinced myself he was an arrogant man who was expecting me to perform like a circus act, until I saw how hard he tried to mask his insecurity behind a façade. Over time I learned that he was good at his job—really good—and he struggled with asking for help. He cared what other people thought about him, and asking for help was weakness in his eyes, which is why he was hesitant to give me a chance.

It was Mark's trust that I worked to earn from that first encounter, and that same trust was what allowed me to truly pursue the career I loved so dearly. He advocated for Carsen-Thorne Consulting when there were many skeptics in the important positions of power.

As grateful as I had been, we were still work acquaintances at best. Aside from the basic pleasantries that coworkers typically afford, we didn't invest in one another's lives away from the office. I knew he wasn't married, and I knew he lived a lifestyle that lined up with that of the bachelor he was. That was the extent of our relationship.

That being said, when I received that box of evidence, there was zero question in my mind who I was going to call. I had watched Mark deal with suspects, lawyers, victims, and families. He'd even gone to bat for me on several cases, as I had done for him. Everything I had observed over four years told me I could trust Mark.

Today, however, something shifted between us. There was a personal lilt to the conversation that had never been present before our time at the coffee shop. He was genuinely concerned for me and had taken steps to inquire after possibilities that would ensure my safety. I had seen him do the exact same thing for victims in his other cases, but I had never seen it happen with the same level of warmth and concern with which he spoke to me.

Combined with the friendship-affirming handshake that had sent pulses of warmth and excitement through my spine, I was now feeling confused in addition to the plethora of other emotions I was already juggling inside of me. It had been a long time since I had felt something this significant. It had taken me by surprise and left me feeling shaky.

I ROCKED Hayley far longer than it took her to fall asleep. This was easily the most relaxed I could feel in a single moment. The warm breaths on my neck and the tickle of the wispy brown hairs on my cheek gave me the most satisfying feeling of contentment to my very core. Allowing everything around me to dissolve into nothingness, I closed my eyes and breathed in the scent of my daughter and exhaled a prayer.

God, thank you. I don't say it enough, but I am thankful for every blessing you have given me. I am thankful for the wisdom and peace you granted when I asked for it. I need it every day. I need it right now. Since I have known you, I have always wanted to use my gift for your honor and not a selfish advantage. But I know you have also given it to me to use when it's needed. Protect it and strengthen it when it's needed.

As soon as my mind felt crystal clear, I took a few more moments to enjoy the quiet before putting Hayley in her crib. Once she was settled, I went downstairs hoping to talk to Marí.

"I don't want to interrupt anything, but are you free to talk?" I approached the couch where Marí was sitting with a skein of yarn and something like the start of a blanket beside her.

"You will not interrupt. Come sit with me." She moved the yarn and her project to her lap.

"That is beautiful!" I sat and admired her work.

"Thank you. I sometimes like to crochet when I need to think. Tonight, I crochet just to calm my nerves."

Marí nervous? This gave me pause. I had never known Marí to be anything but strong and confident. "Is everything okay?" I asked hesitantly.

"Yes, yes, everything is fine. I just spent a lot of time thinking about the future, and I got myself worked up. I am fine but now that I have started this, I am finding it hard to stop." She held up the yarn and hooked needle as though it was a source of aggravation she couldn't remove.

This made me chuckle. "I can relate to that. But not with yarn. It used to be research projects. Now, certain kinds of cases will trigger my obsessive mode."

Marí nodded, "I have seen your obsessive mode. I prefer mine. I can fall asleep mid stitch and not wake up with computer buttons tattooed on my face." Marí laughed at her own snarky remark, which made me laugh.

"It is so good to see you laugh, again, Jess. I knew it would come. I have missed it."

With a sigh I leaned back on the couch and fidgeted with the partially crocheted blanket. "Sometimes I feel guilty when I want to laugh or find pleasure in something. It feels like I'm expected to feel sad all the time, and that makes me feel sad but also guilty for not feeling sad, so I feel sad and guilty all the time. And saying it out loud doesn't even help it make sense."

Marí put her yarn and needle on the coffee table and turned on the couch to look at me. "If it helps, it makes sense to me. And to that I say, 'weeping may come for the night, but joy comes in the morning.' But joy is a funny thing, you know? You can have joy and be sad. You can be sad and have joy. It is not a feeling. It is a place where pain and purpose bump their heads into each other." She bumped two fists together. "And the one you choose is the one that wins. Joy is a choice. Sometimes it is one you must make every day."

I studied my friend, a sense of awe growing inside me. "Marí, I hope one day to have even one half of your wisdom."

She gave me a dismissive wave of her hand. "You are wise, Jess. Your wisdom looks different from mine. And one day, when you are old like me, I think you will be wiser than I ever will be."

"You're not old," I protested. "And, I doubt that, but it's a nice thought."

She motioned for me to continue talking. "Now, I doubt this is what you wanted to talk about. So, you go."

"Right. First, thank you for choosing to make the move with us. I realized that I hadn't even told you when or where, and you have still been dead set on going with us. That overwhelms me with gratitude for you even more, as though that is even possible. I promise that as soon as I know it's safe to tell you, I will tell you everything you want to know."

Marí patted my arm. "I know."

"Thanks, Marí."

"No problema, mija. Now, if it is all the same to you, I must go to bed. I'm no late-night party animal." She gathered her yarn and hooks.

I checked my watch and laughed. "Marí, it's nine-thirty."

"Mío! Maybe I am a late-night party animal." She did a little jig and gave a wink before walking to her room.

Laughing to myself, I sat on the couch a little longer trying to work through a plan for the next day in my head, trying not to think about the handshake from that afternoon.

Several hours later I jumped awake, finding myself still on the couch. Once I dragged myself up the stairs, I fell into my bed fully dressed and didn't move again until the next morning.

40

JESS

Considering my fractured night of sleep, I was surprised to find myself wide awake before my alarm went off. The energy buzzing inside me was a combination of eager anticipation and an edgy nervousness. With a need for an outlet, I had my running shoes on and had left a note before Marí had made it to the sofa for her quiet time. Then I was out the door.

I drove to Waterfront Park, and by the time I had stretched and sprinted two miles, it felt like all the pent-up energy I had been holding in had vanished. I slowed to a walk and took in the view of the river. Without thinking, I pulled out my phone and pressed Call.

"Only one person can call me this early from an unknown number three days in a row." The voice that answered was gravelly.

"Oh my gosh, I'm sorry. I woke you. I didn't check the time," I said, thoroughly embarrassed.

There was the sound of rustling, which I assumed was bed covers followed by a clearing of a throat. When the voice returned, it still sounded tired but more awake. "I wasn't complaining." There was a sleepy smile behind his words.

Movement to my left got my attention, and I paused to try and find it again. The air was still and not cool enough to warrant the chill that moved over and through me. Not even five a.m., the sky was just brightening as the sun was still below the horizon. The light-sensing streetlamps were still lit, providing plenty of visibility of the immediate area. Turning in a circle, I scanned the empty sidewalks, squinting, trying to bring the pavilion into clearer detail.

"Was there something you wanted to talk about?" Mark broke the long silence.

My attention snapped back to the phone in my hand. "Oh, yeah, sorry. I just had a weird feeling and had to look around for a minute."

"A weird feeling?" His voice was suddenly clear and serious.

A whooshing sound followed by a clatter and a thud made me pull the phone from my ear momentarily. "Yeah, it was just a shiver. Everything okay there?" I tried to make sense of the noises on his end.

"Jess, where are you?" The seriousness of his tone startled me.

"I'm at the Southwest Waterfront Park."

With zero hesitation he snapped, "Go sit in your car and lock the doors. I'll be there in five minutes."

"Mark, this is ridiculous. It was just—"

"Jess, please. Do it." The pleading demand in his words set my feet in motion toward my car.

Almost five minutes later, Mark pulled into the space next to me. I got out and met him at the back of the vehicles.

"Seriously?" I gave him an annoyed look that he didn't see because his eyes were already scanning the park around us.

It was clear Mark didn't like this place. When he finally turned back to me, there was nothing masking the look on his face.

Frustration. Concern. Care.

Mark grabbed my arms, and I wasn't sure if he was going to hug me, shake me, or was trying to hold me at a distance. "I don't like the idea of you going places like this by yourself. Don't do it anymore. Please."

Subtle pulses traveled through my arms then up and down my

spine. Something in his voice connected with something inside me, causing my breath to catch.

His eyes bore into mine, and I could tell he wanted to say something else.

He didn't have the chance as I took a step back and cut in, "Mark, I've been here dozens of times. It's a perfectly safe place. Do you honestly believe someone is watching me or following me?"

"Do you honestly believe it's not even a possibility?" He sounded agitated at my lack of concern.

With a heavy sigh, I lamented, "It's not safe to talk about anything in my house. I can't go anywhere by myself to talk about any of this. I can't even sit in my car and talk about it. How am I supposed to talk about anything if nowhere is safe?"

Mark rubbed a finger over an eyebrow and took a deep breath. "Let's go sit in my car."

Once we were both in the car, Mark turned to face me, but I refused to acknowledge him and instead stared out the windshield, keeping my arms crossed in front of me. I was frustrated, overwhelmed, and tired of not knowing what was going to happen next.

"Jess, I..." He paused then started again. "Here's the thing." Another pause. He sighed then made a frustrated groan and let his head fall to the steering wheel.

This made me turn my head to look at him. "What?"

He raised his head.

Reservation. Timidity. Nervousness.

"I can't keep you safe if you go running off in places that would make it easy for someone to hurt you."

Concern. Desperation.

We sat in silence for several minutes before I quietly said, "I'm leaving town," as I stared across the park in front of us.

"When?" His voice was hushed.

"As soon as I can get all our ducks in a row. I'm hoping to be ready early next week."

"Good." His tone was solemn, like the mood surrounding us. "Jess..."

I met his gaze and waited for him to speak.

Instead, he drew in a deep breath and stayed silent.

"Thank you for coming to check on me this morning." I wanted him to know I truly appreciated his concern for me.

"You're welcome. When the woman with the spidey senses starts getting weird feelings, it sets my nerves on edge. I'm sorry if you think I overreacted."

"I don't think that." I gently touched his shoulder.

Immediately it felt like someone had punched me in the diaphragm, making my breath hitch. A rippling current moved from my fingertips through my arm and into my chest. Slowly, I moved my hand to my lap where my other hand massaged it gently. I didn't know how to define this feeling, but it wasn't a warning.

Mark was watching me with an expression that said he had questions of his own.

Glass behind us shattered, causing me to scream.

"Get down!" Mark yelled as he started the car.

Driving with one hand, he used the other to hold my head down and cover me. Turning my head to see him, I watched him scan the parking lot. Through his window I saw a silver sedan speeding away. He yanked the steering wheel and turned the opposite direction and headed for his office. When we had driven several blocks from the park, he moved his hand and allowed me to sit up.

Feeling panicked and afraid, I kept turning to look out the shattered back windshield.

Mark called the local police to report shots fired. When he hung up, he dropped his phone into the console and rested his hand on mine.

"Are you okay? Were you hit?"

"No, I'm fine. What was that?" I asked, my voice shaky.

"Someone took a shot at us. I don't think your strange feeling was as unfounded as you thought it had been."

It felt like a lead weight had dropped in my stomach, and I started shaking.

Mark gripped my hand tighter.

"I need to get home to Hayley."

"First, we need to get you to safety."

"What if they go to my house? I need to go to Hayley."

"Jess, whoever that was, they know you aren't at your house, and they saw you leave in my car. That person had eyes on you. They won't go to your house."

"How do you know? You have to take me home, now."

"That's not going to happen. But I promise you, nothing is going to happen to Hayley." He pulled into a back parking lot of the FBI HQ that I had never seen before. "Listen, Jess, let me take you inside, and we'll make a plan. But if you go home right now, you might put your daughter in more danger. Okay? Trust me, please."

I took in a shaky breath and nodded. What other choice did I have?

He took us inside through a rear entrance and led me to a small room off a corridor. It had a few chairs and a table on one side of the room and a table with a coffee pot on the other.

Mark placed his phone in my hands and covered them with his. "I will be back in five minutes, max. I want you to call whoever is at home with Hayley. As soon as they answer, tell them not to speak. Then tell them to pack any essentials Hayley needs for a week. If they can pack for you, great. If not, we'll deal with that if and when we need to. Tell them nothing else except you will be in touch with them as soon as you can. Can you do that?"

My words were barely a whisper. "What about Marí and Sadie?"

"Who are they?"

"Marí is Hayley's nanny and Sadie is her seven-year-old granddaughter. They live with us and were planning to leave with us."

Mark ran his hand through his hair while he considered this. "Same plan, but obviously tell her to pack their stuff, too, but only the really important things. The goal is to travel quickly and lightly. Okay?"

I nodded. Mark kept his hands around mine for another second before he exited. When he came back into the room, he dropped a black duffel bag to the floor next to the doorway. He had a renewed energy about him.

"DCPD called. They didn't catch the guy, but there was a car that matched the description wrapped around a telephone pole not far from the park. It was registered to a guy named Pete Stewart."

My blood turned to ice. "Say that again."

"Pete Stewart."

Mark's face went dark. "Why? Do you know him?"

My heart pounded in my ears, and I stumbled backwards as though I had been slapped.

"Jess?" Mark's arms moved as though they were ready to catch me.

I swallowed hard and trained my stare on Mark. "Yeah. He and Bryan were friends in the Army."

Mark's face drained of all color. "Are you serious?" He breathed out hard and stared at me in disbelief.

Barely able to nod my head, I closed my eyes and massaged my temples then my neck. "A few years ago, I met him at a club he owns downtown. He was dating my roommate." All the memories from that night came rushing back to my mind.

Mark pulled out a notepad and pen from his pocket.

Trying not to focus on the memory of meeting Bryan, I gave Mark a quick summary. "In short, he gave off massive negative signals. In the context of the meeting, I assumed he was a womanizer. In the context of that weekend's events, which is a whole different story, my assumptions appeared correct.

"Fast-forward a few days, Bryan was in Atlanta for work. Pete asked to meet him for dinner one night. Bryan originally met with him thinking it was just a time to catch up. Apparently, that wasn't the case. Before Bryan could leave, Pete offered him a job at his new Tech. Investment company. Bryan declined, and it apparently made Pete very angry. That was the last time I heard anything about Pete Stewart. I can only assume the same is true for Bryan, but I don't know. He knew that I did not care for Pete. It's unlikely he would have hidden it from me unless he wanted to spare my feelings or something."

Mark took notes and nodded as he listened. "Okay. Good. That's good. We have a name, and we have a lead. Now we need to get you and your family out of town. You ready?"

I wasn't ready, but I stood and followed him anyway. There were too many thoughts swirling around inside my head and too many emotions threatening to surface that I was not ready to deal with in this moment.

41

MARK

The urgency I felt inside battled against the need for levelheadedness as I drove Jess home in a black unmarked Suburban. Driving the speed limit would keep us inconspicuous, but everything in me kept wanting to press down harder on the gas pedal.

When we arrived at her house, I took a moment to appreciate the domestic curb appeal and its simplicity. It was exactly the suburban scene I imagined Jess being part of, and in that moment, I was sad for her knowing everything she was about to leave behind and not knowing if she would ever be able to return to it.

When we walked into the house, a woman caught Jess in a hug so tight, I thought she might break. The woman, who I assumed was Marí, was mumbling rapidly in Spanish, and the sounds of young girls squealing happily upstairs were accompanied by occasional thuds.

When Jess pried the woman's arms from around her neck, I saw Jess raise her eyebrows as she pointed upstairs and tilted her head.

"They are fine. They wanted to help. I told them to pack the socks. The socks became snowballs."

Jess nodded in understanding and held in a laugh. The amusement on her face caused my lips to twitch upward.

"Who is that?" The woman nodded her head in my direction.

Jess silently surveyed me, and I shook my head. "I will tell you later." Jess pointed to her lips and shook her head, implying they were no longer able to speak freely in the house.

"Did you square everything away like we talked about? Is there anything in the kitchen or living room we need to take care of?" Jess asked.

Marí shook her head.

Jess headed upstairs. "I'll go tell the girls I'm home."

When I came back from loading bags into the back of the SUV, they were all waiting inside the front door. I motioned for them to follow and began helping Marí and the girls load into the vehicle while Jess locked the front door.

I paused to watch as she rested her forehead and one of her hands on the door. That was an image I would not soon forget. I had never seen Jess Carsen show any sign of weakness. In the interrogation room, in the courtroom, even in a conference room she was always the picture of confidence. She wasn't arrogant, but she exuded tenacity and determination.

Today, however, I was seeing a different side of her. It was a softer side, quiet, almost defeated. I wanted to reach out and hold her hand again and tell her that everything was going to be fine. But I knew I couldn't because it wasn't a promise I could make. Instead, I promised myself I was going to do whatever it took to protect these women and these little girls.

Once we were all situated in the Suburban, I turned toward the back seat where Marí had tucked herself away with what looked like a Bible.

"Now that we're in this vehicle, I'd like to tell you that my name is Mark Collins. I'm with the FBI. If you need anything, if we need to stop, just say the word. But I would like to put a good distance between here and us, so if we could hold off for just a few hours, that would be good. Everybody comfortable?"

Marí gave a thumbs up from the back seat. The girls cheered in their seats. I waited for Jess's confirmation, which she gave with a nod.

"Then I guess we're off. Where exactly are we going?" I asked, pulling onto the street.

Jess laughed, breaking the tension growing inside me. "I guess that would be good to know." She dug through her purse and pulled out a piece of paper. After she punched the address into the GPS, we drove south.

After nearly two hours of silence in the front of the SUV, Jess suddenly leaned forward and stared at me. Her sudden movement caused me to snap my head in her direction.

"What?" My hands instinctually clenched the wheel tighter.

"You're driving us to Kentucky," she said.

Relief moved through me, and I loosened the grip I had on the steering wheel. "Yes."

"That's a ten-hour drive," she said, sounding taken aback.

"Technically, it's closer to eight now." I watched the road again.

"Mark, you have a job. You can't just drop everything and drive people to a different state ten hours away from it."

"Actually, I can. You are now in the protection of the FBI as part of an on-going investigation. I volunteered my partner and me to take point. He's working the lead from this morning, and I am protecting valuable assets." I gave her a quick wink. From my periphery I could see her slowly sit back in her seat, her focus turning back to the road.

A few minutes went by before I glanced over at Jess, trying to gauge the situation, my fingers drumming on the wheel. She was staring out her window at the sky. I faced forward again wanting to say something but unsure of what I could say. This case had become personal, and it had done so quickly and exponentially.

Clearing my throat I said quietly, "I'm sorry about all of this you've had to go through."

She turned to face me and smiled, though it didn't reach her eyes. "Yeah, me too. But I am thankful that I have friends who have walked with me through it and have promised to stay with me." She motioned her head back toward Marí.

I nodded.

"Do you have a lot of friends?" Jess asked.

The question forced a snort from me. "I guess you would have to define the term friends."

"Okay. Let's say a friend is someone you enjoy spending time with; someone who stands up for you and sticks by you; someone you can trust and who makes you laugh; someone who accepts you for who you are, and they always want what's best for you."

I considered her words before answering. "That's quite the definition. I guess based on it, I'd say I have very few friends."

"Did I make the cut?" There was a smile behind her words.

"I thought we shook hands on it." I cut my eyes over at her.

Jess chuckled. "That was before you were shot at because of me."

This made me laugh. I was glad she was able to find humor in the midst of this situation. "You make a good point. But we shook on it, so I think it's a done deal."

She smiled and made a *hmm* sound.

"I imagine you have a lot of friends," I suggested.

Her voice was now sad. "Not a lot. But the ones I have are very special."

Our conversation was interrupted by a loud announcement from the backseat.

"Mommy! I have to go potty!" Hayley exclaimed.

"I bet Mark can make that happen." Jess gave me a look I assumed was the question mark to her statement.

With a look in the rearview mirror, I gave Hayley a smile. "Yes ma'am. Right away."

42

JESS

The adults settled on taking a longer break for lunch and stretching, which in turn lifted some of the stress from the entire group. When the girls asked to play in the kids' area of the fast-food restaurant we had stopped at, Mark insisted on checking the space and sitting inside while they played. He smiled as they laughed and chittered nonstop with one another, occasionally trying to bring him into their games.

Marí and I watched from a table in the restaurant, laughing when Hayley tried to pull Mark toward the small climbing area.

He stood and pretended to consider the enclosed steps then put his hands on his hips. We could only see his back, but it appeared he was explaining with very exaggerated movements that he was too big to play on the equipment. The back and forth continued when Sadie emerged from a plastic slide and tried to give him a push toward the steps. He spun and sat on the first step and pretended to get stuck.

This made me laugh even harder.

Watching me, Marí smiled. "He's good with kids. And he's handsome."

Still smiling, I raised a brow at her. "Would you like me to set you up with him? I don't see a ring on his finger."

Marí rolled her eyes.

With a lowered voice I hissed, "Marí, stop. Right now. My husband just died a few weeks ago. Mark is my friend, and he's helping me, helping us, through a very hard situation. It's his job."

Marí waved her hand. "Yes, and I am thankful he was there when you needed him to be. I'm just saying, just because your husband died doesn't mean you have to close your eyes to the future."

My jaw dropped. About that time, Mark came out of the play area carrying Hayley on one hip and Sadie on the other.

Hayley was rubbing his face. "Your face is scratchy."

Sadie joined in on the other side. He was laughing, which made me laugh. Marí sat and smiled like the Cheshire Cat.

"It's probably a good idea to get a move on. We can make it before it gets too late if we get back on the road." Mark slid both girls down to the floor.

After quick trips to the restroom, we loaded back into the SUV. Everyone was more relaxed, though still quiet.

Once we were back on the highway, it occurred to me I should call Cal and tell him we were coming. He answered after the second ring, and his warm, gentle southern twang made my heart swell.

His tone grew brighter when I announced myself. "I wondered when I'd get to see you, again," Cal said.

My throat tightened. Cal had practically raised Bryan and had taken care of Bryan's mom in her last years. He was practically family, though there had never been blood relation to Bryan. Now for him to sound so pleased at seeing me again and under these circumstances sent a pang of hurt to my heart. I swallowed hard before I could respond.

"Cal, it's not just Hayley and me. I have a friend and her granddaughter who is coming to stay with us. I hope that's okay."

Without hesitation he replied, "Jess, you could show up with a crowd and they'd be welcome. There's plenty of room for all of you."

"Thank you, Cal. It's going to be late when we get in, but we thought it best to push through. Want me to call or anything before we arrive?"

"Nah, just show up. I'll be expecting you."

Mark let several minutes of silence pass before asking, "Who's Cal?"

"That's a good question. I only met him once, and that was just for a few minutes."

I told Mark about the place we were going, explaining the history Bryan had one time given me and how Cal had always been a part of Bryan's life, especially after Bryan's dad had passed away.

When I had finished telling Mark about the farm, my mind began to wander, and I let myself get lost in my own mind for a while. Recounting it all brought back the memories of the week Bryan and I had spent at the farm, the days we played and laughed together outdoors, and the nights snuggled up together in front of the giant fireplace. It seemed another lifetime ago and yet it felt like yesterday we had come home from that trip and learned we were going to be parents. I couldn't help but wonder how so much changed in such a short amount of time.

43

MARK

As I listened to Jess give me some background about the place we were heading, I kept wondering how she must be feeling as she drew closer to such an important place in her dead husband's past. This was new territory for me. I'd worked many cases where a spouse had been killed, but never had there been such a personal connection to any of them. On the one hand, I thought maybe I should tread lightly. On the other hand, I didn't think Jess was the kind of woman who liked being handled with kid gloves like she was fragile.

But she was fragile. Yes, she was strong and had shown that strength through everything she'd been through. But I also saw a delicate creature who hadn't deserved anything she had been through in the last year. She deserved to be protected from the very evil she and I fought against every day in our jobs.

Jess had finished talking several minutes earlier and had just let the conversation fizzle. When I thought she wasn't looking, I tried to steal a glance at her, but she was already watching me. Heat rose to my cheeks, and I quickly returned my sights on the road in front of us.

She then turned her head to observe the seats behind them. I checked the backseats from the rearview mirror and saw what she was seeing. The two girls had fallen asleep. Marí winked then held up her Bible. I quickly looked at Jess who was smiling and shaking her head. Before she could see me watching, I snapped my eyes back to the road.

A moment later Jess asked, "Mark, do you believe in God?"

This led to a very hard silence. I didn't look at her, though I felt her continue to stare at me. She didn't say anything else but watched me as I thought about her question. She knew I had heard the question because my jaw twitched when she asked it and because she was Jess, she saw it. Because she saw it, she knew there was an answer, I just wasn't giving it up easily.

After staring at me for several long minutes, Jess turned to face forward and began to speak instead. "I always believed there was a higher power that created stuff. I couldn't imagine the world or people just popping into existence. That never made sense to me. It wasn't until I found myself wandering into a church one Sunday that I heard there was a God who had his hand in and on everything. The pastor had used the word *sovereign* to describe God. He said God was this all-powerful autonomous director of the world. I didn't go back to church for a long time after that.

"Then my best friend, who was young and beautiful, had a stroke. I was the one who had to call her mom and tell her. It was awful. But it was that experience that moved me toward seeing that believing in coincidence was much harder than believing there was a God. There were too many variables that fell into place for it to have been chance."

Her words lingered on the air. The once relaxed atmosphere had tensed slightly.

I gripped the steering wheel as though it could keep me from speaking. The silence permeated the car, and Jess didn't push for a response.

My voice felt thick when I finally spoke. "When I was fifteen, I came home from school one day to find my older brother home on leave after his deployment. I was ecstatic. I hadn't seen him in two years. We hugged, and I remember that being the first time I had ever seen him cry. I cut school the next day just so we could go fishing and hang out. We spent the entire day talking about everything except where he'd been. I tried to get him to talk about it several times, and he would always change the subject.

"He was my role model. I wanted to be just like my big brother. Our mom made me go to school the next day, but as soon as I came home, I ran upstairs to change clothes and force Mike to go fishing with me, again."

I had to pause and breathe as memories threatened to fall from my eyes. "I knocked on his bedroom door, and when he didn't answer I opened it, anyway." I lowered my voice to ensure only Jess could hear. "Mike was on the floor in a pool of blood, his sidearm next to him."

Jess tried to smother a gasp with a hand over her mouth.

"If you had asked me before that day if I believed in God, I would have shrugged and said sure. But after…" The horrific scene replayed in my mind as clear as though it had happened yesterday. "I don't know. I've given it very little thought other than to assume that if there was a God, he's not very good at his job."

44

JESS

His words pierced my heart like a hot sharp blade. I desperately wanted to reach out and put my hand on his arm. He was clearly hurting after having dredged up such a painful memory and sharing his story. I had watched him struggle with the decision to say anything but couldn't have imagined this was what he'd been thinking. Before I said anything, I prayed.

God, you are the ultimate comforter. I know this from my own experience. You have brought healing to my heart multiple times. I pray that you would do the same for Mark. And more than that, show him you are real. Bring him to salvation in yourself.

Letting out a slow breath I said, "Mark, thank you for trusting me with your story. I know it wasn't easy."

His eyes were shining with tears. "I've never told anyone that before."

"And it's your story to tell, not mine."

We rode in silence for a long time after that.

∼

A FEW MORE STOPS FOR restrooms, gas, and food, combined with several tedious hours of intermittent conversation, I was relieved when Mark steered the SUV onto a familiar gravel driveway. It was dark, but the glow of a porch light and those from inside the farmhouse illuminated the area enough for us to unload.

Cal met us at the bottom of the steps and immediately wrapped me and a sleepy toddler in a hug warmer than I could remember in a long time. The common loss between us had bonded us, though we were practically strangers.

Unexpected tears began to fall from my eyes.

"I'm so sorry, Jess," The older man whispered against my temple as we embraced.

"Thank you, Cal. And I'm sorry too. I know how special he was to you."

He released me and wiped his eyes with his sleeve before resting his warm hand gently on Hayley's back. He gazed into her tired eyes and smiled. "She has her daddy's eyes."

Marí carried a sleeping Sadie from the vehicle and made her way to where I was standing with Cal.

Before I could introduce the two, Cal had already seen Marí approaching and moved to introduce himself. If my tired eyes weren't playing tricks on me, Marí's eyes had a sparkle in them even in the dark. It was one I had never seen. This could be interesting.

When I realized Mark was not with us, I scanned the darkness until I found him still standing next to the door of the vehicle. I motioned for him to join us.

"Cal, this is Mark Collins. He is our personal bodyguard, chauffeur, and my friend. Mark, this is Cal."

Cal stretched out his hand. "Mark, I'm pleased to meet you. And I owe you a debt of gratitude for bringing these lovely ladies all this way on such short notice."

Mark accepted Cal's hand, and though something more passed between them in the moment, he said, "Keeping them safe is my number one priority."

Turning to Marí and me, Cal said, "Ladies, y'all go on ahead into the house. Jess, your room is the same as last time, if that's alright. Ms. Marí, yours and Miss Sadie's is next to hers. Jess can show you. Mark and I will get your bags and see you inside."

I led Marí into the house while Cal and Mark retrieved our bags.

45

MARK

When the women had carried the girls inside, Cal turned to me with a serious expression on his face. "I really am thankful that you got them here so quickly. I made a promise to Bryan a while ago that if something ever happened to him, I'd take care of his girls. I never thought it would come to that." The man's eyes brimmed with tears. "I plan to keep that promise."

My throat tightened at the emotion in Cal's voice. I had to swallow before I could speak. "I have no doubt about that. I didn't know him, but through all of this it's clear Bryan was a good guy. Jess told me a little about your relationship with him, and I'm very sorry for your loss."

Cal nodded, trying to hold back his tears. "He was a good guy. The best. You must not be too bad, either, if Jess trusts you."

I chuckled as Cal's eyes never left mine. "I must not be."

Once we had the luggage inside, Cal turned his attention to Marí and began telling her about the farm and the surrounding areas. Jess was still upstairs so I excused myself and stepped outside where I planted myself on the top step of the porch. Elbows on my knees, I rested my head on my hands, replaying the day's events in my mind when the screen door shut behind me.

When I finally acknowledged I had company, Jess was sitting on the other end of the step I was sitting on.

"I figured you would be exhausted after driving all day," she said.

"I am. But I needed a few minutes to decompress."

She moved to get up. "I'm sorry, I didn't mean to intrude."

"No. Stay, please. I just mean I wasn't ready to fall asleep."

"That I understand completely." Jess stared into the dark sky splattered with millions of tiny flickering lights. "I get envious of Hayley, sometimes. She can sleep almost anytime, anywhere. She's like her daddy in that way, I guess. I walked into our living room numerous times to find the two of them on the couch asleep with the television on in the background."

A smile played across her face. Her smile made me want to reach across the steps and trace her lips. I had to turn my face away from hers to regather myself. Here she was thinking of her dead husband, and I was thinking about touching her lips. I had to remind myself there were still boundaries. We sat in silence as the night sounds filled the air.

"It's beautiful out here. I had forgotten how peaceful it was," she said wistfully.

I nodded as I stared into the sky, unable to voice a response.

"Before I had decided to leave DC, I prayed that God would give me peace and wisdom. That night, I dreamed Hayley and I were playing in piles of leaves on a cold day. We were laughing and running together. We collapsed from laughing and running so hard. The yard wasn't familiar at first, but the peace and the joy felt so real. It almost overwhelmed me because I hadn't felt peaceful or joyful in a long time. In the dream, we turned to walk inside, and this was the house we were walking into. That's when I knew that we would be coming here. And looking into this sky so full of stars, I can almost feel that same peace. And to think that the same God who created all of this," she pointed to the sky and farmland surrounding us, "cares about my peace. It's almost too much for me to think about for too long."

I tried not to sound too cynical. "You really believe there's a God who cares about you personally?"

With gentleness in her eyes that tugged at my heart, Jess said, "Yeah, Mark. I do. And I hope maybe one day, you will too."

A huff escaped before I could stop it.

She shrugged. "I didn't say today. I said one day."

There was something about this conversation that didn't sit well with me, and I had the sudden need to escape. With a deep inhale, I rubbed my hands on my pants then stood. Without looking at her I said, "I'll see you in the morning, Jess. There are a few logistics we need to work through before I head back."

I heard her say, "Good night, Mark," as I walked back into the house.

46

MARK

Jess was the last one to get downstairs. She carried what appeared to be a less than sociable Hayley on her hip as they came into the kitchen. As the room greeted them, Hayley buried her face in her mother's shoulder, Jess gave a sleepy smile, and kissed her daughter's cheek.

"We had a rough night last night. I'm sorry if we disturbed any of you," she said before releasing a yawn.

Marí reached to take Hayley from her mom, but the child held more tightly to Jess. Marí patted her on the back.

"I'll get you some coffee," Marí said quietly.

"Thanks." Jess surveyed the room.

Marí and Cal were working together to get breakfast on the table, talking, laughing, and exchanging quiet smiles as they did. I was showing Sadie how to thumb wrestle. She would break into fits of giggles when I let her win and pretended to be devastated and impressed with her tiny thumb's strength. When I lost the final match, I told Sadie my thumb needed a break but promised a rematch if we had time before I went home. She made me "pinky promise" by linking our pinkies together and shaking them.

Jess took the seat next to mine at the table, giving me a tired smile. Hayley sat up with a blank look on her face then reached her arms toward me. Unsure of how to respond, I deferred to Jess. She loosened her hold, and I held out my arms. Hayley crawled over and rested her head on my shoulder and started rubbing my face.

Jess's voice trembled. "She'd never felt a scratchy face before yesterday. Bryan couldn't have grown a beard if his life depended on it. He was always clean shaven. If it bothers you, ask her to stop. Seriously, she might keep doing it until you can't grow a beard ever again, at least in that one spot."

"She's not bothering me," I said quietly.

Hayley's hand rested on my face. A heavy silence fell as Jess stared at me holding her daughter. Slowly, I sat back in the chair and held the little girl. My blood rushed behind my ears and my pulse pounded in my temples.

Marí broke the silence. "Let's eat before it gets cold."

Cal hopped back into action at her words. Jess and I continued to stare at one another. I felt helpless. I had not planned for this. My relief came in the form of Sadie running to the table for breakfast. Hayley's head popped up as she caught her friend's energy and excitement for food. I helped her down so she could find an empty chair of her own before standing to ask how I could help serve.

Jess remained seated and stared at my empty chair. Looking overwhelmed, she picked up her coffee and walked outside to the front porch.

I started to follow her, but Marí stopped me with a hand on my arm. "No. She needs to do this alone for right now. It is how she works through things."

I watched out the door for another moment before turning to sit back down and have breakfast with the others, my heart in my throat.

47

JESS

I heard the door open behind me but didn't turn to see who had come out to join me. There was a brief silence before anyone spoke.

"It's hard, watching the moments you thought were meant for you, happen for someone else." It was Cal's gentle voice. "Mind if I sit?"

Unable to speak, I shook my head. We sat in silence staring across the field.

"Did Bryan ever tell you that I asked his mom to marry me?"

My head turned toward him and with a look of surprise, I shook my head.

"Many times, actually. The first time was before she ever married Bryan's dad."

How had Bryan not mentioned this? Had he even known?

"I fell in love with Lucinda when we were in ninth grade. I called her Cindy. She was the girl of my dreams. When we graduated high school, I proposed the same night. She turned me down because I was drunk as a skunk. I don't blame her. I would've turned me down too. She told me she would never marry a man with a drinkin' problem. When I saw she started gettin' serious with Hank, I cleaned up my act and quit drinkin'. I even went to church a couple times and ended up finding God. I asked her one more time, but it was too little, too late. She was marryin' him, not me.

"When Hank died, I stepped in and helped around the farm, around the house, with Bryan. I asked Cindy over and over to marry me, but she'd just shoo me away and tell me she was too old to start over. That's the way it happened 'til the day she died. I don't tell you that for any reason except to tell you that God redeemed me and my losses over my many years. I didn't get all my wants and wishes. But had I, we wouldn't either of us had Bryan in our lives. You wouldn't have your daughter. And I wouldn't have a house full of beautiful women to take care of."

His words made me smile.

"I know watchin' Mark in there with Hayley made you feel like it should have been Bryan and not him. I think we all felt that for a second. But I truly think if you will let God redeem your losses, you might find that he restores you, too."

After another round of silence, Cal grunted as he stood, and I continued watching a cow roam through the neighboring field.

"There's a young man inside itchin' to come talk to you. Be gentle. He didn't mean no harm."

I nodded and reached for his hand. "Thank you, Cal."

He gave my hand a squeeze. "Sure thing, darlin'."

48

JESS

Mark came outside and paused when I stood to face him. "Do you have a minute, or are you getting ready to leave?" I asked before he could say anything.

"I have some time."

"Take a walk with me?"

He looked down at my bare feet then back at me with raised eyebrows.

"It's fine," I chuckled.

"Gone country so soon?" Amusement tagged his voice.

I smiled and motioned toward the yard with my head. "I like the way this grass feels." I left my empty coffee mug on the porch and started down the stairs.

Mark followed, and we began walking toward the fence. "Jess, I'm sorry about—" His words were genuine and earnest.

Holding up a hand, I stopped walking and studied him.

Regret. Apologetic. Worry.

"Mark, you have nothing to apologize for. You did nothing wrong."

His eyes searched mine. "I'm sorry, anyway. The look on your face when…It came very close to crushing me. I can't pretend to know how you feel. I do know what it is to lose someone you love. And no one can or will ever replace them in your heart. Please don't think that I would ever intentionally do anything to make you feel that way. And if I ever do something inadvertently, it's okay for you to say so."

Sincerity. Warmth. Sorrow.

Tears burned my eyes. "Thank you."

We watched the neighboring cow grazing in her field, and my mind wandered for a moment. "It's funny. I only knew Bryan for a few years. But he became a part of me, which I guess is natural when you love someone. We had all these grand plans for him to retire early and move here to raise a family. Hayley was a surprise, but we were beside ourselves with excitement once we processed it. Bryan was so excited to be a dad.

"After she was born, I thought it was step two in our fairytale. Instead, it was when the story started to unravel. I blamed the physical and emotional demands of having a newborn being piled on top of his work responsibilities. For almost a year I watched the man who had become so deeply a part of me waste away. Every day felt like a layer of my heart was being peeled away until I could no longer feel the pain. I prayed hourly some days for him to come back to me.

"God finally answered and restored him. I got six good months with Bryan after that. Hayley got six good months with her daddy. It wasn't long enough." My voice cracked, and the tears streamed down my cheeks.

Holding on to the fence for stability, I attempted to compose myself before continuing. "There have been days when I'm angry with Bryan, and I blame him for doing all of this to us. There are moments I blame God and ask him why he didn't stop it all from happening. This morning, all I could think was how unfair it is that Bryan wasn't here. But the more I thought about it, the less I could hold onto that feeling. If Bryan were alive, we wouldn't be here. I wouldn't be battling the rollercoaster of emotions I've been on for so long."

After wiping the tears from my face, I turned to face Mark. "I'm glad Hayley feels safe with you. I'm thankful we can both feel safe with you and that you are here. So please, don't feel bad or apologize for being someone we can trust when we need you."

Admiration. Compassion. Desire.

"You shouldn't look at people like that. You might make them cry." I gave a tearful laugh.

Mark's lips quirked up at the corners. "Jess..." He started to take a step forward but was interrupted by a toddler's voice yelling from the house.

"Mommy! I can play outside with Sadie?"

"Sure, baby! Just put your shoes on!" I yelled back.

Mark and I gave each other feeble smiles.

"I know you need to get on the road. We should go work out those logistics you mentioned last night."

Mark nodded, and we walked back to the farmhouse in silence.

WHILE MARÍ and Cal took the girls outside to play, Mark and I sat at the kitchen table so he could walk me through what he thought the next several months could potentially look like.

"I can't promise you won't be needed back in DC at some point. As a matter of fact, I'd go ahead and bank on needing to make at least one trip for a deposition. I'll try and take care of as much as I can before that needs to happen. I'd like your permission to sweep your house and vehicles for listening devices and trackers and any additional evidence that might be out of sight."

"I'll give you my keys before you leave."

Mark nodded. "That would help. Now, is there anything you want me to do for you or need me to do when I get back?"

"Any chance you could find Pete Stewart and punch him in the face for me?"

Mark laughed, and it sent a warm flutter into my chest. "I definitely plan to find him if they haven't already. I can't promise I'll get the chance to punch him in the face, but I will bring him to justice. I promise."

"It was worth asking. I just can't believe he's connected to all of this. I knew he was shady, but I didn't think he was a killer."

Thinking about my first encounter with Pete, I shivered as I remembered the painful shock from his touch. Refocusing on the conversation I was having with Mark, it occurred to me that I had very few possessions with me and obtaining more might be difficult if the goal was to stay off the grid.

"I guess I need to know what I'm supposed to do about money. I have money but accessing it will be difficult if I can't use my card. And I doubt they have the same credit union here."

"I talked to Cal this morning. He said that you'd be taken care of and didn't need to worry about anything. So, your basic needs are covered. As far as your bills and obligations, do you pay any of them in person?"

"No, I pay everything online."

Rubbing a finger over his eyebrow, Mark seemed to be deep in thought. His expression was serious though blank. "We need to ask Cal if he has a computer you can use. Do you even know if there's internet out here? It didn't even occur to me until now," Mark finally said.

"I have a laptop with me."

Mark shook his head. "I don't think you should use your laptop. Honestly, I should take it with me and run scans on it when we do the rest of your house. Have you powered it on since being here?"

"No."

"Good. Don't. I know that it's important, but if someone bugged your house, they could have easily put a tracker on your laptop."

"Okay. I'll figure something out soon." I started to feel nervousness creeping up on me. Locking my hands together behind my neck, I squeezed my eyes closed and let out a long breath.

Two hands gently gripped my upper arms and pulled my hands from behind my head until they were being held in front of me.

"Jess, you're not in this alone. You can ask for help anytime. Got it?"

The slow vibrating current flowed through me, and this time I didn't pull away from it. I nodded. "Seriously, Mark, thank you. I owe you my life and Hayley's."

Color tinged his cheeks pink, and his hands grew warm around mine. "You don't owe me anything. I'll do whatever I have to in order to keep you and Hayley safe. I think you being here is a good start." Clearing his throat, Mark released my hands and leaned back.

Unsure what to do with my hands, I clasped them together in my lap.

Once we worked out the computer situation, Mark installed a VPN on the machine before he decided he needed to get going.

"This will make it harder for anyone to make a connection between your bills being paid and where you are while you are doing it. It's not foolproof, but it's what we can do from here right now."

A SHORT WHILE LATER, we all walked outside to send Mark on his way.

Cal shook Mark's hand firmly and looked him hard in the eyes. "Thank you, again, young man. I hope we get the chance to meet, again."

"Yes, sir. I'd like that." Mark returned the look, once again seemingly communicating something more than his words.

Marí, who was carrying a barefoot Sadie, reached up and patted Mark's cheek. "You are a fine young man, and I thank you for getting us here, safely." She pulled his face to hers and kissed his other cheek.

Sadie gave him a thumbs up. "Bye, Mark!"

He bumped her fist with his thumb up. "Bye, Sadie."

Marí led Cal away and pointed into the distance, leaving Mark, Hayley, and me to say goodbye.

He poked Hayley's arm playfully, and she tried poking him back. It made her giggle when he jumped at her pokes.

"You are such a special kid. Be good for your mom, okay?"

She nodded and squirmed to get down. I let her go, and we watched as she ran toward Marí, Sadie, and Cal. Cal turned and scooped her up into the air. Hayley took his hat and put it on her own head, which made all of us laugh.

After several beats of silence, Mark and I both started to speak at the same time. I motioned for Mark to speak first.

"You're safe here, but if you need anything, call me. Don't hesitate. Besides, I've gotten used to talking to you every day. So, if you just want to talk, you could call then too." He sounded nervous.

"Friends do typically stay in touch." I said, trying not to sound too eager.

We stared at each other in silence.

"You know, you could also call me sometime if you wanted to just talk," I suggested, feeling like I was in high school again.

He smiled, and the same flutters I felt when he laughed tickled my core.

"Sounds good." He seemed to struggle with making himself leave.

I was struggling with letting him go.

"Oh!" I broke the moment when I reached into my pocket and retrieved a set of keys. "Here are these."

Mark took the keys, and as he did, I stood on my toes and threw my arms around his neck and hugged him as though he was a life preserver on the open water. He slowly moved his arms around me and hugged me back.

"Thank you for everything," I whispered over his shoulder.

With a gentle squeeze, Mark let go first.

I had to wipe tears from my face when I stepped back.

"Hey," he said quietly, pulling me back to him. "You're going to be okay. Everything is going to be okay; I promise." He quietly stroked my hair.

With a loud sniffle, I nodded against his chest.

He let go once more and after several moments had passed, he said, "I really should go."

"I know. Call me when you get home? Let me know you made it, okay?"

"I will." His eyes didn't leave mine. "Bye, Jess."

"Bye, Mark."

With that, he closed the door and started the long drive home.

49

MARK

It was close to midnight when I finally got home. During the drive I made several calls to catch up with work. The time I wasn't making calls for work I spent thinking about Jess and how badly I wanted to call her. And then I'd argue with myself about the sensibility of calling her.

To say I was exhausted by the time I got home was an understatement. But I had told Jess I would call when I made it home. One look at the clock told me that calling would not be the best idea. It was late, and she shared a room with Hayley. I didn't want to wake either of them with a phone call so I decided I would send her a message instead.

> Me: I finally made it home.

There was so much more I would like to add to those few words. I wanted to tell her how much I missed seeing her and about the serenity that came over me just by being near her. I decided that might be inappropriate.

Instead, I added, *I'll talk to you, soon* and hit send.

PART III

PART III

50

JESS

Four Months Later

"Hey!" I answered with more gusto than I'd intended without looking at the caller ID, knowing it was Mark. We had talked every day since he had left Kentucky.

"Well, hello, to you too. You're in a good mood." His tone was relaxed.

"What are you talking about? I'm always in a good mood. Except when I'm not." I laughed at my lame attempt at humor, which made him laugh, stirring up those inward flutters that sound always gave me.

"So, things are good?" he asked. There was the sound of him shuffling papers in the background and his office chair squeaking as he moved.

"They are. We just came back inside from playing with new baby goats, which can take any day from a level three to a level ten. How are things there?"

The hesitation and the change in Mark's tone gave me pause. "I'd say about a five." He sounded apologetic.

"A five, huh? Not bad but not great. What's up?"

"It looks like the time has come where you're needed here."

I had known it was coming. Mark had warned me it was unavoidable, though I had still hoped that somehow I could avoid going back to DC. The idea of coming face to face with Pete Stewart caused my stomach to twist into a knot and my chest to tighten.

Mark must have sensed my resistance. "You won't see Pete or anyone else other than lawyers and official caseworkers. And I'll be close by the entire time," he said before I could begin to panic.

I released a breath that I didn't know I was holding. "Tell me what I need to do."

He gave me a date and time, and I promised I'd make all the arrangements to be there.

"I'll pick you up at the airport if you'll send me your flight information," Mark said.

"I'll do that. How's everything else?" Which was my way of trying to ask about the case without asking directly.

"I know I've said it before, but I think there is so much more to this than you or I could have ever imagined. We start unraveling one thread just to find another one to detangle. It's a very wide web. But we're making progress. My job is focused on Pete and his company's role in all of it, and I feel pretty good about it."

"Good." His positivity gave my spirit a boost.

"Alright, well, send me your travel plans when you have them. I gotta get back to work. I'll talk to you, soon."

We hung up, and I went downstairs where I found Marí and Cal in the kitchen talking and laughing with one another. I could see the girls through the screen door on the front porch stacking rocks. When they realized I had entered the room, Marí and Cal both greeted me with smiles bright enough to be seen from space.

"Hey, darlin'. What can we do for ya?" Cal's smile was even detectable in his voice.

There was no way I could help but smile back at both of them. Not wanting to burst the bubble of giddiness that seemed to be settled over the room, I hesitated then let out a sigh.

"Mark just called. It looks like I need to be back in DC in three days for depositions."

Cal nodded as he took in the information, the smile never leaving his eyes.

Marí asked, "Is Hayley going with you?"

"As much as I hate the thought of being so far from her for so long, I think she should stay here. But I don't want to inconvenience anyone, so she could come with me, and I could see if Deborah could keep her while I was busy."

"Don't be silly. I know Deborah would love to see her, but I agree with you. Hayley should stay here. And she is never an inconvenience." Marí's voice sounded more carefree than I had ever heard.

Pressing a kiss to Marí's head, I said, "Thank you, mamacita. Now, you two get back to whatever you were talking about." I wagged a finger at both her and Cal and gave a wink. "I need to go book a flight and make some phone calls."

∼

WITHIN FORTY-EIGHT HOURS, I was on a plane landing at Reagan National Airport. I pulled out my phone and texted my hostess for the week.

> Me: Plane is landing. See you, soon!

As I deboarded, butterflies formed in my stomach. Why was I suddenly so nervous? I'd been thinking about this trip for two days, and I thought I had come to peace with everything.

As soon as I entered the terminal, I locked eyes with a familiar face, and my nerves calmed almost instantly.

Eagerness. Anticipation.

I had to bite my bottom lip to keep my smile from taking over my face. Hoping I didn't look too eager, I took longer strides, though I was most likely fooling no one when I practically flew into a pair of arms waiting for me.

Mark reached to take my bag. "Good flight?"

"It was. Plain and simple. It's so good to see you in person again," I said as we walked toward the exit.

After the initial investigation, my house in D.C. had been declared a potential crime scene. Once it was released from custody, I put it on the market, and it sold almost immediately meaning I was going to need to book a hotel. When I mentioned my travel plans to them, Deborah and John had offered to have me to stay with them while I was in town, and they also invited Mark to join us for dinner.

As we drove to their home, Mark asked questions to acquaint himself with the Parkers. "So, tell me, again, about the friends of yours I'm meeting. You said they were close with Bryan?"

The fact that we could have conversations about Bryan without either of us feeling the need to tiptoe around the topic was not lost on me. I had grown to appreciate Mark's ability to both speak freely and matter of factly as well as be compassionate. I didn't offer a lot in the way of personal information about Bryan, and he didn't ask. But I knew if either of us wanted to, we would each be willing to share and listen. It was as though the professional barriers we'd put up between us had allowed us to learn how to respect one another while building mutual trust, which in turn had allowed us to build our friendship on said trust and respect.

When we first met, I thought Mark was arrogant and rude. By our second meeting, I realized his arrogance was a compensation for anxiety. As he'd become more relaxed around me and his true personality had surfaced, I'd discovered he was funny and witty, which surprised me. His serious persona at work was very different from what I'd learned about his personality away from work.

He was extremely intelligent and creative. His ability to problem solve was unlike anything I had seen in a long time. Puzzles were nothing to him, but he rarely used conventional logic to solve them. And he could sort through piles of information in very little time. He would have made an excellent study subject for one of my research projects. Now, however, he was my closest friend, even though we lived over five hundred miles apart.

"John and Deborah were practically Bryan's second parents. John is the pastor at the church we attended here, and Deborah is one of my dearest friends. I think you will really like them."

"They aren't going to try and convert me or get me to join a cult, are they?" Mark teased.

We'd had numerous conversations in the last several months about God during what had become nightly phone calls. Mark wasn't convinced of anything, though I had noticed he was starting to initiate the conversations more frequently. I took it as a good sign.

Rolling my eyes at him I said, "No, not a cult. Just a pyramid scheme. And if you refuse to join, I will have failed at my attempts to recruit you and I'm afraid you won't be allowed to have contact with me anymore."

He gave an exaggerated sigh. "Being friends with you seems to come with pretty high price tags. I may need to check my savings account balance before we go inside."

I shrugged. "Who says money can't buy friends?"

We both laughed and exited the car to make our way to the front door.

Deborah was ecstatic when she opened the door. Once the hug began, I wasn't sure either of us knew if it would ever end. Hayley and I made video calls to them regularly but there was just something about physically being together that made the world seem right in that moment.

John's hug was just as warm and welcoming.

When I introduced them to Mark, I had to stifle a laugh when Deborah embraced him almost as tightly as she had me.

"We are so thankful you have been there for Jess through everything that has happened. It is so nice to finally meet you," Deborah gushed as she squeezed him.

Mark blushed, not knowing how to respond so he simply used both hands to gently pat her on the back.

When Deborah released him, John reached to shake Mark's hand. "If we had lost Jess or Hayley, I don't know what we would have done. Thank you."

Mark nodded, ears still pink from being put on the spot. "I would do anything to keep them safe," he said, not sounding so much official as he sounded caring.

It felt good to be home with this part of my family.

After dinner, Deborah invited Mark to sit and talk for a while, but he insisted he wanted to give us time to catch up with one another. She made him promise to join us for dinner again before I left town.

"Thank you for picking me up and staying for dinner." I walked Mark to his car.

"No problem. I like them. I am disappointed that they never mentioned the pyramid scheme."

With a sigh of feigned resignation I said, "I guess that means you can still call me later, then."

"You know I will." His real smile always showed a dimple in his left cheek and laugh lines at his eyes.

It usually threatened to send my heart into a-fib. "Good. Will I see you tomorrow or am I on my own for the depositions?"

"I'm afraid you are on your own for the depositions, but if you are free for lunch, you will see me then."

"I will definitely see you then."

Once I was back inside, Deborah and I sat on the couch and stayed up far too late talking and crying and laughing together. It was good for both of us.

After fewer hours of sleep than I probably needed, I awoke the next morning to the sounds and smells of breakfast being made. I felt refreshed, which should not have surprised me. I had been reunited with a part of my heart I had missed dearly, and I was going to ride the wave of happiness as long as it would last.

Deborah greeted me with a hug for what felt like the fiftieth time since I had arrived the previous evening, but I did not mind. I was going to tuck every hug from her away to remember later when we were apart once more.

"Do you want to use my car today? I'm not planning to go anywhere." Deborah returned to the stove where bacon was sizzling in a pan.

"Thanks, but I'm going to take an Uber. I don't know how long I will be out today. Mark said it could be an hour or it could be several hours, it just depends on the attorneys involved. I also told Dr. Thorne I would stop by this afternoon to catch up and look at some of his new research. It may be this evening before I make it back here."

"Okay, well, if you change your mind, the keys are hanging by the door of the garage," she said.

And in that moment, I was transported back to the days when I would sit in the kitchen with my mom on the weekends and we would share our plans and schedules with one another. Deborah would have made an amazing mother, and thinking so reminds me of how good she was to Bryan and how wonderful she is with Hayley. I was nearly in tears as I considered how grateful I was to have this woman as a friend, though she's so much more to me than just a friend.

"I've missed you, Deborah."

Looking up at me with tearful eyes Deborah said, "Oh, sweetie, you have no idea."

51

JESS

When I arrived for my appointment ten minutes early, I was surprised to be escorted to a small conference room five minutes later. If anything, I had expected to arrive early just to be left waiting for far longer. This made me hopeful that maybe Mark's estimation of one hour would hold true. My hopes were soon dashed on the rocks of a three-hour bombardment of questions, most I had no real answers for.

By the time they thanked me and said they would call if they needed anything else, my brain felt like butter melting on a hot griddle. My stomach had also started growling halfway through the meeting like I hadn't eaten for days. Now that my nerves had faded, I was feeling ravenous.

After texting Mark and planning our meet up for lunch, I made a quick video call home to Marí and said hello to Hayley, who was fully occupied with Cal and Sadie as they randomly moved pieces around a boardgame.

When I saw Mark was waiting for me, I ended the call. He offered a quick side hug as I passed him to enter the café. Once we ordered and found a table, I caught him up on the last three hours and how I felt it had been a complete waste of everyone's time since I'd had little to offer.

"I'm sorry you had to go through it, but I'm not sorry you're here." Mark twirled the metal card holder indicating our table number.

"I'm not sorry either." I felt my cheeks turning pink.

Our food arrived and our conversation shifted to updates from Kentucky and his other cases. I even told him about Marí and Cal trying to pretend they weren't head over heels for each other when I was around.

He laughed. "That connection was obvious from the minute he tipped his hat to her."

My face hurt from smiling at the thought. "My mind was preoccupied that day, so I missed that. But I caught on pretty quickly. I say good for them. An old friend of mine once told me, 'When you know, you know.' I found her wisdom to be valid." I thought of the email Mrs. Carlisle had sent me years ago that had given such counsel.

"You believe in love at first sight, then?" Mark asked.

I gave him a bewildered look. "Have I never told you about meeting Bryan?"

"You told me you met him at a club owned by his murderous friend."

"Huh. Well, long story short, though it couldn't get much shorter, we met at the club that night and we got married fifteen days later."

Mark's eyes were huge as he stared at me as though I had sprouted a second head on my shoulders. "Fifteen days? Holy cow, Jess! Seriously?"

His reaction made me laugh, which was unfortunate timing as I had just taken a drink of my water. Grabbing my napkin, I dried my lips and chin before I could speak again. "How have you not heard this story?"

"I don't know, but now I have, and I don't even know how to respond. Fifteen days. That's insane."

I gave him a knowing smile, "Not when you know."

"So, you just knew?" Mark was still reeling.

"It's not like he walked in, saw me, and immediately asked me to marry him. But I felt a connection with him when we met. I literally felt it when he shook my hand. We spent hours talking that night. Then we took a road trip to New York because that was where my friend Stacy was when she had her stroke. She called me, I called Bryan to cancel plans we had made, and he insisted he go with me. And I will forever be grateful that he did for so many reasons."

I told Mark about our two-week relationship comprised of mostly texts, phone, and video calls culminating in a proposal one day and a wedding the next.

Mark stared at me for a long time like he was trying to piece a new puzzle together. "Wow. Just wow," was all he managed to say.

I was about to ask him about his dating history when my phone buzzed with a message from Deborah.

> Deborah: Church member has called and needs us to visit this evening. I'm so sorry, but I don't think we'll be home for dinner. You have a key, right? We'll be home as soon as we can.

My response was short.

> Me: No problem. I have a key. See you tonight.

"John and Deborah are pulling after hours pastoral duties, so I guess the rest of my day just got a whole lot more flexible."

Mark gave me a quizzical look.

"They are going to visit a church member who needs them, so they won't be home until late. I was going to visit Dr. Thorne but had suggested it would be a quick visit. I guess he will be glad that my time is in less demand."

"How long were you planning to be at the university?"

"I think Deborah had planned for the three of us to go out for dinner, so I wasn't staying late." I stacked our empty plates on the table.

"Would you consider having dinner with me instead?" he asked.

Tilting my head, I tapped my chin. "I'd consider it."

He rolled his eyes and smiled slowly as though he might regret the answer to his next question. "What would it take to convince you to have dinner with me instead?"

I began to stroke my chin as though I was thinking through a long list of options.

Mark checked his watch and sighed dramatically before drumming his fingers on the table as he waited.

"I would be convinced if the offer included junk food and the dress code involved sweatpants."

His lips twitched as he repressed a smile. "I will see you at six p.m. You had better be wearing sweatpants," he said pointedly.

BEING BACK at the university made me long for the bygone simpler days. Dr. Thorne was thrilled to show off some of his new work and introduce me in person to a few of our interns and research assistants. When we formed our consulting group, we had initially thought we would work independently of the university. But it became a mutually beneficial arrangement as the opportunity to work with Doctors Carsen and Thorne attracted many new applicants, and we were able to utilize the students and their skills.

I almost lost track of time before realizing I needed to get back to the Parkers' home to ensure Mark didn't arrive to an empty house. With assurances to Dr. Thorne that I would make every effort to stop by again before I left DC, I said my goodbyes and made a beeline for my comfortable sweatpants.

52

JESS

"This is perfect." I spread out the blanket Mark had tossed me. There were families and groups of friends and couples scattered throughout a small park waiting for it to get dark enough for a movie to be projected on a large screen in front.

"I was hoping it met the requirements you laid out this afternoon."

"Well, almost. I see sweatpants. I don't see the junk food."

"Ah, yes. If you are comfortable waiting here, I will fulfill the remaining requirements momentarily."

With an approving nod from me, Mark headed off toward the courtyard.

While I waited, I called and talked to Marí and Hayley. Cal sent his greetings, and Sadie was enamored with the puzzle she and Cal were working on at the kitchen table.

"When are you coming home, mommy?" Hayley's voice was whiney with fatigue.

"Two more nighttime sleeps," I say.

"I miss you mommy. Did MiMi Deb like my pictures?"

"I miss you, too, sweet pea. She loved them."

Mark reappeared with his arms full of food from different food trucks around the park. "Is that Hayley?" he asked quietly.

I glanced up and nodded before looking back at the phone screen.

He laid out the food in front of me before sitting down behind my shoulder and waving at the screen.

Hayley waved back. "Hi, Mark."

Marí, who had been watching something on the television immediately focused her attention on the phone. Cal's head popped up from his puzzle.

"Hi, Mark. It is good to see you. Still taking care of Jess, I see," Marí said with a hint of mischief in her tone.

"Yes, ma'am. I'm afraid it's turning into a full-time job."

Giving Mark a playful tap on the arm I said, "Thank you. I am right here. And quite capable of taking care of myself." I rolled my eyes at my friends.

"Hayley, Mommy is going to let you go so you can play a little more before bedtime. I'll talk to you in the morning, okay?"

"Okay, mommy. I love you, 'dis much." She spread her arms as wide as she could.

"And I love you more." I blew a kiss at the phone. "Good night, my darling girl."

"Bye, Mommy."

Mark was watching me as I hung up the call and put my phone back into my purse.

"You are a great mom. Your daughter has no idea how lucky she is to have you."

Thankful for the darkening sky so Mark couldn't see me blush I said, "There are days where I watch her run and play and laugh and I feel like I've got everything under control. Then there are days where one or both of us spend a lot of time in tears and I question my sanity. But we help each other survive." Rather than look at him I traced the pattern on the blanket.

Leaning forward to rest his chin on my shoulder he said, "You're a great mom on the good days and the hard ones."

I leaned my head over onto his, letting the familiar current pass between us and gave a one-sided smile. "Thanks."

When I raised my head, my attention immediately turned to the copious amounts of food in front of us. "How many people were you expecting to feed?"

"I wanted to make sure I went above and beyond the expectations placed on the evening. When there are only two requests made, I have to assume quality matters."

"Hm," was all I said.

With a formal observation, I gave a single nod. "I approve."

THE MOVIE WAS an old black-and-white from the fifties, and the food truck dinner was amazing. Had there been six more fried Oreos, I would have eaten them and not felt at all bad about it. But my favorite part was the comfortable and familiar company I had with Mark. We delivered commentary on the movie at times and sat silently watching at others.

The ride back to the Parkers' consisted of a conversation on the subpar quality of movies today versus sixty years ago. By the time we pulled into the driveway, we concluded the reason had to be related to the quality of talent surrounding the movies, including but not limited to the accomplished musicians behind the scores, the extensively proper vernacular of the day, and the expectation of actors actually being able to perform all the ways listed on their résumés.

It had been a long time since I had felt as relaxed and content as I had for the few hours at the park. I also enjoyed seeing the laid-back side of Mark in person and not just hearing it over the phone. There always seemed to be something new for me to learn about him with every encounter, and each time I had to remind myself that there were still boundaries between us that couldn't be crossed —not right now and maybe not ever. Only time would make that clear.

Nonetheless, I had enjoyed spending time with Mark face to face.

And discovering he still sent those feelings through me made it hard to remember we were just friends.

Mark walked me to the door where we stood as I dug from my bag the key Deborah had given me that morning. Once I found it, I looked up to find Mark's eyes on me.

"That was fun." I smiled.

He was beaming. "I'm glad you enjoyed it."

"Didn't you?"

"I did. But I didn't do it for me."

"Well, thank you. I enjoyed myself thoroughly. The company was nice too," I teased.

I thought Mark was going to say something else, but he stopped himself and shifted on his feet. He appeared to study the porch and rubbed a hand across the back of his neck before looking up.

"Can I see you tomorrow?" he asked timidly.

"You mean other than here for dinner?"

He shrugged and nodded. "Yeah. I'm off tomorrow. If you're free, I'll be free."

I fidgeted with the key between my fingers. My immediate answer wanted to be, 'Yes, absolutely, first thing,' but I had just reminded myself that we were just friends for a reason.

"Did you have something in mind?" I asked.

"Nothing specific." He rushed to add, "It's okay if you already have plans."

"My plans aren't set in stone. Can I let you know tomorrow?"

"Absolutely," he said with his dimpled grin.

I unlocked the door then turned to face him. "Thank you, again, for tonight."

"Good night, Jess," he said before turning to walk away.

When I opened the door, Deborah, sitting on the couch under a blanket, tossed a book into the air and said breathlessly, "Oh!"

"Oh, my goodness! I'm so sorry. I did not mean to scare you." I laughed.

Deborah laughed, too, as she retrieved the book from the floor then removed her reading glasses.

"No, it wasn't you." She was still laughing. "I thought it was John coming to tell me it was late and that I should come to bed, again. It would have been the third time, and I felt like a schoolgirl getting caught by the teacher."

"Good book?" I asked with an amused grin.

Deborah picked the book back up and held it so I could see it. "It really is. I got sucked in and lost track of time more than once, apparently."

Setting the book down on the coffee table in front of the couch, she sighed and smiled as I took the seat next to her. "Thanks for leaving us a note this evening. It was not necessary. You're an adult, and we aren't your parents. But the gesture was appreciated."

"I know, but I respect you and love you, and I didn't want there to be any cause for worry when I wasn't here after you returned." I picked up the end of the blanket and draped it over my legs.

Deborah leaned over and put an arm around me and squeezed. "Well, thank you."

We sat smiling at each other for several beats. I could tell she wanted me to fill her in about the day's events, but it was more fun for me to watch her desperately wanting to know while trying not to pry.

So…" She trailed off, hoping I would offer up information without her having to ask.

"So…" I smiled at Deborah playfully.

"Since you're playing coy, I'll ask you to tell me about the morning."

I gave her the quick version of the depositions then shared with her about my visit with Dr. Thorne. "He was borderline rapturous when I walked into his office. He reminded me of Hayley at Christmas last year when she had opened all her gifts then had to do a personal walkthrough so everyone could see them. He's doing a great job on this end. I told him I'd try to squeeze in another visit tomorrow to watch some of the interns at work."

Deborah nodded along. "Did you have lunch?"

"Oh, yeah, I met Mark at one of the cafés near his office."

Deborah's eyebrows went up as she gave me a cheeky grin. "Lunch and dinner, hmm?"

A slight tremor of panic rose inside of me as I considered her implication.

It must have shown on my face because Deborah was mortified and began to apologize. "Oh, Jess, no. I wasn't— I don't..." She took a deep breath then heaved a sigh. "I was teasing. Oh, honey, I'm sorry."

I relaxed slightly.

"You know that we love you and want nothing but your happiness. You and Mark just seemed so comfortable with each other last night and then you spent extra time with him today. I thought maybe... I am so sorry if that was out of line." Deborah sounded genuinely apologetic.

Swallowing hard, I stared at the rug on the floor in front of us and focused on trying to see every single fiber. I felt Deborah watching me, but I couldn't face her. Old feelings of guilt started to surface, and it felt selfish to let them in front of Deborah. She had and was still grieving the loss of Bryan just as I was, even if it was on a different level.

When I finally met Deborah's gaze it was kind and gentle. We both had tears forming in our eyes. Deborah reached for a box of tissues and took one before handing them to me.

"Mark is my best friend. I've never actually used those words for him, but if I had to put a label on him, that would be the one I chose. We have talked every single day for the last several months. If I'm wrapping up my day and realize we haven't talked, I have to at least text him just to check in and see how his day went. Those days are rare because he usually beats me to it. And I'm still working through some heavy guilt because I haven't grieved Bryan the way I feel is expected of me because I'd already grieved his absence a lot longer before I lost him. I won't lie and say I haven't considered what ifs and possibilities with Mark. We've never talked about it, but even if we did, there are plenty of reasons those things remain outside of the realm of possibilities."

Deborah interjected, "Such as?"

"For starters, he's not a believer. We have a lot in common. We get along beautifully. He's so sweet with Hayley. But there's a massive connection that just isn't there. And he isn't like I was before I fully accepted Christ. I at least believed there was a God. Mark doesn't even know if he believes God is real."

Deborah nodded. "That is a problem." I could see the wheels turning in her mind.

"I'll go ahead and stop you from thinking whatever it is you are thinking. Because if that isn't a big enough problem, my emotional guilt throws up a brick wall any time I remotely consider the idea. Not to mention we live five hundred miles apart, and we each have careers to which we are strongly committed."

I laid back on the couch and stared up at the ceiling.

Deborah chewed the corner of her thumbnail making several sighing sounds before finally putting words to her thoughts. "Jess, I can't make Mark a believer any more than you can. And I can't make you stop feeling the things you feel when you feel them. What I can do is offer you some advice if you are willing to hear it and take it to heart."

Sitting up, I put my hand on Deborah's and squeezed. "I will always take advice from you."

Deborah squeezed back. "I don't know Mark like I knew Bryan. But John and I are both very impressed by him. He clearly cares about you, he's very nice, and if we're both being honest, he's easy on the eyes."

Feeling my eyes grow large, I covered my mouth so as not to laugh too loudly. "Deborah Parker! I have never heard you say such things."

"I only say things when I think they need to be said. Besides, it's late and my filter may be a little weaker when I'm tired."

This made me giggle, which meant it was definitely late.

"Here's my advice. And it may not be at all what you want to hear, but it's something I think you need to at least hear and think about and pray about. Stop letting what you think matters to Bryan dictate your life."

The mood around us grew solemn. I wanted to protest but

Deborah stopped me. "Think about where Bryan is and what he's doing right now. It should make you jealous. It does me. He has no idea what is happening here on earth, and as much as we might wish he did, he doesn't care. Because he is in the presence of his Lord worshipping and singing and probably trying to dance."

This made me smile. Bryan had been a horrible dancer, so to think of him dancing in front of Jesus was almost more than I could take.

Deborah pushed forward. "Now, think of all the things you told me he put in place to make sure you were cared for and protected even in the event of his death. He wanted to be absolutely sure you and Hayley could continue to live unencumbered by anything in the here and now. Obviously, the ideal situation would be Bryan was still here with us and you lived out your years happily with one another and had fourteen more grandbabies for me to love."

The thought of having fifteen children made me chuckle.

"But what we consider ideal was not what God considered ideal for us. Instead, we trust that He has a plan so magnificent that we awaken each morning knowing that every second that passes means we are still actively part of that plan."

We sat in the stillness together for several minutes.

"I never really considered the fact that Bryan doesn't know what's happening here. If he did, that would defeat the point of heaven, wouldn't it? Seeing his family hurting and making decisions without him would lead to feelings and emotions that can't exist in heaven, huh?" I asked, already knowing the answer.

Deborah nodded.

"I don't think hearing this from anyone else would have the same impact. Thank you for being willing to say what I know had to be hard for you to say."

Deborah let go of my hand and began folding back her side of the blanket. "Now, I have to get to bed before I wind up in the principal's office tomorrow. Do you have plans other than going to the university tomorrow? I have to make a few visits at the nursing home and then run to the grocery store before starting on dinner for our guest tomorrow evening. Otherwise, I'd have you booked for the day."

With a sheepish smile I said, "Mark's off tomorrow and asked if I wanted to hang out with him."

"And you said?"

"I said I'd let him know tomorrow."

Deborah snickered. "Oh, that poor man."

"What?"

"Never mind. By the way, you didn't get around to telling me what you two did this evening?"

I couldn't stop the goofy smile that took over my face as I gave her the quick version.

Deborah's face told me that she was impressed and might have been smitten on my behalf. She stood up and muttered, "That poor, poor man."

Standing I hugged my friend. "Good night, Deborah."

"I will see you in the morning, Jess. Sweet dreams."

I LAID in bed alternating between staring at the ceiling and glancing at my watch as I argued with myself internally about spending more time with Mark. I felt silly even debating it. Mark was my best friend. Deborah seemed to think there was more to it, at least on Mark's end. I guess it was plausible, but had he even given any indication of this being true?

We'd had so many conversations, none of which implied any kind of romantic attraction. Sure, we teased each other, which could be construed as flirting by some people. One of us may occasionally make physical contact with the other in the form of a hug or high five, but friends did that all the time. And yes, he had asked me out for drinks after our second encounter, but that didn't mean he had feelings for me. He hadn't even known me then.

A huge sigh of frustration escaped as I massaged my forehead and temples. Decision made, I reached over to grab my phone, stopping when I saw the shiny necklace glistening by the light of all the small lights in the room. I sat up and lifted it from its resting place and ran the chain through my fingers.

Wearing jewelry on the hands is not safe for hands or for the jewelry when farm activities are involved. So, after being on the farm for a few weeks, I'd called the old man from the jewelry store where I had purchased Bryan's wedding ring to ask if there was a way to turn my engagement ring setting into a necklace. He was extremely humble and apologetic when I explained the circumstances. I had shipped the ring to him with loads of trepidation, but he had provided me with much assurance that his process was safe and secure. A few weeks later, my engagement ring was delivered transformed into a beautiful pendant on a delicate platinum chain.

Running my thumb over the stones caused me to replay my conversation with Deborah. It was true that Bryan had more important things going on at the moment. But would it be a dishonor to him if I ever decided to open my heart to someone again?

I reversed the roles in my mind. Would I see it as a slight if Bryan had been the one in my place? I would want Bryan taken care of as well as I was being cared for by so many wonderful people. I would want him happy. And I definitely wouldn't want him held back by a ghost of me in his memory. I would trust him to make the best decision for him and Hayley.

"Ugh!" I was frustrated with myself and with my thoughts. Tears were already in the corners of my eyes.

God, please. Please make this easier. You have brought me through so much and have given every ounce of strength and wisdom I've needed to endure. None of it was in my own power. I know that my heart cannot go to a man who does not love you more than he loves me. But, right now, I don't feel like my heart could ever go to another man ever again. Not because I don't have the desire to love and be loved by another, but because of the guilt and uncertainty that blurs my mind. I want to ask of you so many things but more than any of them, I pray that your will is done in my life. My desire is that Mark comes to trust you as Lord of his life. Even if he is never more than a friend to me, I want him to know you. You will be more of a friend to him than I ever will be.

And, if it's your will, open my heart to love, again, but not before it should. Bryan will always be the one my heart loved first, teaching me what true love looks like, even unto death. I thank you for that love. If it pleases you, give me the ability to experience that kind of love another day. I know you will take me through these feelings and show me how to navigate these waters. Thank you for never letting go of me.

Setting the necklace back onto the table, I picked up my phone.

> Me: Hang out with me, tomorrow?

It was late so I wasn't sure if he would respond, but I watched the screen, anyway. It came much more quickly than I had anticipated.

> Mark: Did you have something in mind?

> Me: Yes.

> Mark: What time should I pick you up?

I smiled as I thought about how much I appreciated his easygoing nature. For a man whose job involved asking questions and putting himself in dangerous situations on a regular basis, Mark never seemed to be overwrought with concern. Well, that wasn't true. I had seen him worry and anxious, but it was only when he was in protective mode. Otherwise, he was relaxed and at ease and I loved that it was contagious when we were together.

> Me: 9:00

DEBORAH MET me at the kitchen counter with coffee.

"Did you get any sleep after you went to bed?" she asked me.

Rocking my head side to side I answered, "I had a long conversation with God, and then I texted Mark. Both got my mind keyed up, so I struggled to fall asleep. I slept hard but not enough, I'm afraid."

Deborah sipped her coffee and gave me a look with raised eyebrows encouraging me to continue talking.

Mirroring her expression, I smiled behind the cup.

"Why do you always make me ask?" Deborah chided jokingly.

"Because it's something I always did to annoy my mom, and I can't change who I am," I said teasingly.

Deborah's eyes sparkled with tears at the sentiment, but they never fell. She sighed dramatically before responding. "Fine. Did you and Mark make plans for today?"

I repositioned myself on the barstool at the counter. "Sort of. He's picking me up in about an hour. I thought I'd show him the institute and lab at the university. Dr. Thorne might wet himself with glee if he gets to give Mark the grand tour. Mark was his first convert, you know?"

Deborah cocked her head.

"I met Mark at Dr. Thorne's request. Mark didn't think my skills were legitimate until after I helped him on a case. Dr. Thorne prides himself on making a believer out of the skeptical Special Agent Mark Collins."

Deborah chuckled and refilled my coffee.

I glanced at my watch and stood, realizing Mark would be arriving soon. "I need to shower and change. Want help with dinner this evening?"

Deborah shook her head. "No, thank you. John is my partner in the kitchen. I think we can handle it."

Coffee cup in hand, I took in my beloved friend, confidant, and sister. I would always miss my mother and Bryan, but I was thankful God had seen fit to put Deborah Parker in my life to fill so many voids — some I didn't know I had.

53

MARK

"You didn't give me much to go on last night. Am I allowed to know where I'm taking us this morning?" I asked Jess as she buckled her seatbelt.

Having Jess in the passenger seat of my car the last couple of days had felt good; it felt right. Last night had been one of the best nights of my life and had me feeling things I had never felt before.

After I dropped Jess off, I spent the entire drive home replaying our conversation from lunch when she told me she had gotten married after knowing Bryan Carsen for fifteen days. The confidence she'd had in knowing her feelings overwhelmed me. It had me revisiting all my past relationships, and there had been many if you considered first dates that were never repeated a relationship. Only one had lasted more than a year, and I had been young and deployed for most of it. I'd never told a girl I loved her, and I absolutely never considered marrying any of the girls I'd been with.

Since meeting her, I'd been fascinated by Jess, and I won't lie—I'd found her attractive from day one. However, our relationship did not allow for romantic feelings, so any feelings of attraction I had were shoved deep into the recesses of my mind never to be retrieved.

Then, our relationship suddenly changed, and over the last

several months, I may have allowed my repressed feelings to slowly emerge. I hadn't decided if it was a terrible mistake on my part, as I'd yet to work up the courage to tell her how I felt. She was an incredible friend, and probably one of the best I'd ever had, which was strange to say as I never thought I could have a female best friend.

"I'd like to show you the new lab at the university if you're up for it. I think Dr. Thorne would get a kick out of seeing you, too." Jess pulled me from my thoughts.

"Then let's go."

Jess had been right. Dr. Thorne was beside himself when we entered his office. "Ah, the prodigal has returned." He smiled as he and I shook hands. "You know, I remember you entering these halls an unwavering skeptic. I also seem to recall you leaving that same day with far fewer doubts. And now, here you are with the wonder herself. I can tell it's going to be a glorious day!" He clapped his hands together.

The three of us moved through the building together talking about some of the projects in the works. When we would come to an occupied space, Dr. Thorne would enter the room and announce that he wanted to introduce two special guests. Then he would excitedly introduce Dr. Jess Carsen and Special Agent Mark Collins of the FBI.

Jess and I had to acclimate to the disturbance it caused at first. Everyone would stop whatever they were working on and move toward us hoping for a handshake or to discuss some project they were working on. The more I heard it, however, the less of a shock it was to hear her name paired with mine, and the more I actually enjoyed hearing it. I had to shake that thought from my head on more than one occasion.

As we wrapped up the tour, I listened as Jess gushed to Dr. Thorne about his progress and all the potential she had seen. She had relegated herself to mostly behind the scenes work and only the occasional direct consultation for almost the last year with all the personal issues I was unaware she had been dealing with at the time. Dr. Thorne had graciously and willingly stepped in for her when she needed him, and they found their stride quickly.

Now their firm and the university were turning out to be a well-oiled machine and most of it was to be credited to Dr. Thorne, though he would insist that none of it would have been possible without Jess and her abilities.

It felt as though I was eavesdropping, but neither Jess nor Dr. Thorne dismissed me or attempted to talk around me. While I was a liaison between the Agency and their firm, I wasn't on the inside of their company but Jess's willingness to share this with me felt like it meant something. I just wasn't sure what it could mean. Maybe it was another checkmark in the column of trust, and for that I was grateful. It mattered to me that Jess trusted me.

Before we left the university, Jess assured Dr. Thorne she was ready to move back into the direct flow of work but did not want to get in the way of any ongoing work, so they scheduled a more official meeting for the next week after Jess was back in Kentucky.

As we were leaving, she hugged her business partner and friend, and thanked him for all his effort and support for her in the last year.

Then Dr. Thorne turned to me with an outstretched hand. "And you, don't be a stranger around here. I could find a place for you here, if ever you get tired of chasing bad guys."

"I will keep that in mind, though I am pretty sure I'm nowhere near the level of intelligence you seem to keep close at hand here." I motioned toward the labs.

Dr. Thorne put his hands behind his back and rocked on his toes. "Do not discount yourself, son. I know a gifted person when I meet them." He winked at Jess conspiratorially.

After their final farewells, Jess and I moved toward the exit.

"I've always liked him," I said to Jess, holding the door open for her.

"Me too. You know, if it hadn't been for him, we wouldn't have met," she said.

"Now I like him even more."

Jess laughed, sending tingles through me from my chest to my toes. That was new.

"Now what?" I asked, as I tried to ignore the new sensation I was experiencing.

"Have you ever been to the Washington Cathedral?" she asked.

I shook my head.

"Good. That changes today," she said decidedly.

"You want me to go to church on my day off?" I asked wryly.

Jess rolled her eyes. "No. I want to show you a beautiful work of art and architecture."

We paid for parking and made our way up from the underground garage. The building was massive and impossible to take in all at one time. Jess appeared to be immediately carried away in her thoughts as she stared at the building.

I could see why. Turning to stare at the building, all I could think about was how big an undertaking such a work of art had to have been before modern methods of building. Along with the design and the attention to details on the outside, it was clear how any modern man or woman would be awestruck.

It wasn't clear how long we stood there staring at the outside of the building, but at some point, I realized Jess was watching me. She could probably see on my face that I was impressed, though I never said so.

Jess linked her arm around mine and began pulling me to the entrance. My attention once again on her, I considered our joined arms and bent my arm to create a crook for hers to rest in.

Walking through the doors felt like walking through the mouth of a massive cave that, if not for all the natural light from the windows, might have swallowed a person. We wandered slowly, taking in the archways and Jess's self-proclaimed favorite part, the stained glass. Neither of us spoke much, but our thoughts were evident by the smiles and looks of wonder we took turns expressing. This was partly because every sound in the building seemed to echo indefinitely. It was also due to the enormity and intricacy of it all. Words were not adequate.

Once we had made our way through the downstairs, we traveled upstairs where Jess said her second favorite part of the tour was found. I could see why it was one of her favorites. Windows all throughout provided endless views of the city.

"This is incredible," I murmured, the first words I had spoken in over an hour.

Jess gave me a knowing smile. "Isn't it? And the day is so clear, I feel like I could see all the way to a certain quiet farm in Kentucky."

I felt a shift in her. I put an arm around her shoulder, and she surprised me by putting hers around my waist. We stood once again in silence for a while before walking quietly window to window looking out at the vastness beyond us, arms still in place around one another. Buildings and cars covered some streets. Trees and parks lined others. Above us were still more spires and steeples and windows.

Three hours had flown by even in the quiet stillness of the visit. Once we were outside again, everything felt lighter in the open air, and our voices returned to normal. Standing on the sidewalk angled toward one another, we admired the building we had just left.

"That was amazing. Honestly, I was not convinced that I was going to enjoy walking around a church. But seeing the history and the art combined was unbelievable. Thank you."

Jess's look of contentment brightened. "You're welcome. The first time I walked through there was a choir singing. Talk about amazing. The melody just bounced from wall to wall, and I felt like I was being entranced. The sounds were almost unworldly."

Turning to fully face Jess, my heart was ramping up inside my chest, and I could feel myself starting to sweat. I forced my now clammy hands into my pockets and studied her profile until she moved to face me. Never had I wished more that I could read people like Jess could. I wondered what she saw when she looked at me. Did she know what I've wanted to tell her for longer than I would admit?

"Jess." My eyes searched her face as I tried to find the words I'd wanted to say but hadn't been able to bring myself to tell her over the phone. I let out a breath and just let the words tumble out. "Jess, I'm in love with you. I have been for a long time. I never felt like it was a good time for me to tell you. I don't even know that now is a good time to tell you. But not telling you wasn't an option because I felt like if I kept it to myself much longer, I'd talk myself out of believing it even mattered. And that would mean possibly losing you to someone else one day without ever knowing if that someone could have been me."

There was a chance my heart had stopped beating, and I had definitely stopped breathing as she stared at me, her eyes scanning and searching as they always did. I needed her to say something. At this point, I'd be open to her laughing uncontrollably thinking I was joking just so I could breathe again.

Her eyes lowered and she appeared to be examining the sidewalk very studiously. When she finally lifted her eyes to meet mine, hers were swimming with tears. It was like a punch to the gut. The breath I'd been holding released, and it was everything I could do not to take it all back and beg her to forget I said anything.

She reached out and ran her hands down my arms sending a shiver across my spine. She pulled my hands from my pockets and put her hands flat against mine. She silently studied our hands for a moment before lacing our fingers together.

"Mark, you are my best friend." She squeezed my hands. "And I would be lying if I told you I hadn't wished it could be more. There are so many things I want to add to that, but I won't. Because it wouldn't be fair to you."

There was rejection and hope and want and denial in her words, and I didn't understand.

Jess let go of my hands to my chagrin and ran one of her own through her hair before shoving both of her hands into her back pockets. She appeared to be having an internal debate with herself before finally speaking.

"I've told you many times my relationship with Christ matters more than any relationship I have on earth. It's that relationship that has been the cornerstone in the foundation of every solid relationship I've ever had. I won't change that now, not even for you, regardless of my feelings. I appreciate you and care about you more than you probably know, and I hope this doesn't change things between us. It won't change anything for me, but I will understand if what I'm telling you changes something for you."

My breath caught in my throat, and I found myself unable to look at Jess. Instead, I stared at the massive cathedral. Words vanished from my mind, and my thoughts were a jumbled mess. Nothing she had just said made much sense to me, but I understood that we were not on the same page. With that, all I could say was, "Okay."

Jess watched me. "Okay?"

The silence was deafening. I swallowed hard several times before I could speak again. "I don't want to lose you, Jess. But I also can't be the man you want me to be. And I would never pretend that I could be." My voice cracked.

I turned away and watched a small bird hop through the grass, feeling her follow my gaze.

We watched together as she asked, "So where does that leave us? Can we really still be friends even though we both know how we really feel? Because I can't imagine a single day without you as my friend."

If this was all I could have, then I would take it and be grateful I still had any connection to her. Reaching out, I wrapped an arm around her and pulled her to me; she turned and returned the embrace. I kissed the top of her head as we stood there wishing for more and knowing more would never happen.

54

JESS

Neither of us said much until we arrived back at the Parkers home. In the driveway, we sat and stared at the front door as though it was a pit of burning coals awaiting our passage.

Sneaking a look at Mark, his features were just as unreadable as they were after our conversation at the Cathedral. "You don't have to come in if you'd rather not. I can explain everything to them and…"

He turned to face me. His eyes were sad, but his jaw was set. His voice was almost hard. "Jess, my feelings for you didn't change because you didn't tell me you felt the same. I would sit through a thousand rejections from you if it meant spending another second with you."

Then he released a single long breath. "And I really like John and Deborah. I would not want to offend them by dropping you off and skipping out on dinner," he said softly.

"I'm truly sorry if I hurt you, Mark." I tried to blink back the tears burning my eyes.

Mark hesitated before putting his hand on my cheek.

Immediately, I pressed my face into his warm palm and closed my eyes. A single tear rolled down my cheek.

His thumb brushed it away.

After a few minutes I raised my hand and rested it on his. "We should go inside."

Turning his hand over to hold mine, he lifted it to his lips and kissed the top of it before releasing it.

THROUGHOUT DINNER, I tried to maintain an upbeat image, and I could tell Mark was doing the same. When Deborah asked me to help her clear the table when we had finished eating, I was glad for an excuse to leave the room. Mark offered to help but John declined the offer and invited him to sit in the living room instead.

When we had taken the last few dishes from the table, Deborah stopped me from leaving the kitchen. "What on earth happened today?" Deborah was not waiting for me this time.

I sighed deeply. "Is it that obvious?"

"You could have written it on your forehead in permanent marker, and it wouldn't be more obvious that something happened. Talk."

While Deborah made coffee and plated dessert, I told her everything Mark and I had said to one another. When I was done, I hung my head in defeat. "And Deborah, the way he looked at me. I couldn't read him. I still can't."

Deborah stopped what she was doing. "That had to be unnerving."

"You know I typically steer clear of reading my friends and family unless I feel it's absolutely necessary or it happens when I'm not thinking about it. But now, I can't read Mark, no matter how hard I try. I mean, Mark is skilled at masking as part of his job, but this is different. It feels like trying to read a stone. My gift has always been something I could turn off and on and feel in control of it, so unnerving is an understatement."

It was clear that Deborah was trying to understand my concerns as she nodded along with my words. Unfortunately, I was skirting into new territory, and I couldn't explain anything beyond what I was currently feeling. And maybe that was the problem. I was feeling a lot, possibly too much, and it was interfering with my ability to think and process normally. I needed to clear my mind from the distractions currently infiltrating my thoughts.

Taking a deep breath, I closed my eyes and silently prayed for the peace my heart and mind were in desperate need of and waited.

55

MARK

In the living room, I sat on the couch and John took a seat in the chair next to it.

"The first time I visited the National Cathedral was on a field trip as a kid. You think it feels big as an adult. Try being half the size and unaware of how big the world around you really is. I can still feel the sense of awe I had if I think about it," John said.

"I can imagine. It was quite impressive. I think what really got to me was when I thought about the craftsmanship that went into it and how much harder it had to be without all the modern tools we have when it comes to construction. But the creators had been so passionate about the job, it didn't stop them. They put everything they had into it, and they created a masterpiece."

John nodded slowly, observing me, making me feel as though he was looking deeper than my outward appearance.

"Can I ask you a personal question, Mark?" John asked, his voice sincere.

This was a loaded question in and of itself. While I knew this wasn't Jess's father sitting across from me, it may as well have been.

I cleared my throat. "Yes, sir. You can ask me anything."

John gave a gracious smile. "Mark, do you believe in God?"

This was not the question I had been expecting. I repositioned in my seat. "Did Jess put you up to this?" I wondered why this seemed to be a popular question with everyone these days.

John raised his eyebrows, and a grin began to form on his lips. "Jess and I have not had much time to talk about anything this week, seeing as how she has been spending much of her free time with a certain young man. And I am not complaining. It makes me happy to see her happy. She and I will catch up next week when she and Hayley call. However, I ask you this question because I know that it's something very important to Jess, but more so, it's important to me because your answer would determine your soul's eternal destination if you were to die tonight."

Leaning forward, I rested my elbows on my knees and folded my hands. My next words felt important but to what end? My answer hadn't changed since the first time Jess asked me, though I admired her more every time we talked about it because she was so committed to her beliefs.

The only way to answer his question was with the truth. "John, I appreciate your and Deborah's hospitality. I can see why Jess cares for both of you as deeply as she does. Jess and I have had many conversations about God and how big a part he plays in her life. But I just don't get it. And I mean no offense to you or your family." I gestured toward the kitchen. "Evil is practically all I see, every day—hate, death, and people hurting. I try every day to stop it and right as many wrongs as I can, and it's like putting a Band-Aid on an amputated leg. If there was a God, I can't imagine wanting any part of him if he could let the world burn while he just stands by and watches."

John's expression was thoughtful as though he was weighing his words. "Did you know at one time there was no evil in the world? Even after God put humans on the earth, for a short period evil did not exist. There was no hate, no death, and no pain. And God could have kept it that way but instead, he gave humans the ability to choose. Which, I am grateful for, even though at times, my choices can get the best of me and lead me down the wrong path. I'm sure you have no idea what I'm talking about, though, am I right?"

I tried to look amused. "I have definitely made my fair share of wrong choices." I sat back on the couch and crossed my arms over my chest.

John gave me a conspiring look. "I digress. God did not put evil in the world. Humans made a wrong choice bringing evil into the world. God gave Adam and Eve one rule about eating from a certain tree. Eve was convinced to break that one rule and brought her husband into her bad decision. It grieved God to the point of allowing his perfect creation to be brought to its knees under the weight of evil-doing called sin."

The room felt like it was shrinking around me, and it was taking a lot of willpower to stay in my seat.

John continued, "I don't pretend to understand the levels of evil you see on a regular basis. I believe it takes special people to do the job you do. I do know that if I did experience such darkness so often, I would easily find myself trying to cling to anything that brought me peace or relief, no matter how temporary. I know how it felt when we lost Bryan. The sadness and darkness that tried to hover around me was intense. Some days it tries to creep back in, and I have to fight it. And, please, understand that I am in no way comparing our loss to what you have seen in your job. It pales in comparison, I am sure. What I want to offer to you is something less temporal to hold onto when the evil begins to feel like it could win."

John was leaning forward with his elbows on his knees holding his hands out palms up as though his invisible offering was within reach.

My heart was racing. My brain seemed to be unable to carry out any commands I attempted to give it, like forming words or bolting from the house. The memories of my darkest times crept into my mind. How could a God who is so great have let my brother kill himself? Why didn't he stop him from pulling the trigger? Why do scumbags get away with murdering husbands and fathers?

I shook my head to clear the thoughts as well as in answer. "I'm sorry, John. I just don't think I can embrace a God you claim gives hope but still allows terrible things to happen to good people."

John gave a gentle nod. "I can see that's how it might look. But consider with me, that when God created Adam and Eve, his desire was to always have a perfect world. And it wasn't just his desire, but his command. He gave one rule, man broke it. He gave ten rules, man broke them. He gave hundreds of laws to his people, and they broke them. Every standard God ever set for mankind was immediately broken and disregarded. His rules weren't to control his creation but to help give them a future and hope. But his creation wanted nothing to do with it. Still doesn't, for the most part. Even those of us who are known and loved by God and have been sealed with the promise of heaven break rules he's given us every day."

I returned my gaze to the floor as it seemed less likely to consume me.

"Mark, we all deserve for God to open up the earth and swallow us into its depths, no questions asked. But God loves people too much to let them go without giving them the chance to reach out and take the offer of his hope. He offers to acquit us in the courtroom of his eternal justice. We broke his rules, we should pay the price. Instead, God allowed Jesus to die the horrific, bloody, painful death of a criminal on a cross just so he could raise him back to life three days later, making him the perfect, complete, and full payment of anyone who would believe in him."

I was having to put a great deal of effort into steadying my breathing. Why was this feeling like a higher-pressure situation than the missions I ran in Afghanistan?

John continued, "Imagine you are a lowdown criminal who broke every single one of the perfect judge's laws, standing in the courtroom facing a huge penalty you could never afford. And then a man you have never met, have never even seen at the grocery store, walks in and signs his name to your debt and says, 'I'll pay the debt.' He asked no questions; he gave no terms or conditions. He only had one desire, but he left the choice up to you whether you fulfilled his desire. That's what happened when Jesus died on that cross for you, Mark. He didn't look ahead and check your record. He already knew what it would look like. It would never be able to balance against the debt owed. That's even what happened when he gave his life for the vilest criminal offender you've ever arrested. The hard part has been done."

Tears had started to roll down my cheeks without my realizing it. I inhaled sharply trying to hide this unfamiliar emotional state by pressing my index finger and thumb into my eyes and wiping away the wetness.

John's eyes were earnest and pleading when I finally looked at him.

"If God loves people so much, why would he let brothers kill themselves or young mothers lose their husbands to murder?" My voice was hoarse.

John's eyes also became wet with tears. "Son, if I could give you a satisfactory answer, I would be a very wealthy man. What I can tell you is that God is not a stranger to our pain. It was his only Son he gave as a sacrifice in our place. And even knowing he would be raised to life again, he had to watch his son stripped, beaten to a pulp, whipped, pierced with thorns, nails, and a sword. God knows pain. Trusting him won't take away your pain. Ask me, ask Deborah, ask Jess. Trusting him does give us an anchor in the midst of it and a promise that one day our pain will fade away completely."

Dragging both hands down my face, I took a quick cleansing breath. "I have a lot of questions about everything you just said but I will save them for another time because it has gotten late. That is, if there can be another time."

John smiled warmly. "Of course, there can be another time. As many times as you need."

"Thank you." I nodded before looking at my watch. "I really should get going if I'm still taking Jess to the airport in the morning." Standing, I glanced toward the kitchen where Deborah and Jess had hidden themselves away.

They must have been listening as they emerged from the kitchen as John stood and reached to shake my hand. "Mark, it's always a pleasure."

"Thank you. Tonight was, unexpected." I suddenly felt tired.

John reached into his pocket and pulled out a small business card. "Call me this week or better yet, come to church Sunday and then have lunch with Deborah and me after."

Pocketing the card I said, "Thanks."

Deborah made a beeline for me, and I braced myself knowing I was in for one of her hugs. Before letting go she whispered next to my ear, "I'll be praying for you this week."

"Thank you," I whispered back.

Jess walked to the car with me where we stood in silence for what seemed hours though only minutes passed.

"I'm sorry about tonight. Well, I'm sorry that I couldn't warn you it was coming because I didn't know. If I'm being honest, though, I'm not sorry you heard it from someone else other than me." Her smile was hesitant.

"Yeah. That was something." I was unsure of what I was feeling.

"Are you mad?" she asked quietly.

"I'm feeling a lot of things, Jess. I'm feeling like I've been ambushed, like I've been left out of the loop, like my heart has been removed from my chest and pummeled over and over today. Worst of all, I feel like I've wasted the last twenty-something years of my life fighting to believe one thing just to have it deconstructed for me in two hours. Which makes me feel stupid, because I worked really hard to not believe there was even a God. And now, I'm not sure what to believe." I grew agitated with every word.

Before I knew what was happening, Jess's hands were on my face pulling me to her until our lips collided.

Frozen in place, I was afraid to take another breath until I realized what was happening. Slowly, I moved my arms around her and began to kiss her back. The sensation I had felt at her touch before was back. The tension that had been building dissipated for the moment.

When she pulled away and stepped back, Jess's eyes were very wide. "I'm sorry. I..." she whispered, gently touching her lips with her fingers.

All I was capable of was staring at her as I tried to form any word.

"Please say something." Her voice was trembling.

"I'll pick you up at five in the morning." With that, I opened the door, got in my car, and pulled out of the driveway.

56

JESS

Left standing alone in the driveway, hands shaking, my heart was silently crying out, *What have I done? God, please don't let me lose him. Forgive my impulsiveness.*

John and Deborah were sitting in the living room when I walked back inside.

"Jess, I hope I didn't scare off Mark. It seemed like he was wrestling with some things, and I wanted to know where he stood on them," John said with concern in his voice.

"He is definitely wrestling with some things. Probably even more now." I gave Deborah a pointed look of mortification and desperation.

Taking my reaction as a sign he should retire to bed, John kissed Deborah goodnight then stood. "Jess, I will see you in the morning before you leave, okay?"

"Oh, you don't have to get up that early. Really."

"Nonsense. I'm always up that early. See you in the morning. Good night." He bowed his head in my direction.

Once John was out of earshot, I groaned and threw myself onto the couch next to Deborah.

"I kissed him," I admitted, covering my face in humiliation.

Deborah's eyes grew wide, and her jaw dropped. "What? Why?" she asked in a loud whisper as though we might have an audience in our empty room.

"To shut him up. He was ranting about all his beliefs being unraveled tonight, and I didn't even know I was doing it until it was too late. Just pulled him to me and kissed him. He kissed me back. And then, he said he would pick me up in the morning and he left." I snapped my fingers. "Just like that."

Deborah had a strange expression on her face that said she might pass out or hug me. "Jess, did you hear what he was telling you? His beliefs are unraveling. Think about his beliefs. They didn't exist. So, for them to unravel…"

I sat up at attention. "How did I not hear that?" I considered what she was saying.

"You were probably too wrapped up in wanting to kiss him," Deborah teased.

I couldn't argue with her there. Not that it had been preplanned, but clearly some part of me had wanted to do it.

"But he left without saying anything. That has never happened. I couldn't tell if he was mad. It felt like he was mad. It also felt like there was more to it."

"Jess, there had to be a lot more to it. You came to Christ from a very different place. If God is drawing Mark to himself, and I believe he is, think about all the speedbumps he's going to hit along the way to move beyond all the things he has believed for so long. Now, all in one day, you've told him no, he's been brought face to face with his need for a Savior, and you've kissed him. I'd probably be at a loss for words myself."

Holding my head in my hands I moaned. "I messed up so badly."

Deborah rubbed my back. "I don't think you messed up. I do think that if you truly love Mark, you will give him time and space to work through all his speedbumps before you attempt to kiss him again."

Shaking my head and running my hands through my hair I sighed. "Thank you, Deborah. I need to go spend some time praying for a massive share of wisdom and maybe a little self-control."

When I stood, Deborah followed then swallowed me with a hug before wishing me a good night.

In the guest room, I checked my phone and was surprised to see two missed calls from Mark. He had left messages both times.

"Jess, I need to talk to you. Please call me."

He sounded stressed. I listened to his second message. It was less urgent and a little sad.

"Please call me when you get this. It doesn't matter how late it is."

My instinct was to immediately call him back, but after the impulsive kiss, I thought better of making the same mistake twice. I put my phone down and prayed.

Take captive any of my words and my thoughts that would not honor you. Give me wisdom and self-control. Clear my mind of the things distracting me—my desires, my feelings, my emotions, the past, even the future. Give me your peace whatever comes from this.

In the quiet darkness, I sat and listened. After several minutes I squeezed my eyes tightly and took a deep breath. Picking up my phone, I called Mark.

"Jess, I'm so sorry I left the way I did. That was uncalled for, and it will never happen, again. I promise. I felt so awful that I almost came back, but I assumed you had gone back inside, and it was late." Without a hello, his words spilled out as though he had held them in as long as he possibly could.

"Mark, breathe. You don't owe me an apology. I owe you one. I don't know what I was thinking." I paused. "Yes, I do. I was thinking that I didn't like seeing you upset. I didn't like standing there watching you struggle through something that was my fault. All I wanted to do was stop the storm building inside you. And I crossed a line. I crossed a line with you I had drawn, and I am so sorry. Please, forgive me."

I could hear him sniffle in the distance through the phone. He was or had been crying. This was almost too much. In all the years I had known him, I had never seen or heard him as I had tonight. Mark was always cool and confident at work, and when it was just us, I knew his dimpled smile and his playful blue eyes and his kindness. To have seen and heard brokenness in him threatened to break me.

Several moments passed before Mark spoke.

"Over the years I have built many walls around myself to keep out anything that might threaten my ability to do my job effectively. I never let myself become attached to anyone or anything because I knew it could disappear at any moment. I let callouses form around my heart, which meant relationships came and went and I didn't care. It also means that I have done things I'm not proud of and am too ashamed to say aloud. I stopped feeling. I never set out to hurt anyone on purpose, but if someone was hurt because of me, I shrugged it off and moved on. And then I got to know you. I told myself so many times that you were far too good for me and that I would never be good enough for you. You're so pure and sweet and beautiful. I knew I would never deserve someone like you, much less you."

My throat tightened.

"At first, I tried to convince myself that I was just doing my job and being a decent human being. Then the more I talked to you, the more I wanted to talk to you, so the more I did talk to you. Then I would think about you when I wasn't talking to you, and I would wish you weren't so far away.

"I can't tell you exactly when I realized the walls around me had started to crumble, but I can say definitively that you have destroyed every protection I constructed. I knew when you were scheduled to come back, I was going to tell you how I felt about you regardless of your feelings for me because I couldn't pretend any longer you were just my friend. There are clearly a lot of things I need to think through after today, but one thing is certain. My feelings for you haven't changed. Right now, I can't imagine them ever changing, and I don't want them to. But I want to respect you and your wishes and your boundaries. If that means not talking to you every day, then so be it. I will do whatever you ask of me."

His voice was quiet, and he sounded defeated. The words I wanted to say were at war with what I knew I shouldn't say as they were exactly the same thing. It would be so easy to throw my values into the wind and give in to my desires. I didn't want to lose Mark. I loved him, and now I knew he loved me. But there was a huge chasm between us, one that if never closed, would always limit any hope of a future. I knew I couldn't compromise on this. He was not a believer, and it mattered, not just to me, but to God.

I swallowed hard and took a deep breath. "Mark." My voice faltered, but I cleared my throat and pressed on. "Mark, I care about you deeply. You mean the world to me. Second to Hayley, you are the first person on earth I wake up wanting to talk to every day. Your friendship has been life changing. There is a connection between us that I can't explain. I know it's there because I can physically feel it any time your hand touches mine or we hug.

"But none of that is enough for me, as much as I wish it could be. And it wouldn't be enough for you. Our emotions and our feelings are so fleeting. They can change quickly and without warning, but I know that when God is the center of something, it doesn't change on a whim. You said you can't imagine your feelings for me ever changing. But they could. And I'm not going to risk my heart on feelings. I want something that is secure and forever. Right now, you can't give that to me."

"Then tell me what to do. Tell me, please. Because I will do anything." The desperation was back in his voice.

"I can't, Mark. This isn't something I can do for you."

"Jess..." My name came out almost like a sob.

"Mark, do you have a Bible?"

He sniffled several times before answering. "No, not in a long time."

I pulled the phone from my ear and texted him a link. "Download this app. When you open it, use the search feature and look for

Romans. Then read until you can't read anymore. We can talk about it on our way to the airport."

Silence.

"Jess," he said pleadingly. I heard him swallow. "I love you."

Eyes closed, I pictured his blue eyes looking at me, a sad smile on my lips. "I'll see you in the morning, Mark."

57

JESS

My sleep was dreamless and hard for the four short hours I slept. My only thought when my alarm went off was that I really hoped I could sleep on the plane ride home. Showered and packed and ready to go by four-thirty, I made my way downstairs. It was still dark outside, but the lights were on in the kitchen. Walking in expecting to find Deborah with the coffee pot in hand and her everlasting smile waiting for me, I froze when that was not the scene I happened upon.

There, next to the kitchen counter, were John and Deborah with their eyes closed and arms wrapped around a crying man's shaking shoulders. They were praying. I covered my mouth with my hand and backed out of the room as slowly and as quietly as I could. My mind raced at what I had just seen.

"We thank you Jesus. Amen," I heard John's voice followed by movement in the kitchen.

There were sniffles and the sound of tissues being pulled from a box. After the quiet commotion died out, I debated my next steps. I decided to attempt to re-enter the kitchen as though it was the first time that morning. Trying to look surprised to see the three of them already there while pretending they didn't all have blotchy tear-stained faces was hard.

"Well, hello, all of you." I used my cheery voice and smile that worked with Hayley on sleepy mornings. "I thought I was early." I fixed my eyes on Mark.

Something was different. His eyes were a sharper blue, if that were even possible.

Deborah shuffled over, still in her slippers, and wrapped me in a giant hug, which caught me off guard.

Slowly, I wrapped my arms around her as I tried to wrap my brain around whatever I had stumbled into.

"I am going to miss seeing your face in person every day," Deborah said as though it was already time for me to go. "You and Haley should video call this evening once you've gotten home and settled, alright? I packed your breakfast, and there's coffee to take with you. I'm praying you have a safe flight." She patted my cheek.

"Okay." I made the word last several seconds.

John walked over and gave me a bear hug. "We'll take care of him, I promise," he whispered.

Confused was only the beginning of how I was feeling. As I was about to protest their timing, Deborah eyed me as though she was trying to communicate something nonverbally. When I didn't immediately acknowledge her subliminal message, she indicated Mark with a shift of her eyes then gave a subtle shake of her head. I blinked several times trying to process her message before looking at Mark.

"I guess I'm ready to go when you are." I tried to sound more ready than I felt. I hugged Deborah one more time and gave John's hand a squeeze. "Thank you both for everything. I'll call you when I get home."

They waved from the front door as I followed Mark to the car.

He put my suitcase in the trunk then opened my door for me. John and Deborah had disappeared into the house. After he started the car, we sat silently for several minutes without looking at one another. He was obviously processing something, and I didn't want to interrupt. I sipped the coffee Deborah had sent with me waited.

"I have no idea what I'm doing," he said to the steering wheel.

I remained quiet.

He finally shifted in his seat, so I turned to face him. "I read Romans six times this morning."

My eyebrows shot up. "Six?"

He breathed a laugh. "Well, five and a half because I fell asleep the last time through."

"Oh, well, five and a half is much more believable," I said, unable to contain my astonishment.

His lips twitched. "My alarm went off and everything I had read, everything John had said last night, it all crashed over me and threatened to suffocate me. It felt like a panic attack. I saw John's card on my nightstand and without even thinking I called him. The next thing I know I'm in their kitchen pouring my heart out at four o'clock in the morning. John stopped me at some point and asked, 'do you believe in God?' and the only word I could physically utter was 'yes.' No other word would even form in my head."

My heart felt like it was going to explode. It was a struggle to keep my face neutral, and I could feel the corners of my mouth twitch occasionally as I listened.

"I don't know what any of it really means. Some of the things I read went over my head. Some things felt like arrows shooting through my heart. And then there were the parts that made me sick to my stomach because it felt like the guy was writing about me and things I had done and what I deserved for doing those things. At one point I was convinced that I was an absolutely terrible person and I deserved to be struck by lightning right then and there. But the more I read about how bad I was, I also kept reading how God could change me."

The more he talked, the more animated he became. His face was practically beaming. "The more I read it, the more convinced I was that I needed to be changed. Before I fell asleep, I had just finished reading chapter five again. And I guess I prayed; I don't know. I said that I wanted the peace and the hope it said God could give me. And then I fell asleep. When I had told him all of this, John asked me several questions about knowing if I was a sinner and if I wanted to stop sinning. He asked if I believed Jesus had died on a cross and came back to life. I told him yes to all those things because it's true."

He took a deep breath. "And then he and Deborah hugged me and prayed over me. But you saw that part," he said with a teasing smirk.

I wanted to cry, hug him, kiss him, run a marathon, and cry some more. Instead, I just stared at this man who had been transformed overnight. My smile was involuntary. I whispered a prayer in my heart to God thanking him for his constant presence in my life and for the salvation he had brought to Mark.

Mark glanced at the clock. "We had better get you to the airport. I have a feeling you would have one upset little girl in Kentucky if you were late getting home."

EPILOGUE
JESS

One Year Later

"If I were a betting woman, I would put money on it," I heard Marí say matter of factly.

Cal crossed his arms and shook his head. "There is no way."

Squaring my stance, I pulled the trigger and unloaded the magazine. The target shuddered repeatedly. With a smug look on my face, I dropped the magazine from the pistol and inspected the chamber. I set the gun on the table in front of me and removed my protective headphones.

Marí and Cal walked away, holding hands as they went to retrieve the target.

"That was the hottest thing I have ever seen in my entire life," a familiar voice said behind me.

Whirling around on the spot, I found Mark standing several feet behind me. My jaw dropped, and I ran straight toward him and jumped into his arms holding on to him as though he might be a figment of my imagination that could vanish at any moment.

Refusing to let go I leaned back and asked breathlessly, "What are you doing here?"

"Can a guy not visit his girlfriend in a different state without telling her?"

I laughed. "Clearly, he can."

He shrugged. "I missed you and wanted to see you. So, here I am. I hope I'm not interrupting anything important." He gestured to the makeshift firing range in the empty pasture.

Releasing my monkey-like hold on Mark, I slid to the ground but didn't take my arms from him.

"Actually, you are interrupting something very important. Cal challenged me, and I was just beating him severely when you showed up. Now my focus is ruined. I think you owe me an apology."

With a heavy sigh his blue eyes locked on my face. "I'm so very sorry. Will you ever forgive me?"

I shrugged one shoulder as though indifferent to his words. "I'll consider it." I pulled his lips to mine. A current pulsed through me until it was vibrating every fiber of my being.

After my initial return home from DC, Mark and I had several long conversations about his newly found faith, and we decided it would be best if we pulled back on the reins of our friendship to let him focus on growing and nurturing his relationship with God. Our communication was limited to phone calls twice a week and platonic texts throughout the week. After three months, Mark asked if he could come visit and I agreed.

During that visit we talked a lot about his new life and the changes that had come with it. We also discussed what it meant for our future. Our feelings for one another hadn't changed, and in truth, being less connected had made my feelings for Mark stronger.

The biggest roadblock we were facing as we considered moving forward was the distance due to our careers. My job could be done from practically anywhere, even if it involved some travel. Mark's was anchored in DC for the time being. Regardless, we decided we would allow ourselves to openly pursue whatever relationship came with our feelings, even if the physical distance remained.

I'd made an additional trip to DC for work, and I may have tacked on an extra couple of days to my itinerary because honestly, phone calls, text messages, and video calls were not sufficient. Even the two extra days had not been enough, but it was all I could have, and I was determined to make it count.

Now he was here, and it was unexpected, and my heart was ready to soar into the sky.

When we finally pulled apart, Marí and Cal had returned with the target.

"You better watch out for that one, son. She doesn't play." Cal held up the sheet with very few holes in it but had one larger hole near the center.

Mark's look of surprise was genuine. "You aren't kidding."

I gave Mark a coy smile. "I have many skills, Agent Collins. Some I'm sure I don't even know about yet."

"I can't wait to find out what they are," he mused so only I could hear him.

The four of us walked back to the old farmhouse where Hayley and Sadie were playing with several of Carlos's kids. When the girls saw him, they made a beeline for him.

"Mark!" they both shouted.

He bent down to receive them both, and with one in each arm, they hugged him, and he hugged them back. He kissed the sides of their heads and released them back to play.

Following Marí and Cal up the front porch steps, I asked over my shoulder, "How long can you stay?"

When there was no answer, I turned to find Mark still on the ground. He reached into his pocket and knelt on one knee. My hand flew to cover my mouth. I heard Marí sigh behind me and turned to see Cal smiling and shaking his head, arms crossed in front of him as he watched.

"I was thinking forever. But I'll leave that up to you." Mark opened the small box inside of which was a platinum band with a round diamond surrounded by bouquets of small diamonds of different sizes.

"Mark!" I barely rasped as I walked back down the steps until I was standing on the ground in front of him. Looking back and forth between his sparkling eyes and the ring, I couldn't have kept from smiling if I'd tried.

"Forever won't be long enough." I pulled him up from his knee.

He stood and wrapped me in his arms, and I laughed as he spun me around.

"Then maybe we should let forever start right now."

My smile wavered, and my eyebrows creased in confusion.

"Why not? Everyone's here, there's nothing stopping us."

"But..."

What I had thought was still a group of children playing in my periphery was actually two people walking toward us who I recognized immediately. Both hands went to my mouth before I felt the tears.

I ran to hug Deborah and John who had blended in with Carlos and his family so as not to be seen.

"What is happening?" I laughed as I turned back around to face Mark.

"We were invited to a wedding," John answered with his warm smile.

"I don't know how you pulled this off, but we are going to have a long talk about surprises, later," I said to Mark, trying not to smile at him.

Marí and Cal had planned and prepped everything with the help of the small group of women Marí held a Bible study with every week. Deborah had brought a dress with her that Leslie had once again picked out especially for me as well as dresses for Hayley and Sadie.

As the sun began to set, Mark and I were exchanging vows in the front yard before all our friends and family. There were plenty of tears and laughter throughout the evening.

When we found ourselves able to break away from the festivities, Mark pulled me to the back of the house where we found one of the farm trucks with the keys conveniently inside. Eyeing him suspiciously, I stepped up into the truck.

"I have another surprise for you." He wasn't even trying to contain his smile.

Trying not to return his smile, I rolled my eyes. "Of course, you do."

He slowly drove us down a long dirt path until we arrived at a beautiful modern white brick farmhouse with a wraparound porch.

"What?" was all I could say.

Mark threw the truck in park and jogged around to open my door. Taking my hand, he pulled me toward the house.

"What?" I asked again trying to comprehend what I was seeing.

"Do you like it?" His words were hopeful.

Slowly, I turned to look at Mark searching his face for answers.

His eyes twinkled with mischief and satisfaction.

"Mark, what is this?"

"It's a house."

"I see that. Why is it here? How is it here?" I asked bewildered.

His smile was infectious as I couldn't keep myself from smiling.

"It's ours. Do you like it?" He tugged on my hand.

"It's beautiful." I whispered, struggling to piece together the how and the why.

"Come, see." Mark scooped me up, causing me to laugh as I wrapped my arms around his neck.

"Seriously, no more surprises." I chuckled as he carried me up the front steps and through the front door.

He shrugged. "I don't make promises I can't keep."

Before he could put my feet back on the ground, I drew him to me and kissed him long and deep. This man had uprooted his entire world for us, and now he was here giving me one more reason to fall more in love with him.

"I'm starting to think bringing you here was a bad idea." He gave me a suggestive, flirty look as he helped me regain my balance after he put me down.

"Give me the grand tour?" I threaded our fingers together.

We walked room to room holding hands until we were finally on the front porch again.

"Mark, I don't understand how any of this is even possible. I'm overwhelmed and completely speechless."

Leaning against one of the posts, Mark pulled me to him. "Maybe I'll spill my secrets another time. Suffice it to say, I love you and would move heaven and earth to make you happy, and I plan to spend the rest of my life doing just that."

Lost in his eyes, I settled against him wondering what I had done to deserve such a beautiful second chance at love. "I love you, Mark Collins. And I will spend the rest of my life showing you just that. For now, however, I think we have a wedding to get back to."

Mark threw his head back and groaned loudly. "Do we have to?" he whined.

"You're the one who invited all those lovely people to be here. I think you kind of have to be there."

"Ugh, me and my ridiculous surprises," he growled.

Never having seen this side of Mark before had me throwing my head back and laughing loudly.

He took this as an invitation to plant his lips on my neck working his way up to my jaw, my cheek, then my lips.

Not wanting him to stop but knowing we needed to get back to the party, I cleared my throat. "Mr. Collins, the wedding?"

"Fine," he mumbled into my neck.

WE SMILED AND DANCED, talked and laughed, and even shed a few tears the rest of the evening with the people we loved most.

Hayley started getting sleepy and fell asleep as Mark danced with her, swaying back and forth to a song. Before her eyes closed, she reached up and put her hand on his face. He brushed her hair back with his lips and kissed her small forehead. I offered to take her and put her in bed, but he declined, taking her inside and walking her upstairs where he tucked her in.

I followed and waited in the doorway.

Hayley opened her sleepy eyes and said in her sleepy voice, "Mark, are you my daddy?"

My gut clenched and all the air left my lungs.

He smiled gently and whispered, "No, sweetheart, I'm not."

"You act like a daddy."

"Hayley, I will always love you like a daddy loves his little girl."

"Can I call you daddy?" she asked, rubbing her eyes.

"Is that what you want to call me?"

She closed her eyes and nodded.

"Okay." He kissed her cheek. "Sweet dreams."

"Sweet dreams, Daddy."

He sat on the edge of the bed wiping at his eyes.

Tears streamed from my eyes as I stood at the door with my hand over my mouth holding back my sobs.

He closed the door as he exited the room and wrapped me in his arms where we stood together embracing each other and embracing the future.

THE SUN HAD BARELY STARTED RISING when I began to wake. Taking a deep breath and stretching, I was immediately aware of the warm body curled around me. I sank back into it and locked my fingers with his.

Mark stirred and tightened his hold and kissed my shoulder. "Let's stay right here forever," he said in a half mumble, half whisper.

"Okay," I whispered back.

BONUS MATERIALS

But Wait, There's More!

For a bonus epilogue to find out what happens next with Mark & Jess, scan this QR Code!

ACKNOWLEDGMENTS

As an author I'm supposed to avoid clichés but you'll have to forgive me as I pour them out in excess and not because I am being disingenuous but because clichés exist for a reason. They can speak to the heart of a matter directly.

First and foremost, I honestly believe God allowed this story to come to me as easily as it did and for that I am immensely grateful. My hope is that it glorifies him and that it reaches people who are searching for hope and redemption.

To my husband who is also my biggest cheerleader, the first reader of every draft of every word I write, and my favorite human being on the planet - THANK YOU. Those two words are inadequate for the gratitude I hold in my heart for you. I appreciate your time and patience and encouragement. It's an honor to have you in my corner.

To my daughter who has been a huge encourager and sounding board, even at such a young age - THANK YOU. You have inspired me and driven me to new levels. Maybe one day we'll team up and work together.

To my family who encouraged me, read my book, provided editing services, design services, counseling services, and overall general support - THANK YOU. From my mom always bragging on and encouraging my writing abilities to my dad instilling his mastery of the English language and offering up his mad editing skills, to my sister being a sounding board/editor/design contributor, this book has really been a family project. Just like life, I wouldn't want it any other way.

To every person who read my work before it was made public and provide honest feedback - THANK YOU. You are true heroes. Putting my imperfect work into the hands of others required me to trust differently than I ever have before, and I am indebted to each of you for being trustworthy.

To my editor, Jennifer Crosswhite - THANK YOU. I've said it a hundred times and I'll say it again. This book would not be what it is without you.

ABOUT THE AUTHOR

Jennifer Carr

Having always enjoyed books, writing, and daydreaming, Jennifer wanted to know what it would feel like to combine the three and write a book. Once she started writing, everything changed. Within a matter of months, she had multiple projects started and found a love for writing in a way she never knew was possible.

Married to her childhood best friend and the mom of a creative daughter, Jennifer enjoys the quiet life on their farm in Alabama, baking, and reading romance novels.

You can connect with Jennifer on Social Media

@jcarrwrites

POSTLUDE